Dear Reader,

Do you believe in destiny? Do you believe in a love that can transcend time and space?

ESSENCE OF MY DESIRE *brings you into a world where passion can take you into another place, and desire can fulfill your deepest dreams. One hundred and fifty years ago, two lovers disappeared on the same night...*

Today, two lovers find each other again, but they are sworn enemies because of a wrenching betrayal. Together they must search for the ultimate element of love. They must search for the ESSENCE OF MY DESIRE...

St. Martin's Paperbacks Titles
by Jill Jones

JILL JONES

ESSENCE OF MY DESIRE

St. Martin's Paperbacks

This is a work of fiction. Resemblance of any of the events to real episodes or characters to real persons either living or dead is purely coincidental.

ESSENCE OF MY DESIRE

Copyright © 1998 by Jill Jones.

ISBN: 0-312-96415-3

Printed in the United States of America

St. Martin's Paperbacks edition/March 1998

St. Martin's Paperbacks are published by St. Martin's Press, 175 Fifth Avenue, New York, NY 10010.

10 9 8 7 6 5 4 3 2 1

For Jennifer Enderlin

A most talènted and creative editor,
a superlative cheerleader, and a good friend

ACKNOWLEDGMENTS

I wish to extend my gratitude to the following people who helped me in so many ways learn about the fascinating worlds of fragrance and magic:

For the loan of your books, photographs, tapes, music, scented products, and for sharing your personal knowledge of and providing input on the various aspects of this story, I thank you, Cheryl DeWitt, Carmela Firstenberger, Light and Brian Miller, Robin Tolleson, April and Jeff Moore, Elaine Hamil, Brooke Kurek, Caroline Wood, Joanna Schulman, Lezley Suleiman, Susan Alvis, Jeffrey Brown, Glenn Palmer, Alan Coppens, and Macgregor Gray.

For the fragrant tour of International Fragrance and Technology, Inc., Canton, Georgia, and the invaluable insight into the business of perfuming, I thank Master Perfumers Deepak K. Shah and Philippe Lorson.

For responding so kindly, completely, and promptly to a fax from a stranger inquiring into the business of fragrance in the United States, I thank Annette Green, president, the Fragrance Foundation, New York, New York. For a similar prompt and complete response to my inquiry about the fragrance business in the U.K., I thank Andrea Jones, publisher of *Esprit* magazine, the trade journal for the fragrance industry in Britain. I am also grateful to Ms. Jones for so generously giving of her time to read the manuscript for correctness of content and detail.

viii ᔓ *Acknowledgments*

My special thanks go to my agent, Denise Marcil, my editor
Jennifer Enderlin, my husband Jerry, daughter Brooke, and
good friend Dea Growden for their encouragement and support of varying natures that have allowed me to pursue my
own incredible dream.

Come to me in the silence of the night;
  Come in the speaking silence of a dream;
Come with soft rounded cheeks and eyes as bright
  As sunlight on a stream . . .

Christina Rossetti, from "Echo"

PROLOGUE

ॐ

Bombay, India
1997

"Must we go in there? This place is making my skin crawl," one of the native workers complained in heavily accented English. The powerful beam of his hand-held light pierced the gloom of the long-forgotten basement, revealing a pair of ancient wooden doors set into the dank orange dirt of the wall. The wood was old, rotten, and permeated by the smell of decay.

"Mr. Rutledge said to search the entire building," Pritchett insisted with undaunted British determination, although he, too, had no enthusiasm for the job. The basement was tomb-like, dark and silent and somehow unholy. The only thing to recommend it was its coolness, and this subterranean exploration provided a break from the sweltering heat above. "Go on, now. Chop away. Likely there's nothing in there anyway."

The two hired workers exchanged glances, then raised pick-axes and felled them simultaneously against the wood, which splintered into crumbling, moldy shards. In only a few strokes the barrier was downed. Pritchett kicked at the debris with his polished leather boot before stepping up to the gaping black hole. At least, he thought gratefully, nothing had slithered out of it or brushed by his face with leathery wings. He flashed his own light into the blackness.

The cubicle behind the doors was small, for which Pritchett was also thankful, as he had no desire to delve into some underground labyrinth such as he'd feared this might be. The earthen walls were bare on two sides, but along the far wall, three thick wooden shelves had been anchored into grooves carved from the claylike soil. Pritchett frowned, speculating on what purpose such a closet might have served.

Shining his light high, he ran the beam across the top shelf. It was empty. The second revealed the same, nothing but a thick layer of dust, collected over the course of a hundred and fifty years, perhaps longer. Pritchett sighed, relieved that their search had turned up nothing and he could return to handling the problems that awaited him in the main part of the building.

The sooner he finished this duty, the better, he thought. If he'd known beforehand the difficulties it entailed, perhaps he wouldn't have hired on as Nick Rutledge's hatchet man. He half expected the employees of the firm, whom he had recently and abruptly fired, to blow up the building or set it afire in their outrage at so suddenly losing their jobs. He'd had to hire a veritable private army to stand guard around the premises while he finished up. He was anxious to get the job over with, shut down the old perfume factory for good, and return to the civility of London. He regretted that he hadn't charged Rutledge more for doing his dirty work.

Squatting in the gloom of the small underground chamber, Pritchett beamed his light across the bottom of the three shelves, expecting to find it empty as well. But to his surprise, the light disclosed an object huddled in the shadows, guarded by the webs of long-dead spiders, their gossamer filaments weighted with the pervasive red-orange dust.

"What's this?" The tall Englishman stood again and signaled to one of the other men. "Say, there, fetch that into the light," he directed.

The dark-skinned man shot his coworker another uneasy look, but then gave his gloves a tug and stooped to pull the whatever-it-was from its hiding place. It proved to be a box, not too heavy, and he carried it into the main part of the basement, placing it beneath one of the high, grated windows. The afternoon sun slanted across it, highlighting the dust and casting an orange patina over the rusting metal surface.

It was a small trunk, about the size of a ladies' makeup case. A very old trunk, Pritchett surmised. And it was locked.

"Shall I, sir?" the man asked, lifting his heavy crowbar.

But Pritchett shook his head. In spite of his curiosity, he would follow the directions of his employer, who had told him to preserve intact any relics he might come across. He walked around the chest, his head cocked to one side, speculating. What was in there? Gold? Jewels? Had the underground closet served as a safe once upon a time? The idea of buried treasure teased at his imagination, but then another thought struck him.

Instead of a safe, what if the cache had been a tomb?

Pritchett shivered involuntarily and told himself it was a ridiculous notion. But the very oddity of finding the ancient, dust-encrusted trunk alone in the obscure hiding place warned him it obviously was meant not to be disturbed. If he opened it, would he find the bones of a long-dead infant? Or someone who had been murdered and chopped into small pieces? He laughed nervously at his runaway imagination, but the possibility set his teeth on edge. He suddenly wanted the trunk out of his hands, as quickly as possible.

"Take it upstairs to the main office," he said, finding his voice at last. "Clean it up and prepare it for express shipment to the London office."

It was perhaps an unnecessary expense, but Pritchett's nerves were already shot, and he didn't much care if Rutledge complained about the cost. Whatever the trunk contained, riches or bones or the curses of Pandora, was none of his business. Let Rutledge deal with it. Pritchett's only job was to secure and pack up every last usable object in the building that had housed for a century and a half the Bombay Spice and Fragrance Company, and ship everything to the new owner, Mr. Nicholas Rutledge, in London. What on earth the man could want with the shabby, antiquated furnishings and equipment was beyond him.

But that, too, was none of his business.

ONE

*

New Orleans

Though it was only the middle of May, spring had forgotten New Orleans, and summer already had its tentacles entwined tenaciously around the city, suffocating it in a simmering wet heat. Simone had lived here nearly ten years now, but she was still unaccustomed to the sultry weather that maintained an almost year-round stranglehold on the sullied streets and decadently decaying buildings of the old French Quarter.

"The South," as they called it here in the United States, was not at all like the south of France, her homeland, and when the atmosphere grew oppressive like today, she longed for the Mediterranean breezes that swept the gentle countryside and cooled the fragrant fields surrounding the city of Grasse.

With a heavy sigh, Simone Lefèvre twisted her rich, dark hair into a knot and pinned it high upon the crown of her head. She rolled up the sleeves of the brightly flowered oversized shirt she wore, then fluttered the garment to create a breeze against her sweat-dampened skin. This morning, as she prepared to unpack some boxes for her aunt, Grasse and her childhood seemed as if they belonged in another lifetime altogether. The only tie that bound her to that past was her beloved Tante Camille, her father's sister, in whose arms and

home Simone and her mother had taken refuge when Jean
René Lefèvre had died so suddenly.

With grim determination, Simone thrust aside the memories
of all that. She tried never to think about those terrible times.
The recollection was too brutal. *Pense seulement au futur!* she
ordered herself, squaring her shoulders and heading toward
the back room of her aunt's tiny *parfumerie.*

Think only of the future.

The future.

Simone knew she must face it soon. She could no longer
hide behind the excuse of getting an education. She had completed an undergraduate degree in chemistry, then spent several months training to become a perfumer at a fashion
institute in New York.

It had not surprised her greatly to learn that her knowledge
of perfuming and her skill as a perfumer were far more advanced than the expertise of her teachers there.

She was, after all, her father's daughter.

Jean René Lefèvre had been of one of the most talented
and respected perfumers of all time. She had grown up under
his exacting tutelage and been schooled since childhood in the
art of perfuming. Her "nose" had been trained from an early
age to sort out and arrange scents into beautiful harmonies,
works of aromatic art, exquisite perfumes that few others
could create so easily.

At the institute, when her identity, heritage, and evident
talent as a nose became known, she was courted aggressively
by independent fragrance firms as well as major American
manufacturers who sought her out, hoping to hire her to create
new fragrances with which to enhance their consumer products—soaps, fabrics, deodorants, diapers, automobile interi-
ors, floor cleaners, medicines, even rubber tires. Americans,
she thought with a fond snicker . . . they are warm and wonderful people, but they do not like the way they smell.

Like her father, Simone preferred to use her talents in a
more traditional manner. She wanted to create great scents,
grands parfums. But unlike Jean René, Simone did not want
to cater to an exclusive private clientele, although she had

deep respect for his work. Her father's talent at the console of perfumery had drawn Europe's royals, Arabia's sheiks, America's movie stars and magnates of commerce, South America's drug lords—the rich, the famous, the elite of the world—to his small but legendary perfumery, La Maison Lefèvre, in Grasse. There, for a substantial price, he had created a personal scent for each, a private perfume unavailable to anyone else in the world.

Unavailable, Simone thought bitterly, until "Nathaniel Raleigh" had knocked on their door. Ten years had passed, and still a knot formed in her stomach when she thought about the handsome young man who had become her father's apprentice . . . and her first lover.

And who had exploited them both.

Simone opened the door to the storage room, again repressing memories she thought best remain buried. That old pain was one reason she wasn't interested in trying to reestablish her father's type of business. It all belonged to a past she had no desire to resurrect in any way.

Unless she found a way one day to destroy the man who had hurt them so terribly. But that seemed unlikely, and she did not dwell upon the impossible.

Instead, she focused her attention upon another, far more distant past, hoping it would provide her with an inspiration and a plan for a future that would return the name of Lefèvre to prominence in the business of perfuming.

La Belle Epoque.

The golden age of fashion and perfume at the turn of the last century, when the venerable houses of Houbigant, Guerlain, Caron, Coty, and others had created *grands parfums,* classic scents that remained legendary in the industry a century later. True perfumers these were, not just *couturiers* who developed fragrances as accessories for the fashions they designed.

During her last semester at the university, while experimenting with various synthetic and natural combinations in the laboratory, an idea had occurred to her, one that she had since secretly nourished and embellished over the past few months. Could she, at the end of this century, develop *grands parfums* of her own? Truly great scents reminiscent of the elegance and beauty of yesteryear, yet available to a wider market, perhaps in Europe as well as the United States? It was a dream worth investigating. She owed that much to her father.

Standing in the dimly lit storage room behind La Parfumerie Camille, Simone ran her fingers over the old-fashioned "organ" of her father's perfume console that stood in one corner, draped in sheets. Perhaps no one in the United States knew better than she how to "play" this instrument, which physically resembled a pipe organ, but which in the place of music-bearing pipes held hundreds of small bottles containing essential oils, resinoids, and absolutes—naturally produced or "nature identical." Her father had rarely used the pure chemicals common to modern perfuming.

Simone had the ability to identify literally thousands of different odors, and using the contents of these vials, she could "listen through her nose" to the harmonies of their scents and blend them into perfectly balanced aromatic chords.

But it took more than just talent as a perfumer to achieve what had become in her heart her dearest wish.

It took money. Lots of money. Because fine fragrances were no longer the products of a cottage industry.

Perfuming today was big business. Today it was more than creating a winning fragrance. It was also creating the hype. The packaging. The marketing. Simone's shoulders slumped. She could be the most talented perfumer in all the world, but without that megastructure of business behind her, her *grand parfum* would likely remain a *petit parfum* instead.

Thanks to her Tante Camille, Simone did not have to decide immediately what to do with her future. She had her small room in the apartment above the shop for as long as she wanted. "My dear little pet," clucked the elderly woman fondly, "stay here with me. Together, we'll run the *parfumerie*. It is a good business. I am getting old. I need the help of a younger woman such as you."

Simone could not bear to tell her aunt that she'd had about all of New Orleans she could stand. Her time in New York had given her a taste for the wider world beyond either Grasse or the French Quarter, and she liked the flavor. She had decided to make up her mind firmly about which direction she would take with her career, then tell Tante Camille when it was a *fait accompli*. She knew the older woman meant well, but Simone did not want to end up as Camille had, a mediocre perfumer in a derelict shop catering to tourists on Esplanade Street.

Until she made a decision, however, she would do all she could to aid the woman who had been like a mother to her since her own *maman* had died shortly after arriving in America. Today, that meant unpacking a cardboard carton of vintage perfume bottles Camille had purchased from a friend who imported antiques by the case lot from around the world. Camille was away having her hair done, so Simone carried the box from the storeroom into the small, cramped showroom where she could wait on customers as she inventoried the contents.

These proved to be English in origin. Some of the bottles packed inside were standard amber vials of the type used in apothecary shops in Victorian times, old but not particularly valuable. Still, visitors to her aunt's shop would perceive them as romantic when filled with Camille's own concoctions.

But at the bottom of the box, Simone felt a larger item, wrapped in heavy brown paper. She brought it out and set it on the counter. It was about six inches wide, four inches deep, maybe eight tall, and it was heavy.

Carefully removing the paper, she let out a delighted exclamation at what she had uncovered. It was an exquisite nineteenth-century toiletries box made of smoky agate, ornately gilded. Raising the lid, she counted five crystal perfume bottles, the stopper of each adorned with a tiny silver bird, nestled in the blue velvet lining like a family of argentine robins. Alongside were some manicure files, a tortoiseshell comb, and a small mirror.

"How beautiful!" she murmured. Taking the largest bottle

from its holder, Simone pressed the tail feathers of the silver bird, opening the vial to the air. A scent spilled out, saturating her senses with a fragrance unlike any she had ever smelled. Or felt. An odor so heady it almost made her dizzy.

"Mon Dieu!"

She blinked her eyes and released the lid, staring at the vessel as she was instantly overcome by the most startling sensation. She felt as if . . . she had just been embraced by a lover. Her cheeks burned and her heart raced as surely as if an intimate caress had ignited her passion. Her skin tingled, and she felt an ache building from deep within, a physical, sexual desire.

Hastily and with shaking hands, she replaced the bottle in the box and took a seat on a tall stool behind the counter to regain her composure.

"What on earth?" she murmured, stunned. Simone had no lover. She was unaccustomed to these kinds of sensual, almost erotic, feelings. And yet, she could not deny them.

Had they been caused by the fragrance? Surely it could not be!

And yet . . .

She reached for the crystal bottle again and lifted the lid a fraction of an inch. Placing her nose close to the opening, she took a cautious sniff, hoping to identify the mysterious substance. Instead, she felt her body heat begin to rise again almost immediately.

"What *is* this?" she repeated, astounded. She inhaled another exploratory whiff, but her olfactory senses failed her utterly in identifying the scent. The only thing of which she felt certain was that this was a pure essential oil extracted from a single plant, not a blended fragrance.

"Hmmm." She replaced the vial in its holder. Whatever was in the old bottle, its scent was powerful. Potent. Alluring.

The very qualities needed in a *grand parfum*.

Excitement suddenly coursed through her, overcoming the residual tingle of sexuality. Today, when her aunt returned, she would take the bottle to the lab at the university. With the modern equipment available there, it shouldn't take long to discover its identity. With its apparent power to "turn her on," as they said in America, Simone knew she had the inspiration for her first *grand parfum*. She would include it in a blend, using only the finest, most expensive natural ingredients, and create a perfume more sensual than Houbigant's Quelques Fleurs, more provocative than Caron's Narcisse Noir, more mysterious even than Guerlain's L'Heure Bleue.

Simone's preoccupation with her fantasy perfume had removed her from all present reality, and when the metal chimes attached to the front door of the shop jingled loudly, announcing a visitor to the cluttered boutique perfumery, she nearly fell off the stool. Then she looked up to greet the customer, and her eyes widened.

The man who entered was as astonishing as the perfume had been only moments before.

He looked like something right out of Mardi Gras, only it was the middle of May, not February.

But this *was* New Orleans, prone to attract the crazies at any time of year.

He had to be almost seven feet tall, Simone surmised, and a large white turban coiling around his head afforded additional height. Made of a gauzy fabric, the headdress was twisted so it enshrouded his beard as well, giving him the appearance of a mummy. But the bright brown eyes that peered at her from beneath shaggy brows glittered with keen vitality.

A mummy in drag, she thought, biting her lip to hide her amusement as she took in the outrageous robe that draped from his shoulders to his ankles. Made from a dark red fabric that shimmered slightly in the sunlight filtering through the front window, it was banded around the neck and down the edges with wide gold filigree braid that was literally encrusted with rhinestones in every color imaginable. Beneath the robe, his clothing was nondescript, something that looked like black pajamas, and he wore sandals on his coffee-colored feet. He was not altogether unhandsome, Simone decided, unable to determine his age. Just bizarre.

"May I help you?" she said, remembering her duty as sales-person.

"I seek Mademoiselle Simone Lefèvre." His voice was rich and deep, his tone polite, but the hair on Simone's arms stood up in alarm. Why would this strange man be looking for her? She suddenly wished she wasn't alone in the shop.

"I am Simone Lefèvre," she replied tentatively, moving farther behind the counter and drawing her overshirt together to cover her scantily clad figure.

He stared at her for a long moment. "Can it be?" he whispered. "Have I found you at last?"

"What can I do for you, Mr. . . . ?" Her stomach knotted, and she placed one hand on the telephone, just in case she might need to call 911.

At her words, the man snapped out of his semi-trance. "A thousand pardons, Mademoiselle Lefèvre," he offered, bending into a deep bow. "Let me introduce myself." He flowed rather than walked toward her. "I am Shahmir, humble servant to one whose name I cannot reveal, but who once long ago contracted with your father for a personal fragrance."

Simone stared at him in shocked silence, then said, "My father is dead."

"So I have learned. I am sorry, mademoiselle."

"What do you want of me?"

The elongated face softened into a kind smile. "Do not be afraid, mademoiselle. I come only to see if you can complete the perfume for which my master paid your father."

"He paid my father . . . ? But, sir, uh . . . Mr. Shahmir, Papa has been dead for over ten years. I hardly see how you can hold me responsible . . ." Panic replaced fear. What if he wanted his money back? She had no money. And for certain, she had no record of any proceedings between her father and any of his clients. Beads of perspiration broke out on her brow.

"My master sent me to your father's *parfumerie* in Grasse, longer than ten years ago. He wished to know if Monsieur Lefèvre could synthesize a certain ingredient and re-create an ancient formula which called for the essence of a plant that appeared to be extinct. Your father agreed to attempt it, and he accepted a retainer.'' The man tilted his head, his eyes narrowing. ''A rather large retainer.'' He hesitated, then added with a solemn nod, ''But I am not here about the money.''

Simone knew better. ''I have none of my father's records,'' she replied, her voice hard and even as it forced its way over the strained muscles inside her throat. ''They . . . they were stolen. By . . . my father's apprentice.'' She could not bring to her lips the name of the thief, so great still was her rage over what had happened.

The tall man's brows lifted. ''Stolen? This is indeed bad news.''

Simone found it hard to believe that after all this time, one of her father's clients did not know the story. It had been the scandal and outrage of the French perfume industry for several years after the fact, especially when the British House of Rutledge flooded the market with its line of fragrances known as Royalty, each fragrance a cheap synthetic copy of those great, and expensive, natural perfumes developed by her father for his exclusive clientele.

''I fear, sir, that your master's formula, if my father indeed was able to determine the ingredient, is now on the shelf of every supermarket and discount store in Europe and America,'' she told him, working hard to control her emotions. She raised her chin rather defiantly when she saw the dark look on Shahmir's face. ''I am sorry, but if you wish to discuss the creation of the perfume, perhaps you should seek . . . Mr. Nicholas Rutledge, who once appeared in our home, presenting himself as Nathaniel Raleigh, asking to be taken in as an apprentice. My father . . .'' She paused to clear her throat, then started over. ''Nat, or Nicholas rather, proved he had great talent as a perfumer, and my father took him in, treated him like a son. Trusted him. Agreed to teach him the secrets of the trade.''

A flicker of guilt passed through her, for she knew her father had agreed to take on the apprentice because he had looked upon ''Nathaniel Raleigh'' as a potential son-in-law, a perception she herself had encouraged, for she had fallen in love with the handsome young Englishman the moment she laid eyes upon him. Papa was of the old ways, always wishing for a son, even though from the time she was old enough to understand the nuances of perfumery he had taught her, his only child, everything he knew about the family business. When he'd learned of Simone's feelings toward "Nathaniel," he had broken his own rules and shared his secrets with an outsider.

"In return for this kindness and trust, Mr. Rutledge stole every formula my father had created," Simone continued, determined to get through the whole story. "It killed Papa. His heart could not stand the pain of such a betrayal. He died the morning the theft was discovered. Perhaps it was best, for he never had to know that a year or so later, his formulas would show up in stores everywhere as cheap imitations, packaged and priced to attract the bourgeoisie."

"But this cannot be," murmured Shahmir, obviously distraught. "It . . . it would be a terrible danger . . ." He straightened abruptly, piercing her with his gaze. "I do not believe your father was successful in determining a substitute for the ingredient required by my master," he said, and Simone detected a hopeful note in his voice. What terrible danger did he mean? Would his master beat him or punish him in some way if his formula had been mass-produced? This was becoming stranger and stranger.

"Perhaps not," she agreed, hoping he would leave now.

"Where can I find this Mr. Nicholas Rutledge?"

"I suppose Mr. Rutledge is still the master perfumer at the House of Rutledge. I believe their headquarters are in London."

"Then I will go there." His expression turned grave. "Tell me, Mademoiselle Lefèvre. If this terrible thing has not come to pass, and your father did not have a completed formula when Mr. Rutledge committed his crime, and if my master's perfume was never created, will you fulfill your father's obligation to make the potion? I have heard it said you are an even greater talent than Monsieur Lefèvre, no disrespect intended toward your father."

Simone felt her face grow hot, and she was troubled, wondering how this very disturbing man had learned such things about her. "What makes you think I would be any more successful than he in coming up with the missing ingredient?"

Shahmir's expression remained impassive, but his eyes belied his composure. Behind them she saw a flicker of . . . what? Exultation? Or madness . . . ?

"Perhaps, mademoiselle, that may no longer be necessary. For now, I bid you adieu."

Before Simone could question him further, he ended their interview with a brief bow, then swept out of the front door, leaving behind him the waning jingle of the door chimes and Simone staring at him openmouthed.

TWO

London

The deathly quiet in which Nicholas Rutledge worked was shattered by the unexpected sound of the front-door buzzer, startling him so badly he knocked over his coffee. "Damn!" He moved a stack of papers away from the pool of dark liquid and rose abruptly, searching for a napkin or towel to wipe up the mess before it spread and made its way to the computer terminal.

He'd been working alone, deep in concentration, setting up the accounting system for his new fragrance company on the computer. He was not expecting anyone, or anything, until the shipment arrived from Bombay, and he frowned as he went to unlock the door of the modest offices he'd rented in London's Esher area. Nearby, other international perfume companies such as Givenchy, Lancaster, and Giorgio Beverly Hills were housed in more elaborate quarters, but Nick counted himself lucky to have enough resources just to become their neighbor.

Someday, he vowed, he would outsell them all.

His first caller was the FedEx man, perspiring in the unusual warmth of the early spring morning. "Delivery for Mr. Nicholas Rutledge."

Nick's frown furrowed more deeply as his eyes took in the large, square parcel that rested on the pavement next to the man's feet. It was crated in pine boards and measured about three feet in each direction. He signed for the delivery, both curious and annoyed when he saw it had been sent by Pritchett. What could be so important, he wondered as he carried the heavy box inside, that the man had sent it by express delivery instead of shipping it more economically along with the rest of the items on board the freighter? He'd warned Pritchett against unnecessary expenditures. Every pound counted as he started his fledgling enterprise.

Nick carried the crate into the back room of the office/warehouse space and placed it on a large table he'd bought recently at a jumble sale. The room was mostly empty at present, but he hoped that soon it would become the heartbeat of Britain's newest, most innovative and successful fragrance company. Soon the scents of thousands of essences would mingle inside these walls of gray concrete, where he would create the most exciting perfumes and other scented products the marketplace had seen in years.

And soon, after ten years of miserable enslavement to that French bastard Antoine Dupuis, he would call his life his own once again.

Soon.

Maybe.

He thrust the familiar anger and raging doubts from his mind, forcing himself to remain in the moment. Locating a hammer, he began to pry loose the wide slats of the crate. The nails squealed in protest as he pulled them one by one from the wood. Whatever was inside must be either terribly important or quite fragile for it to have been so sturdily packaged.

The inner box was made of cardboard, and inside that, Nick could feel still another box of some kind nestled among cushioning foam pellets which spilled onto the floor when he retrieved the object.

It appeared to be a small trunk, very old. As he set it carefully on the table, the exterior metal crumbled into particles of golden-brown rust beneath his touch. Suddenly, for no reason he could fathom, a shiver rippled involuntarily down

Nick's spine, and he was overcome by a strange premonition, as if the trunk held some kind of danger or threat.

A foolish notion, he reproached himself, throwing it off with a shrug of his shoulders.

Carefully, he set about opening the trunk. He released the old-fashioned buckles of the two straps that encircled it, then with his letter knife picked at the ancient lock that hung rusting in the center fixture, breaking the fragile barrier with little effort. When he eased the lid open, the trunk seemed to exhale, releasing a pungent, musty odor into his face. He almost gagged as the scent of air imprisoned for a long, long time commingled with a strange, sweetly cloying smell.

He coughed and stepped back, waiting a few moments for the reek to dissipate, then peered into the chest, his interest now thoroughly piqued. The trunk was lined in dark, faded satin, and against the fabric nestled several items . . . a book, a packet of what looked to be letters, a small amber bottle, and a brooch on a thin golden chain.

Nick felt his heart inexplicably pick up a beat, and he reached for the necklace. The old-fashioned locket was cool against his skin. A dainty cameo glowed on the front, a delicately carved image of a woman's face in three-quarter view. He studied the miniature sculpture for a moment, wondering who it had belonged to and if it was the likeness of anyone in particular. Turning it over in the palm of his hand, he read the initials engraved on the back.

M. R. H.

Curious, he edged his nail into the groove and pried the locket open. Inside curled a slender braid, with strands of deep russet woven among threads of light brown. He raised a brow. Was this a lover's token of some sort?

The idea turned Nick's thoughts abruptly and unexpectedly to his own love life. Or rather, lack thereof. His seven-year marriage to one of England's most beautiful socialites had been little more than a sham, ending in divorce only last year. She'd grown tired of his obsession with restoring the House of Rutledge, accusing him of being wedded to his work, not her. Nick hadn't argued. Phyllis was a fine woman, deserving of a better husband than he could ever be. It had been a love-less match from the outset, one he'd made primarily to please his mother, to whom a place in society meant everything and who had lost so much upon her husband's disgraceful exit from the world.

Lady Rutledge had now departed this world as well, and with her had gone Nick's primary, maybe his only, reason to remain in that hellish relationship.

Besides Phyllis, there had been no other. Well, unless he counted Simone. The image of the young French beauty who had so unexpectedly captivated him during his summer as her father's apprentice in Grasse sprang instantly to his mind, and simultaneously, a slash of guilt shot through his heart.

Nick snapped the locket shut. He mustn't think about Simone. She belonged to a past that was unspeakably painful, a past he'd worked very hard to bury in a far, unreachable corner of his heart.

Annoyed that he'd allowed his thoughts to wander in such a dangerous direction, he laid the cameo locket roughly on the table. Reaching into the trunk again, he brought out a small book with a faded red cover. Stamped in gold on the aging leather were the words "A Gentleman's Diary." Nick opened the fragile volume, and his heart almost stopped beating when he read the inscription written on the flysheet in a strong, distinctive handwriting: *"For the eyes only of John Hamilton Rutledge. Do not trespass."*

Nick stared at the inscription, astounded.

John Hamilton Rutledge. His mysterious ancestor who had founded the Bombay Spice and Fragrance Company and who had provided generations of Rutledges with fireside tales about the unsolved puzzle of his sudden disappearance.

Nick had hoped Pritchett might come across some historical artifacts as the ancient company was dismantled, perhaps something that would enlighten him about what had actually taken place in those long-ago days. That's why he'd given the man explicit instructions to preserve any relics that might turn up. But a diary! Nick shook his head, astonished at his luck.

According to the stories Nick had heard at his grandfather's knee, sometime back in the middle of the nineteenth century John Rutledge, the second son of an earl, had had an affair with a woman of whom his parents, Lord and Lady Rutledge, disapproved. Nick recalled that supposedly the woman had not only been a commoner, but also, some claimed, a witch. He found the concept quaint.

The story went that because of their illicit liaison, his ancestor's family had forced John into the military, and he had been sent posthaste to India. A couple of years later, after he'd established the Bombay Spice and Fragrance Company, he had vanished suddenly one night without a trace. The local police and the British Army alike had turned the city upside down in their search for him. There had been no sign of foul play. No body was ever found, and eventually the case was closed.

Within the privacy of the family, there was some conjecture that he might have run away to Europe and eloped with his forbidden lover. Nick thumbed the pages of the diary lightly. Was John Rutledge's story recorded here? Would the mystery of his disappearance at last be explained?

Nick considered his ancestor's mysterious disappearance. He guessed that an elopement was possible, but more than once, he'd suspected that perhaps John Rutledge might have been as unstable as his descendent, Horace, Nick's own father. Had they shared in their genetics an acute fear of failure? Like Horace, had John Rutledge taken his own life?

Lack of a corpse did not mean there had been no suicide.

Horace's body had never been found either, although divers had searched the Thames for days. The two disappearances differed only in the fact that Horace had left a note explaining his.

Nick swallowed that old grief one more time and laid the diary next to the cameo. He'd get back to his uncle's story when he could digest at his leisure the family secrets those pages might reveal. As it was, he felt almost guilty at taking time away from the important tasks at hand to indulge in this little jaunt into the past.

The package of letters came up next. It was tied with a

wine-colored ribbon, which he released with a slight tug. The faded handwriting was as delicate and feminine as John's was strong and sure. Nick unfolded the top piece of correspondence. It was dated 15 June 1846. *"My dearest John, . . ."* it began, but the legibility became difficult after that. Had these been written by the woman in question? Nick worked his way through the first few sentences, but again decided to wait until later to finish deciphering the letter. Although he was intrigued by the trunk and its poignant contents, it could be nothing more than a diversion. At present, he had too much on his mind, too many things to accomplish, to waste time on old family gossip.

Refolding the fragile paper, he set the stack of letters next to the other artifacts on the table. The only remaining item in the trunk was a small amber glass vial, sealed with a cork. He frowned. A medication of some sort? Carefully, he tried to pry loose the stopper, but it crumbled under his efforts. Digging out the residue with the slender letter opener, he raised the bottle to his nose.

A single sniff instantly filled his senses with a powerful, heady floral fragrance, a remnant of which had escaped with the staleness of the trunk when he'd first opened it.

"Whew!" he exclaimed, wrinkling his nose and quickly reaching for a tissue to stuff into the neck of the bottle. The heavy sweetness of the solution was almost nauseating. Nick blinked, puzzled at having come across a perfume among his ancestor's private possessions. But John Rutledge, after all, had been in the fragrance business too.

Then with a start, Nick realized an astonishing thing was happening to him. A tingle seemed to be spreading throughout his body. A glow. An expectation of pleasure.

Sexual pleasure.

He felt a warmth permeate his skin. His breath quickened for no reason, and his heart began to race. Slamming the bottle onto the tabletop, Nick stepped away from it, shocked and alarmed as he felt the tension of a forceful, potent arousal tighten his gut.

"What the bloody hell?"

And then, like demons released from perdition, every memory he'd ever suppressed of Simone Lefèvre assaulted him. She was everywhere—in his mind, his heart, his body. He was catapulted in memory back to a time ten years before, to a place among the fragrant hillsides of Provence, and into the arms of the young and beautiful French girl whom he had so brutally betrayed.

The memories were both powerful and loathsome, and Nick groaned and left the room, fervently willing the ghosts of the past to leave him even as the residual scent of the perfume conjured them ever more clearly in his mind's eye. He made his way back to his frugally furnished office and sank into a chair, fighting the sick, heavy feeling that always landed in his stomach whenever he relived his treachery.

How could he have done that? he raved at himself as he had a thousand times in the past ten years. How could he have been so stupid, so naïve to believe in Antoine Dupuis, and to let the crafty, unscrupulous French financier convince him wrong was right?

Nick's throat tightened painfully, and for a moment, he thought he might lose control over his usually closely reined emotions. As hard as he'd tried to justify his actions, telling himself that at the time it seemed the only way out of a desperate quagmire, he'd never succeeded in quelling his guilt, and now the scent of the perfume invoked his shame all over again.

After his father's suicide, Nick, the sole heir to a once-vast family legacy, learned that the House of Rutledge, Britain's fragrance giant owned by his family since the reign of Queen Victoria, teetered on the edge of bankruptcy. The scandal of the suicide, combined with the threat of financial ruin, had nearly destroyed his mother, and Nick, only twenty-three and barely out of university, was desperate to set things aright. In his youth and inexperience, in grief and anger and panic, he had allowed himself to believe that the end justified any means, when that end was saving what was left of the once-proud Rutledge family heritage.

Nick's mood blackened as he relived his degradation. He'd

been approached by the French investment banker not long after his father's death. Antoine Dupuis had offered to buy fifty-one percent of the company, for cash. He wanted Nick to stay on, to give the appearance of Rutledge family continuity to the outside world. As Nick was something of a natural "nose," with a keen olfactory sense and a desire to work in the fragrance business, it had seemed a perfect solution.

Nick rubbed his temples and shook his head, still incredulous that he'd actually believed Dupuis when the Frenchman had promised that Nick could repurchase the majority of shares once the company had returned to a strong financial footing. What a young and utter fool he'd been.

It soon became clear that the problems of the House of Rutledge stemmed from the company's failure to introduce any new products under Nick's father's management. Dupuis had insisted that Nick could turn the business around almost overnight by developing perfume knockoffs, cheap synthetic imitations of expensive fragrances. But rather than having Nick try to mimic famous perfumes using his nose, Dupuis proposed instead that the young man travel to Grasse, to the heart of France's perfume country, and learn the secrets of a master perfumer there, one Jean René Lefèvre, who was renowned for the private fragrances he created for the world's wealthy and powerful.

It was the first time Nick had seen Dupuis's true colors, and he also learned how low *he* was willing to crawl to get what he wanted. He grimaced, remembering.

He had followed Dupuis's plan precisely. Using a pseudonym, he'd managed to become the old perfumer's apprentice, and shortly thereafter had stolen the formulas for Lefèvre's exclusive perfumes. A year later, the House of Rutledge introduced a new line of inexpensive perfumes called Royalty that ultimately set the firm back on solid financial footing.

Yes, Nick thought ruefully, everything had gone according to Dupuis's plan. Except for a couple of things. Nick hadn't counted on becoming instantly fond of the old perfumer.

Or falling in love with his daughter.

Nick dropped his head into his open palms. He had to stop thinking about all this. It was history, and no matter how much he regretted it, there was not one bloody thing he could do to change any of it. Instead, he must look to the future.

Despite his promises, Dupuis had refused to sell the now-profitable business back to Nick, and a few months ago, Nick had understood for the first time that he had become nothing more than the Frenchman's lackey. He despised himself as much as the man who had "rescued" him and realized that if he were ever to reclaim his honor and his long-lost self-esteem, he would have to leave the House of Rutledge. It had been an agonizing decision, for it had cost him almost everything. But it was the only way he could bear to live with himself.

He took some small satisfaction that at least he'd come away with something by negotiating the trade of his shares in the House of Rutledge for total ownership of a division of the company, an antiquated perfumery in Bombay. The old fragrance factory had been started by his ancestor whose diary he'd just come across, John Hamilton Rutledge. It was a worn-out scrap of a business, but the equipment and inventory were valuable, and Nick trusted his abilities to use them to start his own perfumery, Bombay Fragrances, Ltd. He believed he could propel the business into the twenty-first century as a major British player in the international fragrance industry, honestly this time, without resorting to the underhanded techniques of Antoine Dupuis.

Nick believed he could make it, *if* he worked quickly and with consummate creativity. As a marketing strategy, he had decided he must develop a product line so bold, so daring, that Bombay Fragrances would become synonymous with adventure and intrigue and instantly capture the imagination of the consuming public.

But ideas for such ingenious products had sadly eluded him. Nick stood up and went to the window, not looking out but rather into the depths of his imagination, searching for inspiration. Then the obvious hit him, and he struck his forehead with the palm of his hand.

The perfume in the antique vial.

It had actually turned him on. Physically. Sexually. Of course, perfumes always promised sexual allure. But he knew of none that actually delivered the physical reaction he'd just experienced.

He rushed back into the room where he'd left the vial. What could be bolder, more daring than a fragrance that invoked actual physical sexual stimulation?

Removing the tissue, considering that his first reaction could have been just a fluke, Nicholas Rutledge closed his eyes and sniffed the fragrance again.

To his enormous relief, the scent again reached into the depths of his libido and stirred the fires of passion and desire. A slow smile spread over the features of his face.

"Yes!" he whispered. "Oh, yes." Then he raised the vial in silent salute to his long-lost ancestor.

THREE

Relief suffused Simone when the tall, exotic man took his leave. Although she had not exactly promised him she would make the perfume for his "master," she knew that if he was able to obtain the formula, she would hear from him again. Obviously, her father had had no luck in reproducing the mysterious missing ingredient, and how she was expected to create a perfume from a plant that was extinct escaped her.

She doubted, however, that the man who called himself Shahmir could lay hands on the formula, if indeed it still existed. By now, Nicholas Rutledge, she supposed, had either used it or destroyed it.

Shaking her head in amazement at the whole episode, Simone made her way to the front door of the shop to make sure the peculiar man had really departed. From the floor a glimmer of red caught her eye. It was one of the plastic jewels from his opulent coat, sparkling like fire in the strong morning sunlight from where it had fallen to the linoleum. She picked it up and gazed at it momentarily, then stepped out onto the sidewalk, thinking to return it.

She looked to the left, then the right. There were the usual passersby . . . the tourists, the homeless, the early-morning drunks. But no seven-foot-tall man dressed like a maharaja, or a mummy ready for Mardi Gras. It was as if he'd just . . . disappeared. Vanished in broad daylight. Simone shivered despite the muggy heat and stuffed the heavy red ornament absently into her shorts pocket.

She hoped Mr. Shahmir would not come back. He gave her, as her American friends would say, the creeps.

Returning to the job at hand, she continued to unpack the myriad of interesting perfume bottles her aunt had purchased. She carefully washed and dried each one, marked the price, and put it on display. It was a pleasant chore, as Simone had always been fascinated by the containers used to hold perfumes. Her father had told her how the famous glassmakers of Paris such as Baccarat and Lalique had worked hand in glove with the great perfumers, like Guerlain and Coty, to combine the visual and the aromatic into a work of art.

She daydreamed, inventing in her mind the perfect container for her first *grand parfum,* which she thought with growing excitement might be based on the remarkable essence she'd just sniffed in the crystal bottle. Maybe she would reproduce the faceted bottle with the small robin on top. It was a charming, old-fashioned design.

When she had finished the unpacking and her aunt had returned, ready to take command once again of her little perfume shop, Simone picked up the ornate Victorian box and took it with her to her room above the shop. She checked all of the perfume bottles inside to see if any other contained the fragrance that had so captivated her earlier, but they were empty. Only one held the precious essence, and she could see through the crystal there was little more than an inch of the liquid inside. Not much to work with, but sufficient to learn its identity, if she were careful.

Although she had already graduated, her professor and mentor in the chemistry department had given her permission to continue to use the university's chemistry labs, at least until she settled on her future and had other facilities available. He believed so much in her abilities as a chemist and her talent as a perfumer that he had convinced the college to purchase a used gas chromatograph and mass spectrometer and had encouraged her to experiment with both naturals and synthetics to create new fragrances. It was just a matter of time, he told her, until she was picked like a ripe cherry by one of the megacorporations that were exploiting the current popularity of scent among consumers around the world.

But Simone was not interested in the idea of spending her life scenting toilet paper and the like.

Settling into her familiar surroundings in the school's lab, the daughter of Jean René Lefèvre began her investigation of the newly discovered fragrant oil, finding it disturbingly difficult to concentrate because of the strange erotic effect the fragrance seemed to exert over her. But it was that very effect that stirred her imagination. What if she could create a *grand parfum* that would be truly aphrodisiac in nature, not just a whiff and a promise like most other scents? No doubt, she would make her mark on the world of perfumery.

But what of the lives of those who used it? Would they be enhanced, made more pleasurable? Or would this substance unleash dangerous desires, sending people out of control in their search for sexual gratification? She laughed to herself. No fragrance on the face of the earth could have such power, and she knew it. Scent had its place and could indeed make the wearer feel more beautiful, alluring, sensual.

But it was all in the wearer's mind, not in the chemistry of the perfume.

Still, she was curious to know the name and the complexion of this substance, which as she'd thought, appeared to be a single essential oil. Her determination mounted with each failed attempt, but three hours later, she was no closer to knowing its identity than she had been in the beginning. Even using the sophisticated lab equipment, she'd been unable to mechanically define and put a name to the sweet, compelling aroma. Confounded, frustrated, and feeling disturbingly sexually tense, Simone gave up.

Returning to her room above the perfume boutique that overlooked the small but exquisitely designed and lushly profuse garden she nurtured in the inner courtyard, she replaced the vial in its ornate holder. She stared at it for a long moment, intrigued with the possibilities it held. She felt certain this elusive substance could be the foundation for her first *grand parfum.* But not unless it gave up the secret of its identity.

And it appeared adamantly reluctant to do that.

Simone stretched and rubbed her back, which ached as it often did after long hours in the lab. She looked at her watch. Four o'clock. She had time for a bath and a nap before supper with her aunt. As usual, she had no other plans for the evening.

In the small bath across the hall, she drew hot water into the deep, claw-footed tub that took up most of the room, reminding herself that as interesting as it was to play around with things like the evocative perfume oil, she really must get on with making a decision about her future. She could not remain here, in this tiny apartment, in this cloistered life forever. She was twenty-seven years old. There was a big world out there, and it was past time for her to join it. Ten years was long enough to hide behind the skirts of Tante Camille.

Simone removed her clothing and caught the fragrance of the inscrutable essence where it lingered on her apparel. Whatever its source from nature, it was a truly beautiful scent, and she could stand to enjoy some of its pleasurable effects right now.

Quickly, she returned to her room, picked up the crystal bottle and brought it with her into the bathroom, where she splashed two drops into the steaming water. Instantly the room filled with its sweetly provocative scent.

Simone sank into the water, feeling totally decadent as she immersed herself and began to experience raw, sensual pleasure. Leaning back against the tub, she closed her eyes. The water became a caress, the brush of a gentle lover's kiss. It was only fantasy, she knew, but then, her love life was nothing but fantasy anyway. Although many men seemed to find her attractive, she'd loved only one, and it had been a horrendous mistake. But that had been years ago, and she knew it was time to get on with that aspect of her life as well. She slipped drowsily into a sweet sleep, vowing she would work on that too.

*　　*　　*

On bare feet, she stepped tentatively into the vast space. It seemed to have no ceilings, no floors, and yet she had no difficulty in moving through it. There were no walls either, she realized, only curtains of deep blue, purple almost, highlighted with red the color of claret, that swayed like mist in a midnight breeze. She felt welcome here, invited, safe, as if it were her own home or that of a beloved friend. She floated freely in the rarefied atmosphere, which was scented with something wonderfully exotic but unfamiliar.

Suddenly, she sensed the presence of another being there, but at first she saw no one. Her heartbeat picked up in anticipation, but she was not afraid. She knew intuitively whoever it was would not hurt her.

He came to her from out of the mists, his face hidden in shadow but the shape of his unclothed body highlighted eerily as if it were under some ethereal spotlight. With a sharp intake of breath, she surveyed the width of his shoulders, the narrowness of his hips, the strength of his muscular arms and legs. He seemed somehow familiar, and yet she'd never known such a man, certainly never in such intimacy.

She heard him call out to her, although no words were exchanged. Come to me, *he bid her. Unused to being alone with a man, she hesitated, although her body was responding in ways she'd forgotten it could. Looking down, she saw that she, too, wore no clothing. Her breasts, usually soft and supple, pointed slightly upward and were crowned with tight crests knotted with a desire to be suckled. Her skin tingled, her lips longed to be kissed, and she felt a blaze of desire inflame an unfamiliar sexual ache in that secret place which had received no visitors in many years.*

Come to me!

She heard it again, and it did not occur to her not *to go to him. She was* supposed *to be here, now, with this man. She took herself to him, although she trod not upon any floor. She was simply there before him, and she saw his eyes feast hungrily upon her body.*

He took her hand and kissed her fingertips, arousing her passion further. She did not pull away. Instead, she nodded, ever so slightly, and allowed herself to flow into his embrace. It was an odd sensation, being held so fiercely by a stranger whose face she could not see. But she felt no fear. It was more than just being comfortable in his presence. It was as if she knew she should become one with him. He kissed her, and her lips melted against his, searing with a need to taste more of him. She parted them, invited him, and felt the strength of his desire harden as his kiss deepened.

She wanted to make love to him, with every inch of her body. Not just with her lips or her hands or her sex. She wanted to make love to him with her total being. She arched her back and felt herself begin to sway against him. Slowly, deliberately, she allowed her breasts to graze against the wall of his chest, the rasp of his dark hair against them hardening her nipples even more. She drew in her belly until her skin was scarcely touching him, then like an erotic dancer, let her navel trace a circular pattern over the flat hardness of his abdomen. Her efforts were rewarded when he cried out for her to end the sweet torture.

He swept her into his arms and seemed to place her upon a cushion of clouds, then lay down by her side. He kissed her again and murmured into her ear words that touched her heart, inflamed her body. She wanted this man, desperately, and she let him know it, by opening her lips to his impassioned kiss and her body to his desire. In one motion, she draped her leg around him and brought him into her fiery depths that raged with unquenched need. She felt him inside of her, filling the void, matching her passion. And for the first time in what seemed all eternity, she knew the delicious completeness of being a woman. She opened her eyes, hoping to see the face of the man who so fulfilled her, but his features remained veiled in the deepening shadows.

Simone's eyes fluttered open, and she took in the reality of her surroundings. A small, high window with French lace curtains. Wooden tongue-in-groove walls, painted lavender. A pedestal sink, old and chipped, but still gracious by design. A commode. Towel racks. And herself, languid in a now-tepid bath. The dream, and that's all it had been despite its intensity, was fading already, its delight and satisfaction vanishing as well with the return of consciousness.

And yet, a whisper of it lingered, as did a hint of the scented perfume oil, sending a shimmer of renewed sensuality through her. With an effort, Simone pulled herself out of the tub and dried her tingling skin on a thick towel. If only it could be like that in real life, she thought dolefully, missing her lover's touch already. But *could* it be like that? Was it possible for a man and a woman to make love so totally, so completely, so selflessly that each not only fulfilled but almost *became* the other?

Her experience was limited, but she remembered that once she had given herself to someone she'd thought she loved, and that the loss of her virginity, as much as she would come to regret it later, had been in the arms of an equally passionate lover.

A lover whose real name she had not even known, she added in disgust as she donned bikini panties the color of the reddest rose and topped them with a matching silk camisole. Maybe it was better to stick to the kind of fantasy lover she'd just enjoyed.

It was a a great deal safer, *certainement*.

But as she buttoned the front of the long, loose sundress she'd chosen from her closet, her body cried out for a real lover, a man in the flesh. Was there someone out there in that big world who would be right for her? Would she have the courage to try to find him? Or, she wondered, picking up the perfume bottle and eyeing it thoughtfully, would she have to be content to use a substance such as this to make her dreams come true?

With his usual unflinching discipline, after his initial probe into the trunk and its intriguing contents, Nick spent the rest of his day working to set up a complex accounting system on his computer. But he found it difficult to concentrate, wanting instead to explore the possibilities presented by the perfume with such potent aphrodisiac effects. What essences were contained in that vial that could cause such an instantaneous and erotic reaction? Would his ancestor's diary, or the packet of letters, reveal the secret? His heart virtually leapt at the thought, but he kept to the task he had assigned himself for the day, before discovering the vial of perfume.

Only when the late spring sunshine filtered through the windows at a certain angle, indicating that twilight was not far behind, did Nick shut down his computer at last and straighten his desk. He had not, as he'd hoped, completed his task, probably because he was distracted by the perfume, but he reminded himself that he had plenty of time to accomplish all he must do before the shipment arrived from Bombay.

Driven by his need to succeed where his father had failed, Nick felt compelled to make certain that each moment of his life was filled with accomplishment. Even his dreams were often interrupted by memos from his subconscious, telling him to do this or that the next day. He had made some monumental mistakes in his life, and he felt pressured to accomplish a lot very quickly to overcome his past errors. Every minute counted, now that he was free of Antoine Dupuis.

He slung his jacket over his arm and picked up the trunk. Pulling the outside door shut, he locked it behind him, a gesture made more from habit than need. Other than his computer equipment, there was nothing in the offices of Bombay Fragrances, Ltd., for anybody to steal, unless the thief was after secondhand furniture. Except for the few boxes of old records and papers he had stashed away in his junk room at home, most of which were likely useless, Nick's life's work, and the venerable firm that bore his family's name, now belonged to Antoine Dupuis.

Now, for all intents and purposes, Nicholas Rutledge was a nobody, starting over with the scraps of an antiquated perfume factory, the money he'd been able to accrue through shrewd investments and divestments, and an indomitable will and determination to overcome the odds against him. Still, the thought of losing the House of Rutledge to Dupuis made his stomach burn.

Nick drove the short distance to his home, a modest two-story brick town house in a quiet neighborhood in an inner suburb of London. He'd bought it after his divorce for its very dissimilarity to the opulent mansion where he'd lived with Phyllis, where she still resided. It was decent enough, but unpretentious and certainly not the dwelling of one who by birthright could use the title "Lord" before his name. He could have afforded better, but chose not to. Part of his frugality stemmed from his desire to keep liquid as much cash as possible, in case he needed it for the new company. But there was more to it than conservative business sense. There was a part of him that said, "You don't deserve better."

And he wouldn't provide himself with better until in his mind he'd earned it. It was part of the ongoing punishment he seemed to keep inflicting on himself. He must make amends, for his father's cowardice, for his own shameful behavior. For his failed marriage. For his inability so far to restore the dignity of the Rutledge name.

Maybe he ought to get a hair shirt.

He pulled his small, classic, but high-mileage Triumph roadster into the drive and braked abruptly, sending pebbles flying. His mood had darkened, subtly, just as the sky had let slip its last hold on daylight.

Opening the large oaken door, Nick went directly to the room at the rear of the house which he used as a study. He placed the trunk on a table beside a wall of bookshelves, eyed it briefly, then turned and went upstairs to change into more comfortable attire.

He hung his suit carefully in the immaculate closet, then slipped into his favorite black running pants and pulled a black T-shirt over his head. He left his socks on but donned no shoes. Going into the WC, he bent over the lavatory and splashed cold water across his face, then peered at himself in the mirror. The face that peered back looked haggard, worried, tired. It needed a shave.

Nick didn't want to look at it.

Hastily, he dried himself and returned to the tastefully decorated but too-quiet study, where he poured himself a stiff drink and slipped a CD into each of the player's three slots, music to match his mood. Somber. Melancholy. Angry.

Tchaikovsky. Mahler. And for good measure, Wagner.

All he needed now was a raging thunderstorm.

He turned his attention at last to the trunk and his thoughts to the perfume that lay hidden inside—the perfume that had caused the unmistakably erotic sensations in his body. Had that been just some kind of weird aberration? His deprived libido calling for attention?

Or could it really have been the effect of the perfume?

He allowed himself to consider that he might have experienced an actual physiological response to the chemistry of the essence. Nick lifted the trunk's lid, determined to arrive at a logical answer.

With the darkly resplendent classical music framing the drama of the moment, Nick placed the cameo, the diary, the letters, and the perfume bottle side by side on the table that stood next to his favorite easy chair. He switched on the lamp, settled his drink into a coaster and himself into the leather seat, eager now to get to the task at hand.

Savoring the moment, he did not go straight for the perfume bottle. Instead, he again picked up the cameo first and studied the intricate detail of the woman's face carved in the shell. She was a delicate beauty, with hair swept back from her slender neck, her lips pouting just slightly, her eyes, though tiny, swept with long lashes. Who was she? Nick wondered again, stroking her image lightly. A real person, or just the creation of the carver's imagination?

A familiar ache washed through him, a symptom of the chronic loneliness in which he lived, and he pondered for a moment what it would be like to have in his own life such a woman as he fancied this one to be. His mind began to wander down that forbidden path, the one lined with regrets and self-recrimination, and he pulled himself together just short of the brink of the depression that descended upon him with those thoughts.

Maybe this wasn't such a good idea.

But that perfume. If it proved to have a sustained capability of producing erotic responses in the wearer, he believed it would be his deliverance. With a deep sigh, he replaced the cameo brooch on the table and picked up his uncle's diary. He was saving the perfume for last.

For the eyes only of John Hamilton Rutledge.

"Sorry, Uncle," he said, opening the book with a small smile and turning to the first page.

FOUR

꙳

19 August 1846, Aboard HMS Valiant Lady

If I disliked my brother before, I swear I hate him now, for every dreadful event that has come to pass of late has been of his malevolent doing. Not satisfied with being the firstborn son, the favored one who will inherit all our father's wealth and the title of Earl, he has always been consumed with a jealousy I have never understood, as if I somehow pose a threat to his inheritance. Always in our childhood days, he freely took or destroyed anything that I held dear, but this time he has gone too far. Perhaps it is best I shall spend the next two years with a vast continent between us, for if I were near to him, I fear I might kill him.

For this time he has managed to take from me what I treasure most in this world, nay, the only thing I truly treasure, my sweet love Mary Rose. Or should I say, rather, he has arranged that I be taken far from her? My imperious mother and insipid father listen to everything James says, thinking him an appropriate guardian for their younger son, when in fact, he uses their trust to manipulate my life. He saw that I fell in love with Mary Rose the moment we came across her collecting mushrooms in the forest, and he took vicious delight in tormenting me with the fact that it was an impossible liaison. She was a commoner, he pointed out, and worse, it was said she was a witch. These things he duly reported to Mother and Father, embellished to my detriment no doubt, and set in motion the events that have torn my heart from my breast even as they have torn me from my native land.

I fear for the safety of my true love, now that I am no longer there to protect her. James is such a bastard when it comes to women, and I fear that he might attempt to harm Mary Rose, perhaps even ravish her. The thought sickens me. I expressed my anxiety to her on the eve of my leave-taking, but she only laughed. She swore that his arranging for my military assignment to India had already caused her the greatest hurt possible, and that nothing he attempted in the future could hurt her more. She is a strong woman, of independent will, and I pray to God she will be safe from that miscreant.

I also swear before God that I will find a way to be with Mary Rose again for the rest of our lives. She is the only woman I will ever love, and I scorn the chasm which my birth into the aristocracy has placed between us. A great deal of good that birthright is to me! I will find a way to bring her to India, or to rejoin her when my duty is completed. Perhaps an elopement to the Continent or America is to be our fate, although I must find a way to finance our lives if it is to be so. I swear on all that is holy I will find a way. I will. J.H.R.

Nick lowered the book and stared unseeing into the subdued atmosphere of the room, uncharacteristically moved by what he'd just read. So it was true, that legend. John Rutledge had been in love with a commoner, a reputed witch. Mary Rose. Mary Rose who?

He picked up the cameo again. Was this Mary Rose, John's beloved? He remembered the initials engraved on the back and turned the brooch between his fingers to study them again. *M.R.H.* Mary Rose H——. He smiled sadly, wondering vaguely what her last name had been, this woman whom John

Rutledge had loved and from whom he had been heartlessly torn, apparently through the machinations of his older brother.

The idea of their cruel separation caused Nick's throat to constrict with emotion, which he cleared with a sip of scotch and a warning to himself against becoming maudlin about the affairs of his long-dead ancestor. But the demanding voice of his curiosity would not be silenced. Had John been able to keep his oath to be reunited with her for the rest of their lives?

Nick flicked through several pages of the diary, but suddenly the weight of his own worries, the lateness of the hour, and the effect of the scotch whisky landed solidly on his shoulders. If he hoped to get even partway through this material tonight, he needed some energy. Laying aside the relics, he padded in his socks into the small kitchen where he threw together a sandwich of cheese and cold meat and wolfed it down almost without tasting it. He poured a glass of milk and drank it while he munched on several of his favorite shortbread wafers. But his mind remained somewhere in the nineteenth century, on the image engraved in the cameo, the outrage expressed in his uncle's private diary, and most of all, the beguiling perfume.

He returned to the study, settling again into the chair and propping his feet on an ottoman. He started to resume his reading, but he could no longer ignore the tantalizing vial containing the perfume that summoned him silently from the tabletop. He picked it up. If he smelled it again, would it have the same sexually stimulating effect he had experienced earlier? The erotic puissance that aromatically crossed the line between the sensual and the sexual?

Almost afraid that it wouldn't, he gently removed the new cork he'd stuffed into the neck of the bottle to replace the disintegrated one.

He sniffed, lightly at first, and then with a deeper inhalation. To his satisfaction, he felt the same glow he'd experienced before as a distinctly sexual response began to arouse his body. Thoughtfully, he replaced the cork, then rested his head back against the supple leather of the chair, unable to repress the smile that seemed determined to cross his lips. He wasn't sure what the smile was all about. Was it the lucrative prospect offered by the perfume if he should be able to discover its contents and reproduce it as the premier fragrance to be introduced by Bombay Fragrances? Or the deeply sensual, pleasurable sensations it was sending in a warm wave throughout his being? He closed his eyes for a moment, thinking of the beautiful woman on the cameo.

She came toward him silently, her feet bare, her body clothed only in the silken mist that swirled about her. Nick's heart momentarily came to a standstill, then thundered in anticipation. He guessed that this was the woman whose face was etched in the cameo, and yet he could not make out her features. She was shorter than he, with exquisite feminine curves that moved in a natural seductive rhythm as she strode gracefully toward him through this haunting, shadowy place. Her dark tresses flowed around her face in appealing disarray.

Where was he? he wondered briefly. What was this place? But it didn't seem important. It was no place, and every place. She was no woman, and every woman. As he watched her move, he felt desire begin to build, the yearning every man has known who has ever sexually longed for a woman.

Come to me.

His command was not voiced, but he knew he'd spoken to her. She appeared to be walking toward him, but she did not seem to be getting any closer.

Come to me!

Nick felt a desperate urgency that she be in his arms. Why was she remaining so distant? Would she not be his? He held out his arms, beckoning her with every ounce of his will.

She must have heard his silent appeal, for suddenly she was there before him, skyclad, wearing only the deep shades of red and purple and blue that floated and swirled around them. Still he could not see her face. He reached for her hand and brought her fingertips to his lips. He grazed their softness with his kiss, begging her with all his heart to allow him to make love to her. He raised his eyes to hers and saw the raw sensuality reflected in those dark pools. He'd seen those eyes before, he was certain of it, but the rest of her face was veiled in the mist. Those eyes gave him the permission he needed, however, and he closed his own as he drew her body next to his.

In her embrace, he was enfolded in an unfamiliar but intensely pleasurable sense of well-being, pure happiness, as if the lover for which he had always subconsciously longed had at last appeared.

He wanted her, and the pleasures she brought him that had eluded him his entire life. He wanted them now. He wanted them forever.

His lips found hers and hungrily fed on their honey. His heart raced as he felt them open to him, returning his kiss with liquid fire.

Their bodies began to sway together, as if in a slow, sensual dance, skin meeting skin, touching, releasing, touching, releasing, then touching again. Burning.

He moved the sensitive palms of his hands over her body, exploring the velvet skin of her neck, the gentle ivory descent of her shoulders, the silken slenderness of her arms. All the while, his lips possessed hers. When his questing hands reached hers, he brought her palms against his and entwined their fingers, drawing her body closer.

He fitted her hands softly against his lower back and left them there, and a thrill raced through him as he felt her begin to trace tiny circles on his sentient skin. With maddening, deliberate slowness, each orbit dropped lower in evocative invitation. His own hands began to imitate her motions on the rounded flesh of her derrière, but his hunger grew fierce, and he was unable to keep his touch light.

He drew her hard against him, pressing his arousal into the softness of her lower body. She responded by beginning to move in a primal rhythm, arching her back, stroking his chest with her breasts, his midsection with her navel, his flat abdomen with her belly, making him burn for her in a ruthless seduction. Nick cried out from both pleasure and pain, his desire desperately in need of satisfaction.

He wanted to bury himself in her, become one with her, at that very moment, but there seemed to be no bed or pallet upon which they could lie to consummate their passion. But suddenly they were together, prone side by side, on the softest of clouds. There was no bed beneath them, for there was no need. Only the two of them existed in the entire universe.

His lips found hers again, and he whispered his longing to her. A murmur, a deepened kiss was her reply, along with the opening of her being unto him. Long legs entwined him, and he felt himself being drawn into what surely must be heaven. Darkness enveloped him. And warmth. The warmth of her arms, the warmth of her woman's body, of her spirit's soul. He moved into that warmth, that home he'd hungered for, deeper, deeper, wanting to deliver his own soul into its eternity. She moved in rhythm to his seeking, until at last he exploded into a thousand shards of exquisite sensation.

His last impression before he rocketed into the star-sprinkled midnight was a glimpse of his lover's face. A sob escaped his lips upon recognition of the fullness of her mouth, the delicate shape of her nose, those dark, absorbing eyes, and long-buried emotions erupted from deep within. Fear and shame commingled with ecstasy that seemed to know no bounds. In exquisite agony, he cried out her name.

"Simone."

Less than a week after Simone's discovery of the perfume, fate intervened to nudge her toward the future she'd been avoiding. Out of the blue, she had received a phone call from a man in London who spoke to her in her native French. His name was Antoine Dupuis, and he had urged her, of all bizarre things, to consider becoming the master perfumer at the House of Rutledge.

At first she'd thought it was a sick joke played by someone who knew her history with Nicholas Rutledge. But Dupuis quickly informed her that Rutledge was no longer part of the business, and that she had been suggested as his replacement by a member of the board of directors.

"Not only do we feel you are a highly qualified candidate

for the position," he'd told her, "but having only recently learned of how Rutledge came to acquire the formulas he used in our Royalty line, we thought offering you the job might in some small measure make up for the unforgivable crime he perpetrated against you. On behalf of the board of directors of the House of Rutledge, I offer my sincere apologies, Mademoiselle Lefèvre. If we had known what he planned, we would have taken measures to stop his contemptible action. Perhaps," Dupuis had concluded, "you will consider this an opportunity to reclaim what was taken from you under grievous circumstances years ago."

Simone was considering it, seriously. That's why she was on board the 747 jetliner, winging her way toward London, sipping champagne in the first-class section. The wine tasted sweet and good, a little like the flavor of revenge. She just might take Dupuis up on the offer, in spite of her trepidations that she was not experienced enough for the job. It would be sweet indeed to be in a position, if Dupuis had described it to her correctly, to finally destroy Nicholas Rutledge.

But the thought, as appropriate as she deemed it, surprisingly did not fill her with any great joy.

The position at the House of Rutledge, however, had another attraction for her. It would give her the corporate structure she needed to develop and market her dreamed-of *grands parfums*. And if the first part of her journey proved successful, her dream might come true sooner than she could have imagined.

After experimenting with the mystifying perfume oil for three successive nights and experiencing in her dreams the same kind of delicious erotic passion and sexual fulfillment as in her first, Simone was driven to learn more about the substance. She warned herself not to become obsessed with it, nor to use it indiscriminately, regardless of the pleasures she'd enjoyed in the arms of her dream lover. A fragrance should not replace reality.

If only she knew that kind of reality!

Still, she recognized the importance of the oil's intriguing qualities, and already it was clearly the inspiration, the basis in theory as well as in substance, for her first *grand parfum*.

Hoping to learn where the fragrant oil had come from, Simone had traced the shipment of the old bottles in which she'd discovered the perfume. They had been part of a consignment to a firm called Ryder and Company of London by a person who was liquidating a property in the country southeast of London. Unable to find out more than that, she'd already decided to travel to England to search further for the source of the perfume, and had been trying to figure out a way to afford the trip when Antoine Dupuis had called. It was he who had paid for the first-class ticket.

Indeed, a strange twist of fate. Maybe some of that serendipity she'd been reading about lately.

FIVE

_ક_

Nick drummed his fingers on the mahogany of his desk, wishing like hell the shipment of the remnants of the Bombay Spice and Fragrance Company would arrive, giving him something at last to occupy his restless mind. He had experimented several nights in a row with the perfume, each with the same unsettling results. No, the dreams had not just unsettled him, he admitted, they seemed to have completely unhinged him. He could not concentrate on the details of his plans that were so vital to his future success. He could not think about packaging or marketing or the all-important product launch. In fact, he could scarcely think at all, except about the woman in the perfume-induced dreams.

It had been Simone, he was certain.

Simone Lefèvre.

It didn't surprise him that he would dream of her. She'd come to him often in dreams, albeit tormented ones, those first years after he had betrayed her. Nick shook his head, still astounded that he could have been so stupid. So cruel. Simone was the one woman he'd every truly loved. So easily, she could have been his. But now, she was the one woman he could never, ever have . . . except in his dreams.

Damnation, he did not want her in his dreams! He slammed his palm against the desk. It was over and done with. He'd made a terrible but irrevocable mistake. He did not want the image of those eyes, dusky and passionate, haunting him. He did not want to remember the silken touch of her skin, the natural sweet scent of her body.

His thoughts raced on, tormenting him anyway, as he relived in his imagination that hot, torrid night in Grasse, when she'd willingly, trustingly given herself to him, her first lover. He could almost feel her body surrounding his, her warm, dark heat pulsing around him as he plundered her virginity.

Oh, God, he groaned aloud, furious at himself for allowing those thoughts to enter his mind, for losing his normal control and composure. All because of the dreams. He thought he had successfully blocked Simone Lefèvre from his mind, even from his subconscious. He'd worked at it very hard for ten years.

But she had crept back to him in the night, every night, and their dreamtime together remained so vivid he could feel his desire rising again in spite of himself. And also in spite of himself, he wondered briefly what had ever happened to her. He'd heard she'd gone to America, and he'd halfway expected her to surface at some time, taking on some role in the perfume industry. Actually, he had dreaded that happening, for if it did, he would likely encounter her sooner or later at some conference or international meeting.

Perhaps she was married now, maybe had children, and somehow he hoped, had either forgiven or forgotten "Nathaniel Raleigh," that lying, deceitful bastard.

She might be married, have children. But he doubted if she would ever forget, certain she would never forgive, what he had done.

Nick's tie seemed suddenly too tight, the air in the room too close. He had to get out of here, go someplace where he could pull himself together. His presence in these small offices was not necessary, wouldn't be until the freighter arrived in England bearing the equipment and records of the dismantled perfumery in Bombay. Until then, there was nothing toward establishing the new enterprise that he couldn't accomplish on his laptop from his study at home, or better, from Brierley Hall.

Brierley. Just the thought of it relieved some of the tension that had its claws deeply embedded into his shoulder muscles. He took a deep breath. Yes, he decided, he would escape for a few days to the ancestral country estate that now remained virtually his sole link to the aristocratic heritage of the Rutledges. As derelict as it was, it was the one place in which he could find inner peace.

A trip to the country would give him the opportunity to read the diary and letters in the tranquillity of his favorite chair in Brierley's drawing room, or perhaps outside in the garden, beneath trees that had been there longer than the stately but crumbling manor house. While he was on the estate, he could also check on the renovations that had finally been completed on the old servants' quarters at the edge of the property. Although he hated having had to resort to such commercialism, he had decided to turn the quaint old cottage into a holiday rental to raise money for his new enterprise. His first tenant was due to arrive shortly. Perhaps he would stop by to say hello.

But should he take the perfume with him to the country?

Nick was convinced the fragrance had triggered his unquiet dreams, and although he was not afraid of it, he allowed it due respect. He'd been around perfumes most of his adult life, and he knew that scent was the sense of memory. He knew how a single odor could travel through the nasal passages, past the olfactory receptors, and drop directly into the limbic region of the brain, the domain of the emotions. There, it was capable of stimulating memories, no matter how old, how buried.

But never had he known a perfume to stir up such an intense sexual experience. Fragrances were simply pleasures for the senses, like art or music. They had limited power over one's mind, virtually none over one's body.

And yet . . .

If indeed the perfume was capable of conjuring up erotic, sensual, sexually explicit dreams, Nick thought for the hundredth time in a week, would it not be the perfect product to launch Bombay Fragrances, Ltd.?

Was not the world starved for some magical elixir to mend

its universal broken heart? Did not fashion designers prey upon everyone's apparent desperation to attract the opposite sex? Was that not why there was such big money in plastic surgery these days? And in fragrance?

This craving, this demand for beauty and sexual acceptance was what drove fragrance and cosmetics giants like America's Revlon and Estée Lauder, France's Lancôme and L'Oréal, Britain's House of Rutledge.

A redder lipstick.

A silkier skin.

A sexier appeal.

Why not a perfume that, if nothing else, caused incredibly evocative dreams? Would that not provide at least some satisfaction for the hunger to be loved?

Nick picked up his laptop and his jacket with a sneer. A damn lot of good it had done him. If anything, it had made his hunger worse, whetted his appetite for a morsel he could never savor.

The English countryside in late spring was an explosion of flowers, and despite her weariness, Simone drank in the beauty of it all from the window of the train that took her from London's Gatwick Airport through the green countryside to the small town of Redford. From time to time, she felt inside her purse, making sure she had the address of the estate agent's office where she was to pick up the key to the place she had rented.

Excitement and expectation coursed through her. She would be staying in the same cottage from which the secretary at Ryder's had told her the Victorian perfume bottles had likely come. Actually, the secretary had kindly arranged the lease for her, telling Simone that the owner of the house was a friend of Mr. Ryder's who was eager to let it out for holiday rental, as he needed the money.

Whether or not she came across any evidence of the origin of the fragrant oil there, Simone would be within walking distance of the village of Redford, where she thought she might discover something in the library or historical archives.

At any rate, it sounded like a lovely place, the price was within her means, and a few days there would give her time to sort out her thoughts concerning Dupuis's offer before meeting with him in London.

The cottage did not disappoint her. It was very old, built in the Tudor style, its whitewashed walls crosshatched with dark timbers. Protecting it from the weather was a thick, neatly trimmed thatched roof, the fairy-tale kind she had seen only in picture books. Charm dripped from its setting as well, with purple lilacs, blue columbine, brilliant white daisies and dapple-faced pansies nodding their brilliant blossoms from the cottage garden. "It's lovely," she murmured to the agent who had brought her from the village, thanking her profusely and following her into the house for a quick tour.

Inside, the rooms were tiny but cleverly appointed in modern reproductions that lent authenticity as well as the practicality of sturdily built furniture for a rental property. "The owner sold the valuable antiques," the agent apologized, "and replaced them with inexpensive replicas." She sighed. "It seems a shame, although the impoverished aristocracy is doing that a lot these days."

At the moment, the furnishings of the house and the owner's apparently dire straits became inconsequential as Simone was overcome at last by the fatigue she had been battling for the past several hours. She said goodbye to the agent, shut the door behind her, and went into the bedroom. She did not unpack her suitcase, but took out a ruby-red satin chemise sleeping gown and matching robe, her toiletries, and the ornate Victorian box that held the precious perfume. She placed the box on the nightstand, carried the rest with her into the shower, and twenty minutes later emerged refreshed and ready for a nap.

Sitting on the bedside, she lifted the vial containing the perfume from its velvet nest and ran her slender fingers across the silver bird roosting on top. Should she? With each use, which before she had rationalized to be in semiscientific experiment, the amount of the precious liquid that remained available for analysis dwindled. She knew she should not indulge frivolously in the sensuality of it, but maybe, just one more time, to celebrate the good fortune that had brought her to this place.

She set the bottle down on the nightstand, brushed her silken ebony hair and removed her gown, laughing at her preparations a little self-consciously. It was as if she were readying herself to meet a real lover in this bed. As she slipped between the crisp linen sheets, she allowed one deep inhalation of the magical fragrance, then slipped easily, eagerly, into her dreams.

Seated beneath the tall trees in the garden of Brierley Hall, Nick held the small diary in both hands to keep the eager breezes from fanning the pages. Although he'd read it through twice, the tale held him spellbound. The entire account of his uncle's bizarre and unhappy life in India fascinated him, as did the letters from Mary Rose that told the other half of their mutual misery. Together, the relics revealed a haunting, heartbreaking story with an astounding, altogether unbelievable resolution. After his first reading, he'd come away convinced that his uncle was at best unstable, at worst insane.

And yet, there was a truth and a passion that ran through the diary that gave Nick pause. It wasn't so much what was said toward the end but rather what his uncle had left unsaid that disturbed him. There was more here than could be comprehended without further study. Nick looked down at the page where his thumbs served as bookmarks and reread a passage:

16th February 1847
  India is infernal. Never have I seen such wretched poverty juxtaposed against obscene wealth. And I believed our class system was rigid! It is nothing compared to the caste divisions in this unholy land. I have dwelt here six months, and each day my aching loneliness mounts. My mind is constantly upon my green homeland, and the woman who awaits me there. I hear from Mary Rose often, but each letter only makes me

*long for her more. How can I bear to remain here for
another year and a half?*

*My young assistant, a native, is witness to my tor-
ment, and he has been urging me to visit his relative
who lives in a monastery high up in the mountains. He
tells me the monks there concoct some kind of potion,
an oil made from the blossoms of a so-called magical
plant, that massaged into my skin will take away my
pain and relieve the loneliness. Thus far I have fought
his suggestions, as I doubt not the liniment must contain
some opiate derivative, and I do not need such dulling
of my senses. But the idea is tempting. As is my latest
diversion.*

*I have been in discussions with others in my station
concerning the possibility of developing a private enterprise. I have heard stories of Englishmen deriving
huge profits from organizing shipments of the exotic
products of this land—tea, spices, fragrances such as
sandalwood and patchouli, madras cloth & etc.—to England. The thought intrigues me, and I am investigating
the possibility of participating in that trade. It could buy
my freedom perhaps. With a substantial private income
I could afford to estrange myself from my family ties
and follow my heart's desire . . . straight to the altar
with Mary Rose Hatcher.*

Nick allowed the book to drop to his lap, his gaze to wander
to the lush green meadow just beyond the garden gate, his
mind to consider this woman who appeared to have held his
uncle so spellbound that he was not only ready, but eager to
renounce what Nick was fighting with his life to repossess,
his family name and heritage.

Mary Rose Hatcher.

M. R. H.

The woman on the cameo? Perhaps not, but surely it was
her hair entwined with John's that was secured in the old-
fashioned locket. It was a common practice in those romantic
times.

As was the creation of scent by Victorian ladies. It was not remarkable that Mary Rose would have created a perfume for her lover, as she'd written in these letters. Nick knew the Victorians loved pomanders and potpourris, flower waters, bath oils, and tonics. The Victorian garden, such as the one behind the servants' quarters where Mary Rose had lived, furnished not only vegetables for the table but also herbs and flowers for creating beautiful scents and home remedies.

But he doubted seriously if any Victorian lady, no matter how talented at such things, had ever created a substance the likes of which was recorded on these ancient pages. *If* this tale was true. He shook his head. It was just too implausible. Perhaps John Rutledge had gone insane, and to cover his disgrace the family had kidnapped him or something. That made more sense than what he'd written in his diary, especially the last entry. It read like a piece of science fiction.

But the rest of it . . . Mary Rose had written of a "perfume essence" she'd derived from something she called the *mahja*. Nick supposed this was the fragrant aphrodisiac oil he'd discovered alongside the diary and letters. But what in bloody hell was a *mahja* plant? Even if its claimed magical effects were only the wistful wishes of his demented ancestor, Nick could not deny the essence had unusual powers. Every time he had used it, he'd experienced incredibly erotic dreams.

But unlike what it did for John Rutledge, who claimed that the "balm" of the *mahja* had assuaged his heartache, it had done just the opposite for Nick. It had wreaked havoc with his emotions, for the lover in each of his dreams had been Simone Lefèvre. Although he made love to her with fiery passion in his fantasies each night, his torment upon waking was unspeakable. He was tempted at one point to empty the vial down the sink and be done with it.

Yet Nick sensed that he had at last inherited something of value from his Rutledge lineage. If he could re-create this perfume, even get close to replicating it and its sensual effects, he would have what he needed to make his comeback.

Nick rose and returned to the house, considering the dilemma he faced. He must find out more about the plant known as the *mahja*. His nose had been of little help in identifying the source of the essence, and he had not come across any reference to such a plant in his own botanical books. He was certain he could chemically analyze and identify the substance, but not until the lab equipment arrived from Bombay and was set up in his London office.

Wait. All he could do was wait. But waiting was not something Nick did well.

He paced. He drank a cup of tea. He cursorily scanned the newspaper. He jumped a mile when the phone rang. The elderly housekeeper, whom he'd hired for the fortnight he planned to be here, summoned him to the phone.

"Hello."

"Mr. Rutledge, it is so good to speak to you again," a feminine voice cooed at him. "This is Virginia Stuart, with Stuart and Sutherland Estate Agents."

Nick frowned, vaguely recalling having met some woman by that name who came by to have him sign the contractual agreement for the agency to represent the rental of the carriage house. "Ah, yes," he half lied. "Miss Stuart. I understand we have our first tenant."

"Indeed. The American woman I told you about. She arrived early this afternoon. I believe by now she should be settled in. She plans to stay for several days."

"Very well," Nick said, glad to know his strategy for offsetting at least part of the upkeep on Brierley Hall through tenant rentals was working. He regretted, however, that he had so hastily disposed of the original antiques that had furnished the servants' house. It had been home to Mary Rose Hatcher, and quite possibly, the information he needed to recreate the perfume oil might have been among the items he'd turned over to his friend Jeremy Ryder for sale. Well, it was too late now. "Thank you for calling, Miss Stuart. I hope you are able to keep the place occupied for the entire summer."

"I'll do my best."

"You have my gratitude. Goodbye, then."

Nick hung up the phone, considering his new role as landlord. He was ashamed to have to stoop to renting out part of the Rutledge estate just to try to make ends meet, but if nothing else, Nick prided himself on being a survivor, and he would do whatever it took to get past this latest challenge. Meanwhile, if he was to be a landlord, at least he would be a courteous one.

"I'll be back in time for dinner," he told the housekeeper, heading for the stable where he kept his one indulgence, an Arabian stallion with blood so blue he earned his own way in stud fees. Mounted, Nick felt the power of the horse beneath him, which somehow transferred to him, raising his spirits, and together man and animal took off at an energetic pace, both glad of the exercise. He'd planned to go directly to the renovated cottage to greet his first tenant, but he decided instead to allow himself a good ride beforehand. His visit to the half-timbered house at the edge of the estate would, after all, only take a moment.

SIX

❧

Indigo mist, soft as baby's breath, enfolded Simone as she slipped out of consciousness and into the space that had become her familiar trysting place with the man whose face, like Eros, had remained hidden from her view. His identity did not matter, for she knew he would not hurt her, indeed, that he would fulfill her every desire in a way no man ever could outside this fantastic realm of dreams. Eagerly she searched the vapors, drifting ghostlike through the rarefied atmosphere, breathing in a scent both beautiful and haunting as she mentally summoned her lover to her.

He was a *knowing* before he became a *being*. She sensed his heat first, a physical fire that flickered and licked against her skin, inflaming the desire that already glowed red-hot in her sex. She felt him brush her lips with the tips of his fingers, as he had done in each dream, a signature greeting, a sensual salutation. She tasted the size of his fingers, felt their masculine texture against her impatient skin, and she kissed them with hungry invitation.

But he was not to be hurried. He traced the outline of her full lips, then let one finger slip between them, bidding her to nibble. Even as she allowed her tongue to play with his touch, she felt the whisper of his other hand moving down the length of her throat, the back of his fingers tracing lightly from just beneath her chin to the rise of her breasts. She arched her back and bit harder into his finger when his hand cupped her breast and his thumb began caressing her nipple in slow, firm strokes.

No words were spoken between them, and yet the message she heard quickened her already racing pulse. He wanted her, now and for all time, he told her. He loved the beauty of her body, the softness of her flesh, the roundness of her breasts, the scent of her hair. He loved the dark passion he saw in her eyes, the ripeness of her lips.

And suddenly, she wanted to see his eyes as well, to read their passion. She wanted to know his face, to view the man whose touch she craved so fiercely she thought without it she might die. She attempted, slightly, to pull away, to demand of him that he reveal himself, but his hand slipped to the warmth of her sex, and she lost all reason and determination.

With his lips, he trailed kisses across her face and along her throat, stopping in his tender travels only to suckle at the dark berries of her nipples, all the while allowing his fingers to explore the dark, wet heat of her.

She felt him part the petals that folded around the doorway to her inner being, and her body quaked as he knelt before her and kissed those feminine flowers.

Simone Lefèvre ceased to exist at that moment. The spirit that possessed her body was of another nature, an animal nature, a creature stalking a quarry, seeking consummation of its fiery hunger. The creature divested the woman of all inhibitions, filled her with feral energy, turned her from acquiescent to aggressive.

With her hands on his jawbones, she drew the man closer and moved against his own now voracious attack with seductive rhythm, feeling the intensity of her desire become almost unbearable with each stroke of his tongue within her heat. He seemed innately to know the circle of pleasure to trace, and he suckled the sensitive clitoris the way he had made love to her nipples moments before. The wild woman cried out just before she was rescued from her torment by the waves of sexual release that at last engulfed her.

She felt his hands upon her buttocks, drawing her down into a gossamer pillow, where she lay, momentarily sated,

*until he began again to arouse her with deliberate slowness.
"I am not through with you, my lovely wanton." She heard
his words although they were not spoken aloud, and instead
of offending her, they only re-ignited her desire. For in them,
she also heard his love, his own aching need, and she became
again an aggressor in the game.*

*Determined to inflict upon her lover the kind of exquisite
pain, and then release, he had perpetrated upon her, she
rolled onto the man's broad chest, holding him beneath her
with her will more than her weight. With the flat of her hand
against his skin, she felt his heart thundering and knew it
would not be an extended torture. She placed her lips to his
pectorals and tasted the salt of his sex-moistened skin. She
inhaled the scent of him, trying to fill her consciousness with
his essence. Against the inside of her thigh, she felt his hardness, and she aggravated it by stroking it with the sensitive
skin of her leg. She let her hand slide to his belly, and then
lower, to allow her fingers to play among the dark curls that
adorned his sex. She traced a path along the crease of his
groin, all the while placing kisses ever lower on his body,
moving deliberately slowly in the direction of his virile erection. When she attained her objective, her lips moved naturally and skillfully along its fine skin, although she had never
before tasted a man thus.*

*At her touch, she felt him take in a sharp breath, and sud-
denly, she was no longer in command. He lifted her up and
away from him, then settled her against his swollen need. She
opened to him and felt a fierce thrust that took her own breath
away. She sat astride him, her hands splayed across his chest.
He filled his own hands with the fullness of her breasts, and
they moved in a race to completion until at last, together, they
found the end to their impassioned agony.*

*Gasping for breath, Simone leaned her full weight into her
arms, which she still held stiffly against his chest, and like a
starving person who has just enjoyed a feast, allowed herself
to lick the plate, to luxuriate in the lingering pleasure of the
tiny pulsations that continued to throb where their bodies
were intimately joined.*

From somewhere far away, she heard a sound like thunder, and she wondered vaguely if it ever rained in this place. With infinite love in her heart, she looked upon her lover, who felt her movement and rolled her to his side. She caught at last a glimpse of his face, the solid jaw, the broad forehead, the fine nose. It was an unutterably handsome face.

And it was a face she knew.

It thundered again, and Simone jerked out of her lover's arms. She stared at him aghast, her heart pounding, her face draining in horror.

''You!''

But her lover only nodded and gave her the dimpled smile she remembered so well, before his face, and the rest of the dream, dissolved.

Simone bolted upright in bed and threw back the covers, frantic to get away from the man. Then she gradually regained her senses and remembered where she was. But the face in the dream remained crystal clear, and she began to gasp for breath, hysterical at the revelation.

''Nat,'' she croaked over the tightness in her throat. ''Don't do this to me.'' Anger flared. ''Nat or Nick or whoever the hell you are!'' She flung a pillow across the room as if it would dispel her anguish. Only then did she hear the sound again, the one from her dream, and she realized that it wasn't thunder, but someone knocking at her door. Probably the grocer, delivering the order she had left in the village. At any rate, she was glad for a diversion from the appalling discovery of the identity of her dream lover.

She sprang out of bed. ''Coming!'' she yelled toward the door as she donned the floor-length satin robe, not having time to put on the chemise that lay in a carmine puddle by the side of the bed. She hurried on bare feet to the door, hoping the delivery person was a woman.

It was her worst nightmare.

Instead of groceries, hell had just arrived at her door.

Hell, or a cruel hallucination. She stared at her caller, frozen between horror and fury.

''You!''

*   *   *

She was even more beautiful than he remembered. More lovely than in his dreams. As she stood before him, her supple body shimmered in a sensual, lace-trimmed robe, its deep red satin hiding nothing from his imagination. Her hair flowed around her shoulders in a soft, dark halo, and her eyes, wide now in surprise and shock, were the eyes that in his dreams invited him to ravish her with abandoned passion.

Nick felt as if he'd been hit in the stomach with a brickbat, and it took every ounce of willpower to maintain an outward calm.

"What . . . are you doing here?" His voice grated the question that screamed through his mind.

Simone stepped back slightly and pulled the robe closer to her, covering her breasts with her crossed arms. "Obviously, I have made a grievous error," she replied, her quavering voice revealing her own shock at seeing him. "Why . . . how . . . what . . . are *you* doing here?"

He did not reply right away, his voice lost in long-buried emotions, his eyes lingering on her loveliness. He couldn't help himself. At last he gathered his wits and replied, "I own the place."

He saw her eyes widen even further, just before her expression turned to disgust and she visibly regained her senses. "That figures," she snapped. "You must be very content, Mr. *Rutledge,*" she went on, emphasizing his real last name with a curl of her lip, "to have such a lovely country home, along with everything else you have managed to accrue in your life. Tell me, did you steal it too?"

Nick flinched beneath her righteous castigation, but his blood began to boil. He didn't need her censure to remind him of his crime. Not here. Not now. Not after ten long years of bitter self-recrimination. Would he never be free of it? "Get out," he told her.

"With pleasure. Had I known this place had anything to do with Nicholas Rutledge, I assure you I would have planned my holiday elsewhere. You are the last person on earth I wish to see!"

The door slammed in his face.

"Go to hell!" she called from behind it.

Simone Lefèvre was the last person *he* wished to see as well. Nick stood for a long moment, staring in shock and disbelief at the door that was all that stood between them. Simone, once his lover, now his bitter enemy, was in there, in his house, just the other side of this portal.

His mind had difficulty grasping that reality.

Stunned, he turned away and strode to where he had tethered his horse by the garden gate. He mounted the steed as if in a daze, then his initial shock began to turn to dismay. What *was* she doing here? Nick did not believe in coincidence, nor that she was here on holiday. There was only one thing that came to his mind.

She knew something about the perfume.

She was here because this was the place where Mary Rose had created the magical essence.

No, his reason argued as he spurred the horse out onto the lane, taking the short way home. There was no way she could know anything about the perfume, or Mary Rose, or any of it. He was just paranoid. It had been a fluke that he had come across it when the old trunk had surfaced from the basement of the Bombay Spice and Fragrance Company after a century and a half. No. Simone Lefèvre must be up to something to have turned up here at Brierley, but, he decided, she did not, could not, know about the perfume.

But what in God's name was she doing here?

His thoughts clashed like Titans as he gave the horse free rein.

How could anyone be so lovely? His body had jolted in immediate response to the voluptuous vision she had presented at the door, the sensations of which lingered yet. She'd always been beautiful, but the intervening ten years since he'd seen her last had added the finishing touches to her womanhood.

Could she, after all this time, be seeking revenge? Nick decided that was a definite possibility, but if so, he couldn't fathom what her plan could be. The questions hammered at him more rapidly as the horse broke into a gallop.

Was her body as lush as he'd known it in his dreams?

Why in hell had he ever listened to Dupuis?

And why, oh God, why had he ever left her?

Nick arrived at Brierley Hall without knowing how he got there. He was heartsick and filled suddenly with those old feelings of dread and defeat he had worked years to overcome. Christ, had he ever made one right decision in his life? Had he made such a mess of his life, dug his hole so deep that he could never climb out? Was he his father's son after all?

Seeing Simone again had brought it all back. Those exquisite warm summer days in sunny France, when as a young man, brash and eager to prove he was *not* cut from the same cowardly mold as his father, he'd managed to become Simone's father's apprentice. He shuddered to think now of the audacity of his behavior then. He hadn't really wanted to undertake the plot, which had been outlined to him carefully by Antoine Dupuis. But at that time, he'd felt he had no choice. He should have backed off the moment he first laid eyes on the old perfumer's daughter.

Simone. He loved her still. He knew it. And the knowledge nearly ate him alive.

With guilt.

With grief.

With longing for what could never be.

Perhaps she *was* here with some plan for revenge. Perhaps she would destroy him. Perhaps if she did, he would at last be able to forgive himself for the terrible injury he had caused her.

Absently, he turned his horse over to the trainer and walked on unsteady legs back into the house. His peace was shattered, his world turned dark all over again. He had to get out of here. He could not stand the idea that Simone Lefèvre was at that very moment living, breathing, *being,* so close to him.

He slammed the door, which brought the housekeeper shuffling into the large foyer to see what was the matter. "Would you like tea, sir?" she asked, peering up at him through thick glasses.

He glared at her, forgetting momentarily who she was. "What?"

He saw her step away from him slightly, and recalled that Simone had done the same. God in heaven, did every little thing have to remind him of her?

"Tea?" the servant squeaked.

"I will be leaving immediately," he informed her brusquely, but when he saw the confusion and disappointment on her face, he apologized. "I'm sorry for the inconvenience. I won't be needing your services further, but I will pay you the amount we agreed upon for the full fortnight, and I do hope you will consider coming to work here when I open the house again." Nick regretted that he was treating the woman so inconsiderately, but maybe the money and the promise of future employment would assuage any ill feelings she might have.

At any rate, she gave him a nod and a smile. "Yes, sir, thank you, sir," she said, then shuffled back into the kitchen, where in a moment he heard the banging of pots and pans.

The brief conversation with the housekeeper served to bring Nick back to the present, and to the reality of his life. He had a business to build. A life to get on with. That disagreeable encounter with Simone was only that . . . an encounter. *Get over it*. He gritted his teeth and went upstairs to pack his valise. He'd find out soon enough what she was up to. Until then, he must keep up his guard, both professionally and emotionally.

Placing the diary and Mary Rose's letters carefully in the trunk, Nick picked up the amber perfume bottle, now sealed tightly with a twentieth-century cork. One thing was certain, he must never experiment with this stuff again, at least not to induce the evocative dreams. For he knew that within the shrouds of the indigo mist, Simone Lefèvre waited for him like a siren, calling him to his destruction.

Simone felt as if she were going to be sick. She raced to the bathroom and stood over the sink, trembling, heaving, her skin clammy. Gulping several deep breaths, she gradually began to regain control, but not before tears welled and spilled down her cheeks. Damn him! First in her dreams, and then in the flesh! How could it be?

Seeing him, being with him in both realms took her back to that night ten years ago when, restless and unable to sleep, she'd wandered in on him—he'd been known to her then as Nathaniel Raleigh—in the tiny office of the perfumery in Grasse and found him rummaging through her father's rather disorganized filing cabinet. She should have followed her first instincts to cry out, to warn the household that a theft was taking place. But she could not believe it. Not Nat, her tender, passionate lover to whom she had given herself freely and willingly, whom she wished in her deepest heart to wed.

It was bad enough that she had not alerted her family, but worse was the reason why. Although he'd seemed disturbed that she'd discovered him, Nat had quickly covered himself in the cloak of both lover and trusted apprentice, assuring her as he took her in his arms and kissed her thoroughly that he was there at her father's request, to help put the place in better order. It seemed reasonable to Simone, only seventeen at the time and not wise to the wickedness that existed in the world.

Simone sank onto the bed, as crushed at the moment as she had been the morning following Nat's deception, when she awoke and hurried eagerly down to breakfast, hoping to meet her lover before he began the day's work. In the kitchen, she'd come upon her family in a state of extreme agitation and learned that the apprentice had *not* been in the office at her father's request. When she'd come upon him the night before, he had indeed been in the middle of stealing everything Jean René had worked for his entire life. Simone had watched her father die right before her eyes when he learned what had happened.

Why had fate brought her face to face with that despicable man again? And why in God's name was she dreaming about him? *Those* kinds of dreams. For she knew somehow that even though she had not seen his face in the earlier fantasies, it had been him all along. Seducing her. Pleasuring her.

Lying to her once again.

Fury replaced despair at the thought, and she straightened. *Mon Dieu!* She would not allow that to happen again. In her loneliness, she'd been a fool to use the perfume oil to rendezvous with her unidentified lover, giving him her body in every intimate way imaginable as they lay together, hidden among the mists.

The perfume oil.

Her thoughts slammed into it like hitting a brick wall. It was the sweetly scented oil that had brought her here, to this place owned by Nicholas Rutledge. Did he know about the fragrant essence as well?

What if Nicholas Rutledge somehow had the same substance? What if he were to use it to create a fragrance very much like Simone had designed in her mind to be her own debut *grand parfum?* Antoine Dupuis had told her he believed Nick would attempt something sensational in his desperation to make a comeback. Had he stolen ''her'' perfume already?

Déjà vu.

But giving it further consideration, she decided it was unlikely he had the perfume oil. Or even if he did, she reasoned, like her, he possibly had not been able to identify it. Dupuis had reported that Nick's disassembly of the Bombay Spice and Fragrance Company had left him with no lab and no manufacturing facility, at least temporarily. If he had the essence, unless he had a better nose than hers, which Simone thought unlikely, he had probably not been able to replicate and mass-produce it yet.

Her thoughts tumbled over one another. The essential oil she had discovered in the robin-crested perfume container had come from this very house. Who had created it? When? And of what? The bottle itself was from the Victorian era. Did that mean the fragrance was of that vintage as well, or had a more recent owner filled the antique bottle with a later concoction?

Simone refused to give up, to lose to Nick Rutledge again. A smile slowly crept across her lips as it occurred to her that with the perfume oil, she had the perfect opportunity to exact the revenge upon him of which she'd always dreamed. Not only would she take his job at the House of Rutledge, she would also use the ultramodern labs and manufacturing facilities which Nick himself had set up there to dissect this essence that itself was somehow connected with Nick's property and create a truly *grand parfum*.

A scent so sensational it would outsell Nina Ricci's L'Air du Temps, or perhaps even surpass the world's all-star perfume, Chanel No. 5.

A scent that would capture the world's wildest imagination.

A scent so successful there would be no room for a has-been like Nicholas Rutledge to take even a tiny fragment of the market share.

The idea made her laugh out loud.

But, she remembered, sobering, first she had to learn the origin of the sensual oil. Well, she thought, this was the place to do it. Not here in Nick's cottage, of course, but perhaps in Redford. She'd find someplace else to stay for a few days, or long enough to try to uncover some information about the essence so that when she met with Dupuis in London, she would be prepared not only to accept the position as master perfumer at the House of Rutledge, but also to move swiftly toward the fulfillment of her dreams—creating a *grand parfum,* and destroying Nicholas Rutledge.

SEVEN

❧

Nick squelched the urge to kick the small car that absolutely, unequivocally refused to start. Triumph. He snorted. There was nothing triumphant about this vehicle. If he didn't love it so much, he'd hate it. The damned thing didn't work half the time, and Nick had never learned how to fix it. Auto mechanics was not a subject that was stressed at the elite boys school he'd attended. It was late Saturday afternoon. He was certain it would be Monday before he could get a mechanic from the village to take a look at it.

Damn.

Since he'd seen Simone, Nick's mood had shifted several times, going from shock and confusion to dismay to wary concern, finally returning to a renewed resolve to get on with his plans for Bombay Fragrances, Ltd., and the development of the perfume. It was the only thing that gave his life meaning, and without it, all that had gone before would have been for nothing.

Nick could not accept *nothing*. Mistakes and all, he'd worked too hard to accept anything less than total success. He was anxious to return to London immediately, and this latest car trouble only darkened his mood further.

He slammed back into the house, which once again brought the now thoroughly confused housekeeper into the main hall to investigate the noise. "You'll have to stay until Monday," he informed rather than asked her.

"Yes, sir. That will be fine, sir. I hadn't had time t' change my plans."

"I'll take my evening meal upstairs in my room."

"Very good, sir."

"But not for another hour."

"Yes, sir."

Dining was the last thing on Nick's mind, but he knew the woman loved to prepare food, and he'd already treated her in a beastly manner. His mother, God rest her soul, would have been appalled. Rutledges, in spite of their financial impoverishment, *were* Rutledges, after all. And Rutledges did not behave like boors. He could almost hear her voice.

At the moment, he wished he'd never been born a Rutledge. He wished he wasn't haunted by this obsessive need to restore the Rutledge name, to prove to the world and perhaps even more to himself that Rutledge blood was still blue. Nick climbed the wide stairs and made his way to his room at the far end of the house, remembering a passage from his ancestor's diary. In his anger and pain, John Rutledge had written . . . *A great deal of good that birthright is to me!*

Nick could relate.

He poured a scotch whisky neat and stood looking out of the window, his gaze traversing the wide meadow that stretched behind the house. His mind's eye entered the forest beyond and made its way to the carriage house. To Mary Rose's house. To Simone. Was she still there?

Nick tossed back the tot, consuming it in one swallow, and the whisky burned all the way to his gut. He poured himself another. How in hell had she turned up at Brierley Hall? He was still astounded at the improbability. And still suspicious of it being an innocent coincidence.

Stop thinking about her, he commanded himself, pacing the room. It was an unfortunate accident, nothing more. But his thoughts would not leave her. He needed action. Something to keep his mind occupied. He wished he could call up the club and schedule a tennis match. Or go to the polo fields where he could act out his aggression like a gentleman. Instead, he felt like a prisoner in his own home.

He picked up the 'Gentleman's Diary,' and it fell open to an entry Nick had marked with a bit of paper. Although he knew the story well already, he read it again:

I have just returned from a remarkable journey. After long avoiding the entreaties of my loyal Indian servant, I succumbed to his insistence that I visit his relative in the monastery. After a difficult journey, we reached the sanctuary and were guests of the strange, quiet men who go about their lives in the cloistered environment in the foothills of the mighty Himalayas.

The trip was worth it just to gaze upon the majesty of those mountains. The view was breathtaking—I wish I could have shared it with Mary Rose. But the journey has resulted in something even more intriguing. I was initially reluctant to believe that any ointment on earth could assuage my anguish and loneliness, as my assistant had assured me the monk's potion would. But in truth, the sweetly scented oil with which my body was anointed by one of the young neophytes infused me with such equanimity of spirit and peace of mind, I nearly lost my senses. I found I did not wish to return to this hellhole that is my existence, and had not my good assistant led me away from the monastery almost by force, I would have become a runaway from the Army.

Use of the balm is forbidden outside the monastery, for my assistant tells me the monks believe it contains the secret to life eternal, a benefit only those holy few are worthy of. Being of rational mind, I doubt that claim, but the effect of the redolent unguent on my misery was so remarkable I wish to attempt to set it in writing.

At first I fell into a deep and pleasant sleep, not remarkable after a long journey, a soothing bath, and the application of the oil. I dreamed that I was home again, at Brierley Hall. I rode across the meadow and entered the forest wherein I encountered Mary Rose, pretty as a woodland sprite kneeling by the beck, gathering herbs. Again, not remarkable, as I dream of her every night. But this dream was different, and I find at the moment I cannot bring myself to record it openly upon these pages after all, for in it, we were together as only husband and wife should be, and then the most daring!

Upon awakening, I thought at first my longing for Mary Rose would only become worse, our separation underscored by the very reality of the dream. But it was not so! Instead, it seemed as if she had become somehow physically closer to me, as if the thousands of miles between us meant nothing.

The next morning, I asked for another treatment with the liniment, to which the monk agreed in hesitation. He warned me that it was not to be used to avoid reality, only to temporarily relieve private pain. I did not understand fully his meaning, but for many days upon my return to Bombay I longed for its extraordinary gratification, and I can see that it would be easy to fall into habitual use, much like with opiates.

Although the monks jealously guard their mahja plants, which supposedly will not grow anywhere else on earth, I managed to nip several pods from one of the bushes that grow in abundance on the monastery grounds. I planted some of the seeds here, but having seen the resplendent results of the nurturing touch of my lady love in her garden, I have decided to send the rest to her in England. Even if my specimens do not grow, with her ability to cultivate plants, I may obtain the mahja oil after all. Perhaps there will be a use for it in my new enterprise, which I am calling the Bombay Spice and Fragrance Company.

*   *   *

The more she thought about Nicholas Rutledge, the angrier Simone became. Swearing furiously in French, she flung the last of her belongings into her bag and dug in her purse for the number of the estate agent she'd decided to call to come get her. Of all the improbable coincidences that this cottage should belong to Nicholas Rutledge!

A knock sounded at the door and Simone froze. Had Nick come back? Damn it all. If he'd just waited a few more minutes, she would have made her escape.

"What do you want?" she yelled, yanking the door open, expecting another confrontation. But before her stood a woman who looked like somebody's benign little grandmother.

The woman's expression reflected bewildered uncertainty, but then she laughed. "I beg your pardon," she said, "but I walk this way frequently, and I was in the lane and saw the, uh, scene that occurred a few moments ago. I don't mean to intrude on your business, but if you are in need of other lodging arrangements, I have a few rooms in my home that I rent out."

The Fairy Godmother. Simone smiled at the woman. "Yes," she said. "Yes, I do need other arrangements."

An hour later, the pair sat across from one another over tea. "So you are a perfumer?" The elderly woman's eyebrows rose right into the silver-blue waves of hair that rolled across her wide, lined forehead. "How very exciting."

Simone felt her face burn at the woman's almost childlike enthusiasm. Granted, being a perfumer was something of an unusual occupation, but Esther Brown seemed unduly enthusiastic about it. Perhaps she was just trying to make her guest feel welcome and important.

"My father was also a perfumer," Simone added, sipping the excellent Earl Grey. "In Grasse, in the south of France."

The round little woman opposite her let out another exclamation of delight. "Oh, dear, this is just too, too much. My spells are working, they're working . . ."

Her voice trailed off into pensive silence, and Simone shifted uncomfortably. Spells?

"I'm afraid I don't understand."

"Wait here just a moment, my dear. I want to show you something."

The aging but energetic woman all but hopped from her chair and hurried into an adjoining room, emerging momentarily with a small brown bottle in her hand. "I just know you can help me," she puffed, out of breath from both exertion and excitement. She gave the bottle to Simone. "Take just a small sniff," she said. "It is very potent, and too much can do strange things to a body."

Humoring the woman, Simone did as she was asked, but her heart almost stopped when she smelled the fragrance. "What on earth?" she managed, her voice barely a raspy whisper. It was without a doubt the same scent as the perfume oil she'd discovered in the old bottle in New Orleans. Her face grew warm as her body responded as it had to the other essence. She raised her eyes to the woman's face. "Where did you get this?"

"It's lovely, isn't it?" was the evasive reply. "But it is unfortunate that what you have there is all I have left, and I'm most desperate for more of it. Can you, Miss Lefèvre, possibly reproduce this essence for me?"

Simone's eyes widened, unable to imagine this sweet old lady using the perfume oil for the erotic effects it seemed to have. But her heartbeat pounded in her ears as she thought it all through. Esther Brown had the perfume. Simone's sample had come from the cottage. It stood to reason that the secret of its source must lie close by. "Where did you say you got this?" she asked again.

Esther Brown gave her a long, appraising look before she answered, as if weighing her reply. "What I'm about to tell you may sound like the invention of a batty old woman," she began, "but every word of it is true." She poured each of them another cup of tea, her silence and the promise of her story building the suspense until Simone thought she might fall off her chair.

"This perfume is actually a healing oil, created over a century ago by my ancestor in the craft," she said at last. "By craft, I mean witchcraft." Simone's saucer rattled in her hand, and Esther laughed. "Now, don't get all unsettled by that. Our craft is of the whitest kind. I have spent my life dedicated to the healing arts, using the herbal medicines our foremothers in their wisdom developed before science and chemistry gave us synthetic drugs." She leaned forward and added confidentially, "Frankly, I don't trust the doctors much these days. I believe that Mother Nature has given us all the remedies we need to stay healthy. We don't need manufactured chemicals in our bodies."

Her fervor struck a note with Simone, who preferred perfumes created from natural essences to those contrived from synthetics. But she didn't want to discuss the ethics of the medical profession at the moment, or the pros and cons of the use of chemical synthetics in either medicine or perfume. "What does that have to do with the oil?"

"Ah, yes, I do tend to digress. Sorry." She leaned forward and took the bottle gently from Simone. "For generations, this essence has been passed down from the village healer to her protégé, and each has used it to help women . . . uh, become more comfortable with their sexuality." She let out a low laugh.

"I doubt if our modern doctors would find this important to a woman's health, but from my own experience, I know that women, especially those brought up under rigid religious circumstances, often feel shame and guilt about their bodies. I'm not a scientist or a physician, of course, only an old herbalist, and I don't know how it all works. But with this," she said, holding up the bottle, "I have successfully treated women for physical illnesses, everything from chronic headaches and heart palpitations to constipation and debilitating menstrual cramps."

Simone's mind reeled. The perfume oil was used in a medicinal manner? "I don't understand."

"I think the problems were all in their minds," Esther said, rocking back in her chair and touching her head with a wrinkled finger. "When I gave the women 'permission,' if you will, to use this and to relax into their natural sexual functions, many of them reported that their symptoms completely disappeared. I don't know how else to explain it, because in most of these cases, this lovely healing oil was all I recommended. No other herbs or drugs of any sort."

"How does it work?" Simone was on fire to understand the substance.

Esther shook her head. "I have no idea. I've never used it myself. I just followed instructions given me by my craft-mother."

But Simone knew how it worked. It worked in dreams.

"What is in it? What is it made of?" Simone's questions were more like desperate demands. She was close, so close, to discovering the secret.

The old woman looked at her long and hard, then frowned. "That, my dear, is what I was hoping you could tell me."

The sun dipped low in its final salute to the day when at last Simone found herself alone in the small bedroom that would be her home for the next few days. She was both exhausted and exhilarated after her long afternoon with Esther Brown, for even though she was disappointed that the so-called white witch did not know the plant from which the perfume oil had been extracted, Simone had learned much that might be helpful in her search for its origins.

Although part of the story Esther had spun would have made a good episode for that television show *Legends, Lore, and Lunatics,* she knew the old woman obviously believed every word of it. Simone was also skeptical of anyone who fancied herself to be a witch. She'd lived too long in superstitious and voodoo-infested New Orleans.

Still the story haunted her, as did the witch's warning, which disturbed her greatly. "There is great danger in that potion if it is misused," she'd told Simone, "and I believe my craft-ancestor who created it must have gravely misused its powers."

Her warning echoed in Simone's mind. Could such a substance be dangerous? Did it have harmful side effects? If she was able to reproduce it, would it even be legal?

Simone stared out into the gathering darkness, attempting to get a grasp on the whole strange story. She tried to envision the creator of the mysterious essence. According to Esther, her name had been Mary Rose Hatcher. She was the daughter of a family who served Nick's ancestors on the nearby estate of Brierley Hall sometime during the middle of the nineteenth century. Simone had learned from Esther that Nick still owned the estate, and that the cottage she'd rented had once been the servants' quarters.

Apparently Mary Rose had fallen in love with the younger Rutledge son, but their liaison was forbidden, and he was sent away to serve in the British Army in India.

And that was where the story had become really interesting.

Simone had listened in amazement to the legend. After creating this essence and teaching her protégée in the craft about its healing powers, Mary Rose mysteriously disappeared one night and was never seen or heard of again. The very same night, her lover, John Rutledge, vanished from his bungalow halfway around the world. Esther told Simone that those in the craft believed they died and that the potion was responsible for their deaths. She also believed that their bodies were somehow dematerialized by the chemistry of what she considered to be the "magical" oil.

"Wrongly used," Esther had warned, "this could be a curse rather than a blessing." Her next words had sent cold chills up Simone's spine. "One thing is certain, it must never fall into the wrong hands."

In all her years in the business, Simone had never come across an aromatic oil or essence that had any real power over the physical body. Most scent worked on the mind and the emotions. Although she granted these had their own effects on the physical self, she could not imagine a perfume oil dematerializing a body.

Still, she could not dismiss the power of the "potion," as Esther referred to it. She herself had experienced the mystical erotic dreams the substance seemed to induce. A deep frown creased her brow. Maybe part of its danger was that in dreams it made you give yourself over to your worst enemy.

The most important detail that Esther had shared with her was that likely Mary Rose had recorded the secret to the concoction of the essence in her witch's diary, a Book of Shadows, the old woman had called it. "But to my knowledge none has ever been found. Even though Mr. Rutledge sold off the contents of the cottage, I believe it could be still around there somewhere,'' she mused. "Mary Rose might have buried it on the grounds or hidden it someplace in the house that wasn't renovated, such as the the the attic.''

Simone attempted to sleep, but she tossed restlessly on the bed, her mind cruelly insisting on taking her back in time. To Grasse. To that fateful summer and the beautiful face of Nathaniel Raleigh . . .

It was a younger face she saw, more open and vulnerable than the Nick of today. A boyish face that grinned at her almost shyly when she opened the door to him.

"Bonjour, mademoiselle." His attempt at French was delivered with a strong English accent. His voice sounded mature and yet innocent somehow. It was a pleasing voice, a voice she trusted instantly. His vivid blue eyes were guileless, and seemed to see into her very soul. Her cheeks grew warm, and she had to work to summon a reply.

"Oui, monsieur, how may I help you?'' she answered him in her own French-laced English, and saw the relief on his face that he did not have to make his way in a language he had not yet mastered.

He gave her another lopsided smile, the kind that formed a dimple in his cheek. She had loved him instantly. But it was not her he'd come to see. It was her *papa.*

Papa had loved him instantly as well, she could tell, in spite of the older man's pretended gruffness. Papa did not casually invite strangers to their table. He had invited Nathaniel that very day. Perhaps Papa had seen into her soul, too, seen that she'd lost her heart to the handsome young Englishman who had come seeking an apprenticeship.

Tears leaked from Simone's eyes and soaked into the white linen pillowcover. Why couldn't Nat have been what they'd believed him to be?

Then her mind took her to another day. They were together in the countryside. The sun warmed her skin, and the air was sweet with the scent of lavender from the fields. Papa had given his apprentice the day off, and Simone had convinced Maman to let them take a picnic to an olive grove nearby. Maman had warned her then against men in general, but Si-

mone knew that her mother approved of the young man and
trusted him with her daughter.

They laughed and chattered like two magpies as they
walked up the hill. She wished to take his hand but did not
dare, thinking it too forward and that Maman would not ap-
prove. But as soon as they were safely out of view of her
family's house, her wish was answered beyond her imagination. Like a handsome prince in a fairy tale, Nat drew her
into his arms and kissed her until he took away her breath.
She could still smell that kiss. It held the scent of sunshine
and lavender and the salty perspiration that mingled on their
lips. She had never been kissed like that before.

Deeply. Openly. Hungrily.

Nat's kiss had changed her life.

He had sworn his love that day. And she hers. And she
knew that every childhood dream she'd ever had of marrying
the most handsome man in the world was about to come true.
Happiness swelled in her heart until it almost hurt.

That night, long after Papa and Maman had gone to bed,
Simone lay awake in the darkness, staring out the open window into the star-sprinkled night sky and feeling more alive
than she could remember. She was filled with a trembling,
inexplicable anticipation, frightening and delicious all at the
same time.

She had not invited him into her bed, but she had known
he would come. She had only a vague idea what would happen, from stories her girlfriends had told her, but she knew
she wanted it. Even though she understood such acts were
reserved for marriage, it did not matter to Simone. She knew,
after all, that Nathaniel Raleigh was likely to ask Papa for her
hand in the near future. Maybe even tomorrow . . .

Simone rolled to her side and sat up on the edge of the bed
upstairs in Esther's house, hugging the pillow to her face to
suppress the sobs that threatened to choke her.

"Goddamn you, Nathaniel Raleigh," she whispered, looking out of this window into this night sky, ten years and many
miles later. "Goddamn you."

EIGHT

❧

Simone gave up trying to sleep. Forcing thoughts of those days in Grasse from her mind, she padded to the window and opened it wide. A full moon crested the treetops, its light spilling through the window and shimmering on the scarlet of her silken chemise. A warm, rain-prescient breeze wafted in the smell of lilacs and beckoned her into the fragrant darkness. The scent reminded her of the perfume and the story of Mary Rose and the old cottage she'd so suddenly vacated. Did she dare return there? Not by day, for certain. But perhaps under cover of darkness, when no one would know of her intrusion . . .

She did not recall locking the door when she'd left in such haste. Maybe she could get in and explore the house where Mary Rose had lived, even though Nick had pillaged it of its historic contents. Perhaps Esther was right, and there was an attic or a cellar that he'd left untouched. With only the light of the moon to guide her, Simone doubted she could search the grounds for the Book of Shadows, but the house was a possibility.

Without giving herself time to change her mind, she took a black woven scarf from her suitcase and tied it loosely around her shoulders, covering the bare skin exposed by the low-cut, sleeveless knit top she wore. She pulled on some black leggings, donned flat black canvas shoes, then tied her hair up and away from her face in a tight ponytail. She laughed when she surveyed her cat-burglar image in the mirror, but Simone Lefèvre felt few qualms about breaking in and entering the cottage belonging to Nicholas Rutledge.

Esther's house was dark as Simone crept down the stairs, and she surmised that her hostess had gone to bed. She slipped silently and unobserved out the front door, making sure it did not lock behind her so she could return unnoticed. Reaching the stoop, she hesitated for a long moment, allowing her eyes to become accustomed to the night before proceeding down the road. It couldn't be more than a mile, she'd decided, and the exercise would do her good.

She headed out on her journey, her heart beating hard in spite of her attempts to assure herself that she was perfectly safe alone here at night. Redford was a small village. She had not seen any unsavory characters loitering on the picturesque streets. There was little traffic along the road at this hour, and when she saw the lights of an approaching vehicle, she stepped into the protective darkness of the hedgerows that lined the byway. No one would hurt what they couldn't see.

At last she reached the small gravel lane that led away from the main road, branching off in the direction of the servants' quarters. Beyond, she surmised, lay Brierley Hall. Was Nick still there? The thought made her uneasy. But there was no way, unless he himself was out snooping at night, that he would know of her nocturnal adventure.

Simone tried the door to the house, the same one she'd opened earlier from the other side to find herself face to face with Nick Rutledge, but to her disappointment, it was locked. In her haste to vacate Nick's property, she'd given the key back to the estate agent in return for a full refund of her money. Now she wished she hadn't acted so impulsively. She stood on the steps and peered into the darkness of the forest that surrounded the house, trying to decide what to do next.

Any rational woman would turn around and go home to get a good night's sleep.

But the night was enchanting, with moonlight fringing the leaves that quivered in the rising wind on the branches of the ancient trees. Lunar luminescence washed the walls of the house in silvery blue and outlined the stepping stones that led from the front of the cottage toward . . . what? Simone followed them as if they were the breadcrumbs left by Hansel and Gretel.

The path, although cleared in the front of the house, became snarled with brambles and overgrowth behind the dwelling, and Simone had to pick her way through the sharp thorny branches that clawed at her ankles. At last she came to a gate in the tall garden wall. It was old and rusted, obviously not part of the modern renovations, and encrusted with prickly vines. Gingerly, she reached through the overgrowth for the lever and raised the latch, and with an effort, pushed the gate open.

Inside, Simone stopped to catch her breath. She surveyed the enclosed space and decided that this once must have been an impressive garden, although now the weeds reigned supreme. She spotted a low bench to one side, next to the wall, and stepped up on it for a better view. From that vantage point, in spite of the weeds, she could make out the outline of a garden bed that once must have been quite grand indeed.

The perimeter of the bed was circular, bordered by light-colored stones that gleamed in the moonlight from beneath their covering of weeds. Rocks also divided the garden into pie-shaped beds meeting at a smaller circle in the center. The four walls that enclosed the garden space were only murky curtains in the night, woven over as well with the tapestry of thick, twining vine.

Simone knew instantly this had been Mary Rose's garden. Here, on this moonstruck plot, she was certain Esther's "craft-ancestor" had grown *something,* some unusual plant, herb, or bush that she'd used to create the fragrant, sensual essence.

Had Mary Rose hidden the Book of Shadows here as well? Perhaps, but Simone lost hope of discovering it by poking blindly around the garden in the middle of the night. This place had been neglected for so long, it was virtually imprisoned by weeds, and she had no desire to fight her way through them. Oddly, however, the part of her that loved gardens, that had planted and nurtured the small but lush and fragrant beds in the courtyard of her aunt's apartment, felt an immediate bond with this place. She wanted to rid it of the overgrowth, the brambles, the ruin, and restore it to its former beauty.

Ha. She came to her senses again abruptly. She would do no such thing. This wasn't her garden. And she had no desire to benefit Mr. Nicholas Rutledge with her horticultural skills. At the thought of the handsome bastard, she jumped down from the bench, suddenly eager to leave this place and make her way back to Esther Brown's house.

Simone heard a strange noise, muffled by the sound of the restless wind in the trees, and she turned her head sharply to discern its source. It sounded like the baying of a hound. The hair stood up on her arms. It *was* a dog barking! And it was not too far in the distance. In fact, it was getting louder, more excited, by the moment, and it seemed as if it were coming directly for her.

Quickly, she dashed through the gate, leaving it open behind her. She had barely made it to the front of the house when a bright light shone directly in her face, blinding her. "Who goes there?" a rough male voice demanded.

Simone froze, then shielded her eyes with her hand. "Don't shoot," she managed, unable to think of a better response. "I'm not a thief."

The dog's hysterical barking sounded more like "yarking," high-pitched and menacing. Simone could see the black, squarely built beast straining at the leash, and she shuddered involuntarily. This animal was no pet.

"Y' mayn't be a thief, but you're trespassin'," the man replied in a thick accent. "I'm wonderin' what a person like you would be doin' here at this time of night, 'specially on a night like this, with th' storm brewin' and all?"

Simone hoped if she answered his questions quickly, she could talk him into letting her go. "I . . . I rented this place," she began, but he cut her short.

"Y' must be th' tenant Mr. Rutledge told me about," he said, his eyes narrowing. "Th' tenant that wasn't plannin' t' take th' place after all." He took a step closer, winding the leash around his arm to further restrain the animal. "Shut up,

Heathcliff," he yelled at the dog, who stopped barking but remained staunchly on guard. "In fact, he told me t' keep a close eye on th' place, in case anybody came snoopin' around. But I never expected anyone t' be about at such an hour, 'specially no woman. I think he'll find that very interestin'. Come along with me now." He took her roughly by the arm, but she jerked away.

"I will not," she said indignantly, brushing the skin of her arm as if to rid it of the man's touch. "You have no right—"

The man took out an identification wallet and showed her his credentials. "I'm paid by Mr. Rutledge t' patrol his property," he growled, replacing the wallet in his pocket. "If he tells me t' bring any intruders t' him first, then that's what I do."

Simone's heart sank. Now what was she going to do? "Please, no," she tried begging. "I—I meant no harm. It was just such a lovely night, I thought I'd take a walk—"

"C'mon, missy, I've got no time t' listen t' you. Tell it t' the boss." He loosened the leash ever so slightly, and the dog strained toward her, growling. "And old Heathcliff here, he's gettin' anxious."

"Where are you taking me?" she wanted to know, doubting that she could outrun the dog.

"T' Brierley Hall, of course. Mr. Rutledge's car broke down, and he didn't go back t' London as he planned."

"I . . . I can't," Simone said, drawing the scarf closer around her shoulders, her voice breaking in anger and fear. "You don't understand—"

"I understand I got a job t' do. Now, are you going t' come along nice and easy, or am I going t' have t' let Heathcliff here convince you?"

Simone glared at the man, then at the dog. She knotted the scarf securely around her shoulders and straightened to as tall a height as she could. "I am certain that Mr. Rutledge will reprimand you for your rude actions," she said, summoning an exterior outrage to hide her inner terror. "He will probably fire you."

But she thought it more likely that Nick Rutledge would give the man a raise.

"Come along," the guard said, undaunted. Simone looked around, desperate for escape, perhaps through the woods. But the enchanted forest was gone, the silvery moonlight covered over now by clouds. A freshening wind, foretelling a coming storm, whipped the trees about in a frenzy. Simone glanced over her shoulder toward the garden. The secret was there. She sensed it. And somehow, someway, she would have it.

But obviously, not tonight.

Turning her attention to the problem she faced at the moment, she gave in to the guard's insistence that she follow him to Brierley Hall. She was not afraid of Nicholas Rutledge, although she did not relish the confrontation that she knew lay ahead. Squaring her shoulders, she summoned thoughts of her father to give her the courage, and the anger, to face the man who had killed him.

Nick tossed restlessly in the large bed upon which his ancestors had slept for eons. Normally, the high bed carved of ancient oak gave him at least a fleeting feeling of that elusive commodity that had driven all of his actions since his father's death—continuity with his heritage. He'd even had it lengthened to accommodate his height. But tonight it felt lonely, empty.

As did he.

He had tried, first with whisky, then with reading, finally with sleep, to rid his mind of the vision of Simone Lefèvre, but she would not leave. She appeared behind his closed eyes, a lustrous, sensual phantasm in the robe of molten silk. A disturbing specter, come to haunt him, first in his dreams, now in the flesh. What had brought her here, to his property? The question resounded through his mind again and again, filling him with unreasonable foreboding. She posed no threat, he told himself. How could she? He tried to imagine some evil she must have planned for him, her long-overdue revenge, but he was unable to picture a vindictive Simone.

But he no longer knew the Simone Lefèvre who had become his lover so long ago. She'd been a young girl then. Innocent.

Too innocent.

Had she hardened into a calculating, spiteful woman set out to bring about his downfall, or was his own guilt just working overtime, riddling him with paranoia? He felt his heart racing and realized his skin was damp. Was he afraid of her? Ridiculous! He sat up in the dark. The digital numbers radiating from the clock by the bed mocked him. Twelve o'clock. The witching hour.

Suddenly he heard a banging sound and became aware of the rumble of thunder outside his window. A shutter must have come loose in the wind. He switched on the light and drew on the pair of lightweight running pants he had removed when he'd gone to bed. The banging seemed louder, and when he stepped into the hallway outside his bedroom door, he saw a light go on downstairs. Hurrying to the top of the stairway, he arrived in time to see his housekeeper, wrapped in a pink quilted robe and crowned with a head full of curlers, approach the door with a broom in her hand.

"Who's there?" she called, her voice high-pitched, fearful.

"It's just me, Clyde th' watchman. I need t' speak t' Master Nicholas." The man's voice hesitated a moment, then added importantly, "I've captured an intruder."

Nick raised an eyebrow. An intruder? He paid Clyde to keep an eye on the property during his extended absences, but the man had never reported even a vandal in the past few years. This was one of the safest neighborhoods in rural England.

"I'll handle it, Mrs. Nelson." Nick hurried down the stairs, curious more than concerned. He opened the door. On the other side stood Clyde Covington, one of his gnarled hands grasping the arm of a small woman who glared at Nick with an expression of pure hatred.

Simone.

Again.

"I caught her snoopin' around th' cottage," the guard explained, proud as a retriever dropping a pheasant at his master's feet.

Nick's body seemed to have turned to stone. His limbs would not move, his eyes would not leave hers. Between them passed a silent communication that screamed of mutual distrust. Shock. Outrage. But their locked regard of one another held something more, a palpable if perverse fascination. They were a mongoose and a cobra, each waiting for the other to blink first.

Mrs. Nelson broke the awkward silence. "Well, don't just stand there, Clyde. Bring her inside. There's a storm comin' on. Th' sky's likely t' open up any minute now."

Her brisk efficiency brought Nick back to the moment, and he managed to step aside just before a squat, stout, and incredibly ugly dog preceded Clyde and Simone into the great entry hall. "Take them to the kitchen," he directed the housekeeper, nodding toward the man and the dog. "See if you can find something for them to eat."

Mrs. Nelson hesitated pointedly, as if waiting to be instructed as to what to do about the "intruder," but Nick's scowl and curt "Go on, then" sent her away with her charges. When they were out of sight, Nick turned at last and faced Simone Lefèvre.

Lightning flared, and a loud crack sounded nearby.

Neither spoke.

Forcing a return of his senses, Nick attempted to react rationally in the face of this most irrational situation. He opened the door to the drawing room and switched on a small lamp which cast barely enough light to illuminate the center of the huge room. The corners remained in shadow. "Please, be my guest." His words were both formal and ludicrous, but he didn't know what else to say. To the outside observer, he appeared unperturbed, the quintessential country gentleman politely determined to learn why his sleep had been disturbed by this unlikely intruder. But on the inside, he was completely undone. His composure was a sham, and he realized with a start that it was a reflection of his entire life since he'd betrayed this woman, and his honor, years ago.

A sham. A lie. A pose.

As she passed close by him upon entering the room, the scent of her assailed him further. It was sensual, a mix of the wild night outside, of wind and rain and lightning stirred up with her own feminine fragrance. He caught a hint of passion flower, its light fruity floral note jolting something deep inside. It was a scent he remembered, one that summoned painful memories from the nether reaches of his heart. One that brought to mind the passion they had shared, the fierce love-making, the broken promises.

Shutting the door behind him, Nick furtively caught a glimpse of her figure while her back was turned. He wished he hadn't. The ebony clothing fit like a second skin, silhouetting the lithe yet curvaceous body.

He ached, with grief, and need.

She turned abruptly to face him, and he saw in the dark pools of her eyes, not the fear of an apprehended thief, but instead an ominous gleam that bespoke a deep inner anger, a rage she'd likely nursed against him for over a decade. It was the moment he'd dreaded for ten years. The moment he had known would come sooner or later.

Her moment of truth.

His moment of shame.

"Well, aren't you going to phone the police?" Simone demanded curtly, crossing her arms and planting her feet, wet in mud-splattered canvas shoes, firmly apart on the worn Oriental carpet of Nicholas Rutledge's drawing room. She was cold and uncomfortable and thoroughly embarrassed that she'd allowed herself to end up in such a predicament. But she would not let the man who stood magnificently bare-chested before her know she harbored one ounce of regret for her actions. He'd certainly never expressed any regret over his.

"I hardly think that's necessary," he replied, and the sound of his voice triggered memories that caught her off guard. She remembered that voice from the past, deep, masculine, sensitive, soliciting her unquestioning trust. She shivered involuntarily, a gesture Nick misread as physical discomfort. "Perhaps I should light a fire," he said, going toward the enormous hearth across the room from the door and stacking the wood into a tall pyre.

Simone watched him in awkward silence, trying to think of all the words she'd saved up over the years to hurl at him if such a moment as this ever presented itself, all the accusations and expletives and bitter reproofs. But no words would come. She stood tongue-tied and overcome with emotions she couldn't even begin to identify. Or accept.

For a part of her, incredibly, still found Nicholas Rutledge desirable.

She tried to will her gaze away from the square shoulders, the lean torso, the long legs that soon became an outline in black against the red-orange blaze of the firelight. She could not make out his face when he turned to her, just as she had been unable to discern the features of the lover who came to her in the dreams. Her heart pounded, and she swallowed an unnamed fear.

"Don't you think you overdid it on the fire?" she managed at last, rekindling with acerbity the enmity she felt toward him.

"What are you doing here, Simone?"

His icy words doused the last unwanted notion of Nick's sexual appeal. Simone raised her chin.

"Does it really matter, Nicholas? Or should I call you Nathaniel?"

She heard him release a long, slow sigh. "Simone, that was a long time ago. I know I behaved in a brutish manner, but—"

"Brutish manner!" Red-hot hatred flamed on her cheeks. How could he consider what he did merely brutish! "I should have had you thrown into prison for the rest of your miserable life for what you did."

"Then why didn't you?"

Nick left the hearth and took a seat on the arm of a long, Victorian-style sofa, giving Simone a clear view now of his face. She was surprised at the sorrow etched there.

But his question was one she'd asked herself a thousand times. Why *had* they let him get away with it? Why hadn't her mother pressed charges at the time? Why hadn't she herself insisted at least that he be outlawed in France? She didn't even know if that would have been possible. But she hadn't even tried.

In part, what had happened had been their own fault. By not calling in the police, they had allowed Nathaniel Raleigh to slip away and return to England, where he'd surfaced a year later as Nicholas Rutledge, the successful young heir to the House of Rutledge, and made a fortune from the formulas he'd stolen.

Why, indeed, had they not pursued him?

The only answer she'd ever been able to come up with was that their grief and her own sense of guilt had made it seem a futile gesture.

The memories brought Simone's emotions to an even hotter burn. "It is something I have regretted ever since," she replied bitterly. "You killed my father, and I let you get away with it."

"Your father was an old man. His heart failed him."

"If you believe that, then you're a deluded idiot as well as a thief!" Her voice edged upward a notch, and she felt her throat contract. "His heart failed him because his beloved 'Nat' betrayed him." She emphasized the nickname her father had given to the young man with whom they'd both fallen in love.

Nick leaned on both arms and dropped his head. For a long moment, he said nothing. Then he raised his eyes to hers. They looked dark as midnight in the firelight, and they smoldered with anger. "What the hell do you want of me?" he rasped. "I can't undo what happened."

What *did* she want of him? An apology? No. It was easy to say you're sorry. Simone wanted him to hurt, to feel the kind of pain and destruction he had inflicted upon her and her family. "I want to see you in hell," she hissed.

His lips twisted in a humorless smile. "That would imply you would be there with me."

If she'd had anything close at hand, she would have thrown it at him. Instead, she remembered some of those words she'd been saving and cast them at him instead. "You bastard! I have already been in hell. You sent me there ten years ago."

Abruptly, Nick bolted from the sofa and came to her, grasping her arms painfully. "Do you think I haven't seen my share of hell?" he growled.

"Let me go," she demanded, genuinely frightened, both of his rough manner and of her own response to the very nearness of him. The skin of his chest gleamed golden, the light of the fire glinting off the wisps of hair that curled there. His eyes were fierce, a deeper blue than she remembered. In them she read an anguish to match her own.

"No, Simone," he uttered, lowering his lips until they almost touched hers, "I won't let you go. Not yet. Not until you understand some things . . ."

His lips met hers. She felt the warmth of their seduction, the strength of his demand as he drew her closer to him. Once she would have melted into the planes of his chest, opened to him fully. Once she would have allowed the heat within to build until only his love could quench that exquisite fire. The heat that threatened even now. But Simone pushed against him with all her might.

"Bastard!" she lashed out again and slapped him hard across the cheek. She jerked free and ran toward the door. "You must be the most arrogant of all men to think I would fall for that again."

His body was in silhouette again, his face hidden. He did not speak. She wanted him to fight back, but he did not. She wanted him to come after her, so she could get close enough to pummel the daylights out of him with her fists. But he did not.

Would he not even give her the satisfaction of a good fight? Simone's rage flared white-hot. Goddamn him to hell. She opened the door and made her way down the now-darkened hallway to the front entrance. Still he did not follow.

Outside, rain fell in torrents. Deadly fingers of lightning singed the branches of a nearby tree. The wind whipped her hair against her cheeks. The storm's fury seemed to match her own, and its very violence brought her to her senses. It was dangerous, and so were her out-of-control emotions. If she wished to inflict pain on Nicholas Rutledge, beating him with her small hands was not the way to do it. No, she had been offered a much more effective means of destroying him, and tomorrow, she would call Antoine Dupuis and let him know she had decided to accept his offer.

In the meantime, she needed to put distance between herself and the man whose kiss still burned on her lips. She turned and drew in a sharp breath when she saw Nick's half-naked body leaning against the door to the drawing room.

"You can't go out in this storm," he said, his voice toneless, as if he were the waking dead.

"No, I can't," she agreed, the quaver in her voice betraying her agitation as her gaze took in every inch of him. "May I use your phone to call a taxi?"

NINE

❧

"There's no one in the village who will come for you to-night," Nick replied, his voice hoarse over the painful emotion that seemed stuck in his throat. He'd deserved the slap in the face. He deserved her contempt. He loathed himself for having lost control. But the temptation to kiss her lips had been too great.

He'd tried to gather himself together again as she left the room, making no effort to restrain her, indeed wishing she would somehow simply disappear so he would not have to deal with all the old wounds she had reopened. But as his heartbeat finally slowed and his reason returned, he knew he could not allow her to go out in this storm.

"You may stay the night at Brierley Hall," he continued, wondering if the guest room was made up and working hard to convince himself that the invitation was born only of Rutledge good manners.

"Are you out of your mind?"

He wasn't surprised by the utter astonishment he saw in her expression. He also saw her great beauty, the dark eyes that lifted slightly at the outside edges, the full lips, the slender nose. Her ebony hair was pulled away from her face, revealing high cheekbones and a square forehead. The black scarf she'd covered her shoulders with earlier was now draped over one arm, leaving her throat exposed, her breasts accentuated by the low cut of her jersey. He felt the stirrings of an erection again and knew his desire for her must be evident against the soft fabric of his nylon running pants, but he could not help it. All he could do was maintain a safe distance.

"I won't harm you," he said. "There is a guest room upstairs you may use."

He saw her hesitate, but a clap of thunder made both of them jump. She stared at him a long while before speaking. When she finally broke the silence, her words sliced like a stiletto.

"If you ever touch me again, I'll kill you."

Simone saw him approach, wearing only elastic-banded trousers made of a soft, liquidlike fabric that caressed his lower torso as he walked and that outlined the maleness of his being, the other half of her that she desired so fiercely yet fought to escape.

No! she cried out, even though no words came from her lips. She recognized this familiar place, knew somewhere in her deep subconscious that it was the indigo dreamworld where she and her forbidden lover had trysted in recent nights. But something about it was different now.

Before, she had felt no fear. No inhibitions. Before, she had welcomed the man whose face remained in shadow, whereas now, she wanted desperately to run away from him, to hide where he could not find her, to elude his false seductions. Before, she had not known him, but now he wore the face of the enemy. Nick.

She felt naked, vulnerable.

The twilight mists parted, and Simone watched him as he approached, a leopard stalking its prey. She struggled but could not free herself from some invisible bond, an intangible tether that somehow held her steadfast. He at last was upon her, his eyes gleaming darkly, filled with animal hunger.

No! she tried to cry out again, but he did not hear her. He began to feast on his prey, taking small nibbles along the sensitive skin of her ears. Simone swallowed as the touch of his tongue and teeth raised the hair on her arms and hardened the bud of her nipples. Why couldn't she run? What held her here, a helpless victim? His nibbles became suckles upon her neck, passion bites that aroused her and sent hot moisture to those regions of desire. No! she struggled to communicate again, but her will was ebbing even as those treacherous inner fires began to singe her soul. His suckles lowered to her tight nipples, where he fed hungrily, almost painfully, at her breasts. Her belly contracted, and in spite of her intellectual desire to run, her traitorous body arched against him, wanting more of him.

More.

Her breath came in sharp spasms as she felt him answer her desire. He entered her now-molten core, and her bonds slipped away into the nothingness that surrounded her. There was only him, in her. Together. One.

Simone jerked awake, her face burning, her entire body erotically on fire. She blinked and looked around, trying to reorient herself to reality. Her neck was stiff, and she was cold beneath the light blanket that covered her where she'd fallen asleep in one of the high-backed chairs in the drawing room. Then it all came crashing back. Her misadventure in Mary Rose's garden. The guard and his monster dog. Nick.

Nick.

She sat up abruptly, wishing she hadn't fallen asleep here, even though she'd adamantly refused Nick's offer of a guest bed. She had to get out of this house. His house. The storm had passed, and gray daylight seeped around the edges of the drawn velvet draperies, revealing the old-fashioned furnishings of the room and giving her an unreal sense of having been transported into a bygone age. Just as the dream had transported her into an equally unreal dimension. Simone sat very still, considering the dream a moment. It had been like the rest, and yet different. In this one, she had known fear. In this one, she had been seduced against her will, rather than giving herself freely to her lover.

This dream was different, more based in reality, she thought with a cold hard knot forming in her stomach. It had obviously sprung from her own subconscious, not from the seduction of any perfume.

Her body began to quake. Her hands trembled. Tears burned in her eyes, and fear crept into her heart. Had her earlier indiscriminate use of the mysterious aromatic substance opened a Pandora's box? Had the aphrodisiac effect of the oil somehow preempted her free will and allowed the demons she feared the worst to take libertine pleasures with her in the dreamworld? Every time she slept, would she be ravished against her will by her most hated enemy?

She felt sick to her stomach.

Then another, darker thought frightened her even more . . . what if somewhere deep within her own psyche she *wished* to be ravished by Nick?

A brisk knock sounded at the door, and the housekeeper bustled in with a tray. "Mr. Rutledge ordered up breakfast for you, miss," she said, her face professionally unreadable. "He asked me t' give you this and apologize for him." She handed her a small piece of paper. "He had t' leave for London. It was a blessin' that Clyde turned out t' be a handy mechanic. Fixed that stubborn little car right up." All this was spoken in a breathy rush as she laid out the dishes on a sideboard. The smell of bacon, sausage, eggs, and roasted tomatoes wafted across the room and into Simone's nose, heightening her nausea.

"Thanks," she said, feeling the notepaper slick against her clammy fingers. "But I must be going right away. Is there a phone I can use to call a taxi?"

The stout woman turned and surveyed Simone critically. "You're too thin. You should eat something before you leave. Here." She buttered a piece of toast. "Eat this, and I'll give a call t' my friend in th' village t' come for you."

Simone accepted the cold, rather limp piece of bread, staring after the housekeeper, bemused. Then she unfolded the note Nick had left for her.

Please leave Redford at once. No good can come of us running into one another again. Sincere apologies for my abominable behavior last night. Nick.

* * *

Simone sank into the chair, thinking of the dream, wondering if he knew just *how* abominable his behavior had been.

Nick sped along the motorway, oblivious to the horns and rude gestures of the other motorists into whose lanes he cut, weaving back and forth in the traffic, trying to put as much distance as quickly as possible between him and the woman he'd left at Brierley Hall.

His eyes were haggard, his face unshaven. Thank God that man Covington had been able to coerce the Triumph to start and he'd been able to leave without running into her again. He could not have borne to look upon her after the dream he'd had of her in the night.

Jesus God, what was happening to him?

First he'd kissed her. Kissed her! In the real world. Not in the dream. That was bad enough. But in his dream, which had come upon him unbidden by any damnable perfume, he'd . . . he had taken her. He'd heard her silently resist, but his lust was out of control. He had wanted her with the intensity of a wild creature. He'd been unable to stop himself.

Nick Rutledge prayed to a God he'd never really believed in that she would do as he'd asked in the terse note he had left for her. He did not know what had brought her to the servant's cottage. It was hard to believe it was only coincidence, but at the moment he didn't really care. All he wanted was to never have to face her again.

In reality or in dreams.

Those dark eyes, hate-filled and accusing, sapped him of the determination to proceed with rebuilding the Rutledge name, reestablishing the family's lost fortune, all he had left to hold on to in his life. And without the will to go on, all that he had done, the crimes he had committed, the sacrifice he had made in leaving the House of Rutledge . . . would be for nothing.

Nick had worked too hard for it to come to that.

He clenched his jaw tightly as he finally reached the town

house. He must quit thinking about Simone, for thoughts of her would lead only to disaster.

Half an hour later, Nick emerged from the shower to answer the phone that jangled insistently from the bedroom. His face drained of color as he listened to his new secretary's message, then flushed again in anger. "I'll be right there. Call the police."

"Dupuis!" he snarled, slamming down the phone. "You son of a bitch." He knew that the slimy little Frenchman wouldn't let him out that easily. It didn't surprise Nick that Dupuis would try to destroy Nick's new enterprise before it could pose any real threat to the House of Rutledge.

But he'd never expected him to attempt something so blatant.

A police car stood in the parking lot in front of the square, nondescript concrete building that housed the offices of Bombay Fragrances, Ltd. Inside, the place was torn apart. File drawers yawned open, papers were scattered everywhere. Brenda, the woman he'd hired only days before, was pale but remained a pillar of efficiency, pouring coffee for the two investigators who were waiting for him to arrive.

"What happened?" Nick asked, his gaze taking in Brenda's frightened countenance, the havoc around him, the curiosity on the face of the officers.

"Looks like the place was ransacked." The senior officer stated the obvious. "What were they after?"

Nick looked at Brenda. "Dupuis is obviously behind this," he said, trying to control his anger. "But I don't know what he thinks he is going to find. He already has everything I've ever worked to develop. Is anything else disturbed?"

"Your office looks just like this one," his secretary answered grimly. "It's a good thing the equipment hasn't arrived yet. He might have destroyed it too."

The idea turned Nick's stomach. He'd thought this site would offer adequate security. It was fire-safe and patrolled, and there were other similar businesses in the office park. But then, he'd never thought Dupuis would stoop to breaking and entering. Or actually destroying his property.

Nick answered the investigators' questions as best he could, his wrath mounting as the minutes ticked by. At last they were finished and left with an admonition that Nick repair the broken door lock immediately.

"Do they think I'm an imbecile?" he growled, looking out through the panes of the heavy door that had been jimmied open with a crowbar. "I'll have the whole damned door replaced and an alarm system installed by tonight."

And that wasn't all he would do. Going into his office, he made a few phone calls. Then he went back into the reception area.

"Are you afraid to stay here by yourself?" he asked Brenda.

She hesitated only slightly. "No, sir. Not during the day."

"Good. I've made arrangements for the security company to come out and make this place burglarproof. I would appreciate it if you would stay until that is accomplished, then you can take the rest of the day off."

"I'll try to straighten up some of this mess," the woman offered, giving Nick a reassuring, somewhat motherly smile.

Nick left the office and ground the starter on the Triumph until the engine kicked in. He shot out of the parking space and sped down the tree-lined street of the industrial park, jerking to a halt at the stop sign at the corner. In his rearview mirror, he noticed a long black car pull out of the lot across the street from the offices of Bombay Fragrances and into the lane of traffic behind him. The glass on the limo was tinted, and he could not make out the face of the driver, but as it stayed on his tail, making every turn just behind him, Nick became uneasy. Was this Dupuis's henchman? Was he out for Nick, as well as the company?

The idea seemed ludicrous, like something out of a James Bond film, and Nick decided that his paranoia was getting out of hand again. He drove steadily back to his town house, watching the following vehicle carefully as he turned into the drive. It slowed, but it did not stop. When he got out, he saw it resume a normal speed for the traffic and disappear around the corner.

Anger and outrage dispelled any fear, and Nick slammed into the house determined to put a stop to Antoine Dupuis's funny business then and there. He raced up the stairs, changed into a navy blue suit, white shirt, red tie, shined shoes. He knew how to play the power game. Dupuis had taught him well.

The House of Rutledge stood like an icon of British tradition, its red-brick Neoclassical architecture grand beneath the summer-green boughs of the mature trees that lined the avenue in London. Simone paid the taxi driver and turned to face her future. Her heart thundered, her pulse raced, but she gave herself no time to change her mind. She'd left Redford on the train to London a little less than two hours before, returning to Esther Brown's only long enough to shower and change clothes and make a single phone call.

As she saw it, she had two choices. She could run away now, return to New Orleans, and put the distance of the Atlantic Ocean between her and the man who kept invading her dreams. In the United States, she knew she could find a good job in the fragrance industry, and there she would never have to encounter Nicholas Rutledge again.

Or . . .

She could at least fulfill the desire for revenge that had eaten at her for the past ten years. The opportunity quite literally stood right in front of her.

Simone brushed the skirt of the tasteful cream-colored suit she wore with a red silk blouse. Her hair was pulled back and fastened with a pearl-studded clasp at the nape of her neck, and she wore modest pearl earrings. Other than the color of her blouse, which should have been white or cream, this was the kind of outfit the school had suggested students wear when interviewing for a job. She took a deep breath.

She knew she looked better in red than white. And that she was after more than just a job.

Ascending the steps, she opened one of the tall, ebony doors with a firm grasp on the brass knob. Inside, a woman looked up from the reception desk and gave her a warm smile.

"Miss Lefèvre?"

Simone was impressed that the receptionist remembered her name from the hasty call she'd placed to see if she could set up this meeting with Antoine Dupuis. "Yes. Thank you for your help today."

"Monsieur Dupuis was most pleased that you wished to meet with him so soon," she said, getting up. "I'll let him know you have arrived."

Simone surveyed her surroundings while she waited for the man who likely would become her employer . . . today, she hoped. The building was quite large, obviously once a grand residence. Home to Nick's ancestors? The reception area was to the right of the entrance, in a large, sunny parlor furnished tastefully in period pieces. An unused fireplace was framed by a marble mantel, above which hung the portrait of a woman dressed in the fashion of a long-ago era. A Rutledge? she wondered. Could she work in a place so pervaded by the heritage of the man she abhorred?

Her thoughts were interrupted by the sound of rapidly approaching footsteps, and she turned to see a short, balding man hurrying toward her. When he reached her, he took her by complete surprise when, instead of taking her hand to shake, he bowed slightly and grazed her fingers with a kiss. "Mademoiselle Lefèvre, this is indeed a pleasure," he gushed in French. "I am delighted that you decided to come earlier than we had planned." He raised his eyes to hers, and his expression grew serious. "I hope it portends a decision on your part to join the House of Rutledge."

Simone withdrew her hand. Although the man in front of her, immaculate in his Italian suit and suave manner, had done nothing to affront her, he made her uneasy. Even if she considered his greeting too personal, it wasn't out of line. He was French. At least he hadn't kissed both cheeks. But his words betrayed an eagerness that didn't make sense to her. How did

he know she would suit as a master perfumer? Wasn't he even
going to test her abilities?

"It is a rather awesome responsibility," she hedged in reply. "I am not certain that I will be qualified."

Dupuis took her by the elbow and escorted her down the
long center hallway into an opulent office toward the rear of
the building, reassuring her as they went. "I have taken the
liberty of checking your background," he told her, indicating
for her to take a seat on a velvet couch in the office. The
surroundings in this room were decidedly French, but a little
too rococo for her taste. "Not only did I find you have an
excellent record in your university study of chemistry, but the
people at the institute in New York told me that you were the
greatest natural *nez* they had ever seen."

Le nez. The nose. It was the one tool of the perfumer that
science and technology had not managed to displace with
computerized equipment. Technicians can assemble fragrance,
but only a nose can create a great perfume.

Yes, she was a great "nose," as her talent was called in
the business. Her father's genes and a childhood spent among
the finest essences of the world had given her a gift few people shared. It was not a matter of simply being able to dif-
ferentiate between the scent of a rose and a lily. It was the
ability to detect in a mixture of more than a hundred ingredients the precise amount of the substances that contributed
to a formula. She was able not only to recognize instantly by
their smell the raw ingredients in a mix, but could tell whether
a certain lot of labdanum was from Mediterranean soil or that
of the Middle East, whether the oil of ylang-ylang came from
the Philippines or the Moluccas. Her skill as a chemist was
just icing on the cake.

"Perhaps they exaggerate," she replied modestly, although
she recalled the astonishment of the faculty at the institute
when she completed in a day the most complex battery of
tests designed to evaluate a person's ability at creating fragrance. "Don't you think it would be wise to put me through
the tests, as I am certain you would any other candidate for
this position?"

Dupuis pulled a chair opposite her, took a seat, and leaned forward, his hands on his knees. His eyes were bright. Like a fox's, Simone thought. "I was able to read the results of the tests you were given at the institute," he revealed. "They faxed them to me. There is no need to replicate the effort. Besides," he added, leaning back into the chair, "you are the daughter of Jean René Lefèvre. Some members of the board of directors of the House of Rutledge were clients of your father. They know the talent that courses through your veins."

Mention of her father caught Simone off guard and brought a clutch of emotion to her throat. "They knew my father?"

"Some of them. It was how I came to locate you in the first place."

Simone felt unexpected moisture spring to her eyes, and she blinked it away quickly. It was as if her beloved papa had somehow reached out from beyond his grave and given her a personal reference. As if he knew her desire to become a true perfumer, not a slave to the commercial fragrance industry, and had found a way for her not only to fulfill that dream, but also take long-overdue revenge on his former apprentice as well.

"I see," she croaked, pulling herself together before her emotions got away from her.

"I have no doubt that you are the talent we need to take over as master perfumer here," Dupuis went on, his voice serious, almost silky. "But what is it *you* want, Miss Lefèvre?"

Simone shifted in her seat, thinking before replying. "I want a place where I can create," she answered at last. "I do not want to be merely a technician, or the perfumer who makes fragrances for the toilet bowl," she laughed nervously.

"You want to be your father's daughter," Dupuis finished for her, nodding knowingly.

His understanding encouraged her. "In a sense, yes," she said. "But I do not wish to create great perfumes for only a few. I . . . I wish to create *les grands parfums,* like in the days of *la Belle Epoque.* Truly great scents, packaged in crystal or gold, fragrances that will honor the memory of my father and place the name of Lefèvre right up there with Guerlain and Caron and Coty.''

She saw a smile widen across Dupuis's face. ''Then we are of like mind,'' he replied. ''Although the House of Rutledge has made its comeback through the success of the Royalty line and the development of common bath and body products that have become favorites in the mass market, I believe the time has come for us to step above the mediocre, where Nick's limited talent has kept us for the past ten years. It is time for the House of Rutledge to move onto center stage, to create the finest perfumes in the world.''

He leaned forward and took her hand. ''And I believe it is time once again for the name of Lefèvre to become synonymous with the finest perfumes of the world. *Les grand parfums*. Yes, I think we are of like mind, mademoiselle.''

TEN

Nick pulled the Triumph into the small car park behind the House of Rutledge, fighting the anger that surged through him to know that this place, which had once belonged to his ancestors, and should have belonged to him, was now the property of Antoine Dupuis. But it was Nick's own damned fault, and all he could do now was work harder than he ever had to fight his way back. He got out of the car and strode toward the back door of the building, as he had every day for the past ten years. But then he remembered he no longer had a key.

It hurt.

His jaw set, he turned to the narrow sidewalk that led from the parking lot to the imposing front doors, determined to confront Dupuis about the ransacking that had taken place in his own, far less pretentious offices. When he opened the door, he saw first the surprise then the distress that came over the face of Sarah Addington, the receptionist who had long had a crush on him and who had been distraught to learn of his departure from the company. Was she still his ally?

"Hello, Sarah," he said, feeling painfully like an outsider now, like one of the sales reps who called on the company.

"Nick!" She gasped his name, then glanced nervously over her shoulder, down the hall toward the office that had once been his. "What . . . what are you doing here?"

"Is Dupuis here? I need to speak with him."

He could tell by her agitated manner that Antoine Dupuis was here, but that she didn't want the unpleasant job of announcing Nick's arrival to him.

"Yes, but he wasn't expecting you, was he?"

"I doubt it," Nick replied dryly. "Where is he? I'd like to catch him unawares anyway."

"Oh, Nick, don't," Sarah pleaded. "He's . . . he's taken your old office, and—"

But that was all he needed to know. He marched down the familiar hallway, ignoring Sarah's flurry of protests. The bastard, he thought. But he wasn't surprised that Dupuis had wasted no time in displacing Nick in every respect possible. He was, after all, the quintessential predator, hovering, waiting to pick clean the bones of his prey.

"Nick, stop!" Sarah's voice reached his consciousness, its urgency finally registering. But it was too late. He had already opened the door, already discovered the secret that lay beyond.

And suddenly everything fell into place.

"So that's what you are doing in England." He voiced the realization in a low growl. If the world hadn't started to crash around him, he would have found ironic humor in the little tableau that remained frozen for an instant in front of him. Dupuis had jumped to his feet, a look of startled irritation on his face. Simone sat on the sofa, her eyes wide, her hand at her throat, her mouth slightly open, as if she wanted to say something but couldn't find the words. Both of them looked like the proverbial rats caught in a trap.

Before, he'd been unable to picture a vindictive Simone. Now, she was right before his eyes. In league with the very man who had masterminded the plot that had led to the theft, to her father's death. Did she know? She couldn't. Dupuis was a master at deceit. At engendering trust, however misplaced.

Nick's first impulse was to warn her against Dupuis, but at the look on her face, he stopped short. She had recovered from the surprise of his intrusion, and now her gaze bored into him with undisguised venom. She hated him, and he knew intuitively she could only be here with the intent of doing everything in her power to destroy him. Was she the new master perfumer? Did she have her father's talent? If so, she would bring to the House of Rutledge what it needed to remain the leader in the market, and his own young enterprise would have a harder time than ever competing.

This was not the Simone he had once loved, the young girl whose face had haunted him for the decade of despair and regret that had been his existence since his night of crime. Not even the lover in his dreams, for except in last night's variation, she had been his eagerly.

This Simone was dangerous. Deadly.

Nick managed at last to tear his gaze from her face, turning his attention to Dupuis, determined to finish the business he'd come here for.

"I won't take much of your time, Dupuis. Just enough to let you know that if you, or your henchmen, ever set foot onto my property again, I will sue you on every charge I can come up with." For a fraction of a second, he saw what appeared to be pure bewilderment on the Frenchman's face, but he didn't believe it for a moment. Dupuis was an actor. His responses were always controlled.

"I do not know what you are talking about," Dupuis professed, a scowl deepening on his face. "But it is you who are trespassing at the moment. Get out, or I'll call the police."

But Nick would not be intimidated. Instead, he stepped right up to the man, thrust his face squarely into the other's. "You've got it all now, you stinking little bastard," he said, his voice low and menacing. "Just as you planned all along. Be content with what you've acquired through my own naïve trust and stupidity, but leave me alone. I warn you. Stay out of my way, or you'll be sorry."

Nick knew about Dupuis's many "fringe activities," his involvements with shadowy characters and the underside of politics.

And Dupuis knew that Nick knew.

Nick's testimony in certain investigations could probably send Dupuis to jail, and if there was such a thing as guilt by association, Nick would likely join him there. But at the moment, he did not care. He was ready to do anything to be rid of Dupuis once and for all. He regretted that Simone was likely to be caught up in the man's web, but it was her choice, and he knew, she would neither listen to nor believe him, if he tried to convince her otherwise.

Dupuis pushed him in the chest. "Don't threaten me, Rutledge," he hissed, "or you are the one who will be sorry. Now get out."

Blood thundered in Nick's ears. His face was crimson with anger because the man had laid a hand on him, and he wanted to tear the vile Frenchman apart on the spot.

Control, Nick, stay in control. A voice inside of him shouted over his raging emotions, reminding him it was when he had been out of control that Dupuis had been able to best manipulate him.

He glared at Dupuis, then turned a contemptuous eye on Simone. "He is all yours, mademoiselle. And good luck."

Simone sat in stunned silence after Nick left the room. There was no question in her mind that these two former allies were now bitter enemies. She wondered what exactly Dupuis had done that had brought Nick storming into his office. Wondered, in fact, why Nick had decided to leave the House of Rutledge in the first place.

"What was that all about?" she inquired cautiously. It really was none of her business, except that she had every intention of making Nick's downfall very much her business, and any information she could glean about him would be helpful.

"I have no idea," Dupuis replied in a tight voice, going to close the door behind the intruder. "I'm afraid our man is regretting his decision to leave us. He has delusions that he can make it on his own." He shrugged and gestured with his hands. "Maybe he can. I doubt it, however. He is not a self-made success. It is I who gave him his chance after his father had practically destroyed the company. It was the money I invested that rebuilt this firm into the fiscally strong company it is today.''

Simone frowned. ''What about the Royalty line? I thought you told me that was entirely of Nick's doing.''

Dupuis took his seat again and gave her the warmest of smiles. ''I assure you, Miss Lefèvre, the manufacture and marketing of that line was accomplished in my complete ignorance of the source of the formulas. I never questioned Nick in those early years. He seemed a highly talented perfumer when he developed those fragrances. Synthetically reproducing them instead of using all natural ingredients as your father did was nothing short of genius, since it made them so affordable. So in that respect, the Royalty line *was* entirely of his doing. But the money that paid for it was mine.''

Simone chewed on that for a moment, then digested it as likely being the truth. Nick had deceived her and her father. It stood to reason he would have deceived his financial backers as well in not revealing how he'd come up with those formulas.

''May I see the operations?'' she asked, suddenly curious to know the kind of technology that would be available to her if she accepted the position Nick had recently deserted.

''But of course,'' Dupuis said, jumping up instantly and helping her from the couch. She didn't like the way he seemed to want to put his hands on her, although he had been consummately courteous. She slid the strap of her handbag over her shoulder and put her hands in her jacket pockets before following the sweep of Dupuis's arm as he indicated for her to precede him into the large hallway.

''This house has been the headquarters of the firm known as the House of Rutledge since it was created in 1848 by James Rutledge,'' he began, and led her into a large conference room across the hall, where a number of portraits lined the pale green walls. ''That's James.'' He pointed to the painting above the mantel.

Simone saw the resemblance between this man and Nick Rutledge in an instant. He had the same broad forehead, outlined by a handsome, square hairline. His straight nose was the same as well, and the intense blue eyes.

"James started this company as the British liaison of a firm instituted by his brother out in India called the Bombay Spice and Fragrance Company." Dupuis gave a disdainful snort and added, "That's the division Nick thinks he can salvage and rebuild in today's market. Fat chance."

But at the mention of the brother in India, Simone's curiosity stood at attention. "What was the brother's name?" she wanted to know, recalling the story Esther had told her.

"John. John Rutledge was the younger son of the earl, an officer in the British Army in India. Nick told me once he was sent there by his father because he was having some kind of illicit affair with a commoner. The British are such snobs," he added in French.

"Please, go on," Simone encouraged him.

Dupuis gave her an odd look, as if he were surprised she was so interested in Rutledge family history. "John Rutledge disappeared while he was in India. He'd started the export business, and it was apparently thriving. The old records show that there was quite a trade between the firms owned by the two brothers, although they reportedly were not friendly toward one another. Then one night, John supposedly just vanished. Poof! Like that." Again the Frenchman gestured dramatically.

"What happened to him?" Simone could scarcely conceal her excitement at this confirmation of Esther Brown's story. Did Dupuis believe, as Esther did, that John's disappearance had something to do with a perfume?

But when he answered, he didn't mention any magical perfume or dematerialization of dead bodies, and Simone didn't bring it up. "Nobody knows. They suspect he was murdered, but no body was ever found. His family thought perhaps he'd eloped with his forbidden lover, but again, there was never any proof of that either."

"People don't just disappear," Simone murmured, staring up at the portrait, wondering what had really happened to John Rutledge. Had he looked a lot like James? Like Nick? And what had Mary Rose been like? She allowed her concentration to drift into that bygone era until her escort's voice brought her abruptly back to the present.

"Well, it's just a tale at any rate," Dupuis said. "This is our conference room, as you can see. The department heads meet here every Tuesday morning to keep abreast of what is going on within the company. You will be expected to make a weekly report on the activities of the perfumery operations." He came to stand behind her and put his hands on her upper arms. "It is my great hope, Simone, that we will hear soon of your first *grand parfum*."

Simone shuddered involuntarily at his touch. *"S'il vous plaît, Monsieur Dupuis,"* she said, removing his hands and turning to face him. "It is uncomfortable for me to become too familiar with my prospective employer."

"I beg your pardon," Dupuis replied properly, but she could see he was obviously put off by the polite rebuff. "I intended no such familiarity."

Simone hoped she hadn't just shot down her chance for the job, but she'd meant what she'd said. If Dupuis wanted her, it must be for her talents as a perfumer, not for her body. Better get that understood right from the beginning. But for the rest of the tour, which took the better part of an hour, Dupuis was all business, and if her words had offended him, he didn't show it.

Simone was duly impressed with what she saw. The House of Rutledge was streamlined, completely state-of-the-art, with every resource she could imagine available to her. It was a perfumer's dream. When at last they returned to Dupuis's office, she had decided that she would accept the position, if he still wished her to take it. She would be a fool to pass up this opportunity.

"Well?" Dupuis said. "Do you think it would suit you to become the master perfumer at the House of Rutledge?"

Simone could think of nothing that would suit her more. *"Mais oui, Monsieur Dupuis,"* she replied. "It is a wonderful opportunity, one for which I am extremely grateful. I only hope I can measure up to your expectations."

"I am certain that will be easy for one of your talent. Now, a few business matters." He offered her a salary that was quite acceptable, along with a number of fringe benefits. "Of course you will have to relocate to London," he added. "You may use the company's flat not far from here for the time being, until you find a place of your own. The House of Rutledge will assume all the expenses of your move."

He extended his hand. "Is that agreeable?"

She laughed. She'd be an idiot not to agree. "Yes," she replied, and they shook on the deal.

"You will be my guest for lunch, then, to celebrate?" Dupuis beamed at her, obviously pleased with her decision, and Simone scolded herself for her earlier suspicions that his overt familiarity was out of line. It had been many years since she'd lived in France. She'd forgotten that such gestures were cultural, not lecherous.

"It would be my pleasure," she said, relaxing and beginning to assimilate her new role at the House of Rutledge, assuring herself that as CEO, Dupuis would have invited his new master perfumer to lunch whether the successful candidate had been a man or a woman.

Nick left the building without even looking at Sarah Addington at the front desk, afraid his steaming temper would erupt in her innocent direction. He slammed the door of the Triumph and steered it recklessly through the heavy traffic. The balls of that man! Dupuis's audacity never ceased to astound him. But he had to admit that hiring Simone Lefèvre to replace him was a stroke of pure, if cruel, genius.

At least now, he thought bitterly, braking abruptly and skidding when he realized the car in front of him had stopped, he knew his competition. And even though he didn't like it that she had taken over his job, he was undaunted. Simone Lefèvre was an unknown, riding on her father's reputation. Did she have talent in her own right? Was she a true nose? Or had Dupuis hired her in some sort of sick revenge for Nick's departure?

As shaken as he'd been to see her again under such unexpected circumstances, in a way, Nick felt sorry for Simone. Did she have any idea what she was getting into by going to work for Dupuis? Did she have any suspicion of his shady background, his unscrupulous character? He doubted it. Nick was certain that Dupuis had blamed the theft of her father's formulas entirely on him.

Although he respected the irony, Nick failed to find any humor in the fact that if Simone was indeed a talented perfumer, she was now in a position to exact revenge on him if she so chose, a revenge that would be financed by the very man who had orchestrated the whole sordid plot to begin with.

Nick decided to stop off at his house and change his clothes before returning to clean up the mess at the office. After successfully avoiding disaster from his reckless driving in the heavy midday traffic of London, he wheeled the Triumph into the protection of his driveway and knew instantly something was wrong. The front door stood open a few inches, its black paint scraped, the wood gouged. What the hell? First his office, now his home . . .

Nick reached for the heavy lug wrench he kept beneath the passenger seat. Was the intruder still inside? A part of him wished it so, because he was angry enough at the moment to bash his head in. He pushed the door open cautiously with the tool, keeping his body against the outside wall of the house in case the burglar might have a gun. The door thumped against the inner wall. Nick heard nothing stir within. He peered around the corner and into the darkened house, aware that his breath was coming in short rasps.

He crouched down and dashed into the hallway, shutting the door behind him and taking cover behind the large armoire that stood in the entry. Still no sound revealed the presence of a trespasser. With courage born of anger and outrage, Nick stepped quietly down the hall and into the study, not surprised to see that his bookshelves were in disarray, the drawers of the desk plundered, the room in general a mess from someone's search through his personal belongings. His rage increased. Who the hell was doing this to him? And why? Had Dupuis faced him calmly during their earlier encounter, en-

joying the knowledge that Nick's house was being torn apart
even as they spoke? The idea nearly drove him mad. Then
another terrible thought struck him.

The trunk! Was Dupuis after the contents of the trunk?
How could he even know about it? But a quick search revealed that although someone had opened it, rifled through
the letters and probably also scanned the diary, nothing appeared to be missing from among his ancestor's treasures.
Thank God he'd had the good sense to place the vial of perfume securely in his bank vault. Nick frowned, thoroughly
perplexed.

Upstairs, the scene was much the same in the small guest
room that also served as his junk room. But oddly, nothing
was amiss in his own bedroom. His closet retained the im-
peccable order in which he kept it. His drawers were unopened, his nightstands untouched.

Nick returned to the junk room and stared at the mess,
totally confounded. What *was* Dupuis after? He started to
straighten things, then decided he'd better call the police first.
He still had the card of the detective who had investigated the
break-in at the office, and he dialed the number rotely, his
mind preoccupied, searching its very nether reaches to think
of what Dupuis might possibly be seeking.

Two hours later, the police had come and gone, the report
had been duly filed, and Nick was left alone again to clean
up the mess. He started in the upstairs room. The contents of
the old boxes that contained his "jumble collection," as he
called it, had been dumped on the floor, and he began to sift
through the useless but nostalgic memorabilia they had contained. Old photos. Articles he'd clipped during his years at
Harrow and Cambridge. The newspapers that carried the reports of his father's suicide. Those, he decided, wadding them
in his fist, could go into the rubbish.

Under the newspapers were several manila folders, all of
them empty, their contents used long ago to create the Royalty
line. He looked at the labels. *Katherina. Diana. Grace.
Ivanna. Evita.* Each the name of the woman for whom Jean
René Lefèvre had created his great perfumes. Some he had

designed decades ago, others were more modern.

Nick recalled with a grimace having helped Jean René label these very folders after he'd convinced the aging perfumer to write down his formulas instead of carrying them in his head. Like a good apprentice, Nick, or rather "Nat," had offered to help get him organized and had served as an eager scribe. Just part of the web of deceit he had wrought upon the old man. Nick felt the familiar sickening regret all over again.

Why had he saved these? Frowning, he dashed them in the trash pile alongside the suicide reports.

ELEVEN

❦

Three weeks passed, and with each day Nick's frustration mounted. He had tried everything he could think of to learn about the plant described in the old papers. He'd contacted a horticultural expert at Kew Gardens, called on a scholar who was an expert on mystical sects in India, sought reference to the plant in the library, even gone on-line to try to discover its contemporary name. But the *mahja* had remained elusive. No one had ever heard of such a plant.

Nick knew that at one time it had existed. He held the proof in his hand:

June 1847
My dearest John,
   Summer has arrived this year with a lushness that is rare even in our lovely shire. The weather has produced a passion of color in the garden. Every seed I have planted there has sprung to life, blossoming fuller and more beautiful than at any time I can remember. Perhaps it is because every seed was sown with thoughts of you, of our love, and my firm belief that we will one day be reunited.
   I received your packet, which was transmitted by our friend in the village, and immediately planted the seeds that you sent. Not knowing the species or requirements of the mahja, *as you call it, I kept them in the green-*

house which I have fashioned on the north side of the garden wall to protect my seedlings during the winter. You wrote that this plant could not be cultivated outside a certain region of India, but to my delight, the seedlings sprang eagerly from the soil. I transplanted them alongside one wall of the garden where they get ample sunshine, and they have rewarded me by blooming rapidly and in profusion. The showy blossoms come only at night, however, and they are fragile and short-lived. Even so, I managed to derive from them an essence, a lovely perfume, and before sending you the enclosed specimen, I cast a spell over it, meant to bind us together for all time. I know you do not believe in my "magic," but thoughts are powerful things, and my spells are cast with powerful thoughts. I urge you to invoke the power of this magic, my love. You need only place a few drops of this lovely essence upon your pillow each night and dream of me. Promise me you will, and somehow, some way, we will fulfill our love despite the obstacles that have been set against us.

Forever yours,
Mary Rose

Nick let out a long breath and shook his head. Had they pronounced it *mah'-ja? Mah-ja'?* Had they even got the name right in their own time, or had his ancestor misheard the name to begin with? Or had the wily monks given him a false name all along? He wished Mary Rose had sketched the "showy" blossoms, but there was no such artwork in any of her letters to help him solve the mystery.

Laying the letter aside on the smooth surface of his desk, he drummed his fingers impatiently. He must break the secret of the *mahja*. He needed that essential oil now, in large quantities. Because he knew it was his ticket back into the mainstream of the fragrance market. To its forefront, he hoped.

His sense of urgency bordered on panic. Dupuis would move quickly to capitalize on Simone's famous name. If indeed Simone were anywhere nearly as talented as her father,

Dupuis would be a fool not to shift the focus of the House of Rutledge from bath and body products, and move into the more upscale and lucrative arena of fine perfumes.

And Antoine Dupuis was no fool.

With the financial clout of the House of Rutledge, he could easily outpromote Nick's first creation, no matter how fantastic it might be.

Nick leaned back in his chair and considered his one advantage in being a one-man company. He did not have to answer to anyone but himself. There was no corporate bureaucracy to deal with, no financial backers he had to please. That thought gave him some small satisfaction. He could move quickly, while the House of Rutledge might have to lumber on for weeks in pursuit of progress.

If he only knew *what* to move quickly *upon*. Would that blasted shipment from Bombay never arrive? Included in it was some rather beat-up equipment, but perhaps it would be sufficient to learn the identity of the *mahja*. If it was not, he would have no choice but to take a chance and make arrangements to dissect the fragrance using someone else's more sophisticated equipment, perhaps at a university somewhere. Although in doing so he risked exposure of his secret, he did not want to spend any of his limited funds at the moment to purchase a lot of expensive high-tech computerized equipment. However, Nick hoped going elsewhere would not be necessary, for he sincerely believed that he might be on the verge of a breakthrough in the science of perfumery, and he didn't want anyone to have an inkling what he was about.

The possibility that something in the chemistry of the *mahja* oil might actually enable the user to go beyond the illusions usually summoned by a scent into an actual physical experience was an outrageous, mind-boggling concept. Nick wasn't even certain it was possible. The only similar phenomenon he could think of was the use of hallucinogenic drugs. Users of LSD often claimed to have "tripped" physically into other realms.

But from what he'd read of LSD and the like, he believed the dream journeys on which the *mahja* oil had taken him were even more physical in nature than those drug-induced "trips."

He wondered, too, if his reaction to the perfume oil was an isolated response, or if others would have the same intensely sexual experiences? Eventually, he would have to experiment with the substance on others, providing of course that the oil of the *mahja* proved to be neither harmful nor illegal.

He'd contacted his friends in several of England's most prestigious department stores, all of whom assured him they would help him gain distribution of his new line of perfumes. But they had no idea what type of perfume he intended to introduce as his first product. He laughed to himself. What would those friends think if . . . when . . . they tried the stuff and were whisked away into an erotic dreamland where they could indulge safely and privately in every sexual fantasy of which they could ever conceive?

He could think of several who might not want to wake up.

Nick took the scenario further, to the investigations that were sure to follow. When the "morality squad" learned about the "love potion," surely the perfume would be put to the scrutiny of those who were charged with protecting the citizenry from the decadent influences of the world . . . the drugs, the porn, the sin and smut that seemed to attract humankind. Would his perfume be outlawed?

Or, he thought more hopefully, perhaps its inherent sensuous nature would stir up free publicity and create a huge demand for it. A demand he would find difficult to fill, thereby driving the price skyward.

The shrill buzz of the intercom interrupted his reverie. "Mr. Rutledge, I have good news. The transport company just called. Your shipment from Bombay will be arriving at the docks within twenty-four hours."

Nick's heart leapt, but he growled an answer. "It's about damned time." Then he softened, wishing he hadn't been so short with the long-suffering Brenda. "Thanks. If you're finished with those letters, you can go home early if you'd like. We may be putting in some longer hours in the next few days."

Nick wasn't surprised she took him up on the offer. He turned off the intercom and reached for the ancient amber vial that almost matched the wood on his desk. Although he had been tempted, he had not removed the perfume oil from the bank vault until today. The police had come up with no conclusive evidence linking the Frenchman directly to the break-ins, and Dupuis had made no more attempts to disrupt Nick's new enterprise. Hopefully, that funny business was behind them. Perhaps Dupuis was not as threatened by Nick's departure now that Simone Lefèvre had brought her talent to his doorstep.

At any rate, Nick had succumbed to his temptation to take personal possession of the substance once again, and he spoke to it as if it were a living thing, his voice barely above a whisper. "A lot is riding on you," he told it. "You'd better give up your secret, and you'd bloody well better do it soon!"

Antoine Dupuis had never expected the daughter of Jean René Lefèvre to be so beautiful. Of course, he had never seen her, having remained scrupulously in the background during the theft he'd orchestrated ten years ago. But he wondered why Nick had never mentioned her, and how the young man could have avoided falling in love with her then. Surely she had not changed so much in those years, although perhaps she had become, as young women often do, more maturely attractive.

If he'd been in Nick's shoes . . .

The collar of his starched white shirt pressed into his fleshy neck, and he levered his tie loose with two fingers. These were not thoughts he should be entertaining about his new master perfumer. It was not important whether she looked like a goddess or a toad. What mattered was her nose.

And that goddess-shaped nose had Antoine Dupuis worried.

Simone had been at the House of Rutledge for three weeks, and even though he conceded that it was a relatively short time, considering she was having to relocate from another continent as well as settle into her new job, Dupuis had hoped she would produce at least one fragrance over which management could become excited. The company's morale needed a boost. Since Nick's departure, the place had suffered from an inexplicable congregate depression, as if their leader had defected, leaving them helpless. Dupuis detested the idea that Nick had commanded so much respect, but he knew the young Rutledge heir had been popular with everyone but himself, and he did not take it personally that the entire staff had so openly expressed their regret at losing the talented perfumer. They would get over it. In the meantime, he had come up with a brilliant replacement in Simone.

Or so he had thought.

Although fragrances had always contributed a substantial percentage to the bottom line for the House of Rutledge, since Dupuis had been there the company had focused on producing economy-priced scents for the mass market, such as the Royalty line, as well as moderately priced bath and body products and cosmetics. But when Simone had expressed her strong desire to create instead the *grands parfums*, as she called them, Dupuis saw in an instant the potential of allowing the daughter of the world-renowned Jean René Lefèvre to take the staid old firm into a more upscale market.

Fine perfumes were the glamour end of the fragrance business, a highly lucrative end, and Dupuis had given Simone carte blanche to create fragrances so fine they would command the respect of the entire world.

But he had yet to see, or smell, any such perfumes. In fact, he'd not seen any results at all, any evidence of the great talent she supposedly possessed.

Maybe he'd been too hasty in hiring her, he mused, standing at the tall multipaned window that overlooked a small garden behind the building, watching the shadows of late afternoon deepen into evening. Maybe he *should* have given her the battery of tests one normally demanded of a new perfumer. Maybe her friends at the institute had rigged the exam results.

Mais non. That was ridiculous. Certainly, she must have the innate talent those tests indicated. Still, he had expected more from the daughter of Jean René Lefèvre, even though it might be unfair to compare her fledgling attempts at perfumery to her father's awesome reputation.

So far, however, even though she'd worked long hours in virtual isolation, concentrating at the console and the scientific equipment of modern-day perfumery, Simone Lefèvre had come up with nothing.

Nothing!

Be patient, he told himself, buffing his immaculately manicured nails with his handkerchief. She will produce. Still, her lack of some kind of dramatic, instant performance irritated him.

Was it that, he wondered suddenly, or was it her attitude? Was his disappointment in her due to a perceived lack of productivity or to her continuing aloofness toward him? Although always polite and professional when she was around him, she seemed too quiet, restrained, almost withdrawn. Why did she not like him? He could think of nothing he had done to offend her. Had Nick somehow managed to cause her to distrust him? Impossible. Other than Nick's brief, nasty intrusion the day she was hired, Simone had not seen Nicholas Rutledge in ten years. And from what Dupuis had heard about her reaction to the theft, Rutledge was likely the last person on earth she would ever speak to again, much less take advice from.

Perhaps she didn't trust men in general. After all, Nick had dealt her a heavy blow. Yes, that could be what was causing her to remain so reserved. It could be that she was wary of men, and her coolness was not directed at him personally, he thought, nodding. It could also be that she was having difficulty adjusting to surroundings that must remind her of the man who had so betrayed her. Dupuis considered that a moment, knowing he should feel some twinge of guilt in the matter. But he didn't. It had been a business decision to send Nick after those formulas. Nothing more.

Dupuis turned away from the window, consciously examining his feelings toward Simone and acknowledging they were more complex than those of an employer toward an employee. He was attracted to her. Man to woman. It disturbed him. Antoine Dupuis had never let such emotions stand between him and good judgment. And yet he feared he might now be in just such a position.

He went to a small cabinet across the room and opened the door to his personal closet. On the back of the door was an oval mirror framed in ornate gilded plaster. He peered at his reflection. Was he an old fool to think she could become attracted to him? Probably. He was a good twenty years older than she. Slightly balding. Not tall or broad of shoulder, but expensively dressed. His suits were handmade by the finest *couturiers* in France and Italy. His ties pure silk. His shoes Italian leather. He gave himself an appreciative smile. He might not be as tall or handsome as someone like Nick Rutledge. But he had the one thing that all women found attractive.

Money.

He would, he decided, smoothing back his graying sideburns, bide his time with Simone Lefèvre. Give her a chance to settle into her new position. Give her the benefit of the doubt concerning her talent as a perfumer. He would court her, not overtly or personally, but corporately. He would keep things strictly business, until she trusted him and lowered those lovely defenses.

He smiled to his image in the mirror. It was a safe and appealing strategy. He would not risk appearing the fool, and yet from a relatively intimate vantage point, he could admire her sensual beauty without exposing his true feelings. He had already made a practice of dropping in on her at work, and he decided he would continue to do so, to let her get used to his presence.

The perfume lab was located upstairs in a large area that was sealed in an attempt to prevent the riot of scent at play there from escaping into the rest of the building. Antoine wondered how anyone could concentrate among the intensely aromatic surroundings. He could not remain long in the perfumery. It gave him a headache.

He entered the room and stifled a sneeze as a virtual cacophony of scents assailed him. He found Simone where he'd expected, perched on a chair in front of the computerized equipment used in modern-day perfumery. He hesitated before approaching her, allowing his eyes to feast for a moment on the young woman's allure. Even in the white lab coat, she exuded an innate sexuality. Her hair spilled down her back in rich, dark waves, forming a tantalizing contrast to the severity of the uniform, the clean lines of which could not hide the curve of her hips, the gentle slope of her shoulders. *Ah, qu'elle jolie jeune femme*, he sighed. What a beautiful young woman.

Now, if only she proved to have the talent he sought in a master perfumer . . .

    . . . and if he could win her trust . . .

    . . . and then win her affection . . .

He would have it all. The House of Rutledge. The woman. The power. The prestige.

It was a challenge. But he *would* have it.

He would have it all.

"Bonjour, mademoiselle," he said, coming to stand directly behind her. She jumped as if she'd been doused with a bucket of water and whirled the swivel chair around to face him. He was astounded to see she wore a filter over her nose. *Mon Dieu!* What kind of perfumer covers her nose, even in this aroma-laden environment? Most "noses" claimed that their olfactory senses became accustomed to the sensory overload, that they simply did not smell the scents mingling in their immediate environment. His earlier doubts came screaming back.

"Oh, good morning," she replied, hastily removing the white mask. She turned back to the computer table and with a single swipe, covered with a piece of heavy plastic a syringe, a small vial, her notes, everything that lay on the surface. "You startled me," she added, turning again to face him. "I get so engrossed in my work, I'm afraid I lose track of everything else. Is there something I can do for you?"

Her face was very pale, her eyes strained, her demeanor intense and nervous. She acted almost . . . guilty. Curious, Dupuis watched her closely, but he remained casual, moving to the edge of the console and leaning against it.

"*Pardon,* Miss Lefèvre," he said with thick charm, "I did not mean to frighten you."

"Yes, uh, yes, thank you," she replied, pushing the rolling chair away from him and standing, brushing imagined wrinkles from her black silk trousers.

God, but he loved the way she dressed. Hip. French. Daring. Sexy without knowing it. Today beneath the lab coat she wore a tightly fitting long-sleeved shirt in a bright geometric techno print. Two buttons were unfastened at the neck, a fashion statement, nothing more, and yet he perceived a subtle invitation there. He swallowed over the unexpected desire that seemed suddenly lodged in his throat.

At the same moment, a scent made its way through the myriad smells that permeated the room and traveled up his nose. A lovely scent, unlike anything he had ever smelled. So she *was* working on something! And from its delectable aroma, he knew instantly he had been wrong to doubt her talent as a perfumer. But suddenly he realized with a start that something else was going on here . . .

He seemed to be experiencing some kind of physiological reaction to the scent. His pulse began to pound in his temples. His skin tingled. And incredibly, he felt himself growing . . . hard! He felt younger, vibrant, more alive than he had only moments before.

He regarded Simone with open astonishment. "*Qu'est-ce que c'est?* What is this?"

TWELVE

֍

"What is what?" Simone was alarmed by the expression that had suddenly come over Dupuis's face. It was the unmistakable look of the predatory male. She'd seen it on the men who had sometimes come on to her both at the university and the occasional times she'd visited a bar with friends in New Orleans. The look that clearly indicated a sexual advance was on its way.

It hadn't been there when she first turned to face him. In that instant, she had perceived he was all business, checking up on her the way he had since she'd joined the company three weeks before. At first it had annoyed her, these little drop-in visits of his. But she'd become accustomed to them, and she figured he had the right to keep an eye on her, at least in the beginning.

The problem was, she did not want him to learn anything about the project in front of her, the search that was driving her crazy. Until she discovered the identity of the floral essence and, if it was unavailable from nature, came up with a synthesized version of it for use in her *grand parfum*, she wanted no one to know about it. She herself was unsure of its safety, and for that reason, and to avoid the pleasurable but disturbing sexual arousal it caused in her, she had begun wearing a face mask during her analytical work at the computer. She also kept her materials covered in plastic so no one else would be exposed. She couldn't imagine a perfume being dangerous, but she wanted to take precautions all the same.

But she'd been careless, and she knew from his reaction Dupuis had caught a sniff of it. In one respect, this proved it *was* dangerous, and powerful, because he now stood before her, obviously horny as a schoolboy. He hadn't been when he'd entered the room.

It had to be the perfume.

"That scent," he murmured, taking a step toward her. "It . . . it is the most beautiful fragrance I have ever known."

Simone backed away from him and began protectively buttoning her lab coat. "It's . . . just something I have been working on. But I'm not ready—" Her eyes widened as he reached to pull back the plastic. "No!" She rushed to place her body between him and the perfume. The last thing she needed was for her boss to truly fall under its spell and get out of line.

Crossing her arms in front of her, she took on her father's attitude, behavior that bordered on arrogance. She, like Jean René, was an artist and must be allowed creative freedom. The trick had worked for Papa, and her father's clients had always respected his wishes and demands, because he was, after all, the master. Simone hoped it would work for her as well. She pulled herself up to her full five feet six inches, almost as tall as the Frenchman. *"S'il vous plaît,"* she said sternly. "I must insist that I be allowed to work in privacy until I am ready to introduce my fragrances. If you wish me to remain as your master perfumer, it is imperative that I work in my own way, alone." She stared him in the eye and didn't blink.

In his eyes she read a series of conflicting emotions. Desire, clearly, dimmed by her brusque and resolute insistence on having her way. Then she saw curiosity, a flicker of thoughtfulness, and finally, the glitter of greed.

"Oui," he said at last, his professional demeanor returning. "But of course. Every great perfumer must have his . . . uh, excuse me, *her* creative freedom. I apologize for interrupting your work, mademoiselle."

With that, he gave her a slight bow, turned and left the room. Simone sagged into the chair again. She glanced at the

tools of her trade visible through the clear plastic that enshrouded them, wondering what, if any, secrets they would
eventually reveal. There was no longer any doubt in her mind
that the essence created by Esther's ''craft ancestor'' Mary
Rose was more than evocative, more than sensual, more even
than just a perfume. She knew it had had the same effect on
Antoine Dupuis as it had on her, and she forgave him his
temporary lust. She, too, had fallen victim to the lure of the
scent, and it had only been through her determination to end
the dream encounters with Nick that she had avoided letting
it become a habit.

A habit-forming perfume. Hmmmm. That *would* be prof-
itable, she thought with a wry smile. And she supposed a
fragrance that brought about intensely sexual dreams was fine
too. It might make an unhappy world a little brighter.

But a scent that created instant sexual arousal frightened
her. That, she decided, could definitely be dangerous. There
were a lot of sexually repressed nuts out there. Would the use
of her perfume turn them into perverts? Rapists? Libertines?
On the other hand, maybe some of those repressed sorts could
use a good dose of healthy sexuality, she thought, smiling.
Maybe her *grand parfum* would have the effect of freeing
people, especially the puritanical Americans, from some of
their ridiculous inhibitions concerning their bodies.

Simone looked at her watch, surprised to see that the day
had fled. She stood and stretched away the hours she'd sat
hunched at the highly sophisticated computerized equipment
with software that should have made her search for and re-
construction of the chemical makeup of the perfume easy.
Using this advanced technology, she had been able to discern
the molecular structure of the essence, but she had not been
successful in replicating it. She had come close, but nothing
had smelled exactly like Mary Rose's perfume.

Or performed like it.

This kind of chemical trial and error was a time-consuming
process that could also be expensive, and she sensed Dupuis
was getting impatient with her lack of productivity.

How long would he allow her to continue her experimentation before he demanded she move on to something else? she wondered, gathering up her materials, turning out the lights and stepping into the upstairs hallway. She was becoming frustrated herself. Maybe she ought to give up on it. Why was she so obsessed with re-creating the perfume anyway?

Summer evening sunlight slanted through the windows on the upstairs landing, casting a dusky, caramelized glow down the stairs. She descended to the back hallway, noting that no one else was around. Apparently the others had already left for the day. She'd been given instructions on how to lock up if she worked late. Her footsteps echoed on the hardwood floors as she approached the front entrance, and her keys echoed a loud jingle when she withdrew them from her handbag.

The front parlor was in shadow, the only illumination at the entrance coming from the recessed lighting in the center hallway. Simone was almost to the door when a motion at the corner of her eye caught her attention, and she turned with a gasp as a man stepped from the shadows into the lighted foyer.

A tall man. Dressed in a splendid, opulent, and completely ludicrous red coat that literally dripped with rhinestones.

"Good evening, Mademoiselle Lefèvre," he greeted her, bowing so low his turban almost touched the floor. She stared at him in astonishment. It was the man who had come to her aunt's perfumery in New Orleans. She reached to remember his name, but it wouldn't come.

"Mr. . . . uh . . ."

"Shahmir," he reminded her gently, a benign smile on his lips.

Simone knew she ought to be afraid, but for some reason, she was not. The man did not appear to wish her any harm. He was just some kind of madman, she decided, wishing she could make the perfume for which his master had paid her father long ago and get him out of her life.

"Mr. Shahmir, I find it a little surprising that you are here. How did you know where to find me?"

A twinkle lit his dark brown eyes. "It is not difficult for me to find anything, or anyone," he replied enigmatically.

"Please, do not be afraid. I have come to return something to you." With that, he moved his arms from where they had rested behind his back and handed her a manila folder.

She reached for it, confounded by Shahmir's presence and curious as to what he might be "returning" to her. The tab on the folder was marked "Project X," in a handwriting that seemed vaguely familiar. She opened the file, her fingers trembling slightly. Squinting to read in the dim light, she saw that it was a formula for a perfume.

"What is this? And where did you get it?" she asked.

"It is the missing formula for my master's perfume. Where I got it is not important. I simply request that you finish the perfume," he said, bowing his head slightly, "now that I have provided this formula for you."

Simone's eyes widened as she suddenly comprehended the implications of Shahmir's return of the formula. This file must have been among the rest of the materials that had been stolen from her father that night. Still in the possession of Nick Rutledge? Simone thought of the afternoon Nick had barged into Antoine's office, accusing him of trespassing, and she was certain now that Dupuis's surprise had been genuine, his innocence in any theft beyond doubt.

She glanced at the formula again. The ingredients listed were nothing extraordinary, a blend of primarily Oriental scents that should give the perfume an exotic Far Eastern personality with a slightly leathery green undertone. Patchouli. Sandalwood. Myrhh and its cousin opoponax. Ylang-ylang. Cinnamon. Oak moss.

But at the bottom, in a handwriting different from the rest, in a style she recognized immediately as her father's, she saw inscribed a large question mark and a notation in French that something was missing, an ingredient that Jean René had wished the client to supply him, but which might have to be re-created synthetically. Simone smiled briefly, knowing how her father deplored the use of synthetics in his perfumes. It did not surprise her that he'd requested the client to come up with the missing ingredient. But apparently, the client never had, and her father had died before the perfume could be completed.

"This is as useless to me as it was to my father," she told the tall man. "It appears that there is an ingredient missing, one that must have been critical to the perfume that he was unable to find, or synthesize."

"That is true, mademoiselle," Shahmir replied.

"I have no idea what it could be," she explained. "I cannot make this for you, unless you can give me the missing ingredient, or at least some clue to what it is."

Again, the strange smile. "You are closer than you know," he replied with benevolent patience, "but I have brought you something that will perhaps serve to hasten the process." With that, he took her hand, opened it palm up, and dropped into it seven small seeds that lay like black pearls against her fair skin. "I am not certain," he told her, "but I have reason to believe the plant from which these seeds came might give you what is missing in my master's formula."

Simone looked down, studying the seeds for a long moment. "I . . . I don't know," she said, wishing the man had not tracked her down, wishing he would go away and leave her alone. He was obviously not in his right mind, dressed as he was and obsessed as he appeared to be about "his master's" perfume. How could she gracefully disengage herself from his presence, and from her father's obligation he obviously intended for her to fulfill? "I don't have anywhere to grow these. I don't know what they are, or what they need in the way of cultivation. I—" She lifted her eyes, hoping Shahmir would understand.

But when she looked up, no one was in the room.

Thoroughly frightened and dismayed, Simone turned on all the lights in the front of the building and searched for the man who called himself Shahmir, but he was nowhere to be found. She could not explain his sudden disappearance, but she did not doubt that he had been there only a moment before. The proof of his visit was in her hands.

Seven seeds and the formula for a perfume he'd somehow managed to procure, probably by theft.

It was too much. Surely she must be losing her mind. Maybe it was the frustration of the project she'd been working on. Or the long hours she was spending in the lab. Or the stress of it all combined . . . new surroundings, new job. Running into Nick Rutledge after all this time. The strain must be taking its toll, she decided, but even so . . . where did the seeds and the formula come from, if not from the man who now seemingly had vanished into thin air?

Simone had never paid much attention to magic, but she guessed that Shahmir must be some kind of stage magician who had a very effective disappearing act. Every sensible part of her said to ignore him and his request, that he was mentally unbalanced, maybe even dangerous. She looked again at the seeds. They were small and black, like beads, and she did not recognize them.

What kind of plant produced these seeds? She shrugged and slipped them into her pocket. She reached to turn the lights off when she noticed a glimmer on the floor. She knelt and picked up a red rhinestone, similar to the one that had fallen from Shahmir's coat in New Orleans. The man needed a seamstress, she decided, placing the bit of heavy plastic in her pocket alongside the seeds. His ridiculous bejeweled coat was raining away its glory.

Simone returned to the corporate flat owned by the House of Rutledge that she had been loaned until she could find a place of her own. It was modern and sterile, rather like a hotel room, and its very utility made her long for the cozy room above Tante Camille's shop. Homesickness washed over her, and she plopped onto the bed, a lump forming in her throat.

What on earth was she doing in London? What had possessed her to go chasing after that perfume oil when she had so many opportunities open to her in the States? Was her hatred of Nick so strong that she would make such an impulsive decision just to attempt to seek revenge against him? Revenge had been on her mind for a full ten years, but never as a real possibility, and now that the possibility was upon her, she found to her surprise that it had somehow lost its appeal. In fact, she felt a little sorry for Nick. From what

Dupuis had told her, Nick had given up all holdings in his family's firm to start over with an insignificant little perfumery stuck somewhere out in the suburbs of London.

Leaning back against the pillows, Simone kicked off her shoes. Nicholas Rutledge was such a mystery to her. If she could only understand, find some logical reason for his behavior all those years ago, maybe she could at last put closure on the incident and get on with her life, emotionally speaking. She supposed the time must come when she would get over it. But her father's face loomed behind her closed eyelids, and she knew that time had not yet arrived.

And she knew that revenge was still very much on her agenda. It just seemed anticlimactic that Nick had chosen to give her such an easy victory.

Simone's stomach growled, and she got up and went into the postage stamp–sized kitchen, but there was nothing in the place to eat. The emptiness of the small fridge reflected in microcosm the macro emptiness of her life. One day seemed just like the next in her futile search to identify the nature of the perfume oil. She had to look at the calendar to remind herself what day of the week it was. Thursday night. She had nothing to do. Nowhere to go. No friends to call. Tomorrow was Friday, and Friday night promised a repeat performance.

She bit her lip to keep from crying. *What's going on here?* Simone was not a crybaby. And yet here she was, wallowing in some sort of misguided self-pity. She had everything she wanted.

Didn't she?

An idea occurred to her. Instead of spending another lonely weekend in London, perhaps she would return to Redford. Esther at least was a friendly face, and Simone had enjoyed hearing the old woman's tales. She thought of the seeds, and of the lush garden Esther cultivated around her home. Maybe she would let Simone plant them there. What did she have to lose? Maybe they would produce some kind of exotic plant and she could make Shahmir his perfume. Maybe then he'd quit popping in on her.

The thought made her grin, and she shook her head, still

amazed at the ease with which she accepted the impossibility of his disappearance. There was a logical explanation, she was certain. Maybe when she had his perfume, he would let her in on the secret.

But how would he know if she successfully created the perfume he so adamantly desired?

He just would, she guessed, and decided not to worry about it further. She placed a phone call to Esther and made plans to travel to the country the next evening when she got off work. Then she changed into more comfortable clothes and went to a nearby Indonesian restaurant, where she ate more than she should have, as if trying to fill the inexplicable emptiness within her that hungered for satisfaction.

THIRTEEN

ॐ

Nick was in a dark mood as he headed back to his office from his tennis match. The pro had bested him in two out of four sets because Nick had been unable to keep his focus on the game. Instead, his thoughts kept tumbling back to the mystery of the substance that continued to confound him, and to Simone. To the enormous task that lay ahead of him in starting the new fragrance house. To Simone. Simone.

Simone.

She was driving him mad. Her name had seemed to echo with each contact of the ball against the racquet. He must stop thinking about her.

And yet, he could not. Because now she was part and parcel of his most forbidding competitor, the House of Rutledge. He'd read the announcements of her employment in the newspapers and received numerous calls from curious friends who wanted to know if Nick knew the Frenchwoman who had taken his place. He'd been vague in reply. Yes, he knew of her, but more so her father, he'd told them, a knife twisting all the while in his gut. If Dupuis had intentionally contrived to continue to torment Nick, he couldn't have chosen a more effective device.

Somehow, he must put her out of his mind.

The cellular phone rang in his car, startling him. Nobody ever called on the car phone. He didn't even know why he continued that expense.

"It's Brenda. Your ship has come in," she quipped merrily. "It arrived in Southampton this morning."

The news cheered him, and he smiled. "Thanks. I think I'll drive down to check on it. Don't expect me back in the office today."

Nick turned the Triumph in the direction of the motorway to Southampton, gratified that this particular ship had finally arrived. By showing up at the dock in person, perhaps he would be able to arrange for the crated perfumery equipment to be delivered to the office tomorrow. He wouldn't be able to get the technicians started on setting up the lab until next week, but at least he could supervise the off-loading of the crates. It would make him feel as if some progress were being made.

He was acutely aware that time was of the essence, and he'd already waited nearly a month to start on his first fragrance. He hoped it was worth it. He mustn't disappear from the fragrance scene too long. People forget, or change jobs, and he might lose his valuable contacts. He must move quickly now, before Simone came out with her first perfume, and more importantly, before he ran out of money.

Bringing out a new perfume was an expensive proposition. It wasn't just the fragrance itself that was so costly. It was the bottle, the packaging, and the hype. He was aware that Calvin Klein had spent fifty million dollars to launch Eternity worldwide. Thank goodness he could introduce his fragrance in Britain alone, where the cost wasn't so exorbitant. He had enough money to properly develop and promote one fragrance.

Just enough.

For just one.

One that would be successful enough for him to use its fame and the proceeds to bring out subsequent products.

His first perfume had to be the right perfume.

Reaching home after the long trip to Southampton, Nick took off his shoes and poured a stiff scotch. Then he clicked open his briefcase and took out the familiar amber vial and placed it on the table. In only a matter of days he could undertake the scientific examination of the oil inside, he thought with relief. He fully expected to discover that the mysterious *mahja* was in actuality some familiar plant, the scent of which would become immediately recognizable once he knew its identity. And he also fully expected to feel foolish because his nose had been unable to tell him what it was.

He couldn't believe that his nose had let him down so miserably. Normally, he was able to identify hundreds of scents, singularly or in complex combination. He frowned. Maybe he ought to give his nose one more chance.

Determined to keep this final olfactory experiment exactly that, an experiment, he set up the investigation in as formal a manner as he could construct at home. He covered the small table in the study with a white cloth, placed the bottle in the center, and took a seat in a hard-backed chair. He was determined not to allow himself to slip into the pleasurable sensuality he knew could be engendered by the scent of the perfume.

Two hours later, he still had no answer, and he was exhausted from consciously fighting the effects of the perfume, resisting the force of its provocative titillation. Even so, he'd had a hard-on for most of those two hours. He stood and stretched, then headed for a cold shower before his unsatisfied sexual appetite became too painful.

Nick read long into the night, afraid to drop off to sleep, afraid of the dreams and the lover he expected awaited him there after having exposed himself to the perfume. But nature at last took command, and he drifted into a deep sleep.

It was not a sleep, however, that remained undisturbed.

He heard the sound of water falling, trickling over rocks and past cool vegetation to collect in a pool somewhere nearby. He heard a woman's voice, singing in lilting tones, and he was drawn to the music.

Around him, a familiar indigo mist swirled in a light breeze, tinting everything with its ethereal blue. The glade where he stood was tropical in nature and should have been washed in a hundred shades of green. Instead, it reflected the almost luminescent colors of the mist. The large flat leaves of some of the plants were blue-black rather than jungle-green. Smaller leaves were tinged with purple, or ruby, or indigo, while underfoot, tiny flowerlets drooped their bell-shaped heads gracefully, nodding in an almost silvery light. It was an enchanted forest, a magical glen, a secret, mystical garden.

The indigo mist was familiar to Nick, but this place was a fantasy he had never before visited. He felt himself relax into the moment, allowing the sensuality of his surroundings to suffuse his entire body. Breathing deeply, he inhaled a sweet essence, the fragrance of flowers mixed with the fresh green of the woodlands, and he shivered in delicious anticipation of the pleasure it promised.

The song of the woodland sprite who beckoned him was sweet as well, drawing him in a wordless melody. He parted the foliage and stood silently, watching the woman who stood hip-deep in a pool, her back turned to him. Her hair was dark as the midnight-blue shadows that hovered in the forest beyond, and it was piled high upon her head, exposing a slender neck and gently sloping feminine shoulders. She played with the water, dipping her hands into its shimmering depths and raising them to watch the drops dance as they fell from her fingertips to splash into the placid pool.

With her arms upraised, he could see the inviting outline of her breasts, the curve of her waist, the silhouette of her hips just above the water's surface. She was as mystical and dreamy as the rest of his surroundings, chimerical and corporeal at the same time. A twig snapped as he took another step toward her, and she turned to him, smiling, as if she had expected him all along.

It was Simone.

And it was not Simone.

It was someone who looked exactly like the French beauty who seemed to have ensnared his heart, his mind, and his soul. But this Simone was guileless. There was no hatred in her eyes. No artifice. No revenge. Her expression instead evinced a willingness to transcend all that had gone before, a wish to forgive, an invitation to start anew—all those impossibilities he'd long ago despaired would ever happen. She stretched her arms toward him, a goddess offering her body in a gesture of intimate reconciliation. Nick thought he would explode with joy.

She began to sway sensually in the water, and he watched transfixed as the ripples caressed the flat of her belly just above the triangle of dark curls that were barely visible below the waterline. She released her hair from its confinement, and he saw it spill down and across her shoulders in sensual abandon, coming to rest in gentle curls upon her breasts. Not daring to breathe lest the illusion fade, Nick clenched his fists to contain the raw energy coursing through him. Could she really forgive him? Could there be a chance . . . ?

He did not hesitate to accept her invitation, as astounding as it was.

There was no need for him to remove his clothing to join her. He wore nothing and stood before her unashamed in his nakedness, like a primal warrior. His desire for her pressed hard, and he paused for a moment before going to her, as if to allow her to gaze upon him and understand the force of his passion. Her regard indeed dropped from his face, traveling slowly down his form, understanding his message. He saw her tongue edge between her parted lips.

Advancing to the rim of the pool, his eyes locked on hers, and he saw her move toward him, emerging from the water until she stood only ankle-deep in front of him. She took his hands in hers, and he felt himself being drawn toward her with surprising strength.

When their bodies met, a force sizzled between them, like water dropped onto a hot skillet. Her body heat appeared unquenched by the cool waters where she had just bathed, its glow turning the light sheen of dampness on her skin to steam. She tilted her head, closed her eyes, and leaned into him, her full breasts crushing against his chest. Her arms slid to the small of his back, and she pressed him even more closely to her.

This garden must surely be paradise. Nick could think of

*no other explanation. He must have died somewhere along
the way, and somehow the gods had forgiven him for all his
errors and transgressions and sent Simone to tell him so. He
was pervaded by a strange and powerful sense of peace and
love. If this is what it is like to be dead, he thought briefly,
he never wanted to live again.*

*His heart thundered in the misty night as he and the woman
he loved more than life itself were reunited in a place that
removed them from all time and space, a place where the past
didn't matter, and the future would never arrive. They were
one, in the moment, in the now of the bliss that showered
them in fulfillment.*

Nick awoke abruptly. His eyes flew open and his heart sank
as reality returned. He lay very still upon his bed, closing his
eyes again, trying with all his might to regain entrance to that
magical garden in his dreams. But the gates to the subconscious were closed, shut tight against him, and he felt the
moisture of unshed tears behind his lids.

God, what he wouldn't give for one moment of the grace
he'd just dreamt of. One moment in Simone's arms, one moment of her love and forgiveness. For that, he would sell his
soul.

Groaning, he rolled out of bed, his feet landing heavily on
the cool floor. The clock on his nightstand said five thirty-
five. Too early to get up, too late to go back to bed. He
shuffled to the bathroom, then made his way downstairs to
the kitchen, where he foraged for a prebreakfast snack. His
mind was numb, his body recovering as best it could from
the effects of the erotic dream. It had been a mistake to experiment further with the perfume. He'd known that. Just as
he had known, on some level, that he *wanted* to enter another
dream, *wanted* to meet Simone in that eerie world of shades
and mists.

He bit into an apple. The truth was, and he forced himself
to face it here in the dim light of the breaking day, the truth
was, he wanted exactly what he had just dreamt of . . . that

incredible sense of peace and happiness that had been his so fleetingly in the arms of his dream lover. That sense of being forgiven, of being loved, of having another chance with her.

He threw the apple across the room. Damn.

Angrily, he returned to his bedroom and switched on the television to catch the early-morning news, determined to cling firmly to the reality of his world—Simone would never love him. There was no second chance. He didn't deserve to be forgiven, and he certainly did not deserve to know such incredible peace of mind, or to feel such joy in his heart. His dreams of her castigated him with such precision no human jury could match its vengeance.

He stared at the images on the screen, but he saw only the garden he had just visited in his dreams. Simone in the garden.

Simone in the garden.

Wait. Nick froze. Simone in the garden. Clyde Covington had told him she'd been snooping in the garden behind the carriage house when he'd apprehended her. What was Simone doing in that garden? Mary Rose's garden?

A thought he'd dismissed earlier suddenly slammed through him again, and this time, he considered it a possibility. Maybe Simone *did* know about the perfume. Why else would she have been there, in that particular garden? At midnight, for God's sake? Nick had no idea when or how she'd learned of it, but he knew in every cell of his body that she was after the same perfume oil that he sought to identify and use in his debut perfume.

Even if he were to work fast and furiously once he broke the secret of the *mahja,* with the resources of the House of Rutledge behind her, Simone's version of the perfume, heavily marketed as it would be, would bury him. Nick leaned back into the pillows, nauseous. What irony, if she beat him to it and created the perfume that he'd counted on to be his salvation.

But it would be Antoine Dupuis who would end up the big winner in this game. The nausea turned to a knot that wound tightly in his gut.

He'd be damned.

It was too early to accomplish anything, but Nick decided to be at the office, ready to supervise the off-loading of the crates. With luck the shipping line would have scheduled a morning delivery. While he waited, he could line up for next week the team of technicians who would install the rather antiquated but still functional electronic equipment.

Once that was accomplished, Nick decided he would spend the weekend at Brierley Hall. It might be his last chance to go to the country for a long while, and he was anxious suddenly to explore the garden behind the carriage house, once cultivated by one Mary Rose Hatcher, witch.

Simone thought the day would never end, and she was like a child out of school when at last five o'clock came. She hurried to her flat to pick up the suitcase she'd already packed and headed for the train station.

The evening train was filled with commuters. It passed from London's heart, stopping frequently as it made its way into the sprawl of the suburbs. At last it reached the open countryside, where it picked up speed, racing past villages seemingly older than time. Summer was ripe on the hillsides, the yellow of rapeseed and gorse glinting in the late sunshine, contrasting with greens deeper than any she'd ever seen. England was beautiful in its own way, she decided, although in her heart she longed for the Mediterranean slopes surrounding Grasse.

"Ah, it's good t' see you again." Esther greeted her with a warm embrace, and Simone's spirits lifted discernibly. She settled into "her room," as Esther called it, and joined her hostess for a light supper of sandwiches and tea in the small dining room, over which she told the older woman all about her new job.

"But are y' happy up there in London?" Esther wanted to know.

Simone paused. Was she happy? Not really. She was frustrated, lonely, and more than a little insecure in her job. But it was a start, she assured the woman, and she was certain she would get used to it.

"Have y' been able t' learn how t' make the perfume I gave you?" Esther said, her blue eyes glittering in expectation.

Simone frowned and stared into her teacup. "Actually, no," she replied regretfully. "I have been working on it for over three weeks now, and it just eludes me. Even the computer is scratching its head."

"I see." Esther's smile faded. "I thought that might be the reason for your visit."

Simone reached out and touched the papery skin on the back of Esther's aging hand. "I came because I was lonely, and I wanted to see you again." When she saw the other woman brighten, she added, "And I have some seeds I want to know if we could plant in your garden."

"Seeds?"

Simone told Esther about Shahmir, leaving out the part about his ability to disappear. "He gave me these," she said, digging into her handbag and showing her the seeds. "He said they might produce a plant that would give me the missing ingredient to a perfume my father promised to make for his 'master.'" She laughed. "Who in this day and time has a 'master'?"

"We all have our masters," Esther replied more soberly than Simone would have expected. "Some are in human form, but more often, they are our obsessions."

Simone considered that a moment. "Yes, I suppose so," she said, wondering if her obsession with taking revenge on Nick had become her master. She did not like the idea.

Late the next morning, after a more restful sleep than she'd had since arriving in England, Simone spent a pleasant hour walking the extensive garden Esther had cultivated for many years in the gently sloping terrain surrounding her house. The older woman pointed out the many varieties of herbs and medicinal plants that were interspersed with those that produced a riot of colorful flowers. Simone was enchanted and hoped aloud that someday she would have such a magnificent garden.

"Someday," Esther said, plucking a weed. "Sometimes,

someday never gets here, you know, unless you make it happen.''

Simone remained silent. What did *someday* hold for her? What *did* she want to happen in her life? She'd thought it was to be a master perfumer, to create her own *grands parfums,* like her father before her. But that dream had come true, only to prove to be a rather empty ambition. She had found no joy in the work, no *raison d'être,* other than revenge. Of course, she'd only given it a few weeks, and those weeks had proven highly frustrating. She shared this with Esther.

''It's a short time,'' her friend agreed. ''Maybe you ought t' work on something else for a while. You mustn't let our little perfume become your master.'' She winked.

But Esther did not know the real reason Simone was obsessed with uncovering the secret of ''their'' perfume, or that she would not, could not, rest until she was successful.

Esther took up a shovel and helped Simone plant the seven seeds, each in a different part of the garden, so that some would receive full sunlight, others partial shade. ''I'll keep an eye on them for you,'' she assured Simone. ''I've never seen seeds like these, so I don't know whether they will grow quickly or slowly, or at all.''

''Thank you for planting them,'' Simone replied with a smile. ''I don't know if they will give me what that Shahmir person thinks I need for the perfume, but if they do, I will be glad to honor my father's promise to the man, especially if it will get him off my back,'' she added with a laugh, feeling more lighthearted than she had in weeks. She was glad she'd come to see Esther.

Then her companion startled her. ''Oh, I forgot,'' the old woman said, touching her hands to her cheeks. ''We must cast our spell.''

''Spell? What spell?'' Simone vaguely recalled Esther mentioning something about a spell at their first meeting.

Esther laughed. ''I have told you I am a sister in the craft,'' she said. ''I never plant anything, a seed, an idea, a plan, unless I send it off with an appropriate spell.''

The ''craft.'' Witchcraft. Simone knew there were those

who practiced black magic in New Orleans, and she shivered. But she took in the loveliness of the garden around her, smelled the bouquet of all the flowers that bloomed here, and decided that she would humor the old woman. She could sense nothing dangerous in her "craft," and if her belief in such susperstitious nonsense made her happy, Simone was willing to indulge her.

Esther led her back to the house, where they entered the small but charming kitchen that overlooked the back gardens. Herbs of all kinds dangled in bundles upside down from the ceiling, scenting the room in a bouquet of aromas as they dried. Copper cooking vessels hung on hooks along the walls, decorating the space with their warm glow. A tea kettle squatted on the stovetop, and dishes gleamed from behind immaculate glass panes in the cabinet doors. Simone was enchanted. This kitchen was filled with life, and warmth, a pleasurable sense of well-being, the antithesis in every way of the cold, lonely kitchenette she'd left behind in her flat in London. This cozy place reminded her of Maman and the aromas of her childhood that had filled the air in their home in Grasse.

Suddenly, she missed her mother, whose grief had cut short her life after they'd arrived in the United States. She longed for France and her childhood home again. The home and the security that had so suddenly vanished from beneath her when . . .

Not now! She forced her attention to Esther's activities. The old woman was digging through a jumble of small items in a drawer and at last came up with a stub of a pencil and a small pad of paper.

"I knew it had to be in there," she muttered, handing the items to Simone. "Now, write on this paper your dearest wish."

Simone stared blankly at Esther. Her dearest wish? Several wishes came to mind. But which one was dearest? To create her *grands parfums*? To revenge her father's death? To destroy Nicholas Rutledge? It occurred to her suddenly that one wish could accomplish all. She wrote, "I wish to know the secret of Mary Rose's perfume."

She had no idea what this spell-making was all about, and she had to squelch a giggle at the thought that she was even doing this. But she handed the paper and pencil back to Esther, who did not look at what Simone had written, but rather took the paper to the table upon which sat a round black iron pot filled with sand. It looked to Simone like a miniature witch's cauldron, a small version of the kind she'd seen on the Halloween cards in the United States, where a witch in a pointed hat hunched over a steaming vessel with a black cat arching at her ankles.

As Simone watched, Esther took out a long wooden match, and without any explanation, set the paper on fire. She placed the flaming note on a small metal tray that nestled on the sand inside the pot, then began to chant in repetition:

> "Smoke and fire, smoke and fire,
> Bring to us our heart's desire,
> Ash and seed, ash and seed,
> Bestow upon us all we need."

In an instant, the paper had turned to ashes, which Esther then briskly scooped up into her hand. "Come," she said, indicating for Simone to follow her back outside. She went to where they had planted one of the seeds. "Take the shovel and turn back the soil."

"But . . ."

"See if you can find the seed," she instructed. "We're going to give this one a little extra nourishment. Should have done this first," she added under her breath. "Must be getting old."

As if by magic, the seed was unearthed with the shovel full of dirt and rested on the soil in plain sight. "Good, good." Esther chuckled. Then she emptied the ashes into the hole. "Now, just slip that back into place. When this seed blooms, your fondest wish will come true."

Behind the woman's back Simone could not resist a roll of the eyes. Esther was such a dear, but her "spells" were a bit too much.

Back in the house, Simone went upstairs to wash up, then rejoined Esther for lunch. They sat at the table in the snug kitchen and watched as a gentle rain began to fall.

"It's a good omen," Esther murmured. "The seeds will get just what they need." She turned a beaming face to Simone. "And so will you."

"Let's hope," was the most enthusiasm Simone could summon in reply.

A silence fell between them, broken only by the clink of their spoons in the teacups, but at last Esther cleared her throat and spoke. "There's something I'd like t' ask you," she said, and Simone looked up, surprised at the change in her tone of voice.

"Of course."

"Did you . . . have you mentioned . . . our perfume to Nicholas Rutledge?"

Simone's face grew instantly hot. "Of course not! I've only run into him twice, quite by accident . . ." She remembered his intrusion at Dupuis's office, and amended, "Well, actually, three times. But he and I are not exactly friends. I would never mention it to the likes of him. Why do you ask?"

"I was just curious," Esther returned, a questioning look on her face. "Some of my friends here in the village were hired this morning to do some landscape cleanup work on the grounds at Brierley Hall."

"I don't understand. What does that have to do with the perfume?"

"Mr. Rutledge has hired them to clean up the garden behind the cottage. Mary Rose's garden," she added with emphasis. "I know he's in the perfume business, and I just wondered if he might be looking for information about our little perfume."

"How could he know about 'our' perfume?" Simone asked, alarmed.

"I don't know that he does. It's just a feeling I have."

The teaspoons clinked again against the china as each woman became lost in thought. Simone's thoughts traveled swiftly back over her brief encounters with Nick. Had she inadvertently said something to him about the perfume? She thought not. If he knew about it, he had come up with it from some other source. "If that essence was originally made there in Mary Rose's house, and since I discovered it in a set of antique bottles from there, I suppose it's possible that Nick found some of it when he sold the antiques from the carriage house," she said, sorting her thoughts out loud. An uncomfortable suspicion began to form in her mind.

"That is possible," Esther agreed with a sigh. "I am sure Mr. Rutledge is above reproach," she added, "but I am in earnest when I say that the potion must not fall into the wrong hands."

Simone thought about her own intent for the use of the perfume oil once she found out what it was, and shifted uncomfortably in her seat. "What . . . what *would* happen if someone, uh, like Mr. Rutledge, for instance, discovered the perfume and . . . reproduced it for sale to the public?"

Esther looked at her gravely and shook her head from side to side. "It was never meant for such purposes," she said dolefully. "I don't want to even imagine what might happen."

FOURTEEN

It had taken until almost noon for his hastily recruited land-scape crew to remove enough of the thick nest of vinelike weeds from the garden behind the carriage house for Nick to get an idea of its shape and form. It was less than a quarter of a hectare in size, enclosed behind a crumbling stone wall. But apparently at one time it had been a gardener's pride. Meticulously outlined in white stones, the main bed was in the form of a circle. It was divided into wedge-shaped beds by the same kind of stones, and a small circular bed was outlined in the center. The rocks forming this smaller circle were charred, as if it had been used as a fireplace. Nick frowned, finding the idea of a fire in a flower bed curious.

Along the south and east walls he came across another puzzle. Stubs of small trunks stood like dwarf soldiers in a row. A miniature orchard of some kind? He wished his men hadn't been so hasty in chopping them down. But then, he'd given orders for them to clear everything to the ground.

The west wall backed up to the house, with a small portal giving access to the residence. Nick had had that door sealed, however, when he renovated the property to be a rental cottage. He had not considered renovating these gardens as well. Maintenance was too costly, so he had simply decided to leave them in their wild state, guessing that no guest would dare venture among the prickly vines.

Which was precisely what his first tenant had done. He set

his jaw at the thought of Simone prowling these grounds. What had possessed her to do such a thing, on a stormy night he recalled . . . unless she was looking for something she wanted very badly?

Something like . . . the secret to a very unusual perfume? He scratched his head. How on earth could she know about Mary Rose's perfume oil? What would make her think that information about it might be hidden here in this garden?

Early-afternoon sun finally pierced the clouds that had brought sporadic showers and illuminated the north of the garden. Nick caught a glint of sunlight reflecting on a shard of glass. Frowning, he made his way through the piles of beheaded weeds that rested in prickly disarray ready to be hauled away, until he came to the place where he'd spied the glass. Upon the ground at his feet, the remains of a shattered windowpane lay half-buried in the rich earth, along with the outline of a wooden frame, long since weathered and worm-eaten into a spongy pulp. Pulling away the remaining vines that clung to the wall, Nick saw that it had apparently been used to support a crude structure of some sort. A primitive greenhouse? he wondered, glancing again at the glass at his feet. He remembered some mention of a greenhouse in one of Mary Rose's letters.

His gloved fingers brushed at the wall, which sent a crumble of pebbly rock to the ground. Odd, he thought. This wall had stood for centuries. It shouldn't crumble so easily beneath his touch. He brushed it again several times, and with each swipe of his hand, more of what appeared to be loose mortar showered away from the wall. It tore away in roughly a square pattern, as if at one time it had been a patch of some sort.

A patch. Or a seal . . .

Nick's curiosity clicked into high gear. He borrowed a heavy ax from one of the workers and chopped at the mortar, which fell away freely. Carefully, he began removing the rocks it had held in place and to his amazement discovered they had indeed sealed over a niche in the wall. He tore away the rest of the rocks, exposing a dark, dank compartment about three feet wide and half that deep. At the back of the hole in the wall sat a square object.

Nick laid the ax aside and reached for whatever had been sealed inside this odd hiding place, obviously for quite a long time. His fingers encountered a small, heavy box. Bringing it into the light of day, he saw it was made of metal, like a rustic safe of sorts, except that it bore no lock.

The latch squeaked and the hinges rained rust when he raised the lid. Inside lay a single item . . . a moldering book, or what might at one time have been a book. The cover was rotting away, and the pages were yellow and soft with age. But clearly discernible on the first page, in a handwriting he recognized, were the words: "The Spells and Enchantments of Mary Rose Hatcher."

Simone was uneasy with the plan, but Esther had been adamant. Even though Simone had told her about Nick's betrayal years ago and about the enmity between them, Esther insisted that Simone must pay a call on him to find out if he knew about the magical perfume oil, and if he intended to mass-produce it as a commercial fragrance. "He must understand th' danger of putting that essence into th' hands of th' whole world," the old woman had warned.

Simone, who had not told Esther that creating a marketable perfume was her intent for the fragrant oil as well, believed the "white witch" was being overly dramatic in her insistence that the potion was dangerous.

However, Simone herself wanted to know if indeed her archenemy had somehow obtained the mysterious substance. If so, and if his intent was the same as hers, it would make her first attempt at creating a *grand parfum* that much more difficult, for time would no longer be on her side. If Nick had discovered the sensuous effects of the scented oil, and if he had already learned its secret ingredient, she had no doubt he was working diligently toward launching his first fragrance made from it. With the connections and friends in manufacturing and retailing she'd learned he had, she believed he just might pull it off.

Simone needed to know where she stood in the race with Nick, if indeed there was such a race, and so she'd agreed to pay a visit to Nick at Brierley Hall.

The sun cast shades of late afternoon through the trees, although daylight would linger far into the night on this mid-summer's eve. Simone was not accustomed to such long hours of daylight, for at home, even the longest day of the year began to darken by nine o'clock. Carefully, she steered Esther's borrowed car along the left-hand side of the road. It was her first driving experience in England, and she was ter-rified she'd forget and cross into the wrong lane.

In spite of her attempts to concentrate on arriving in one piece, Simone's thoughts wandered back to Esther's admo-nition. Why was she so insistent that the lushly fragrant oil was dangerous? She'd offered no proof, only her homespun theory that somehow it had caused the deaths of Mary Rose Hatcher and her lover, John Rutledge. What was Nick's take on that whole episode? she wondered.

Nick.

Her face grew warm at the thought of Nick's visitations to her in dreams, and the unabashed pleasure she'd taken in his arms disturbed her greatly. Only last night she'd once again experienced an incredible dream in which she and Nick had made passionate love beneath a waterfall in an exotic jungle-like forest. In this dream, she was no longer afraid of him, no longer his prisoner. In fact, she had invited him to enter the pool, and her body, and had relished the delicious comfort of being in the arms of a man who truly loved her.

Truly loved her?

Who was she kidding? Nicholas Rutledge did not truly love her. Never had. Never would.

So why was she obsessing about him? That was the danger of the perfume, she thought darkly. It created dreams that made you believe in the impossible. Become delusional. Per-haps sometime, some way, there would be a man who loved her like that. But she was certain his name would not be Nicholas Rutledge.

Lost in thought, Simone drove past the front entrance to

Brierley Hall and had to turn around and retrace her course. But when she again approached the gray stone pillars that marked the entrance to the estate, she lost her nerve. This was insane. She didn't want to talk to Nick Rutledge. She loathed the man. And except in dreams, where it seemed impossible to avoid him, she had no desire whatsoever to encounter him again. Ever.

She passed the gates by again. But her car slowed when she reached the small lane she recognized as leading to the cottage. She looked at her watch. Seven forty-five. Probably late enough for the landscape crew to have gone home. And she hoped, their employer as well. With this much daylight left, she could see what work had taken place and perhaps decide if Nick had unearthed anything, if he was actually searching for something like Mary Rose's Book of Shadows. Of course, she would have no way of knowing what he might have found, but a hole in the ground would be telling.

There was no car in the drive, no horse tethered to a tree, and Simone guessed she had the place to herself. Remembering Clyde Covington and the dog Heathcliff, however, she parked Esther's car facing the lane, just in case she might need to get out of there in a hurry. Her pulse pounded as she stepped onto the gravel, and she wished she'd worn more sensible shoes instead of the trendy but slippery sandals that were on her feet.

She made her way down the stepping stones she'd followed in the moonlight the night she'd been apprehended here for trespassing, and wondered if Nick's too-efficient watchman was lurking nearby. By the light of day, or rather early evening, the place looked totally different, innocuous, nonthreatening. Just the typical picture-postcard charm of a restored sixteenth-century dwelling. Briefly, she regretted that she had been unable to stay here for a few days.

Behind the house, the brambles and briars had been cleared away, some ripped from the earth by their roots, others sawed at their gnarly bases. It looked like a miniature layout of a new subdivision raked of growth by an aggressive developer. Still, sometimes to make room for new beauty one had to destroy old chaos, and in her mind's eye she could see planted here a garden as lush and lovely as Esther's.

She came to the gate and saw that the scene behind the garden wall was much the same, only here, many of the brambles remained in a huge pile in one corner, ready to be carried off or burned, she supposed. Slipping past the intricately designed, rusting iron barrier, she entered the sheltered area. The circular outline of the central garden was now naked and clearly visible. Simone walked slowly to the outer edge and knelt and felt the soil. It was rich, fertile, but had been uncultivated for a long, long time.

What plant had Mary Rose grown here that had provided the oil she'd used in her magical essence?

Obviously, nothing Simone was familiar with. Could John Rutledge have sent her something from India, some exotic plant from the Far East? Or perhaps seeds or bulbs?

Simone allowed her gaze to scan the enclosure, wondering if anything sent from India could survive an English winter. Only if it were properly protected from storm and cold, she was certain, but she didn't know if a place like this would have had a greenhouse or solarium in those days. She doubted it.

Suddenly, her eye came to rest on a fresh scar on the face of the north wall. What appeared to be recently scraped white mortar gleamed like a beacon even in the last of the sunlight, framing the dark hole it surrounded.

With a lurch of her stomach, Simone knew that if Mary Rose Hatcher had hidden her Book of Shadows in that niche, Nick had beat her to it.

Damn him!

She made her way across the soft earth of the garden to the hole in the wall and hesitated before feeling inside with her bare hand. Simone had never trusted dark places not to be inhabited by spiders and other creepy things. She stood on tiptoe and strained her eyes to see what, if anything, the cache might hold, but as she'd expected, it was empty.

"You seem unreasonably fond of this place." A deep voice filled with undisguised sarcasm sounded behind her, and Si-

mone nearly collapsed in alarm. She turned, expecting to see
the watchman leering at her, ready at any moment to unleash
his ugly dog. But the source of the comment was far worse.
Leaning against the garden gate, looking sexier than hell in
tight jeans and an open-necked shirt, Nick Rutledge studied
her speculatively. "Want to explain what keeps bringing you
to my property?"

At that moment, Simone hated him more than ever. His
face was like stone, with just a hint of a sneer on his lips. His
arms were crossed, his intense stare calculated to intimidate.
His stance was arrogantly casual, with one knee bent, his foot
resting on a lower bar of the iron gate.

She hated him, and yet, something inside of her stirred
instantly, a fire she'd fought to extinguish over the long years
since their days together in France. To her dismay, she felt a
familiar sexual hunger, an appetite she'd been able to satisfy
only in her dreams.

She desired him still. How could it be?

Damn him again.

Simone hated herself as well in that instant. Hated her
weakness. Her vulnerability. She'd found him attractive when
she'd seen him earlier, but her feelings had not been this blatant, this naked, not even when he'd kissed her that night at
Brierley Hall. What had happened since then that caused her
defenses to crumble so suddenly and easily at the mere sight
of him?

A clip from a remembered dream, like a film short in a
movie, rolled into her consciousness, filling her with impres-
sions of a sweet sensual union beneath the gentle flow of a
tropical waterfall. A sense of being loved totally. Of being
able to trust her lover implicitly.

It was the perfume, she thought, panic-stricken. Or at least
the aftereffects of the perfume, playing tricks with her mind
and her body. Now, instead of its control over her impulses
being limited to her dreams, its powers appeared to have taken
over in the real world. She cringed against the wall, her skin
suddenly ice-cold. "No," she hissed in a low groan. "No!"

*   *   *

The dark-haired woman with her back to the garden wall stared at him like a cornered animal, a mixture of fear and hatred in her dark eyes. Nick's gut wrenched. In spite of her expression, she was exquisitely beautiful, dressed all in white, like some mystical enchantress on this midsummer's eve. She was a modern-day sorceress, however, clad in a stylish white sleeveless linen blouse tucked at her slender waist into white slacks that hugged her body possessively. Her feet tantalized him from within high-heeled sandals. Against his reason, Nick's body responded to her appeal with alarming fervor.

The lengthening rays of the sun pierced the leafy protection of the ancient trees overhead and shone upon her, as if spotlighting her beauty with pretwilight shades of misty blue and silver. The image was reminiscent of the dreams he'd experienced recently. Dreams in which he had been with this woman, known her intimately, loved her fully. He ached for her, longed for this to be the dreamworld where time—past, present, and future—did not exist.

But this was not the dream world, no matter how he wished it so. And Simone was here, trespassing again, and this time, Nick knew why.

Somehow, incredibly, Simone knew about the essence he'd discovered in the old trunk, the potion which he'd read more about this very afternoon in Mary Rose's strange and enchanting journal. It was the only rational explanation for her repeat appearance here in this garden. She must have somehow come into possession of the fragrance. Had she found some remnant of it in her brief stay at the cottage?

No. It was why she had come here in the first place.

Intrigued, and knowing how much of his own future might be riding in the balance, he decided to press her for an answer.

"Relax," he said, forcing a calm he did not feel. He wanted to assure her, get her to talk to him in a rational manner. "I'm not going to hurt you."

She took a step away from the wall, defiance replacing her irrational fear. "I'm not afraid of you. You are despicable, but I doubt that you would murder me right here and now."

Her words stung, their impact eroding his careful emotional

control. He laughed bitterly. "Are you quite sure?" he baited her, irritated that she would not be at least civil toward him. "I could do away with you, bury you here in the garden, and set fire to those brambles over your grave. No one would ever suspect . . ."

Nick was surprised to see her eyes widen at his diabolical joke. She believed him! "But then, I'm only despicable, as you say, not a murderer." God, but he was making a bloody botch of this. He needed her cooperation, not her antipathy, if he were going to learn anything from her.

He moved away from the gate, going to the far side of the circular garden, enabling Simone to escape if she wished. "You may leave at any time, Simone. But I do believe you owe me an explanation. What is going on? What's brought you here again?" He knew he was pushing it, doubted if she would bother responding.

To his surprise, she did not run. He saw her shoulders relax slightly beneath the open-throated blouse. She looked down at her hands, as if examining her manicure.

"I suppose I do owe you that," she said after a long moment, her tone unreadable. Then she raised her head suddenly, and her eyes were cold and hard. "But I will not give it to you until you explain to *me* why—"

Nick's heart sank and his stomach knotted. "Stop it, Simone," he interrupted her roughly, striding still farther around the circle until its full diameter lay between them. He shoved his hands deep into his pockets. "What happened in France is history. And it's best left buried in the past."

"Why? Do you think I am still a foolish, naïve child, that you can wave me off so easily? Don't you think *you* owe *me* an explanation? An apology?"

Nick turned to face her fury. She had every right to an explanation. An apology. If he could only come up with something that made sense. For a decade he had avoided facing the truth of what he had done, tried to justify his actions in terms of having had no choice.

But he knew better. Everyone has choices. He could have chosen to fail in his mission to obtain those formulas from

Jean René. He could have opted to try to convince Dupuis of another strategy for the recovery of the House of Rutledge. He could have chosen . . . Simone.

Instead, he'd allowed his obsession with overcoming the shame of his father's suicide, with reclaiming his family's heritage and good name, to distort his thoughts and drive his actions. It was not something of which he was proud, but at the time, it had seemed indeed as if that had been his only choice.

He wanted desperately to make it all go away. Wanted time to spiral backward to when they'd been friends. Lovers. He wanted worse than life itself to take her in his arms and say he was sorry.

But too many years, too many lies, prevented that from ever happening.

His heart bled as he stared into Simone's face, which was nearly as white as her clothing. Only her full lips retained a hint of color. Her lips, and her dark, demanding eyes.

Yes, he owed her.

But it was a debt he could never repay. In his dreams, perhaps. But only there.

His dreams reminded him of the perfume, of all that he must protect if he were to survive and emerge successful once again. "What," he made himself ask again, "are you *doing* here?"

FIFTEEN

Simone was shaking from the unleashed emotions that raged through her. She hadn't meant to confront Nick about all of this. It did not serve her purposes. She should have been subtle, used his own device of seduction rather than raving at him like a madwoman. But his arrogance, the sneer that had greeted her when she turned to face him, summoned in an instant all the anger against him that she had stored inside. If she'd had a gun at that moment, perhaps *she* would have become a murderer.

"You are unbelievable," she said, finding her voice again at last and shaking her head at his refusal to give her even so much as a verbal apology. The man was without remorse. He was hard. Selfish. Devious. Criminal. And if she wanted answers concerning the perfume, she'd better gain control over her emotions and start playing hardball. Perhaps her best offense was the defense he was seeking.

"Very well," she said, straightening, preparing her strike. "It's no secret I've taken your place at the House of Rutledge." She thrust her verbal dagger and was gratified to see a flicker of chagrin flash in his steel-blue eyes. "But to perform at my best, I must know all about the materials available to me. As you well know, I have every fragrant substance known to man beneath my fingertips in the perfumery. But I am not like other perfumers." She brushed her long hair away from the heated perspiration on her neck, wondering if her improvised "explanation" would end up making sense to Nick. Wondering why she cared. Why she didn't just get the hell out of here.

But she seemed compelled to continue. She raised her chin slightly, looked directly into his eyes. "I am my father's daughter," she told him, taking a step toward him across the perimeter of garden, daring him to look away, wanting him to know she was out to avenge his wrong against her family. "I do not wish to use synthetics unless there are no other options. Truly great perfumers go to the source, the flowers and plants and animals that give us of their essences. Being new to English soil, I came to this area because I've heard the English gardens here are second to none. I came to smell the earth and the flowers and the plants so that I will understand their nature, for I plan to use them to create my own *grands parfums*, just as my father once did."

As the last words escaped her, she wanted to bite off her tongue. She'd agreed with Dupuis not to let anyone know about the new direction in which she planned to take the House of Rutledge until they had worked out a corporate marketing strategy and cut their deals with the manufacturers of the containers. Now, in a fit of pride and passion, she had just spilled their plans to their prime competitor.

The expression on his face told her that he understood clearly the implications of what she'd just revealed. But his cold, hard reply ignored it, demanding instead that she answer his original question . . . why was she here? "There are no flowers in this garden, Simone."

"I did not come here to see flowers," she said, groping for an alternative explanation. Her eye caught the gleam of the last of the sunlight on the circular rock formation outlining the garden and the wedge-shaped beds it contained. "I came to see the mandala, the circular layout of the garden."

Nick's expression shifted from angry to surprised, and his gaze dropped reflexively toward the garden. When he looked back at her, grim suspicion was etched into his features.

"How did you know this . . . mandala, as you call it, was here?"

"Esther Brown told me, the woman I stayed with in Redford after I left here. By the way, I can assure you," she added
with dry cynicism, "that my reservation of your rental cottage
was made in total ignorance that you owned it."

Nick said nothing, regarding her for a long moment. Then
he stepped toward the circle and kicked at one of the rocks
absently. "Why did you come back here, then, after you knew
I owned the place?"

Same question, different format. The man was nothing if
not tenacious. But his quiet tone of voice caught her off guard.
It was devoid of its earlier cold, caustic suspicion, revealing
just a hint of self-deprecation. *Why would you want to be
anywhere near me?* it seemed to ask. It was the closest she'd
seen him come to behaving as if he gave a damn about anyone
but himself, and it stirred an odd sympathy within her.

But she blinked and clenched her fists. She could have no
sympathy for Nicholas Rutledge. Reaching into her imagination, she continued her made-up tale. "I . . . I wanted to see
it by moonlight. That's why I was here when your guard
caught me. I study gardens, you see," she went on, liking the
direction her story was taking. It was the truth. She did study
gardens. "Gardens should be enjoyable by night as well as
by the light of day, and I was intrigued when Esther told me
about the luminescence of the rocks that form this mandala."

"Odd that you should refer to it as a mandala."

The suspicion was back in his voice, and Simone wondered
why he would concern himself with semantics. "Why so?"

"A mandala infers that it is some sort of ritualistic symbol."

Simone considered that for a moment. Esther had described
the garden as a mandala, not a circle. She'd also said she
believed it had been used at one time by her "craft ancestors"
as a sacred place for casting spells. Maybe it was once used
in some sort of ritual, but Simone wasn't inclined to share
this foolish folklore with Nick. "I'm sure Esther was just
being descriptive."

Nick raised his head to her face again. "Yes, likely." He
questioned her no more, but his piercing gaze searched her

own. Silence stretched between them, and with it, a tension so palpable Simone's heart began to beat in apprehension. He wanted something more of her, she was certain of it. But he remained silent, still, like a leopard just before the strike.

The sun had slipped over the horizon, giving way at last to the encroaching night, leaving the garden enshrouded in the indigo of twilight. Fireflies illuminated the shadows with brief, tiny glints of light, and Simone caught the redolent scent of roses and honeysuckle.

Time seemed to become suspended in the gloaming. There was no yesterday. No tomorrow. Only the moment.

The cooling air misted and played upon a light breeze, swirling around them. Simone's skin prickled, from more than just the damp and the changing temperature. It was as if they were no longer in the garden, but had shifted to some other reality. A surreal, ethereal world . . . like that in her dreams.

Nick's expression changed. Instead of the demanding questions, in his eyes she now saw desire, an aching need mixed with incredible pain. His was a sorrow the depth of which she'd never seen before. Despite her determination to hold on to her fury against Nick, his expression filled her with a strange despair. She wanted to look away, to deny the feelings of sympathy and compassion that welled unbidden from her heart, but she could not tear her gaze from his. She heard him calling to her, an unspoken appeal, but powerful and real nonetheless, and as if in a trance, she answered his silent summons. She moved toward him from across the far side of the circle, and he stepped inside its ring, meeting her in the center.

They stood before one another, their bodies not touching, and yet she felt him. Felt all of him, surrounding her, within her, a part of her. She raised her eyes to his, and their gazes locked. Their hands met, palms touching, lightly, ever so lightly.

Every rational part of her screamed out to run from him, to escape while she still could. He was a practiced seducer, and she was apparently still unable to overcome his spell. Yet she stood transfixed, not daring to breathe, watching as his head lowered, waiting for the longed-for taste of his lips against her own. It should not be so. Could not be. Except in her dreams.

But when his lips met hers, the universe shifted, and she knew this was no dream. His touch was light, magical. She felt the caress of his breath against her face, smelled the fragrance of his skin. His scent swept her instantly back to that summer's night long ago, and she leaned into his embrace, for a moment suspending time and tide and all the terrible events that stood between them. They were just Nick and Simone. Man. Woman. In love.

And then it was over. Simone felt Nick's muscles tense where her hands lay on his upper arms. Her own body responded in kind, and she straightened abruptly and stepped away. Whatever had overcome them?

"I . . . I have to go," she stammered, backing over the loose dirt of the encircled garden, almost tripping on one of the outlining rocks.

He stood in the center, still as a statue, and stared at her awkward retreat with unreadable eyes. Then he, too, seemed to come out of the trance. She saw him take a step backward and raise his hands, palms out, in front of his chest, as if to prevent him from getting close to her again. "Go," he rasped. "Just go."

Much later, Nick stared unseeing out the window of his room at Brierley Hall, trying to sort out what had happened between him and Simone in Mary Rose's garden. When he'd stepped into the circle of rocks, he'd felt irresistibly drawn to the center, toward Simone, and he could swear that when he entered the inner circle he had been overcome by some magical enchantment. He had no other explanation for what he'd done.

Nick picked up the crumbling volume he'd discovered that afternoon in the niche in the wall. *The Charms and Spells of Mary Rose Hatcher*. He'd concluded earlier from what he'd read in these pages that Mary Rose indeed must have been a witch, at least in a sense. But he did not believe in magic or divination or witches or spells. And yet, as the sun had set and twilight descended, he had taken Simone Lefèvre into his arms as if it were the most natural thing in the world. And astoundingly, she had come to him. Willingly. Had she been under an enchantment as well?

He knew Simone Lefèvre hated him with every ounce of her being. And he was suspicious of every move she made.

What *had* come over them?

His throat tightened as he recalled the feel of her in his arms, the taste of her lips, the scent of her body. He ached for her from the depth of his very being. If they had been under some magical enchantment, he sighed, he wished he could live forever under that spell. For in those brief moments, he had known happiness the likes of which he'd experienced only fleetingly, in the dreams. He despaired that it had ended so quickly, that they had so suddenly regained their senses and hastily and with great mutual embarrassment departed in different directions.

But they *had* parted, and likely she was struggling to make some sense of the inexplicable interlude as well. He glanced at the book. Did Simone know anything about magic? Nick gave a short, doubtful laugh and forced his attention to the book. It had been barely twelve hours since he'd come across this slender, aged notebook that held a secret that could very possibly change his life. He still found it hard to believe that he'd discovered the place where it had been hidden away for over a century and a half.

He opened the book carefully. The pages were handwritten, decorated with clever designs and illustrations. On them, in the same strong yet feminine penmanship he recognized from his uncle's packet of letters, Mary Rose Hatcher had recorded recipes, set down descriptions of wild plants and herbs and their uses, even made note of the progress of certain of her patients she was treating with different tonics and other medicinals.

But what had fascinated Nick immediately was the inclusion of spells and enchantments among the entries. There before his eyes was proof that the family legend that Mary Rose had been a witch was true.

He turned to a page that had caught his attention earlier. There was a drawing of a five-pointed star within a circle, accompanied by a paragraph on how to invoke a sacred space. On other pages were instructions for creating dolls—Mary Rose called them poppets. They were made of corn husks, and she apparently used them to symbolize real people in her magical rituals. This reminded Nick of an old horror movie about voodoo dolls, and he shivered in spite of himself.

Absently, he turned to the back of the book, hoping for something less ominous, and he was surprised at what he found. Pressed between the pages were specimens of various blossoms, probably plucked from Mary Rose's garden . . . a damask rose, a daffodil, a sprig of lavender. And there, collected with the rest, was a paper-thin skeleton of a blossom he was certain he'd never seen anywhere else before. It was trumpet-shaped, about four inches in length, and although faded, it looked to have once been red. Beneath it was written *"Mahja."*

Nick's pulse began to pound against his temples in excitement. *Mahja.* This was it! According to one of the letters he'd found in the old trunk, this was the flower from which Mary Rose had extracted the mysterious and erotic perfume oil. With trembling fingers, Nick eased the blossom gently from between the pages and laid it across the palm of his hand. He nodded and grinned to himself. So this was the elusive *mahja.*

He held the pressed blossom to his nose, but the eons had stolen away its scent. No matter. Surely now that he had an actual specimen, Dr. Wheatley at Kew Gardens would be able to identify it from its shape and form. He would give it a modern, recognizable British name, and Nick could move forward with the development of his perfume. He'd drive out to the Gardens first thing Monday morning, before even going in to work.

Nervous excitement shot through his body. He was close, so close, to the critical discovery. But with his usual self-discipline, he reined in his high hopes. It was too early to get excited. And besides, there was still the question of whether or not Simone had somehow discovered the essence as well.

If she had the perfume oil, Nick wondered if she also knew the real identity of the *mahja* plant. Had her nose been better than his? Had she already identified the mysterious scent, either from smelling it, or by using the high-tech tools available at the House of Rutledge?

At the thought, his spirits came crashing down, for if she had learned the secret to the perfume, Nick was certain he'd already lost the race to create it first. He drew in a deep breath. Should he even pursue it further? Wouldn't it be smarter to invest his limited resources in something less dramatic but financially more sensible, such as another line of bath and body products?

But as he eyed the exotic blossom on his palm, he knew that a line of bath and body products wouldn't do it for him. He needed a sizzling, dramatic perfume. And he would not abandon his hopes for the future on the basis of his own misguided, paranoid presumptions. He had no proof that Simone knew about the perfume. Maybe she'd been telling the truth when she'd said she'd come to the garden to see its unique shape and the shimmering rocks that outlined it. Maybe her reservation at the cottage *had* been coincidental.

Nick frowned, his paranoia returning. It concerned him that Simone had called the garden a "mandala." Exactly how Mary Rose had described it in her little book. *That*, he thought, was just a little too coincidental for comfort.

The train ride back into London seemed interminable. Simone knew intellectually that it was taking the same time as it had to come to the country, but now instead of pleasant expectations of a visit with a friend, she was left alone with thoughts too scary to contemplate.

Thoughts about Nick Rutledge, and what had happened in the center of the mandala garden. Thoughts about how her body, her heart, her entire being had felt at last fully alive when he held her in his arms and she opened to his kiss.

She wasn't supposed to feel like that.

Staring unseeing at the quaint villages and bucolic scenery passing before her eyes, her mind could behold only the look in Nick's eyes, and the pain that was reflected there. Always before, her hatred of him had precluded any consideration of the circumstances of his life. She had assumed, after learning he was the heir to the House of Rutledge, that he was wealthy, and the thought of being betrayed not only by a heartless thief but also a rich one had added to her outrage.

But during this visit, Esther had told her that Nick's parents, both of whom were no longer living, had been instead part of the impoverished aristocracy found often in British society these days, and that when he had inherited Brierley Hall, it had deteriorated into a nearly derelict state. That explained why he had sold the valuable antiques and put the cottage up for rent.

But she knew it wasn't the despair of penury that she'd seen in his face. It had been a look of loneliness, of regret, of torment, a look so sad that it had struck a chord in her own wounded heart.

Simone shook her head. It had been none of the above, she told herself irritably. It was just her imagination bedeviling her. Her imagination—and her misplaced desire. She was being a fatuous fool again. Falling for his seductions. Again. Nicholas Rutledge, impoverished or not, was still a master seducer, a traitor. And he still wanted something from her.

Was it the perfume oil?

She let her mind toy with that thought a while. Suppose he knew about the essence? Perhaps, as she'd suggested to Esther, he'd come across it when he was disposing of the contents of the cottage. If he'd sampled it, Simone had no doubt that he would immediately recognize its importance as a potential component in a highly marketable fragrance. But suppose he was having no better luck than she in determining the origin of the oil, whose unusual combination of molecules had to be what was responsible for creating the remarkable erotic effects on the human body?

What are you doing here? He'd pressed her for an answer over and over in the garden. Did he suspect she was there because he knew the fragrance had originated there? How could he? And yet, she had to admit, if she were him, she would be highly suspicious of her repeated visits to the cottage, especially if he thought something valuable was hidden there.

She thought about the niche in the wall, the *empty* niche, and decided that if anything valuable had been hidden away there, Nick had found it. It rankled. She'd been so close. Well, there was nothing for it but to keep trying by trial and error to re-create the perfume by synthesis.

She caught the tube from the train terminal, and covered the few blocks from the underground station to the company's flat quickly, suddenly eager to resume her research again. Knowing that Nick was likely on the same trail added urgency to her quest.

At first she was unaware that anything was amiss. The apartment appeared to be just as she'd left it. Until she went into her bedroom and glanced at the fake wooden surface of the inexpensive nightstand.

The vials were missing.

The small bottle into which she had decanted the last of the essential oil from the crystal container and the bottle that held the remnants of Esther's supply simply weren't where she'd placed them before leaving for Redford.

Simone sank onto the bed. Think! she screamed silently at herself. Am I mistaken? Did I hide them someplace else? Panic rose hot and bitter at the back of her throat. How could she have so carelessly mislaid something so important? Her heart thudding, she forced herself to undertake a methodical search for the missing containers, for in them was the essence that could very well secure her future. Bathroom drawers. Kitchen drawers and cabinets. Closet shelves. Beneath the bed. Even in the refrigerator.

Her search led to the end table, next to the sofa, where she usually deposited her handbag and any other personal belongings upon entering the apartment. Of course, she'd taken her handbag with her to Redford, but it seemed as though something else had been on that table when she'd left on Friday evening . . .

The manila file containing the formula Shahmir had given

her. It had been there when she left. She was certain of it. Unless she had absentmindedly put it wherever she'd put the perfume vials and they were missing together.

Simone resisted the urge to scream. Instead, she called upon that trusted emotion that had seen her through so much— anger. She did not think she had mislaid anything. Somebody must have broken into the flat and taken them. But who? For once, she couldn't blame Nick. She knew where he'd been over the weekend, although, she supposed, he could have hired someone to do it.

She thought of the tall, dark-skinned swami whom she suspected had broken into Nick's own house or office and taken the incomplete formula. But why would he want to steal it from her? He'd just given it to her.

Nothing made sense.

She went to the window and stared into the summer street below. Nothing made sense at all. Not this theft, if it *was* a theft and not her own carelessness. Certainly not her misplaced sympathy, as brief as it had been, for Nick Rutledge. Or the ease with which she had let him break the long-standing seige she'd held around her emotions. She shook her head, laughing to keep from exploding with anger and frustration. No. None of it made sense. Not even being here, in this cramped, impersonal apartment, working for a company in England, rather than in France or the United States, the two places she'd called home. Maybe she was losing her mind.

But what would she be doing if she wasn't doing this? She closed her eyes and felt an emotional pain that slashed through her so deeply she could feel it in her fingertips. Here she was, twenty-seven years old, without a life, without friends, without a lover, except in the dreams she now feared might be eroding her sanity. She knew it was foolish of her, but she allowed herself to remember briefly how, just for a moment, all those ''withouts'' had disappeared in the warmth of Nick's embrace. For a magic moment, suspended between daylight and darkness, between yesterday and tomorrow, she had found the sense of home, of belonging, that had eluded her since she had left France.

That was what she'd rather be doing.

She would rather be with someone, not Nick of course, but a man who would take away her loneliness, someone with whom she could share her life, whom she could trust and love and respect, and who would feel the same toward her. Simone exhaled a tired sigh and looked out the window again. Was there such a someone out there for her? It seemed not, for every time she'd met a man in the past few years, she'd backed off, her fear of betrayal too great to allow anyone too close.

In short, she was her own worst enemy. And until she got over her fear, she supposed she'd be stuck just as she was—alone. At least she had a good job, she reminded herself, even if she didn't particularly like her boss. At the House of Rutledge, she had the chance to become what she'd always wanted to be, a truly great perfumer. She picked up her handbag and headed for the door, seeking yet another meal alone in a restaurant.

Maybe she would have to be content with that—being a truly great perfumer, even if she lived alone the rest of her years.

SIXTEEN

❧

It was almost a relief, after weeks of struggle, not to have to fight it out again today with Mary Rose's perfume. Her samples having been stolen, Simone had nothing with which to work. She stood before the console, fingering the myriad little bottles, wondering what she would do now . . . and where in hell those two vials and the folder with Shahmir's formula had gone. She'd turned her apartment upside down upon her return from dinner the night before, searching until she was satisfied that they simply were not there. She had not yet decided whether to call the police, but she felt foolish reporting the theft of a perfume. Unless a person was in the industry and understood the espionage factor that made perfumers tight-lipped and paranoid, no one would take her seriously.

So she'd decided to bide her time and see what unfolded. The robber might reveal himself if she didn't press the issue. Isn't that what great detectives counted on sometimes? The ego of the thief and his subconscious wish to be caught? But did this thief wish to be caught? Or was he a more pragmatic burglar, one who also knew about the perfume and who had decided to make it his own? Since Simone knew of it, as did Esther and probably Nick, she reckoned others might have learned about it and its "interesting" effects. She would wait and see, for in truth, there was nothing else she could do about it.

The phone on her desk buzzed, and she noted the intercom light glowed red. "Hello. This is Simone."

"Ah, good morning, my dear." Antoine Dupuis's voice was just short of intimate. "Did you have a good weekend?"

"It was okay," she said, fingering a strand of hair. Was it just because he was her boss that the man made her so nervous?

"I called at the apartment to see if you needed anything, but no one was home."

"I . . . I spent the weekend in the country."

There was a long pause, then, "Are you busy, or could you come to my office for a few minutes?"

"I'll be right down." What could he want of her? Perhaps she was about to get fired. After all, she hadn't "produced" anything since she'd been at the House of Rutledge. But surely he'd give her more of a chance than a mere three weeks.

Dupuis rose from the chair behind the massive desk when she entered the room and indicated for her to take a seat on the opposite side. Then he sat down again. She gave him a curious glance, and it was then she saw the vials. They sat on his desk, atop the manila folder.

Her eyes widened. "Where . . . did you get those?" She tried to control her shock by speaking in an even tone, but her cheeks burned.

Dupuis gestured and shrugged his shoulders and gave her a calculated smile. "I told you I stopped by your flat."

Simone was aghast. "You went in?"

"The place does belong to the company, my dear, and I have a key. Now, now, don't get yourself all upset. When you didn't answer my knock, I just went in to make sure you weren't murdered in the night or something."

"But . . . but you stole those vials . . ." she sputtered, outrage blinding her to his inferred concern for her welfare. "You entered my apartment and took them. That folder as well."

Dupuis shook his head and gave her a condescending smirk. "You are such an *ingénue*," he replied. "I find that refreshing in a young woman these days." His tone shifted from cordial to serious. "I saw these containers in the lab last week where you were working. I figured you must have brought your work home, and I must admit to a certain amount of professional curiosity about your progress, or shall we say, lack thereof?" He raised a brow and aimed a meaningful look at her.

Simone was not about to let him intimidate her. She crossed her arms and glared back at him. "I told you last week, I must work in complete privacy. What I create is art, as much as a painting or a piece of music. It takes great concentration, and I cannot, will not, tolerate intrusions such as this. You have no reason or right to . . . to burglarize my living quarters."

"I stole nothing, Miss Lefèvre," Dupuis said levelly. He picked up a ballpoint pen and tapped it irritatingly end over end on the desktop. "I believe what is in those vials belongs to the House of Rutledge. That formula, too, although it's nothing unusual. If anyone could be accused of theft, it could be you. After all, you did take the perfume from these premises."

Simone was livid. "How dare you? You have no idea where those fragrances came from, or the formula. Perhaps they were mine to begin with."

"Then you've been working on personal projects on company time?"

The man was despicable. Yet she realized suddenly he did have a point. She had been on a personal quest, in a way. She backed off just a bit and took a deep breath. "Look, Monsieur Dupuis, I do not wish to enter into a fray with you. I . . . I have reason to believe that what is in those vials could be the basis for our first *grand parfum,* and I have spent three frustrating weeks trying—"

He did not let her go on. "What *is* in those vials, Simone?" His eyes narrowed and suddenly seemed to take on a sybaritic glow.

She looked down at her hands, breathing deeply, trying to bring her emotions completely under control. She raised her eyes to meet his gaze directly. "I don't know."

"I beg your pardon?"

"I wish I had a better answer for you, but I don't know what is in them."

The sneer returned to his face. "Some master perfumer you've turned out to be. I thought from the records I received about your talents and abilities that there would be nothing with a scent that you would not recognize instantly. Especially such a remarkable fragrant essence as this." He paused and eyed her pointedly. "I'm sure you are well aware just how remarkable this perfume is."

His words dropped like rocks into the pit of her stomach, and Simone swallowed over her apprehension. How far had he gone in his personal experimentation with the oil?

He held up one of the small flasks. "What is it about this potion, Simone, that makes a man feel half his age and twice his potency? What is it that brings on the dreams . . . ?" The expression in his eyes shifted to pure lust, and his voice took on a husky tone. "I'm certain you know what I am talking about."

Oh, my God. Simone felt a shudder crawl involuntarily down her spine. Antoine Dupuis had experienced the dreams. Her first thought was that she hoped she hadn't played a part in them. Her second was not to rise to his bait. She opted to remain the ingénue. "I beg your pardon?"

He failed to find it refreshing this time. Abruptly, he stood up and came around to the front of the desk and took her arm, pulling her roughly to her feet. His face, directly in her own, was intense. He smelled of fear. And power. And domination. "You claim that you want to create *les grands parfums*. But don't you see? You already have." He gestured toward the desk. "I don't give a damn where you got that fragrance. Make more of it."

Simone wrenched free of his grasp and backed away from him. "I can't." She watched his face go from red to purple.

"What the hell do you mean, you can't? We have every substance known to man upstairs in that perfume lab. It shouldn't be that difficult—"

"*Mais non,* we do not," she countered, gratified in some small way that she truly could not indulge this man his childish tantrum. "This essential oil is different from anything I have ever encountered. I have been working steadily for the past three weeks to break it down chemically, to mimic its scent, to determine its . . . well, its magic, if you will. There appears to be something in it that defies the equipment, the computer, and my own nose!" As she talked, she was aware that her words came more rapidly and at a higher pitch than she would have liked, but she couldn't help it. They reflected her own frustration, and she didn't care if Antoine Dupuis knew it.

The little Frenchman cocked his head to one side and studied her for a long moment. "I hired you because you are the daughter of Jean René Lefèvre. You have the potential for becoming one of the finest noses in the business. I have trust in your abilities. But I warn you, I will tolerate no excuses. I want this perfume. And I expect you to develop it for the House of Rutledge."

"For the House of Rutledge?" she asked petulantly, irked by his attitude. "Or for yourself?"

But he appeared unoffended. "Is there a difference?"

"The flower resembles that of the brugmansia, a cousin to the datura," the botanist informed Nick, bringing out a large illustrated encyclopedia of the plants of the world. He thumbed through it until he came to the page he sought, then turned the volume around so Nick could see the color photo for himself. Next to the photo, Nick laid the ghost of the blossom that had been pressed between the pages of Mary Rose's book and marked *"Mahja."*

"See the resemblance?" Dr. Wheatley remarked, pointing out the elongated trumpet shape. Nick nodded, not wanting this to be the answer. He didn't know much about the brugmansia, but he knew that datura was an ancient and highly toxic hallucinogen. That's all he needed, for the secret to his "love potion" to be a narcotic drug. But it appeared to be a distinct possibility.

"Is there any way to know for sure? I mean, such as doing a DNA test or something?"

"We could take a look at the pollen. It will tell us the genus, perhaps even the species."

Nick left the fragile treasure in the safekeeping of Dr. Thomas Wheatley at Kew Gardens and departed, feeling suddenly disconcerted and uncertain about the future of his perfume. Brugmansia? Datura?

He rolled the possibilities over in his mind and decided it was entirely feasible that the *mahja* could indeed be one of these, or a close relation. He tried to recall his uncle's description of his visit to the remote Himalayan monastery, where he was massaged with an ointment made from the *mahja* plant. Hadn't he written in his diary that it had engendered a mind-altering state that had assuaged his mental pain over being separated from Mary Rose? Something like that.

It didn't sound exactly like the effect of an hallucinogenic drug, but the oil must have had some kind of mood-altering ability that had so impressed John Rutledge that he had stolen the seed pods on his way out.

Discouraged, Nick sped through the crowded London streets, oblivious to the beeps and honks of the cars that whizzed by him. Brugmansia. Datura. If the "magical" ingredient was one of these, or even a close relation, his project would likely have to be abandoned.

It had been foolish of him, he decided, to plan his entire future around the development of one particular perfume. Still, he could not dismiss the power, and the potential, of the perfume oil he'd found in the old trunk. Neither could he dismiss the dreams. If only for his own satisfaction, he vowed to follow through with his investigations until he knew exactly what the substance was that had the ability to vault him into a dreamworld so lifelike, so sublime, he did not want to wake up.

With each dream experience, with each sensual rendezvous with Simone, Nick found what his uncle claimed he was about to do at the end of the diary to be more and more understandable, if not believable.

Nick heard chimes over the din of the city and looked at his watch. Noon. His stomach growled in sync. He should get back to the office to check on the team of computer technicians he'd left a couple of hours ago busily setting up his electronic equipment. But they'd probably be on lunch break, he figured, and decided to pick up a quick bite himself in one of his favorite restaurants, a place he'd often gone for lunch, not far from the House of Rutledge. As glad as he was to be out from under the control of Antoine Dupuis, he missed that aspect of his former position, being around others in his everyday life. He would admit it to no one but himself, but his new lifestyle was a very lonely one.

The restaurant was busy with the noonday crowd, and Nick waved to several acquaintances while he waited to be seated. When at last the host led him to a table for two, he took a seat facing the rear and began to study the menu. Having decided on his selection, he lowered the large, leather-bound folder and looked up, directly into the leering face of Antoine Dupuis.

"*Bonjour,* Nick." Dupuis took great pleasure in seeing the acute discomfort on the face of his erstwhile master perfumer. He was surprised to see him in the neighborhood. Nick had always been sensitive and emotional, and Dupuis had expected him to find new haunts, rather than return to the likely painful memories of his old ones. Interesting that he had come back. And an opportunity to see what he was up to. "May I join you?"

He gave Nick little option as he took the chair opposite. "It is time, don't you think, to let bygones be bygones?"

Nick glared at him. "What do you want, Dupuis?"

"What's this? Why the frown?" Dupuis asked genially. He fluttered his napkin to signal to the waiter, then laid the crisp, white linen across his lap. "There's no need for animosity." He turned to the server who showed up at the table posthaste upon seeing Dupuis's flag. That's why Antoine liked dining here. They had proper respect for a man of his position.

"Two martinis, please. Extra dry. Mine with a twist.

Yours?'' he turned to Nick. "Olive or twist?"

"You know I don't drink at lunch."

"Ah, forever the old maid. Well, then," he said to the waiter, "give him a twist as well. Perhaps he'll change his mind."

Dupuis was almost gleeful at this chance to nettle the supercilious Englishman. He'd had to put up with his superior attitude for ten long years. But not anymore. It always amazed him that no matter how impoverished, how lowered their state in life, the English aristocracy managed to insinuate their sovereignty over those they considered "lesser humans." As he supposed Nick considered him to be.

Dupuis sneered. "Why the sour face, Rutledge? Didn't you get everything you wanted? I didn't stand in your way."

"I came here to enjoy lunch," Nick growled. "Alone."

"It's a busy place, and I'm a considerate man. No need for each of us to take up separate tables." He leaned forward. "Now, tell me, my friend, what has been up with you?"

A cynical smile curved Nick's lips upward slightly. "You're such a bastard, Dupuis. You know damned well what's up with me. You know I've closed the Bombay plant and moved it to England. Just as you and your henchmen know the inside of my new offices . . . and my home."

Dupuis felt a tingle of alarm. "You are mistaken on this, Nick. Yes, of course we know about the Bombay closing. But I have no idea why you keep accusing me of burglarizing you." The look Nick shot him left no doubt that the perfumer did not believe him.

"What are you after, Dupuis? Perhaps I could save you the trouble and just give it over to you. That way I wouldn't have to clean up the mess afterward."

The waiter brought the martinis and placed one in front of each man, then took their orders. Dupuis sipped deeply on his. Nick's was left untouched.

"I don't know how to convince you I wasn't involved in whatever you're talking about, so I won't continue to try," Dupuis sighed at last. "You've always been such a hardhead. But I ask, what I could possibly want from you further?" He twisted the knife a little deeper. "I already have everything."

"You son of a bitch."

Dupuis smiled. "As I said, it is time to let bygones be bygones. What is important is to look to the future." He raised his glass. "And here is to your future, Nick. I wish you every success."

"I don't drink with criminals."

"Your usual charming, hypocritical self." Dupuis drank anyway. "Well, if you won't talk about your future, perhaps you'd be interested in hearing about the future of the House of Rutledge." Although the Englishman didn't reply, Dupuis was gratified by the look in his eye to see he'd gotten Nick's attention. He went on, enjoying this immensely.

"Fate is a capricious thing, is she not? Who would have dreamed ten years ago that the daughter of Jean René Lefèvre would join forces with us? I mean, what with your theft of her father's formulas and all."

"And I am certain she knows nothing of your involvement in that business."

"It was your decision, Nick. I merely made a suggestion." Dupuis picked up a fork and tapped the end of it on the pink linen tablecloth. Then he raised an eyebrow and slanted a smile across the table. "You forgot to mention how lovely the old man's daughter is. I'm surprised you didn't fall in love with her then and botch the whole thing. I have to hand it to you. I doubt if I would have had the discipline to carry through."

Nick's face contorted in anger, and Dupuis thought he might punch him out right across the table. Hmmm. So there *had* been something between them. He kept his finger on the button. "However, I am not the man you are," he continued smoothly. "I find myself profoundly attracted to Simone Lefèvre. And I'm pleased to say, she seems to feel the same about me. We . . . uh, have had a pleasant time getting to know one another, shall we say?"

Nick's face now drained of all color. "You're a filthy liar, Dupuis."

"Careful now, or I won't pick up the check."

The waiter approached with plates of steaming pasta and avoided a collision only by a matter of inches when Nick bolted from his chair. "Go to hell, you slimy little prig," Nick snarled, throwing his napkin on the table. "And keep your hands off Simone."

Dupuis watched the man's back as he made his way out of the restaurant. An irrepressible chuckle welled from deep within and spilled out between gin-flavored lips. "I suppose I'll be needing only one of those plates, *garçon*," he said, making room for the astonished young server to place his lunch in front of him. "But I'll keep the other martini."

SEVENTEEN

༉

Simone threw the stack of *mouillettes,* the slender absorbent testers used by perfumers, into the trash can and swore under her breath in French. Beside her on the large teak worktable was a computer printout generated from her experiments using a gas chromatograph linked to a mass spectrometer, giving her a molecular picture of the chemical structure of the baffling perfume. From this, she should have been able to reproduce it synthetically, but she had worked at it for days to no avail. Her nose did not lie. These synthetic solutions did not even approach the original in scent, although the molecules were as close to identical as she could make them. Even more aggravating, as she worked on the artificially created substance, she experienced no erotic effects whatsoever. She had long since discarded the mask.

She heard the door to the sealed perfume lab whoosh open and close again, but she paid no heed. Her mind was focused completely on the puzzle at hand and her growing sense of defeat. Even though she was under pressure from Dupuis to perform, it was her own desire to break the secret of the perfume oil that had driven her to work nonstop as long as she could physically stand it. She was exhausted, her eyes burned, and her back ached.

"Well, well, how is my little *princesse de parfum* today?" Antoine Dupuis's chipper voice was as irritating as squeaky chalk on a blackboard, his words insulting. Simone threw her head back, glaring at him. "What do you want?"

He stopped in his tracks and tilted his head. "My, my, aren't we touchy? Is it the wrong time of the month?"

Simone resisted the urge to throw the canister of clean *mouillettes* at him. How much longer could she suffer this pompous little man? How had Nick managed to work for him all those years?

"That is none of your business," she answered him, standing and leaning forward on the table with both hands. "It's a good thing I'm a relatively well adjusted woman, monsieur. It's comments like those that get male chauvinists in trouble these days. In America, they call it sexual harassment."

She could see she'd angered him, and she hoped perversely she might get fired. She found it more difficult by the day to come to work in this place. The only thing that kept her going was that here she had every state-of-the-art piece of equipment known to the fragrance industry at her disposal, and she was determined to win the battle between her nose and Mary Rose's perfume.

But Dupuis straightened his tie, cleared his throat, and squared his shoulders. *"Pardon, mademoiselle,"* he said with a slight bow. "I did not mean to offend you. Please accept my sincere apologies."

She stared at him with a contempt she could not conceal. "A professor once told our class in business management that one should never say to a female employee anything you wouldn't say to a male."

"Point taken. Now," he said, coming to the far side of the table that separated them by only a few feet, "about the perfume. Where do you stand on it?"

Simone shoved the computer printouts at him. "That's what it looks like," she said. Then she reached into the waste can and drew out half a dozen *mouillettes*. "And that's what it smells like."

Eagerly, Dupuis snatched up the white fibrous blotters and raised them one by one to his nose. "This will not do," he said, frowning.

"No, this will not do," Simone agreed, collapsing into her

chair again and rubbing the ache in her forehead. "But I do not know what to do next. I have tried everything . . . from what I learned in school to tricks my father showed me." She raised her eyes, feeling fatigue weigh heavily on her shoulders. "I need to know from what plant this essential oil was derived." Simone had used all of Esther's sample in her work. She picked up the only remaining vial of the scented aphrodisiac. "Otherwise, I am defeated."

"You do not know what plant it came from?" Dupuis raised his eyebrows in surprise. It was a little detail she had not shared with him. "You must find out what it is!"

"I've tried everything."

"Surely there must be some way."

Simone hated to divulge what little she knew about the origin of the perfume to the onerous man, but she was tired of arguing with him. "There is only one possibility I have not explored. I . . . I have reason to believe that the name and the description of the plant might have been recorded in a book kept by the woman who created the oil, an ancestor, sort of, of the person I, uh, got my sample from."

Dupuis brightened visibly. "Terrific! Then why don't you just look in the book and find out what it is?" He looked at her as if she were a simpleton.

She almost laughed in his face. "Because I don't have it."

"Where is it?"

"I think Nick Rutledge has it."

"What!" Dupuis almost exploded. "Impossible. What makes you think that? Have you been with him, told him about my perfume?" Simone watched in amazement as he went from suave businessman to raving madman. The man was a chameleon, and she steeled herself against his diatribe.

"You're a fool if you think that," she said quietly. "You know that I have no use for Nicholas Rutledge. But quite by accident, I ran into him when I first came to England." Simone saw no reason to withhold her story from Dupuis. If anything, it would make it clear that the perfume indeed belonged to her before she became a part of the House of Rutledge. She told him about finding the first sample of the essence in the shipment of old bottles purchased by her aunt, of having traced them to England, to a particular estate, which coincidentally turned out to be Brierley Hall, owned by Nick Rutledge.

She read the skepticism on his face, but she didn't care. "I stayed in a B and B in a nearby village, and the woman who ran the place also had a sample of the perfume," she continued. "She claimed that it was originally developed by a woman who lived on Nick's estate over a hundred and fifty years ago."

Dupuis's eyes widened in disbelief. "What? Why, that's astounding."

"Yes, it is. But I believe it to be true."

"What makes you think Nick knows about it?" He glowered at her suspiciously.

She told him about Esther's claim that something called a Book of Shadows might still exist in which the originator of the perfume would likely have recorded the formula, and then told him of her visit to the garden, just after Nick had had it cleared of overgrowth.

She did not tell him about her twilight encounter with their mutual rival. She still did not know what to make of that.

"I think he had the garden cleared because he was looking for something there. Possibly the same Book of Shadows. When I arrived, I found a niche in the garden wall that looked as if it had been recently unsealed. It's my guess that if the book existed, he found it there."

She looked up at Dupuis and was surprised by the look on his face. It was as if his mental wheels were turning furiously. Finally and surprisingly, he smiled.

"This is beautiful," he said, coming around to her side of the worktable and kissing both her cheeks. *"Fantastique!"* He laughed uproariously.

"I don't understand," Simone said, thoroughly confused.

"Listen carefully," he said, edging his body onto the tabletop. "I can understand how terribly hurt you must have been when Nick betrayed you and your father all those years ago. Would you not like to take revenge on him for that?"

Revenge.

The word wrapped around her heart like a thick, dark cloud. Oh, yes, she'd longed for revenge. That was one reason she remained at the House of Rutledge, in spite of her growing antipathy to Antoine Dupuis. And why she was killing herself to discover and re-create the ancient perfume. So she could kill Nick in the marketplace.

"What do you have in mind?"

"How was Nick able to win your father's trust when he first came to the perfumery in Grasse?"

Simone's cheeks burned. "He . . . he was most charming . . ." She saw the corner of Dupuis's mouth edge upward in dry amusement.

"To whom? Your father? Or you?"

"What are you getting at?" she snapped, acutely uncomfortable by the direction of his line of questioning. His insinuations brought back entirely too many unquiet memories.

"I am not blind, Simone. You are a lovely woman. You must have been a beautiful girl when he met you. It is my assumption that he used seduction as his weapon, that it was you he charmed, you who encouraged your father to accept him as an apprentice."

Simone thought she might get sick. She hated Antoine Dupuis at the moment more than she'd hated anyone in her whole life, including Nick. What right, or reason, did he have for bringing all this up? "You're out of line again, monsieur!"

"Am I? Perhaps. But consider this. Suppose he did seduce you and used you for his own greedy ends. But suppose also that he fell in love with you too."

"Ridiculous!"

"Not at all. Men do such things all the time. Stay with me." He hopped off the table and began to pace aimlessly around the large room as his thoughts tumbled out. "Would it not be poetic justice for you to use against him the very weapon he used against you?"

Simone was aghast. "What do you mean?"

He stopped his pacing and turned to face her, an odd little smile on his lips. "Seduce him, my dear. Two can play that game. Gain his trust, learn his secrets, and then . . . steal them.''

Almost a week later, Simone was no closer to success with the perfume, and with each day that passed, her doubts mounted. At home, she sought comfort after a hard day, trying to forget her boss and his licentious approach to solving her problem. She poured water from a large plastic jug into a teakettle provided in the corporate flat and placed it on the burner of the toy-sized stove. Everything in the place seemed to be a miniature of what she was accustomed to in the United States. She knew she should be more aggressively seeking a place of her own to live, but something held her back, warning her against believing that she would be living in London for very long. Perhaps it was her failure to re-create the perfume. More likely, she thought, taking a cup and saucer from the cupboard, it was her intrinsic distrust of Antoine Dupuis.

The man was amazing. She shook her head at the suggestion he'd made about stealing the Book of Shadows from Nick. Had he been serious? Did he really think she was capable of a calculated seduction of Nicholas Rutledge? Seduction, followed by theft?

She poured hot water over a teabag, and a profound sadness washed over her at the same time. Of course, Nick had done that very thing to her, years ago, but even her deep-seated desire for revenge wasn't strong enough to make her lower herself to exact revenge in kind. Were all men so dispassionate about using sex to get what they wanted?

She thought about the most special man she'd ever known in her life—her father. He would never have done such a thing, nor asked a woman to. She was glad he never knew that she had allowed Nick into her bed.

With a lump in her throat summoned by memories of her father, she added milk and sugar to her cup and took the tea to the small table where she thumbed idly through a magazine that lay there. Her gaze lingered upon the many ads for perfumes that glittered from the glossy pages, and she shook her head. Would hers ever be there alongside them?

Simone knew each of these perfumes, could conjure their scent easily in her imagination. In her mind, she could take them apart, note by note, and put them back together in a different formula if she wished. Thanks to her father's training, and his genes, there were no secrets from her nose.

Except one.

She slammed the magazine shut. Damn it all, what was wrong with her? Was she not a nose after all? Maybe she never should have signed on as master perfumer at the House of Rutledge.

Simone considered her options. She could quit. Simply tell Dupuis she'd made a mistake in taking the job, jump a plane back to New Orleans, and figure it out from there.

But in her gut, that did not feel like a valid alternative, just a coward's way out of her frustration. If she admitted defeat so early, she was a loser without the backbone it took to survive in the highly competitive, cutthroat business of perfuming. Her career would be over before it had begun.

Second option. Give up on the stubborn substance and move to something else before she lost her self-confidence. But to do this, in her mind, would be to admit failure, and to Simone, who wanted badly to become a perfumer of the stature of her father, failure was *not* an option.

But what was it going to take to succeed? She slammed her palm on the magazine. She'd never been so frustrated in her life. She stood and moved about the apartment, straightening the minimal clutter, while Dupuis's contemptible suggestion flirted with her conscience.

Did she have it in her to seduce Nick to gain the answers she needed to break the secret of the perfume? The very thought brought a cold sweat to her skin. She couldn't do such a thing.

She drummed her nails on the Formica tabletop, her frustration simmering into a low-boiling anger. She might not have the nerve to seduce Nick to get them, but by God, she wanted answers! And not just answers about the perfume. She allowed the anger to boil higher. She wanted answers to all the old "whys" that continued to haunt her. Nick had refused flatly to discuss it both times she'd tried to get those answers from him. But it was worth another try.

She bit her lip, thinking. Seduction was out, against her principles. But maybe a date, where they could meet on neutral ground, around others, where they could at least talk civilly, at a safe distance from one another . . .

The phone was ringing as Nick walked in his front door, but he couldn't get to it in time to answer before the machine responded to take a message. His heart almost stopped when he heard the woman's voice, hesitant, unsure, speak to the machine in English that was softened by a lilting French accent. "Nick, this is Simone. I would like to talk to you. Please call me at . . .''

Simone.

Why on earth would she be calling him? Red flags went up all around him. Dupuis must have set her up to call, after his own lunchtime snooping had failed to uncover Nick's perfuming plans. He found it laughable that the Frenchman seemed to be so threatened by Nick's new little venture. But he also found it disgusting that he would use Simone as his spy, and also that she apparently was his willing partner in intrigue.

The perfume industry was rife with industrial espionage, however, and he had no reason to believe that Simone was above participating in it, other than his ardent wish that such activity was beneath her. But where Simone was concerned, Nick had lost the ability to be objective.

He picked up the receiver and dialed the number she'd left on the answering machine.

"Hello?" The woman's voice on the other end was soft, perhaps a little nervous.

Nick felt his stomach do a flip, but he summoned his most professional tone. "Simone? This is Nick, returning your call."

"Nick. Uh, yes. Well . . .'' She paused, and he heard her exhale an audible breath. "Look, Nick, I'm not very good at this sort of thing, but . . . but I need to talk to you."

Nick closed his eyes, felt his heart hammering. Oh, God,

how he wished she wanted to talk to *him,* not to probe about his business or spy on him for Dupuis. He knew better, but . . .

"Can you meet me for dinner?" he heard himself say.

A long silence. Then, "I . . . I suppose so. Where?"

"My club isn't far from the corporate flat. I assume that's where you are temporarily lodged?"

"Uh, yes."

"I could pick you up there. Would that be suitable?"

Another quiet stretch. "No. I mean, your club would be fine, but I can take a taxi."

Not knowing how the evening would go, Nick didn't argue. It was best if she wasn't obliged to ride with him. It gave them professional distance. And he was quite certain this was a professional engagement. He gave her the address of the gentleman's club in the heart of London, they agreed to meet at nine, and he hung up with sweaty hands.

Two hours later, he stood in the lobby of the venerable In and Out Club, as it was known, formerly a military club and now open to general membership. He joked with the doorman, cast a glance in a mirror and caught his own image, that of a confident, well-dressed gentleman, and swallowed his fear. Moments later, a black taxi swung through the front gates of what in Regency times was Lord Egremont's private residence, and Nick's élan vanished the moment Simone Lefèvre stepped out.

Dressed in a long, slender, body-hugging gown of shifting soft fabric, with slim straps and no back at all, she looked like a model stepping from the pages of a fashion magazine. Her hair was piled in curls atop her head, leaving a creamy expanse of neck, shoulders, and back exposed to view. Long, exotic earrings dangled to her shoulders, and crimson caressed her lips, matching the hue of the dress.

Nick groaned aloud, not because she was overdressed, which she wasn't, but because of the incredibly erotic vision she presented. Not even in his dreams had she ever appeared so drop-dead gorgeous. How could he survive the night?

He clenched his jaw, took a deep breath, and stepped from

the building to greet her. "Good evening," he said, trying to find his tongue. She turned her large, dark eyes on him and gave him a demure smile.

"Hello, Nick."

EIGHTEEN

✌

Nick's insides melted even as his throat constricted. He swallowed hard. My God, what had he walked away from those many years ago? He did not know what punishment Simone had in store for him this evening, but it was a torture he would happily endure just to be near her.

He led her into the staid old building, where next to the other rather somberly dressed patrons she looked like an exotic flower amongst a funeral arrangement. Heads turned as he escorted her, hand on elbow, to the courtyard. "Would you like a cocktail out-of-doors before dinner?" he asked. "It's very pleasant out this evening."

"That would be nice. Gin and tonic, please."

Gin and tonic. How quickly she'd become British, Nick thought as he hurried to the bar, not wishing to delay their drinks by depending on the services of the elderly and legendarily plodding bar waiter. When he returned, he paused a moment in the doorway. Simone was seated next to the gently rippling fountain, and he stood there mesmerized, captivated by her inexpressible beauty. She looked up and caught him, and his collar suddenly seemed too tight about his neck.

"Here we are," he said, trying for a recovery but feeling very much a schoolboy as he handed her the cocktail. He took a seat opposite her, to give her the comfort of distance between them, to give him a better view. He raised his glass. "To what should we propose a toast?"

Her eyes riveted his. She held her glass up between long, slender fingers. "To honesty."

It would have been easy for Nick to laugh, for he suspected she was here on a distinctly dishonest mission, but something about her demeanor stopped him short. Either she was serious, or she'd been taking acting lessons from Dupuis.

"Honesty? I'm surprised you think I'm capable of it." His cynical answer slipped out before he could stop it.

But it was an honest answer.

She placed the frosty glass to her lips, and he watched, aching, as a small portion of the clear liquid disappeared between the strawberry pout. Her eyes never left his. Then she spoke. "Are you?"

Nick was not so reserved in consuming his drink, and he hoped the cocktail waiter would make an appearance soon. One tonic would not suffice for long. But he did not flinch at her question, nor drop his gaze.

"Only recently have I learned the art."

She raised an eyebrow. "Whatever possessed you to acquire the trait at this late date?"

Nick pondered her sardonic question a moment, but he knew the answer. "Living a lie can be exhausting." He saw a frown of curiosity light momentarily on her delicately arched brows.

"Is that what you were doing, Nick?"

"It's what I have been doing since . . . since my father died." She wanted honesty? He guessed it was time he gave it to her. She deserved to know what had motivated his contemptible behavior where she was concerned, no matter how shameful it was for him to reveal.

She didn't press him verbally to explain, but her questions were evident in her expression. Nick shifted in his seat and caught the eye of the octagenarian who had served drinks at the club since before Nick was born. He signaled for another round, knowing it might be half an hour before they were served.

Then he faced Simone. He'd thought she would have her moment of truth the night she'd been caught snooping around the cottage, but at the time neither had seemed able to deal with it. He'd avoided it then, but it had been only a postponement. He glanced around and was relieved to note that the other tables were almost empty now.

"It . . . won't excuse what I did," he said at last, the words tasting bitter on his tongue. "But perhaps it will explain why."

"I have waited ten years to understand what happened," she replied, her own voice tight with emotion. He took courage, however, from the fact that he saw no hatred on her face at the moment.

"My . . . my father didn't die a normal death, like most fathers," he began. "He . . . took his own life. I was only twenty-three at the time. I wasn't that close to him. I spent most of my adolescence in residence at Harrow and later at Cambridge. I knew little about him, his personal life, his profession. All I knew was that I was supposed to grow up to be just like him, and my grandfather, and his father before him, in other words, to be a Rutledge." He laughed contemptuously. "Lord Rutledge, to be exact."

"Why did he kill himself?"

Nick was surprised that she didn't want to know more about his title, as most others did. And that she addressed his father's death so directly. Most people avoided the uncomfortable subject of suicide. "He was an abominable businessman. He should never have tried to manage the House of Rutledge. But he did, and before he died, he'd nearly taken it into bankruptcy. He was a failure, at least in his eyes, and he couldn't bear it." Nick cleared his throat. "That's what he said anyway, in the note he left my mother."

Silence stretched between them, broken at last by Simone's soft voice. "I'm sorry, Nick. That must have been very difficult for you."

He shrugged and drained his drink. "People die. It was no worse than you seeing your father fall dead of a heart attack, I suppose," he said, suddenly angry, not wanting her to be sorry for him. He didn't deserve her kindness or understanding. He looked up to see tears brimming in her dark eyes.

"Do you have to be so cruel?" she said.

Damn. He'd done it again. In assuaging his own pain, he had hurt her. It seemed to be his demented proclivity. "Please. Forgive me," he uttered.

The waiter arrived with surprising promptness, served their drinks, and informed Nick that if they wished to have dinner, they should proceed to the dining room soon, as it was getting late.

Nick was grateful for the interruption. Perhaps inside he could change the subject. Find out what she really wanted of him. He doubted it was the story of his father's suicide that she'd come for. He stood and picked up his drink. "Shall we?" he said, motioning toward the door.

Simone was irritated that the waiter had broken in on their conversation. For the first time in her life, she felt she was beginning to understand the real Nicholas Rutledge. And she wanted to know more. She wasn't hungry. Dinner was just an annoyance, a ritual that provided them an impersonal social setting for this meeting. But Nick offered her no choice but to accompany him into the dining room.

The enormous room glittered in ornate Georgian style, with heavy, intricately carved molding where the portrait-lined walls met the muraled ceiling. It had been Lord Egremont's ballroom, Nick told her as they were seated, and she could easily envision Lord Byron and Lady Caroline Lamb flirting and laughing in the golden light of the glimmering chandeliers.

At the far end, a small ensemble played classical and popular music, and a few guests had taken to the dance floor. The staff was formally dressed, exceedingly British. It was Simone's first brush with what she perceived must be England's famed "upper crust." Hadn't Nick himself just told her he was a lord or something?

She ordered the lightest thing on the menu, a ladies' filet mignon in burgundy sauce, wondering how she could consume a bite, thinking that perhaps this whole idea had been a mistake. The way Nick kept looking at her made her distinctly uncomfortable. It was the same expression she remembered from years ago, a mixture of admiration and desire. Perhaps she should have worn something more modest. But she was crazy for this dress. It had caught her eye in Harrod's, and she'd bought it on a whim, wondering if she would ever have a place to wear it.

"You said on the phone that you needed to talk to me." Nick's voice jarred her back into the moment.

"Yes. Yes, I do." She fiddled with her earring. She picked up her drink. "We toasted earlier to honesty, and that's what I hope we can maintain between us tonight."

He did not reply, just regarded her steadily. She must approach this carefully or she could blow the only chance she might have to accomplish her secondary mission, to learn if he, too, knew of the erotic perfume.

"Why did you leave the House of Rutledge?" she asked, truly wanting to know, but also hoping the answer would lead to the history of his ancestors in general, and maybe from there to John and Mary Rose. She could tell from the way his eyes narrowed that he wasn't expecting that question from her. Nor did he like it.

"Why do you ask?"

"It . . . it has to do with Antoine Dupuis," she improvised, not sure where that answer came from.

"What about him?"

"Do you trust him?"

"Only to serve his own interests. Why?"

"I . . . I don't know. He has been pleasant enough to me. He's given me total creative freedom with my work. But there's something about him—"

"He's a cold, calculating, self-absorbed, greedy little son of a bitch, if you want my honest opinion."

Simone couldn't help but laugh. "Is that all? I thought you might say something really bad about him."

"Why do you care what I think of him?"

"You worked with him for ten years. Even though he's been good to me so far, I've seen him be . . . ah, difficult, with others. I'm wondering how you managed to stay there so long."

Nick glowered and took a drink. "Birds of a feather, wouldn't you say?"

"I suppose I could think that," Simone said, "but for some reason, I don't."

He clearly disbelieved her. "I left," he responded at last, "because as I said, I was tired of living a lie, the lie that the House of Rutledge still belonged to me. It didn't. It hasn't since Dupuis 'loaned' me the money to salvage it from disaster ten years ago. He invested in the company, and I was part of the purchase," he added bitterly, "although I was too stupid to understand until last year I was nothing more than his lackey. I finally couldn't stand it anymore. I made a deal, if you can call it that, to turn over all my remaining interest in the House of Rutledge to him, in exchange for the Bombay perfumery and my freedom. I only completed," he concluded grimly, "what my father began. I lost the House of Rutledge."

Simone heard the immense pain behind his words and saw it on his face. "You made a business decision," she offered, but she sensed he saw it more as a personal defeat than a business decision. He had failed, just as his father had failed. Could preserving their family heritage be so important to these people that they would commit suicide if they failed? That they would steal so as not to fail? The man sitting across from her did not seem that spineless. She wondered suddenly if the Frenchman had been lying about his involvement in the theft of her father's formulas.

"Did Dupuis put you up to it?" she asked abruptly, unaware that her line of thought had drifted so far.

Nick frowned, perplexed. "What? The trade of the businesses?"

"No," Simone replied, dropping her gaze from his face to the pattern she traced on the snowy linen tablecloth with a long, highly polished scarlet fingernail. "Did he put you up to . . . what you did in Grasse."

She heard him let out a long, heavy sigh, and looking up

again into his eyes, she saw that he seemed suddenly older than his years. "Yes," he admitted at last. "It was Dupuis's idea, but I was stupid enough to go along with it. Look, Simone," he said, taking her hand. "I know it won't make up for what you lost, and it may seem lame after all this time, but . . . I'm . . . sorry." He squeezed her fingers tightly and nervously rubbed at the skin of her knuckles. "I'm truly sorry. I was so wrong. What I did was not about you, or your father. It was a crass, misguided last-ditch effort to salvage the House of Rutledge."

His words shocked and appalled her. So restoring his family heritage *had* been more important to Nick than ethics or morals. More important than her, or the love she had thought they shared. Simone's heart thundered, and her face burned. At last, she had an explanation, an apology even. But it only served to heighten her distress. How could he have so callously used her the way he did? After he'd said he loved her . . . after he had made love to her . . .

She withdrew her hand. "And now you've given it up after all." Her words came out cold, unforgiving in spite of his apology. But she wasn't about to forgive. Somehow the fact that in the long run he'd given up the House of Rutledge made his crimes against her and her family that much worse, the theft that much more futile.

A surge of new anger refocused her thoughts on the other reason she'd called Nick. The perfume oil. She must learn if he knew about it, for in it lay her chance for revenge. Could she get him to tell her about his precious ancestors? About Mary Rose?

"Giving up the House of Rutledge must have been difficult," she said, wishing she could conceal her scorn. "The firm has been in your family for a long time. Wasn't one of your ancestors the founder?"

He cocked his head and gave her a pained smile. "You really know how to pour salt into a wound, don't you?"

Simone winced at her own callousness and relented a little. "I'm sorry. I didn't mean to. I'm merely curious about your obsession with holding on to a losing proposition. Companies change hands all the time. I don't understand why it was so important to you that you would stoop to Dupuis's demands. Why didn't you just sell him the company outright, or close it down?''

Nick's face darkened. "I don't suppose you gave it a moment's thought when La Maison Lefèvre went out of business,'' he bit back acidly.

She glared at him, red-hot fury burning her cheeks while an icy grief encircled her heart. How dare he? But in that instant, a veil seemed to lift, and suddenly she understood. She understood because his grief was the same as hers. They'd lost the same things—a father, a family business, a heritage. But she wasn't about to let him off the hook just because she understood.

He, after all, had *caused* her losses.

"We had no choice,'' she returned with contempt. "I was too young to take over the business when Papa died. There was no other perfumer of my father's talent. Mama decided she'd rather close the perfumery than have it become second-rate, as we were both certain it would under another perfumer.''

Nick swirled the liquid in his glass, and his expression grew distant. "We all have choices,'' he said at last, seemingly impervious to her anger. "You chose to let the business die along with your father. Perhaps that was smarter than what I chose—indenture to the likes of Dupuis.''

"The House of Rutledge lives on,'' Simone pointed out, pain slicing through her. "La Maison Lefèvre does not.''

Nick stared across the expanse of white linen at the woman whose pain was obviously still raw, even after a decade. Why in the hell had she called him? She'd said she wanted to talk, but he was beginning to think it was to attack him. He decided to sidestep the bait he perceived in her last comment and fell silent, waiting to see where she'd take the debate next. She did have a point, however, one he'd never considered before. In a way, he had saved the House of Rutledge, even though he no longer owned it. The idea gave him some small measure of comfort.

Their dinner was served, and the waiter poured the wine Nick had selected. An awkward silence descended between them, broken only by an occasional trivial comment and the sound of knives and forks clanking against heavy china as they ate. Tension tied a knot in Nick's stomach, but he pretended that nothing, not her words, nor her presence, affected him out of the ordinary.

"I didn't think I was hungry," Simone said at last, finishing her meal, "but that was delicious."

"The chef here is French. The food is usually excellent."

"I noticed you ordered French wine as well," she said, a smile lighting up her face at last. "That was very thoughtful. It was excellent, although I probably should not have had wine on top of the gin."

Nick caught himself just in time before he let slip some comment about being spoiled to French wine after living in Grasse. "I'm glad you liked it."

Could nothing between them ever be normal?

Probably not, he decided. But sitting across from her, studying the haunting beauty of her face, his reactions were entirely normal. He wanted to touch her. He wanted to hold her in his arms. He wanted somehow, as in his dreams, to bridge the chasm that lay between them.

"Would you care to dance?" He saw the look of surprise in her eyes, followed by suspicion, and added quietly, "I promise I won't bite."

She studied him for a long moment, then gave him a nod. "I promise I won't either."

Nick led her to the dance floor, aware of the envious glances of the other men in the room. Her hand in his was cool, and she trembled slightly. As they began to dance, he held her at a distance. The ensemble played a classic waltz, and they danced together smoothly and easily, as if they'd been partners a long time and were accustomed to each other's moves. The music shifted into a more recent classic, and Nick recognized it was being played for Simone.

"Lady in Red."

Nick could not help himself. With a smile and a wink at the conductor, he pulled Simone against him. "I think this one's for you," he whispered.

He felt the resistance melt away from her body. The tune seemed to hum itself from somewhere deep inside him, and he closed his eyes, resting his chin alongside her head and recalling the words in his mind.

Surely this must be one of the dreams, he thought, except that he wasn't asleep. Simone was real. Warm and supple in his arms. His heart thundered, and he wished the music would never end. The scent of passion flower and ylang-ylang, wild, fresh, and floral, assailed his senses from the depths of the dark, rich curls crushed by his cheek.

Mixed with the perfume was another, more primal scent— the essence of the woman in his arms, a fragrance he had never forgotten.

He felt the skin of her bare back against the palm of his hand, and he had to fight to control his urge to explore its softness fully. Instead, he pressed her more closely against him and prayed that his overture would not ruin the moment. His other hand closed more tightly over hers.

A knot formed in his throat. Was there no way for him to restore the intimacy they had once shared? The passion between them he had so deplorably misused?

Dreaming. He was dreaming again.

The music ended, and he expected the magic of those moments to be lost as well, but to his utter surprise, Simone did not step away from him. Instead, she tilted her head upward, and when he looked into her eyes, he saw huge, unshed tears.

NINETEEN

꙳

"I think I'd better go now," she managed, blinking back the moisture that had sprung embarrassingly to her eyes. It had been a mistake to come here. And she'd made a *serious* mistake in dancing with Nick. She'd forgotten how his body felt moving next to hers. Her dress imposed almost nothing between them, and when he'd pressed her against him, her breasts remembered more than the feel of his chest against them, as it was now. They recalled the first time he had gazed upon them, upstairs in her room over the *parfumerie* in Grasse. How he had unbuttoned the front of her blouse, agonizingly slowly, one tiny pearl at a time.

Her heart remembered how it had fluttered when he'd reached inside and cupped her youthful fullness in his hands. It was fluttering so even now. And the way her chest rose and fell rapidly as she breathed in both apprehension and anticipation. Wanting him. Afraid of him.

Then.

As now.

"Don't go," he murmured, touching the hairline around one ear. Their locked gazes delivered between them an unspoken message that each clearly understood. A man and a woman, each wanting the other. Fiercely. Hungrily.

She looked away first. "This is wrong, Nick. We both know it," she said, then turned from him and retreated back to their table. She picked up her small handbag. "Please, can you call me a taxi?"

Nick took the bag from her and put it back on the table. "We can at least finish the wine." Even though he clearly wanted her to stay, his reply sounded maddeningly cool and collected. What was wrong with the man? she thought irritably. Was he made of stone? Couldn't he tell what he was doing to her?

But she suspected he knew exactly what he was about, and that he'd turned the tables on her. She must be careful what she said to him.

"I've had enough to drink tonight," she told him.

"Finishing the wine is just an excuse not to end the evening."

"I . . . I shouldn't have called you. I shouldn't have come here . . ."

He touched her chin and raised her head. "Then why did you?"

Simone searched his face for a sign of his earlier cynicism. It wasn't there. His eyes instead almost pleaded with her to assure him that she'd come to make peace. She wished her motivation could have been that guileless.

"Because I wanted to see you. To talk. I never thought to do the dinner thing. Certainly not to go dancing. The whole thing has . . . gotten out of hand."

As had her emotions.

"We haven't talked enough."

"No. We haven't. But I still think I should leave."

This time the hold his gaze had on hers refused to let go. He was silent for a long while, then he said, "Come home with me."

Simone's heart leapt and hammered several beats in her throat before settling in place again. "You must be mad," she whispered.

"Mad about you," he replied, his own voice barely audible. Then he took her hand. "Look, Simone, I know you may never be able to forgive what I did. But I'd hoped tonight I might have had a better chance to explain. Come to my house, just for a while. It's quiet there. Private. Perhaps we can say the rest of the . . . difficult things that likely need to be said. You can yell at me if you want and nobody will stare at us." He gave a short laugh. "You could kill me, and nobody would probably miss me for days."

Simone stared at him in amazement. Yes, she'd like to yell at him. And curse him, and demand some better answers of him. She probably would stop short of killing him, although more than once she'd wished him dead. But . . .

"It's a bad idea, Nick. Call me a taxi, please."

Outside, the night held on to the heat of July with a dark passion. It radiated from the pavement, penetrating the soles of her shoes and warming her entire body. That was the only explanation Simone would allow for the flush that stained her cheeks and raised tiny dewdrops on her bare arms. Nick was close, too close.

In every respect.

Would the damned cab never come?

At last the beetle-shaped vehicle lumbered into the circular drive. Nick paused before opening the door. "Are you certain you won't at least let me take you home?"

She allowed a smile onto her lips, easing her own tension. "To your home or mine?" she couldn't resist teasing. "Thanks, but I'll be better off on my own. And thank you for dinner, Nick."

His hand rested on the door handle, but still he did not open it. "Will I see you again?"

Simone wished with all her heart she could say yes. A very big part of her wanted to see him again, tonight and every night. But she knew her desire was only an illusion, a remnant of feelings from days long past reawakened by tonight's too-personal encounter. Too much had passed between them for that now, and being near him was dangerous. She did not trust her body not to betray her, and she did not trust him not to either.

And yet, as she climbed into the rear seat of the cab and heard the door slam solidly behind her, she heard an unspoken cry from the depths of her heart.

You're a fool, it said.

Go to him, it commanded. *You've wanted answers for ten years. He's willing to tell you everything. Now. Tonight. You may not have another chance.*

She gave her address to the driver, and the taxi lurched forward. As it rolled over the curved drive and through the tall gates, Simone turned and glanced through the rear window. Nick had not moved. His tall, broad figure was backlit by the powerful beams of the building's security lights.

Come to me.

Simone heard his voice as distinctly as if he were sitting beside her. As she had heard it in her dreams.

The cab turned right and entered the main thoroughfare. "Pull over," she said suddenly, behaving more impulsively than she ever had in her life. Her heart was racing, and her mind told her she was insane.

The driver shot her a funny look over his shoulder. "I beg pardon, mum?"

"Pull over, please. Don't go any farther. Just pull to the curb and wait here for a few minutes."

The taxi driver shook his head but did as she instructed. The headlights of several cars whizzed by them, and then a pair of beams, lower to the ground, exited the driveway from the club and turned in their direction. Simone pointed to the Triumph as it passed.

"Please, now, follow that car."

"Sounds like a line from a melodrama on the telly," the driver smirked, but he pulled into the stream of traffic again and kept within several car lengths of the classic sports car.

What the hell are you doing? her mind screamed at her.

Shut up, replied her heart.

She tried to listen to neither as the meter on the taxi kept ticking steadily higher. Simone hoped she'd brought along enough money to fund her madness. How far away did Nick live?

Sixteen pounds' worth, she saw as the Triumph at last turned into a driveway in an inner suburb of London. "Go on up a few houses, then pull over," she told the driver. "What street is this?"

"I believe it's Highcastle, ma'am."

Simone fumbled in her purse for a pen and paper, and when the motion of the cab stopped, she wrote the street name down, along with the driver's instructions on how to call a taxi to come for her later on. She paid him with a twenty-pound note and told him to keep the change. She had another in her purse that would suffice, she felt certain, to get her home.

Before she lost her nerve, Simone jerked the door open and stepped onto the sidewalk.

"Take care, ma'am," the driver said. "It's not good for a lady t' be alone at this hour of th' night, especially dressed like that, not even in this fancy neighborhood."

"Thank you." *Now go away,* she added silently. She wanted no witnesses to her scandalous behavior.

Keeping to the shadows, she retraced the distance to the driveway where Nick's car had disappeared behind a tall hedge, hoping wildly that it *was* Nick's car they'd followed. The Triumph was parked directly in front of the house, its metal crackling and popping as it cooled in the night air. Simone took a deep breath in relief. Yes, it was Nick's car.

She looked at the front door. Number nineteen. She closed her eyes. Dear God, what was she about to do? But she straightened her spine and hurried up the two steps, not giving herself a chance to change her mind.

Come to me! His words resounded in her ears. She hefted the heavy doorknocker in one hand and rapped with it sharply, sending a metallic tattoo into the summer night.

Nick had barely removed his coat and shoes when he heard a knock at the front door. Frowning, he looked at his watch. It was almost twelve-thirty in the morning. Who in blazes was calling on him at this hour? Just for good measure, he reached into his nightstand drawer and took his small revolver in hand before making his way down the stairs again.

"Who is it?" he called from behind the door when the rapping ceased its third set of staccato drummings.

At first he heard nothing, and then he couldn't believe what he did hear.

"Can we still talk?" came the unmistakable lilt of Simone's French accent.

Nick pocketed the gun and nearly ripped the door down. "What . . . how . . . what are you doing here?" He rushed onto the stoop and enclosed her in his embrace before he had time to think what he was doing. His lips were upon hers like lightning, consummating the fierce desire that had held him hostage throughout the evening. He wanted no explanation, needed no reason. All he knew was that the only woman he'd ever wanted, never thought he would have, was somehow, magically, in his arms right now.

By her own choice.

Nick lifted Simone and carried her into the front hallway, hooking the door closed behind him with his foot. His lips devoured hers, and hers returned his passion in kind. He felt her hands threading through his hair, drawing his head closer, insisting that he taste even more of her sweet, delectable, honeyed kisses.

He did not deny her request.

Her hands slid to the front of his shirt, where deft fingers began, incredibly, to pry the button there from its hole. Nick was on fire, but he knew it must only be a dream. He'd just placed the vial of the magical perfume on his bedside stand, thinking to indulge himself in an indigo rendezvous with Simone, in lieu of the real thing. Perhaps he had already fallen asleep, and this was nothing more than a lucid dream.

Simone unfastened the second button, and Nick ran his hands down her bare back, unzipping the short fastener at the edge of the dress, opening even more of her to his touch, peeling away the petals surrounding her exotic nectar.

But she began to peel first, edging his shirt over his shoulders and down his arms, where he hastily shrugged it off. Upstairs, he thought maniacally. They must go upstairs, where there was a proper bed for this sort of thing. If they didn't hurry, he was likely to ravish her right here on the floor in the hallway. She clung to him feverishly, however, so he led her in a dancelike maneuver to the first step. There, one level above him, she was suddenly taller than he, her breasts level with his lips.

Nick reached behind Simone's neck and found the clasp that held the halter-topped dress together. In an instant, it was open, and he slid the silken fabric erotically down her throat and across her breasts before letting it drop softly on the carpeted stairs. She stood stunningly naked before him in the dim light, her dark, sultry eyes molten with desire. She arched her back and brushed his lips with one passion-tight nipple. Nick groaned and tasted her divine gift.

Unable to stand the agony any longer, he placed his hands around her waist, lifted her easily, and carried her up the rest of the stairs. Behind him, he vaguely heard the thud of her shoe as it hit the floor.

His room was illuminated only by the low light of the bedside lamp, and when he placed her feet on the floor, he thought reality would set in and she might vanish into his imagination from whence she'd come.

But instead, a very real Simone reached for the buckle of his belt, released it and the zipper beneath it, and slid away the only barriers that remained between them.

The bed was directly behind her, and they fell together across the cloudlike softness of the comforter. There was no time for gentle love play. Nor desire for any. Urgency, hunger, and desperation drove them into one another like two broken souls mending into the one they once had been.

Union came, flaming hot and painfully exquisite. Intimate closeness surged them forward, thrusting them onto a great white wave, demanding that they crest it, or die.

They rode the wave, climbing, pulsing, crying, burning, calling out into the night before finally crashing into the sweet release of mutual completion.

Nick fell upon her, breath ragged, limbs weak, able to move only enough so that he would not crush her beneath his weight. He heard her gasps, rapid and raking as his own, and felt the tiny, tender tremors that continued to pulsate around him in the warmth of their union.

Unwilling to let her go, he rolled her to one side, and she curled a leg over him to prevent them from parting. She lay beside him, quiet now, eyes closed, her hand gently stroking the hair that curled between his pectorals. Nick slipped an arm beneath the curve of her neck and drew her protectively against him. He kissed her forehead, then her nose, then her lips that she turned toward him. He suckled them gently, with short, still-hungry kisses that even the strength of their climax had not sated.

He felt her move against him, and the motion of her hips, the sensation of being drawn even more deeply into her, banked the inner fires, causing them to burn hotter, if more slowly. Simone seemed unwilling to end their intimacy, although the fluid, sensual movements of her body told him she was desirous of a more languorous lovemaking.

Nick reached up and switched off the bedside lamp, as it was shining into their faces. His hand brushed against the vial of perfume and a wicked, delicious idea occurred to him.

He believed he must be already under the influence of the substance. This *had* to be a dream. There was no other rational explanation for what had just taken place.

What, he wondered, would happen if he used the perfume while already in a dream? Would it increase the erotic possibilities? He couldn't imagine how making love could get any better than what he'd just experienced, but . . .

Easing the stopper from the bottle, he placed a single drop on Simone's skin, just between her breasts.

He heard the sharp intake of her breath.

"Qu'est-ce que c'est?" she whispered. "What is that?"

Simone lay nearly insensate from pleasure, not believing she had found such total and complete satisfaction . . . in the arms of her worst enemy. She shouldn't have come. She ought to feel guilty. Yet her body thanked her for something it had been missing since she'd been Nick's lover long ago.

Oh, Christ, what was she thinking!

But before she could gather her senses or think further, she felt a drop of something cold and wet on the sentient skin between her breasts. She caught her breath sharply. "What is that?" she asked. And then a familiar scent, floral and heady, made its way to her nose.

The perfume!

Nick *did* have the perfume.

Simone was stunned at the knowledge and appalled at the way she had come to it. She'd wanted to know if he knew of it, and she'd used her body to find out. She was no better than Nick, her first thoughts reproached her.

But second thoughts intervened in her behalf. She hadn't come here for that, they tried to convince her.

However, Simone knew that wasn't totally the truth. She was guilty as charged . . . unless this was only a dream, like the rest. A bad dream, but one from which she would awaken into a safer reality.

Her thoughts tumbled about, but she lay torpid and unable to stir. As the power of the perfume stole over her, all cogent thoughts ceased, and she drifted away into the seductive pleasures awaiting within the indigo mist.

Nick waited for her there, and she was surprised to see he was in a marble palace, high on a hill, rather than in the undefined twilight of their usual trysting place. She willed herself to go to him, and when she reached his side, she saw that he stood beside a placid pool that dropped into a second and then farther on into a third, like stair steps. The sound of falling water was soothing and pleasurable.

Simone took Nick's outstretched hand and let him lead her to a nearby bench. Beside the bench, a marble table tendered a slender flute of scented oil, a large rosebud with full, lovely deep pink petals, and two feathers from the tail of a peacock, winking at her with seductive, iridescent eyes. The bench was covered in a soft white cloth, and Simone lay down upon it, luxuriating in anticipation of the pleasure she sensed was imminent. The sun was warm, and she closed her eyes and turned her face to its radiance.

She felt the sensual warmth of the oil as Nick poured a small amount onto the skin at the juncture of her breasts. Just beneath that spot, her heartbeat began to quicken as his hands, with a touch both light and compelling, began to massage the oil into her skin, spiraling seductively around the firm flesh of her breasts until he reached the nipples, which he stroked into hard knots of desire.

"Mmmmm." She felt more than heard the vibration of her voice, like the purr of a cat.

Finished to his satisfaction with that lovely part of her body, Nick moved his ministrations to the flat plane of her belly, where he toyed with her navel. He dropped a brief kiss into it, his tongue darting there like the silky strike of a serpent.

Flames of desire licked into her sex, flaring deeply inward.

Simone drew in her breath deeply, filling her entire being with the light and beauty of this place, and as she did, the exquisite sensual sensations he aroused in her lower body seemed to move upward, into her belly, her heart, spreading an incredible feeling of lightness and ecstacy throughout her upper body. She'd never before experienced anything like it, and she was filled with a joy beyond explanation.

She expected her lover to turn his attention next to the pleasure center of her, and she opened to him with a sensual craving. But she heard instead his low, tender laugh, and felt his touch move to the inside of her thighs, where he massaged the erotic pulse-points there until her skin tingled. Again she inhaled of the fragrant, fresh air, and again her senses reeled.

How long could this last? she wondered from some far corner of her mind.

But it did not end, and neither did Nick's sweet torture. He moved along her legs, anointing her feet with oil and kissing each of her toes. Then, he very slowly stroked the inside of her arches, one at a time, until they, too, responded in sexual arousal.

Her fingers were next, and when he had finished their loving massage, he placed them against his lips. Simone stroked his soft kiss with her fingertips, which delighted in the intimate contact. He completed his journey of arousal by feathering kisses abundantly over her face and throat, then returning to her breasts, where with stronger stokes than before, he raised her inner heat to an even higher degree.

Simone lay before him, completely open and vulnerable, but unafraid. This was a new experience, unlike what had tran-

spired between them, on earth or in the dream state. It had an almost spiritual quality about it.

She felt as if she wore the smile of a saint.

Inhaling, she caught the scent of rose, and she felt the velvet petals of the rosebud beneath her nose. The sweet sensation seemed to fill every cell of her body, until she thought she might be the rose.

And then the rose began to make love to her, as Nick's hands and lips had moments before. With deliberate slowness, Nick traced the ripening blossom around each of her breasts, lingering at each nipple, allowing the rose to suckle there, and to leave its sweetness in its wake. Like a magic wand, the rose moved over her body, summoning every inch of it to new heights of awareness. The curve of her waist, the roundness of her buttocks, the hollow beneath her arm . . . nothing was spared its lover's touch. Her breath became rapid, and her desire for Nick, and completion, surged through her with each intake, intensifying the agony.

But still he had not completed his sojourn over the geography of her body. Her eyes remained closed, but she imagined the brilliant blue-green eyes at the tips of the peacock's plumes. She felt surrounded by a golden glow and tingled at the touch of the feathery light air that stirred across that erotic aura as Nick perpetrated his next delight upon her.

He made love to her with the feathers, beginning this time at her sex, where first he fanned the heat of that tender furnace, then fed the fire with the implement's gossamer touch. When Simone breathed in the sensual pleasure, he followed the intake of her breath with the feathers from the mound of her pubis, over the gentle slope of her belly, across her navel, between her breasts, up her throat and neck, past her lips, her forehead, and beyond. She felt the touch, like angels' wings, bringing the fire energy of her human sexual desire upward, into a higher plane, sending her, it seemed, into a more sacred space.

"Nicholas," she cried out, wanting her lover to share this space.

"I'm here."

TWENTY

Nick didn't know where the temple had come from, or the pools of warm, scented water. Or the oil, the rose, the feathers. Nor did he have any idea how he had known to proceed in such a manner to so erotically play the instrument of Simone's body. It was as if he'd heard a voice, either from deep within, or else from somewhere out in the blue, guiding his actions. His body, now a fiery host to sensations that threatened to overwhelm him, had guided him as well. What he'd done to arouse her had aroused him in turn, as if her body were a reflection of his own. As if they were one body, in two pieces.

He wanted them to become one, for all eternity. He'd known it since the first day he'd laid eyes upon her. She was the other half of him, and if all could be right in heaven, she would be with him forever. Emotions both tender and frightening washed over him, tightening his throat with the love he felt toward her as she lay before him, a feast for his eyes . . . and his body.

Hearing her call out his name filled him with unnamable joy. He laid the feathers aside on the table and knelt next to the bench, taking her hand in his again, feeling their fingers become entwined as their souls moved toward union. "I'm here," he whispered.

She drew him to her, and he eased himself onto the edge of the bench. He bent and placed his lips on hers, gently, *tenderly, tasting the essence of the rose commingled with the nectar of her own sweetness. Her lips parted in tender invitation, like a morning glory opening to the courtship of the bumblebee.*

He parted that other honeyed doorway with loving fingers and entered her with all the strength of his man's body, but gently, reverently, closing his eyes in ecstacy as he felt their separation come to an end. His breath moved slowly within him, flowing from his nose down into his heart, swirling there to calm its rapid beating, then moving still lower to bless their union with its subtle energy.

Time stopped.

The universe stood still.

There was only One.

Completion began with a ripple of bliss instead of a wave crashing around them. Their bodies moved as one, in the glow of the pure essence of the love that surrounded them, that filled them, that became them. They were one, in body, mind, and spirit, moving in a symphony of ecstacy and delight, spiraling ever higher and higher, until a final crescendo brought them to a fulfillment experienced by few.

The lovers slept entwined upon the gentle winds of the cosmos. When at last he awoke, however, Nick thought perhaps he had died, for he awoke to nowhere, surrounded only by the indigo twilight of the scent-drenched dream. It had been a beautiful death, he decided. Holy somehow.

But the woman remained in his arms, her flesh warm, her breathing deep and even. She had not died, and he knew neither had he. But he thought it likely they were in heaven. She stirred and caressed his chest with a sleepy nuzzle.

"Simone?" he whispered, wanting to verify that it was indeed she who had become his sacred lover.

"My darling Nicholas," she replied. "We must never leave this place."

Nick saw no reason to leave it. Nor any way, at the moment. "We shall remain here for all eternity, together, as we have always been, before . . ."

A troubling thought knocked at his consciousness, but he

refused the summons. No! They would not go back there. Here they were together as they were meant to be. There, all things stood between them.

He gathered her more closely in his arms. "We will never leave here," he assured her, whispering into the fragrance of her dark hair. "Never."

Simone awoke just before dawn. She lay naked, sprawled openly across Nick's own unclothed body, with no sheet or blanket covering their dishabille. Her skin was cool, clammy almost, as if it had recently shed a fever. It took several moments for her to assimilate what she had done, and when she did, she was filled with horror and despair.

Mon Dieu! *Oh, my God! I didn't . . .*

Her whole body began to tremble. She rolled away from Nick, pulling herself into a tight ball and covering her nakedness as best she could with her arms and hands. Her throat contracted painfully, and she began to cry.

How could I have done this?

She could not blame Nick for what had happened. It had been all of her own doing. Everything. From the phone call demanding that they talk to the shameless red dress, from the impulsive decision to follow the Triumph in the taxi to allowing Nick to carry her to this bed. Why? Why was she so driven to such senseless, self-destructive behavior? Had she no pride? Was the revenge she'd sworn to take for his betrayal nothing but lip service? She choked back her tears and her shame and slipped noiselessly out of bed. She must not awaken Nick. She could not bear to face him after this.

Ever.

Her cheeks flamed, recalling their earlier frenzy, how they'd stripped off their clothing as if it, and they, were on fire, and engaged in the most wanton sexual behavior.

Oh, God, she groaned again inwardly. On the floor by the bed, she found one high-heeled slipper. But that was the only sign of her clothing she could discern in the bedroom's pre-dawn darkness. Catching a glimpse of a small object on the floor next to the shoe, Simone reached for the shadowy form, and her heart nearly jumped into her throat when she realized she held the vial from which Nick had pressed a drop of perfume between her breasts.

And not just *any* perfume.

The perfume!

A drop of which had taken them beyond the realm even of the indigo mist and into another, more altered state, almost like another dimension.

Even in her misery, Simone shivered at the memory of the exquisite lovemaking they had shared ... where? ... somewhere among the cosmic clouds. In it, they had experienced a sexual ecstacy unlike anything she'd ever known possible, a complete, soul-embracing union that transcended the earlier, earthly rites they had engaged in upon this bed.

In the low light, she surveyed Nick's sleeping form. Stretched over the full length of the bed, he slept peacefully, beautiful in his nakedness. His dark brown hair tousled rogu-ishly over his broad forehead, and his lips were slightly parted. Although he was completely relaxed, there was no mistaking the strength of his masculine body. He looked like a sleeping god, and Simone recalled that he had made love like a god.

Oddly, recalling that near-divine experience, her initial sense of shame and despair vanished, replaced by a surge of intense love that immersed her in a deep peace and content-ment. More tears urged themselves upon her, but this time, they were tears engendered by an unspeakable joy that stirred her heart once again. That lovemaking had been not of this earth. It had belonged in the celestial realms, she decided, and she remembered that she had not wanted to leave there.

Simone forced her eyes away from Nick and stared at the the vial of perfume she held in the palm of her hand. It was more powerful than she had ever imagined. She felt its danger as well ... Even though she'd thought in the dream that she did not want to leave that enchanted scene, what if she and Nick had been *unable* to return to reality?

John and Mary Rose.

The names shot through her consciousness like two well-trimmed arrows.

Is that what had happened to them? Had they used the perfume to meet in dreams, and somehow been caught in that otherworld, unable to return?

The whole idea was both scary and absurd. No substance on earth had that kind of power. At least Simone didn't think so. But she knew nothing about the plant from which the perfume oil had been extracted.

The perfume must never get into the wrong hands . . .

Esther's warning rang in her ears as well, and a shiver of fear crept over her. Could the perfume really be dangerous? Could it be used to manipulate a person against her will? She shuddered again in the darkness, clutched the perfume vial, and tiptoed quickly out of the room and down the stairs, gathering her scattered clothing and her other shoe as she went. She had to get out of here.

She flicked on a light in a room toward the back of the house and found the telephone. Retrieving the number for the taxi from her purse, she dialed it with urgency. Then she slipped into the red dress and fastened it securely around her neck. At least it wasn't the type of fabric that wrinkled easily, but she could guess at the taxi driver's thoughts when he picked up a woman dressed as she was at this hour of the morning.

Simone didn't care what the driver thought. She just wanted to make her escape from Nick's house before he awoke. She was about to turn the light off again when her eye lit upon a small, mold-encrusted volume that lay on a nearby sideboard. Its very state of decay caught her attention. She picked it up, and her heart almost stopped beating when she read the handwriting on the inside front page: *Charms and Spells of Mary Rose Hatcher.*

Mary Rose's Book of Shadows!

So Nick *had* found it, probably in that niche in the wall. Without giving herself time to think or change her mind, Simone tucked the book into her purse next to the vial of perfume, turned off the light, and made her way on bare feet down the hallway to the front door. Her heart slammed in her chest; her pulse roared in her ears, loud enough to wake the sleeping man upstairs, she was certain. With trembling hands, she managed to maneuver the mechanism of the lock and let herself out. She heard it click behind her. *Please let the car come now!* she prayed silently to the gods of the early-morning taxis. Apparently they were listening, because a horn sounded in the street, beyond the row of hedges that separated the busy avenue from the small parking area in front of the town house, and Simone streaked toward her means of escape.

She clambered into the vehicle, slammed the door, and breathless, gave the driver the address of the corporate apartment. Only then did she realize she'd dropped one of her shoes. Too bad. They'd been expensive. But nothing could make her go back after it now.

Nick sat up abruptly, startled awake by the sound of an insistent automobile horn on the street outside. Damned inconsiderate jerk, making such a racket at this hour, he thought, then realized that the other half of his bed was now empty.

Simone. Oh, damn it all. She must have called a taxi. Groggy from the deep sleep he'd been in for hours, Nick swung his feet over the side of the bed and wiped his face with his hands. *If* she'd even been here, he reflected, suspecting he'd dreamt her into his arms. He reached for the pillow where her head would have lain, if she'd been here. He held it to his nose, and her presence returned instantly with her scent. As did the memory of the lushness of her body, the fierce sensuality of their lovemaking. The scent of her was still on his own skin. No, it had not been a dream.

Shuffling on bare feet into the bathroom, Nick marveled that she had come after him. He did not understand her. One minute she seemed to hate him. The next she seemed eager to be with him. He wasn't surprised she had fled. Her ambivalence was understandable. What surprised him was that she had come at all.

He turned on the shower and stood beneath the jets of hot water as his consciousness gained clarity. With clarity came the awareness that he had deliberately experimented on her with the perfume. He shouldn't have done that. She was still, technically, the enemy.

But he was curious as to what she'd experienced after he'd introduced the perfume into their lovemaking. To learn that, and for a hundred other reasons, Nick wished Simone had stayed for pillow talk this morning. Had she found herself in the magnificent white temple? Or did her version of the perfume-induced dream take her to some other place, created in her own imagination, different from his?

Nick had no clue how the perfume trance operated, whether he and Simone went together into the altered reality, or if they experienced separate realities. He knew only that in previous dreams he'd experienced erotic, incredible sex, but when he'd added the perfume to their already sexually intense state last night, the effect had been phenomenal. Pure emotional and physical ecstasy. There was no other way to describe it.

Nirvana.

Had it been good for her too? He laughed wryly at the trite question and stepped out of the shower.

But he really wanted to know. Perhaps he would give her a call later on.

Nick dressed for work and went down the stairs, grinning and gathering up the puddles of his own clothing lying about. He couldn't seem to dampen the euphoria that encompassed him at the thought of Simone's nocturnal visit, and he allowed a tiny candle of hope to light in his heart that perhaps she could, after all, forgive him. That there might be a second chance for them.

Sunlight crept over the windowsill, and soon the smell of freshly brewed coffee permeated the small kitchen. Nick retrieved the morning *Times* from the front step and, for the first time in years, smiled into the upcoming day. Something red caught his eye from the driveway, and he crossed the pebbles to see what it was.

A shoe?

It was Simone's shoe. One of the dainty slippers she'd worn the night before, proof positive that she had indeed been there.

Nick knelt and picked it up, feeling very much like Prince Charming.

Now, if Cinderella would only agree to the rest of the fairy tale.

Paper tucked under his arm, shoe dangling from one finger, Nick reentered his house, whistling to himself. He put the shoe on the kitchen counter, poured himself a mug of coffee, and went into the study to skim the newspaper before leaving for work.

It was then he noticed the book was missing.

It was then it all began to make sense.

It was then his world fell apart . . . one more time.

Of course. How stupid of him to believe she might be willing to forgive him and want to mend the decade-old rift between them. Her call to him had had nothing to do with wanting to talk about that. If she indeed had wanted to talk, he suspected she wanted *him* to talk, about his new business, and what perfume he might be working on as his launch. He could still see those huge dark eyes, listening to him in pretended feminine awe last night, and recalled how she'd tried more than once to direct their conversation to his family, his past. What was she trying to get at? He had no answer for that, but Nick was without a doubt that she'd come as a spy, likely at the urging of Antoine Dupuis.

And he'd played right into her hands. He'd fallen for her charms, welcomed her seduction. Good God, he'd even used the perfume on her!

The perfume.

Nick raced upstairs, but discovered exactly what he'd feared. The vial was gone too. He searched the floor and the bedclothes, but he knew that the sample he'd decanted from the original into another vial for "home use" was now speeding away from him in a London taxicab, along with the witch's diary.

Her ploy was so obvious he wanted to groan out loud at his gullibility. Lady in red. Indeed. Her retribution was so perfect, he gave a short, bitter laugh into the silence of his existence. She'd used him. Just as he had used her ten years before.

Very well, he thought, returning to the study, shaking from rage and humiliation, they were even now. From now on, it was a race to the finish.

And he held one ace in the hole. He not only knew about the *mahja,* he had the pressed flower safely tucked away in his bank vault, along with the botanist's report and the remainder of the perfume. Unless she was more successful than he at discovering its modern-day identity from the name alone inscribed in Mary Rose's book, *and* found the plant, she could never make the perfume.

But, he reminded himself, unless the exotic trumpet-shaped blossom gave up its secret to him, neither could he.

TWENTY-ONE

Shame and elation vied for Simone's conscience as she dashed into her apartment and slammed the door behind her, breathless. She'd skimmed through the ancient little book on the taxi ride home, and she now knew the name of the plant Mary Rose had used to create the perfume oil. She was not familiar with it, not under the name that was inscribed in the diary, *mahja*. But at last she had something to go on.

She was sorry she'd had to steal the book to learn about the *mahja* plant. In spite of Dupuis's nasty little suggestion, theft had not been her motivation for impulsively following Nick home. At the moment, she did not want to consider *why* she had gone to Nick's house, but she knew it had not been to purloin Mary Rose's Book of Shadows. She hadn't even been sure Nick had it.

But once she'd discovered it, she was unable to forgo the opportunity. She assuaged her guilt somewhat by reminding herself that she'd only reciprocated what he had done to her long ago. It didn't make it right, but it might mean they were even.

Simone felt in her purse for the vial of perfume, glad to have a sample of it back in her personal possession. Antoine Dupuis had jealously guarded her own small amount of the solution at work, allowing her access to it only in the perfume lab. At least he'd had the good grace to return the folder to her containing Mr. Shahmir's incomplete formula.

Taking the vial closer to the window, she cradled it in her

hand, staring at it for a long while, remembering vividly exactly what had happened to her after Nick had dabbed a single drop between . . .

Her skin tingled at the memory, and she raised her hand to release the fastener at the back of the red dress. The fabric fell away, exposing the pout of her breasts. How could a drop of perfume, placed there, have led her to that unbelievably sensual experience?

Magic. It had to be magic. There was nothing else in this world to explain it.

Gathering her wits with some effort, Simone glanced at the clock on the wall. She was supposed to be at work in little more than an hour, but she was not at all inclined to report in and sit in frustration all day at her console. She would accomplish much more here. She called in sick, then headed for the shower.

The essence of the perfume, mingled with the scent of love-making, assailed her sensitive nose as the steaming water washed from her body the residue of last night's madness. She felt a surprising sense of loss. It was as if she were washing away all hope of ever making love to Nicholas again.

Idiot! She stepped from the shower and jerked a towel from the bar. Of course she would never make love to Nick again. She shouldn't have last night. Whatever possessed her . . . ? She shook her hair and wrapped another towel around it in a tight turban. Possessed. That could be it. She could be possessed by the perfume.

No. If she were possessed by anything, it was Nicholas Rutledge. He'd possessed her from the moment he'd knocked at her door that long-ago summer morning in Grasse. Damn it all. She had to quit *wanting* him. To quit wanting to go back to that time, to those hopes and dreams in the heart of a very young, and very stupid, girl.

Simone slipped into cool, comfortable shorts and a loose T-shirt. The apartment was equipped with an ancient air conditioner, but it smelled funky when it spewed semicool air into the room, and she preferred to open the windows. Suddenly ravenous, she poured herself a tall glass of orange juice and dug into a bag of cookies she'd stashed in the fridge, then settled into the serious investigation of Mary Rose's diary.

Taking the book out of her purse, she smoothed the cover lovingly with her fingers and blew the dust and mold of well over a century into the air. She turned back the gray, brittle cover and read again Mary's Rose's curious inscription: *"The Charms and Spells of Mary Rose Hatcher."*

Simone's heart beat hard, both in anticipation, and in reverence for this artifact.

The pages were carefully laid out and printed in calligraphy-style penmanship. Many were graced with ornamental embellishments or illustrations. There were recipes for herbal tonics, soaps, rose and lilac waters, potpourri, candles, poultices, tinctures, and other more mysterious and complex concoctions for the cure of ailments such as "women's flow" and "fainting." Accompanying many of the entries were little rhymes, poems that invoked blessings upon the substances. Charms, Simone thought wistfully, enchanted by the sweetness of the sayings. She recalled the couplets Esther had chanted over the ashes she'd buried with one of Shahmir's seeds. Too bad the charms were only that, sweet little sayings, and had no real power.

Still, the entries filled her with hope. Obviously, Mary Rose, the "witch," had been a healer. Simone recalled Esther's claim that their "craft" was of the whitest kind, and she could see clearly from the notations in this diary, it was true. She smiled. A perfume created by a healer could only be of the whitest kind as well.

She turned the pages until she reached the inscription toward the end she had glanced at in the taxi. A lump formed in her throat as she read:

> There is no greater malady in this world than a broken heart. Until now, I have lived without hope of discovering a cure for my own heart's misery caused by the cruel and extended separation from my beloved John, who is the very essence of my soul. As I begin this procedure, I pray to obtain not only a sweet per-

*fume oil, but a sublime one as well, which will allow
us to transcend all that keeps us apart here on Earth.
Herewith are the instructions for extracting the essence
of the* mahja *plants grown from seeds sent by my beloved from the distant land where he now lives. The very
essence of my desire is that the union of his seeds and
my soil will produce for us a "natural child," a potion
that will have the power to unite us in love for all time.*

Simone felt the sting of tears and batted at them with her
lashes. That poor, poor woman. Separated from her beloved
John, the "very essence of her heart and soul," not only temporarily by distance, but forever by societal restraints. Simone
tried to imagine her pain and found that she could relate. No
wonder Mary Rose had nurtured the illusion that a perfume
oil could transcend their hopeless predicament.

She drew in a long breath and thought of Nick. Now *there*
was a hopeless predicament. Simone questioned whether
she'd ever loved Nick with the same fierce passion that Mary
Rose had loved John, but in her heart, she knew that she had.

Suspected that she still might.

A tear fell as she recalled how she, too, had been suddenly
and brutally separated from the man whom she'd thought to
be the essence of her heart and soul. But, she reminded herself
harshly, unlike the way it was for John and Mary Rose, Simone's pain was wrought by her own lover.

And she doubted that any perfume oil could ever transcend
the events of that terrible day.

The recipe in the Book of Shadows was an outline of the process Mary Rose had used to capture the essence of the so-called
mahja flowers, whatever they were. Simone immediately
recognized the procedure as *enfleurage*. Even though a person
like Mary Rose might have had access to crude distillation
equipment, it made sense that she would have used the earlier,
time-honored perfuming method. Simone had herself played
around with *enfleurage*, just to experience how the early perfume had captured scent from the flowers of the fields.

*   *   *

*Prepare a glass plate with a thin covering of suet.
Cut fresh flowers and lay them in the fat. Remove wilted
flowers daily and replace with fresh blooms until harvest is complete and pomade is redolent with the fragrance. Extract with alcohol to render pure perfume oil.*

A simple, traditional Victorian recipe. Easy to dupicate, except for one thing. The *mahja.*

What the hell was a *mahja* plant?

She dug in her purse for the scrap of paper upon which
she'd written Esther's telephone number. "Esther?" she said
into the phone moments later. "This is Simone."

"Simone, my dear. Are you well? Is everything all right?"

"I'm fine, I'm fine. Listen. Have you ever heard of a plant
called the *mahja*? Or something that sounds like that?"

"I don't think so," Esther replied. "Why?"

"Because that's the name of the flower that Mary Rose
used in her perfume oil. I'm certain it must have another name
that's familiar in our vernacular. *Mahja* must have been what
John Rutledge called it when he sent her the seeds."

"What on earth are you talking about, child?"

Oops. Simone forgot that Esther didn't know the full story,
the tale that she herself had only just read in the witch's diary.
How was Simone going to explain to her friend that she'd
obtained Mary Rose's Book of Shadows? Or rather, *how*
she'd obtained it. "Never mind," she said, going on hurriedly. "Speaking of seeds, have any of those we planted
sprouted yet?"

"I was thinking I should call you about them," Esther said,
her words revealing an evident curiosity. "They're th' fastest
growers I have ever seen, especially th' one that received th'
charm."

"Really? Are there blossoms yet?"

"No, no. Nothing that spectacular. But I do think we'll be
seeing buds shortly, and I wouldn't be surprised if it doesn't
bloom by early August."

"Great. Well, I had better ring off now," Simone said, anxious to avoid giving Esther any opening to question her further. She would explain it all when she'd had time to sort it out herself. But she couldn't resist one last reminder. "If you remember any flower by that name, *mahja,* or something similar, give me a call. Bye."

Her next call was to the horticultural experts at Kew Gardens, seeking an answer to the same question.

"It's very strange that you should call," said the polite and very British voice on the line. "We had another inquiry about that same plant just last week. A man brought in a pressed flower he said was called a *mahja.*"

Simone's eyes widened, and she felt her pulse pick up a beat. "You wouldn't happen to recall his name, would you?"

"Let's see. I have it here in my appointment book. Yes. Rutledge. Nicholas Rutledge. Do you know him?"

"Yes, I do, but we're mere acquaintances. How interesting, and coincidental," she said, forcing her voice to remain calm even though she was about to explode. Where had Nick obtained a specimen of the *mahja*? "Did you discern the plant's contemporary identity? Does it have a modern name I might recognize?"

"Actually, no," the botanist replied. "He left the specimen with me to examine the pollen, and my tests indicated that it is likely in the same family as the datura, and its cousin, brugmansia, although it is a species not known at this time."

Simone had to struggle for her breath. Surely his identification was mistaken. Those plants were like poison. "When you say the species is 'not know at this time,' what exactly do you mean?"

"That it is either now extinct or grows so sparsely that it is virtually nonexistent."

"But how can that be? If he had a specimen, surely he must know where the plant grows."

"It was a dried specimen, a flower that had been pressed between the pages of a book a long time ago."

"Oh." Simone considered that for a moment, then asked, "Are you certain that it is in the same family as the datura?"

This was not good news. Although she had not studied hallucinogenic plants extensively at the university, she was well aware that both the datura and the brugmansia were highly hallucinogenic. That they could be toxic even.

"Yes, fairly certain. I, uh, took the liberty of photocopying the specimen before returning it to him. It is here in my files, if you'd like to see what it looks like."

"Yes, I'd appreciate that." Simone thanked the man very much and asked for directions to his office. Then she rang off and picked up the Book of Shadows. At the very back of the bound volume she came across several pages where pressed flowers lay in their papery graves. One page was bereft of its bloom, but Simone knew it was where Nick had come up with his specimen, because at the bottom of the page was written the word *Mahja*.

An hour later, Simone sat in the office of Dr. Thomas Wheatley, staring at the photocopied image of the blossom. It was a graceful, trumpet-shaped flower attached to a stem and adjacent to a small leaf. The botanist brought out a large volume in which he located color photos of both the datura and brugmansia.

"As you can see, even though it is smaller, the flower and leaves of this so-called *mahja* plant are very similar in structure and design to these other two," he pointed out.

"Yes, I see," Simone replied, stunned at this turn of events. It had never occurred to her that the perfume oil might have come from an hallucinogenic plant. "Do you think the *mahja* might have had the same, uh, mind-altering qualities as these?"

"I think it very likely."

Simone sighed. "Could I . . . would it be possible for me to have a copy of this?" she requested, indicating the photocopy of the flower.

"I see no reason why not." Dr. Wheatley left the office for a moment to comply with Simone's request, and she stood staring at the red and yellow trumpet-shaped blossom of a brugmansia in the botanical encyclopedia.

So Nick had an actual specimen of the *mahja*. Would he somehow be able to use it to synthesize the perfume? Knowing it was possibly hallucinogenic in nature, would he dare?

Simone gave a cynical laugh. Of course he would dare. As she well knew, when he was determined to get ahead in life, Nicholas Rutledge was most capable of bypassing ethics and scruples. He would push the envelope, make the perfume, and take his chances that it would not end up on someone's list of illegal substances.

Simone had wanted to develop the perfume as a way to wreak her revenge on Nick, but now, she was no longer sure she was willing to take the risk she believed was involved. If he was successful in making the perfume, it was likely he would be caught in his own greed when the drug-enforcement agencies found out its source and recalled the product from retail shelves. It would mean his financial ruin, and that, she supposed, was revenge enough.

Despite her disappointment at this unexpected turn of events, she thanked the botanist sincerely and returned to the heart of London on the underground, stepping to streetside just in time to inhale a whiff of gray-purple exhaust that belched from a passing bus. God, how she hated living in the city. The smells were dreadful. Simone sighed. After the discovery of the nature of the *mahja* plant, she wondered if there was any reason for her to remain in London.

She had now reached a dead end with the *grand parfum* she'd hoped to create from Mary Rose's perfume. She hated working for Antoine Dupuis. And she found the Nick-look-alike Rutledge family portraits that peered at her from every wall of her workplace depressing.

Stepping absentmindedly off a curb, Simone was almost sideswiped by a speeding taxi that missed her but enveloped her in a swirl of hot, dirty air. She coughed and returned to the safety of the sidewalk, down which she wandered aimlessly until she came to a large park, with a fountain and a statue of a man on horseback. Around her, pigeons clucked and cooed. Homeless people slept on the concrete benches. Tourists snapped shots of the bronze rider.

Suddenly exhausted, she sank onto an empty park bench, clenching her jaw and fighting the raw sadness that strained at the back of her throat. It didn't make sense for her to be so downcast. Other than her dislike of Dupuis, she really did have a great job that afforded her the opportunity to create the kind of perfumes she'd dreamed of, as well as big money to back her work.

Even so, Simone felt more dispirited than she could ever remember. She was lonely, miserable, unsuccessful so far in her profession. She had no home here, no friends or family, nothing at all in this city except a one-time lover with a penchant for betrayal. Her only happiness seemed to be in the perfume-drenched dreams where she could be with that lover while in reality she could not. Maybe, she thought with a heavy sigh, she ought to turn in her resignation at the House of Rutledge and take the first flight back to New Orleans.

But she hadn't been particularly happy in New Orleans either. Where would she be happy? She wondered morosely.

Her stomach growled, bringing her back to the moment. Maybe if she ate something, she would feel better. Spotting a pub across the street, she made her way safely through the rush of traffic, but just before she got to the doorway, a poster in a nearby storefront window caught her eye.

"Come Home to Provence," read the attractive, four-color poster in the window of a travel agency. It depicted a couple dining in cozy luxury in a quaint inn, their plates filled with the bounty of the area's renowned produce, their glasses glowing with the rich red of the wine they held.

Come home to Provence. The image on the travel poster transported her instantly away from city streets and smelly fumes and into the lavender fields surrounding *her* home in Provence. In Grasse. The last place she could remember being truly happy. What if she went back to that home? Would it be the same? Or would all the ghosts of that horrible time come screaming back at her?

She turned away from the window, then walked past the entrance to the pub, her appetite gone.

Home. Where was her home? Did she have one?

Only in her dreams.

TWENTY-TWO

༜

Two weeks had passed since his regrettable encounter with Simone, and they had been among the most futile and frustrating of Nick's life. Determined to create and market the perfume ahead of Simone, he had spent every waking hour at the computer equipment that was now efficiently installed in the lab of Bombay Fragrances, Ltd., using every skill he had to try to chemically re-create the scent of the *mahja*.

Using the last of the perfume available to him, since Simone had stolen the rest, he'd obtained a molecular "picture" of it using the gas chromatograph and mass spectrometer he'd finally purchased, although the expense was enormous and took a large bite out of his funding. Then, using a solvent, he had made a faintly fragrant solution from the pollen remaining inside the pressed flower. With his heart in his throat, he'd asked the sophisticated equipment to compare the chemistry of the two.

It was close, but not close enough. The scent created by the pollen mix was like a mere shadow of the real thing.

Then he'd tried another tack, reconstructing the perfume's chemistry using synthetic products, although he knew that re-constitution of a natural oil is never as good as the true oil. Even so, he'd been pleased with the delightful variations on the theme of the fragrance that resulted from his efforts. Any one of them would make for a very respectable entrée into the world market.

But none of them was quite the same as that made by Mary Rose Hatcher.

And none of them turned him on.

None held the magic of Mary Rose's original perfume.

Nick groaned and rolled his stool away from the desk. His back ached, and his throat felt like sandpaper. What time was it? What day was it? Why did he give a damn anyway?

Life had taken a bleak turn for Nick the morning he'd discovered Simone's treachery. After his initial shock and anger had subsided, a black depression had settled over him, worse than any he'd ever experienced, even in his darkest moments. Her seduction and subsequent theft had indeed been poetic justice, a deadly accurate retribution that had brought back to him his sins from the past, and his bitter regret. His night with Simone had given him a taste of what life could have been like with her, what they could have shared. If he hadn't thrown it all away. And for what? His pride? Fear? Money?

He could think of nothing important enough for him to have carried through with Dupuis's plot to steal Jean René's formulas. Nothing dire enough that he should ever have betrayed Simone's love.

Of all the losses of his life, and they were legion, Nick realized now that losing Simone had been the most monstrous. And the most unnecessary. Having held her in his arms and made love to her once again, he wanted with all his soul to find a way back to her. Knowing she was now forever beyond his reach filled him with despair, and for once, he had come close to understanding how his father could have taken his own life.

For two weeks, Nick had had to force himself to go on. He'd moved, zombielike, from one task to another, his heart no longer truly passionate about such things as restoring his family's good name, or becoming the leading perfumer in Britain.

They simply no longer seemed to matter.

He would give up everything for one chance to reclaim Simone's heart.

His nights had been tormented as well, for like a fool, he

had indulged in applying a drop of perfume to his skin, hoping to induce the dreams in which he could have what was denied him in his waking hours. Simone. But in his dreams, even though she continued to call to him like a siren, inviting him into the temple of pleasure, he found he could not go there. He wanted her with a passion that seared his soul, but some deep inner restraint forbade him to join her. In some of the dreams, the conflict was so severe, he'd felt as if he were being torn in half, and he'd awakened in a cold sweat.

He was fairly certain that any psychologist would tell him it was his guilt that held him back, that his subconscious was telling him he did not deserve Simone, even in his dreams.

But in the most recent dream, the one he'd had last night, when his body had grown hard with desire and his heart cried out for Simone, he'd experienced a different kind of proscription. It had come in the form of a voice, a man's voice, admonishing him to give up the dream visits.

"As if I had a choice," he'd snarled back to the disembodied speaker. The voice seemed somehow familiar. Where had he heard it before? Was it merely an echo of his own?

"But you do," it replied, with a gentleness and understanding that defused his ire. "You use the perfume to come here because you think it is the only way to be with her."

"It is the only way."

"No, my son. This is not the way. There is great danger in what you, and she, are doing."

"She?"

"Your lady love visits her dreams too often as well," the voice continued, and Nick suddenly recognized it. It had been the whisper in his ear the night he'd been with Simone, the voice that had told him those surprising secrets, directed him as to how to pleasure her and bring them both to new heights of ecstacy.

"But it was you who—"

"Yes. There is no harm in learning the secrets of the ancients and discovering the sacred holiness of the joining of man and woman. Such secrets will strengthen the ties between you and your beloved. But such secrets were meant to be enjoyed on the earth. There is great harm in seeking them only in this dreamscape, for there is grave danger of becoming lost here. You must go, and not return. You must prevent your lover from entering this realm again as well. For there is a doorway that will close eventually, and you will be imprisoned here, unable to return.''

Nick heard his secretary open the door to his office, and he snapped out of his reverie, realizing he'd just relived the bizarre dialogue, verbatim, in a daydream.

"Tea?" Brenda said, placing on the desk a tray with a covered teapot, a cup and saucer, and a few biscuits. "Are you feeling all right, sir?"

Nick looked up into the face of concern. Brenda was older than he, and sometimes she acted like an overprotective big sister. He appreciated her thoughtfulness, though. "I'm fine, really," he assured her, knowing that he was anything but fine.

Probably he would never be fine again.

Unless, he mused, he succeeded in losing himself in that land of dreams.

"You have what!" Antoine Dupuis's eyes bulged from his head.

"I have suspended my experimentation with the . . . ah, 'special' perfume." Simone faced the Frenchman squarely. It had taken her two weeks to get up the nerve to confront him. "I have been unable to locate the ingredients I need, and my efforts to build a chemical synthetic have failed completely."

In spite of her knowledge of its danger, Simone had continued to plug away at the console, thinking that if she somehow happened upon some successful synthetic reproduction, she could use it to replenish her rapidly diminishing supply. For against her better judgment, but seeking comfort from her chronic loneliness, every night for the past two weeks she'd used the perfume from the vial she'd stolen from Nick, dipping into its precious fluid at bedtime, seeking solace in the arms of her dream lover.

She'd sought him, but failed. She'd found her way into the

indigo mist, and once or twice even into the realm of the mystical white temple. But not once had she been able to summon Nick's presence. He had left her. In reality. And now in her dreams. For her, the perfume no longer worked. Its magic had disappeared. And she was no longer interested in continuing her pursuit of it in the laboratory.

"You are being ridiculous," Dupuis shouted at her. "What kind of master perfumer refuses to make a perfume? I should fire you right now."

"Then do," she said, shrugging her shoulders, almost wishing he would. She did not like being under the authority of anyone, especially a man like Dupuis. The only thing that had prevented her from resigning two weeks ago was that she'd have no place to live, and no income to live on. Minor matters like that.

But Dupuis did not fire her. Instead, he shifted from his angry threats and took a placating, wheedling approach. "Now *ma chère*, you are just distraught from working so hard. Why don't you take a few days off to reconsider? You can put the project aside for a while. But there is no need to stop work on it altogether."

Simone was not moved. "Why do you want it so much? What is it to you?"

"Why, it is the most spectacular *parfum* this nose has ever smelled," he said, coming closer. Simone cringed visibly and took a step backward. She knew why he wanted the perfume. Why he kept it locked in his private closet. Why each time she checked it out from him to work on, there was more missing than what she'd turned in after her lab experimentation the day before.

Its magic still worked for him.

The wretched little bastard was using it to indulge his sexual fantasies, and she could only imagine what kind of lurid episodes those might be.

But wasn't that exactly what she had been doing? Seeking in the perfume-induced dreams the love and sexual intimacy that was missing in her life?

Somehow, her use of it seemed less licentious. Her use of

it night after night had been, at least in justification, in the name of research.

"There are other, even more *fantastique* perfumes to be developed, Monsieur Dupuis," she told him. "Perfumes I can create quickly. And much more profitably." She stood her ground. "I wish to work in a new direction."

Simone was not prepared for what happened next. Antoine Dupuis pushed her against the wall and pressed his body against hers. She could smell the oil in his hair and the slightly acidic tone of his body odor.

"You will continue to work in *this* direction," he said, forcing his erection against her. "I am almost out of the perfume, and I must have it."

"Get away from me," Simone cried, shocked and frightened, realizing suddenly he'd come into the perfume lab after closing time, when no one else was around.

"You bitch," he snarled at her, pinning her wrists against the wall with surprisingly strong hands. "You think you are too good for me, don't you?"

"Don't do this," she implored, attempting to loosen his grip.

He let her go, but his hands moved like lightning to the neck of her silk blouse, and he tore it open viciously, popping the tiny buttons onto the floor.

"Stop it!" she screamed, and brought her knee upward and directly into his groin. He fell away in stunned agony, and Simone picked up her purse and raced from the room, covering her bare bosom with her white lab coat.

The man had gone mad. And she didn't plan to be around when he recovered his senses.

She ran out the door and into the street, aware of the stares of passersby and not caring. She turned in the direction of the corporate flat and walked rapidly, glancing occasionally over her shoulder. Would Dupuis follow her home? Was he going to rape her?

She tried to calm her panic, to think through what had just happened, to find a logical reason for his behavior. She hadn't known Antoine Dupuis long, but as far as she could recall, he had always been the epitome of control. In fact, there had been a few times, particularly in staff meetings, when he'd seemed to delight in manipulating and controlling his "inferiors."

What could explain this sudden loss of control, except his use of the perfume? The very thought sickened her.

I am almost out of the perfume, and I must have it.

Until that moment, Simone had thought the potion evocative, but even in spite of its hallucinogenic potential, not really dangerous. Now, Esther's warning rang like thunder in her ears. *It must not get into the wrong hands.*

Simone was taking no chances. She had little doubt that Antoine Dupuis was irrational, angry, and capable of following her back to the corporate apartment and attempting to finish what he'd started. She entered the flat and slammed the door behind her, wishing it had a deadbolt. Instead, she wedged a chair beneath the knob, as if that could stop a madman. Still running on adrenaline, she went to the bathroom and surveyed the damage to her new silk blouse in the mirror.

Totaled. The buttons were missing, their embroidered holes ripped apart, the lapels in shreds.

The sight of it heightened her nausea. Simone's knees grew weak, and she leaned against the bathroom wall, crying in both fury and relief. What would have happened if she hadn't been able to escape? She sat on the edge of the tub, hysterical sobs heaving from deep within.

"Well, mademoiselle, you wanted to leave the House of Rutledge?" she said, regaining control at last and talking to herself in the mirror. "I'll bet you just got fired." She forced a bitter laugh to cover her distress. Knowing she'd lost her job filled her with a combination of anxiety and relief. She had little money, soon would have no place to live. But she would never have to put up with the loathsome little Frenchman again.

The thought lifted her spirits in spite of the trauma of his assault. She removed the blouse and examined her throat and breasts in the mirror. If Dupuis had physically hurt her, she would file suit against him. In her opinion, men who beat women were the lowest of creatures, and she felt morally compelled to fight back. But to her immense relief, she didn't see any bruising on her skin. She wasn't into lawsuits either. She would, however, send him the ruined blouse, and a bill for its replacement.

Simone felt dirty. She ran a hot shower and tried to wash away the stink of the incident, all the while remaining nervously alert for the crash of Antoine Dupuis's body against her front door. Fortunately, the crazed animal didn't come knocking.

Still driven by urgency, Simone dressed hastily and gathered enough clothing into a duffel to last her for a few days. She also tucked in the Book of Shadows, the "Project X" folder, the photocopy of the *mahja* blossom, and the bottle of perfume she'd stolen from Nick. Then she picked up the phone.

"Hello, Esther, this is Simone. Is my room available?"

"Yes. Are you coming today?" Her voice sounded startled. "It's the middle of the week."

"I . . . uh, lost my job. Are your mid-week rates lower?"

"Never mind about rates. I'm just glad you're coming. I was going to call you tonight. The plants," the elderly woman huffed into the phone with unveiled excitement. "One of the plants bloomed last night."

"Night blooming?" Simone suddenly forgot all about Antoine Dupuis. A night-blooming plant, such as the cereus, often had the most prized scent used in fragrance.

"Yes. And delicate. By the time I discovered it, the blossoms had already dropped. There are more buds, but we must work quickly."

"I'll be there in a couple of hours."

Simone straightened the small apartment and made sure she had anything of real value with her. She suspected that out of vengeance, Dupuis might enter it with his key and remove anything that belonged to her, daring her to demand him to return them. It would be a control freak's sort of revenge.

Two and a half hours later she disembarked at Redford station. The sun had gone down and twilight washed the small village in hues of blue and silver. Simone inhaled deeply of the country summer night, glad to be rid of the city, of Antoine Dupuis, and the House of Rutledge. She guessed she was just a peasant at heart.

Esther greeted her with a warm hug and a plate of supper, and Simone ate ravenously as she related the whole story to the horrified woman.

"Don't you go back there," she scolded. "I told you th' perfume was dangerous in the wrong hands. Now you've seen it for yourself."

Simone gave the woman a long, perplexed look. "I believe you sincerely. But how can a perfume be dangerous? *Je ne comprends pas*. I don't understand."

"I don't understand either, but it's not important t' understand. It's just important t' know that overuse of whatever Mary Rose concocted can drive a person mad, like this Antoine Dupuis. Or"—she paused—"it could kill them. Like it did John Rutledge and Mary Rose Hatcher."

"Oh, Esther, you don't know that."

The witch sniffed. "I know."

Simone smiled, unwilling to continue the argument. "On the other hand, I know you are anxious for me to make more of it, because you claim it can also be beneficial. How do you know what's safe and what's dangerous?"

"Medicine and poison are often derived from th' same source," Esther explained. "Th' only difference is in th' amount ingested. I think it's much th' same with th' perfume. In limited quantities, used only occasionally, it can enhance a woman's sense of feminine well-being. Maybe it can work in a similar manner for men. But abused, I'm convinced there is no estimating th' mental and emotional destruction it could cause."

Simone's cheeks burned, and she was suddenly uncomfortable talking about overuse of the perfume with Esther. Even though she'd rationalized her nightly use of it as being experimental, she knew that wasn't quite the truth. She'd used it to be with Nick in her dreams. However, Esther didn't need to know that, or worry that she would continue using it. In the dreams, Nick was obviously through with Simone. And Simone was through with the perfume.

Maybe she was through with all perfumes, she thought glumly. It seemed that they'd brought nothing but misery into her life for the past ten years. Maybe she should return to the States and find a good, steady, safe job creating fragrance for baby diapers and soap.

She had only one remaining obligation, and then she would be free to plan her next move. For the honor of her father, she must attempt to make Shahmir's perfume, if the flowers that bloomed in Esther's garden did indeed provide the missing ingredient. She'd brought along the formula, hoping she could create the blend right here in Esther's kitchen, somehow summon the tall strange man to come for it, and be done with him for good.

"What time do you think the plants will bloom tonight?"

TWENTY-THREE

✦

Nick lowered the convertible top on the Triumph, looking forward to the evening drive into the countryside. That feature of the car was useless much of the time in England's dreary climate, but presently there was not a cloud in the sky, and a full moon was to rise later.

He needed to get away from Bombay Fragrances, Ltd., and out of London to clear his thoughts and decide what to do next. The perfume experiment was still unsuccessful, and the clock was ticking. He must decide whether to continue to pursue it, or use his time in another direction. His original business strategy had been to take Bombay Fragrances straight into the high end of the fragrance business—fine perfumes. But when he'd learned of Simone's plan to develop *grands parfums,* as she called them, for the House of Rutledge, he'd been forced to rethink his ideas, especially when Mary Rose's erotic perfume refused to give up its secrets to him.

Nick accelerated and entered the motorway, his dark hair whipping over his forehead and his skin tingling from the rush of fresh air in his face. He urged the powerful engine forward, feeling the speed ease the deep melancholy that had suffused his spirit since his night with Simone. He'd nursed the deep hurt of her actions into a dark anger, trying to convince himself that now that she'd gotten even, he could live at last without guilt over what he'd done to her. But it seemed instead that his life had returned to rock bottom, and at times over the past few weeks he wondered if he cared enough about anything to carry on.

But as he left London behind and drove into the countryside, his spirits brightened, and he forced himself to argue the positive side of things. So he'd lost a couple of rounds. There was always another set, as Scotty, his tennis coach, had so often kindly pointed out after demolishing Nick on the courts. But what would his next round be?

Nick could continue with his original plan and create a perfume other than Mary Rose's to launch Bombay Fragrances. Maybe something decidedly Oriental, spicy, exotic, to match the name of the company. Maybe he could have the designers come up with a package that would look like the old trunk found in the basement in Bombay, and they could nestle the bottle inside. It could even contain a note, evoking a forbidden love affair. Nick allowed a grin onto his lips. If he couldn't re-create the perfume, he could at least re-create the mystique.

It was a good idea, evoking the mysterious, the forbidden. And it was highly marketable.

Marketing, Nick acknowledged to himself, was what he did best. As a perfumer, he had a better-than-average nose. But as a businessman, he had a brilliant sense of what the consumer would buy. Often it was the concept and packaging that attracted the customer, not the perfume itself. They would buy the promise of excitement, adventure, and intrigue offered by the package, and take whatever scent that happened to be inside, providing it did not offend their sense of smell.

But was it smart to enter the field of fine fragrances at the moment, knowing that Simone and the House of Rutledge were primed to make the same market entry? Another option was to go with a lower-end product line, such as aromatherapy oils, bath and body scents, much as he'd developed for the House of Rutledge. They were far less glamorous, but also very lucrative.

Either way, it seemed he was destined to run up against his former financial backer . . . and Simone. He recalled Dupuis's innuendo, that he and Simone were "friendly." Was it true?

The thought revolted him, but it was possible. It would explain why she'd called asking to talk to him. That had the mark of Antoine Dupuis all over it. Smooth talk. Followed by seduction. Nick knew that formula.

It was almost dark when Nick at last arrived in the village of Redford. He wondered as he drove down the narrow winding streets which inn Simone had stayed in after she'd left the cottage.

Simone. There she was again. Damn it! He had to find a way to get her off his mind. She was stuck there, in his thoughts and feelings, almost as if she had become a part of him.

He stopped for a drink and a meal in a pub in town, then headed toward Brierley Hall. He passed the lane that turned off to the old servants' cottage, and the image of Simone answering his knock wearing nothing but the scarlet gown assailed him from out of nowhere.

He gripped the steering wheel tighter and drove on to the twin stone pillars that marked the entrance to the country house. The road leading to the house was lined on either side by tall trees that canopied so thickly overhead they turned the last of twilight to darkness. He envisioned Simone coming down this drive, escorted roughly by Clyde Covington and his ugly dog, with the wind whipping wildly with the ensuing storm. Had she been afraid? She'd shown no fear when she'd lashed out at him. And no mercy in her assault.

Nick parked the car and unloaded his baggage. He'd brought the old trunk and its contents with him, with the intent of leaving it at Brierley Hall. The latent romantic in him had convinced him that his great-great-great-uncle John Rutledge might have started out on his ill-fated journey from here, that very trunk in hand. It seemed fitting that it should come full circle.

After settling in, Nick wandered into the gardens behind Brierley Hall just in time to see an orange glow light up the eastern sky. As if performing just for him, a huge golden moon inched its way into the night sky, cresting the tops of the trees at the far side of the meadow in such a stunning display that it looked surreal. As if it belonged to another world. Perhaps rising over a white marble temple, reflecting in the three stair-step pools, washing two lovers in its glow . . .

Oh, damn it all to hell.

Nick fought the imagery, but he was under the spell of the moonlight now. It drew him like an enchantress across the meadow and into the woods, then led him down a silvery, leaf-quilted path directly to the back of the cottage. Was this how John Rutledge had come to visit his ''lady love,'' as he'd referred to her many times in the diary?

Moonlight illuminated the whitewash of the house, turning it to a silvery-blue, and Nick wondered suddenly why that estate agent—what was her name?—hadn't been able to let it out again but a couple of times during the summer. Maybe his price was too steep. Or he'd gotten it on the market too late for the tourist season. He made a mental note to check on that tomorrow.

Nick knew he ought to avoid going into the garden, and knew just as surely there would be no way he could *not* go there. The memory of the magical, tender embrace he'd shared there with Simone wrapped around his heart and squeezed it until he thought the pain might kill him.

That embrace had not been orchestrated by Antoine Dupuis.

He pushed open the iron gate and glanced around, half expecting to find her waiting there for him. Of course, that was foolish, but this did seem to be something of a magical place. Instead, he was greeted with a space that was still relatively free of the brambly growth he'd cut out. In the center, the rocks outlining the mandala garden gleamed in the moonlight. Fireflies flitted everywhere, like fairies with lighted lamps. His eye followed one particularly bright bug until it lit on a bush next to the south wall. Four other identical bushes were lined in a row next to it.

Nick frowned. His crew had cut those bushes down, he was certain of it. He remembered wondering if the five stumps had been some kind of miniature orchard. Obviously, these were not trees, more like leggy bushes, probably some kind of weed to have grown so fast. For they had all sprouted new growth, branches that were now almost two feet long. He went closer to examine them, and then he saw the flowers.

His heart stopped. His eyes widened. His mind exploded with the impossibility of what he thought he saw. There, growing in profusion on the weed, were delicate rose-colored trumpets, identical to the bloom of the plant Mary Rose had pressed between the pages of her diary and marked *"mahja."*

The light of the full moon outlined the paths that wound throughout Esther's garden, and the old woman led Simone easily toward the plant they had nourished with the ashes charmed with Simone's wish.

I wish to know the secret of Mary Rose's perfume.

Would she ever know? Simone wondered.

"Just as I thought," Esther wheezed excitedly, "they're in full bloom. There's even more tonight than last night."

Simone stared at the plant in shock. She plucked a bloom and held it to her nose. "Don't you recognize this?" she asked the witch.

Esther picked off a bloom and smelled it as well. "My gracious, it smells like our perfume . . ."

Simone placed the red trumpet-shaped flower on the palm of her hand. "It looks like it too," she whispered, barely daring to breathe. Could Shahmir's seeds have been from the *mahja* plant? The whole thing was getting weirder and weirder. Without a word of explanation, she turned and hurried back toward the lights of the house. She raced upstairs to her room and dug in the duffel for the Book of Shadows. When she turned around, she jumped a mile when she saw Esther standing in the doorway.

"What is it, child?"

Simone held the book toward her with trembling hands. "It's . . . it's Mary Rose's Book of Shadows."

Esther's eyes became the size of the China-blue saucers that nested in her kitchen cupboard. "Where did you get this?" she said, taking the book in hand.

"Uh . . . from Nick Rutledge. Never mind that. Look, turn to that page marked with the paper there." Simone had folded

the photocopy of the image of the *mahja* plant and slipped it
between the pages where Mary Rose had written down her
process for extracting the flower's essence.

With fingers wrinkled with age, Esther unfolded the paper,
and her eyes grew even wider. "It's th' plant down there in
th' garden."

Simone had carried the blossom she'd just picked upstairs
with her, and she now laid it alongside the photocopied image.
They were identical. "Yes," she said quietly. "I believe it
is." Then her subdued astonishment turned to jubilation, and
she gave Esther a hug. "We've got it, Esther! We have the
secret to Mary Rose's perfume. The charm worked."

The old woman nodded knowingly. "Was that your fondest
wish?"

Simone stared at her, realizing that for an instant, she had
unquestionably accepted that it was the charm that had
brought about this miracle. Intellectually, she knew better. It
had been Shahmir who had brought it about. But where in the
hell did he get the seeds?

"Quick," she said, "we need to move quickly to harvest
the flowers. In there"—she pointed to the book—"Mary
Rose wrote that they only lasted a brief time. We must hurry
and gather those that bloomed tonight. And"—she paused a
moment, "we must use *enfleurage* to extract their scent."

"What is *enfleurage*?"

Simone took the book and ran her finger over the notation
Mary Rose had made, holding it so Esther could read the
instructions. "Can you take this and prepare the glass plate?
I feel strongly we must do this exactly as she did. Do you
have any suet?"

"I have canned lard. Will that do?"

Simone nodded, her heart pounding wildly. Canned lard
should be clean enough. She grabbed Esther's arms with both
hands. "It will have to do. We must start tonight. We must
use the flowers while we have them. I don't know how long
those bushes will produce, or how much of the essential oil
we can extract. We'll use the lard."

The two women hurried back down the stairs, Esther with

the Book of Shadows tucked under her arm. She produced the lard from her cupboard. "What shall we do for a glass plate?" she wanted to know, looking at the directions given by her craft ancestor.

Simone opened the refrigerator door. "Perhaps these glass shelves," she said with a thoughtful frown. "Take them out and wash and dry them completely. Then coat both sides of them with the lard and put them back in place." She shook her head, feeling almost gleeful. She had everything she needed right here in Esther's kitchen. The glass shelves were very close to what the early perfumers in Grasse had called their *châssis*. It wasn't state-of-the-art technique, but then neither had been Mary Rose's, and it had been successful.

Esther then gave Simone a large basket and a lantern and sent her into the garden. Fireflies flickered in the shadows, and a golden moon paled to brilliant silver as it rose in the sky. Simone's thoughts tumbled over one another as she carefully but rapidly picked the red trumpets from the newly sprouted bushes. Where *had* Shahmir come up with these seeds? It was too coincidental that the missing ingredient in his master's perfume was the very one she needed to create Mary Rose's perfume oil. Somehow, the two had to be connected for any of it to make sense.

But that concept made no sense at all. Shahmir in the twentieth century and Mary Rose in the nineteenth? Simone tried to calm down by inhaling several deep breaths, and with each, the sweet fragrance of the *mahja* filled her olfactory sense with more than just a lovely aroma. She was filled as well with peace and joy and a sense of inner contentment the likes of which she'd never known. It was as if she were becoming intoxicated . . . on love. She thought of Nick and could not suppress a smile. She loved Nick. Why was there such strife between them? It could be healed. She was certain of it. She wanted it to be healed. She wanted their separation to end. And she knew somehow, with the blessing of these flowers, it could be. She held a blossom to her nose and inhaled slowly and deeply.

Nick.

Yes.

Somehow.

She filled the basket almost to the brim, picking only the blossoms that were fully opened, leaving the rest for the next night. The seven plants were all producing flowers, although she had to admit, the one that had received the "charm" was outperforming the others. Probably because it got the right amount of sun, she told herself as she made her way back to Esther's kitchen.

Esther had covered the glass shelves with just the right amount of lard, and they rested at the ready in the small, antiquated refrigerator. "We must dry the blossoms completely," Simone instructed her assistant. "Do you have extra toilet tissue?" It was the softest, most absorbent material she could think of, and these delicate blooms must not be damaged.

At last the harvest was prepared to her satisfaction, and Simone picked up a blossom and stuck it nose-down into the fat. It seemed an unappetizing way to extract the perfume oil, but it had worked for perfumers for eons before anyone knew about distillation. To Simone's mind, there was a certain propriety in extracting Mary Rose's oil using this ancient method. She and Esther worked in silence until all the flowers were immersed in the fat. Then she asked for plastic wrap, which Esther brought from beneath her sink. Simone gently wrapped the shelves, protecting both sides where the blossoms clung precariously to the fat. The lard would shortly assimilate the scent, much like butter absorbs the smell of a neighboring onion in a refrigerator. "This will keep the fragrance enclosed so the fat will take on more of it," she explained. Then she carefully slid each shelf back into its place in the fridge.

"By tomorrow night, these flowers will likely have rendered most of their scent. We'll remove them and replace them with fresh ones," Simone said. "We keep repeating the process until we have no more flowers to work with. Hopefully, by that time, the fat will have soaked up sufficient scent that we can then extract it with alcohol. Then," she added with a satisfied smile, "you will have the oil that you need for your healing, and I'll have it to use—'' She halted in mid-sentence, but Esther was swift on the uptake.

"What *will* you use it for?" the old woman asked, eyeing Simone shrewdly.

Simone sank heavily into one of the wooden kitchen chairs and ran her hands through her hair. Good question. Of course, she'd make Shahmir's perfume. It couldn't be too dangerous, she reasoned, since according to the formula, the strength of the oil of the *mahja* was diluted by several other ingredients. Besides, it was only for his "master's" use anyway.

But knowing what she did about the dangers of the *mahja*, the avarice of Antoine Dupuis, and his perverse nature, she could no longer even consider using it in a marketable perfume.

"Private use," she murmured, thinking of Nick, wanting him.

As if she'd read Simone's mind, Esther said, "You don't need the perfume to be with the one you love. That'd be Nick Rutledge, wouldn't it?"

Simone straightened upright in the chair, her cheeks flaming. "What are you talking about? I hate Nicholas Rutledge."

"Hate is just the other side of love," Esther replied gently. "You hate what he did to you, but I sense that you still love him. Deeply."

Simone felt a cold sweat break onto her skin. How did this woman know what she felt? *If* she even felt that. "How can I love someone who hurt me, and my family, so terribly?" she argued.

"What made him do that?"

Simone crossed her arms on the tabletop and laid her head on them. "I've asked myself that same thing a hundred thousand times over the past ten years. He started to tell me once, but we didn't get very far. Something about his family heritage."

"We all have our problems. Maybe if you understood what his were at that time, you could forgive him."

Simone's head jerked up. "Forgive him? Are you kidding?"

"*Do* you love him?"

To her amazement, Simone began to cry. All the anger and resentment she'd stored against Nick, all the urge for revenge, seemed to well up within her into a wave of tears that needed to break on the sands of her emotions. They came gently at first, a shower she tried unsuccessfully to repress. "I . . . I loved him, once," she choked. "I gave him my heart . . . everything."

"It must have hurt terribly when he left."

Simone felt Esther's hands touch her shoulders, a gentle, soothing gesture, such as Maman used to make when Simone cried as a small child, and it made her cry harder. "Oh, Esther, you can't begin to know . . ."

Simone sobbed for a long, long while, allowing Esther's unspoken empathy to support and comfort her. Her tears brought back the face of her father, her mother, her Tante Camille. They brought back her longing for Grasse, and times gone by. And then they brought back Nick, and the love she still held in her heart for him.

"I'm drawn to him like a moth to the flame," she whispered at last, blowing her nose ungraciously into a piece of toilet tissue. "I should not love him. He was a bastard. But I do . . . still . . . love him."

"Is that what you've been using the perfume for? To be with Nick?"

Simone looked at Esther, feeling as if her face and nose and eyeballs must be swollen like balloons. She started to deny it, but she sensed there was no lying to this wise woman. Esther seemed to be able to see right through her. Simone nodded.

"With the perfume, I meet him in dreams. It's safe there. And all the . . . old problems between us go away."

"It is not safe there, child," Esther said, beginning to rub her hand across Simone's tight shoulder muscles. "It appears safe, but it is only an illusion. A very dangerous illusion."

Simone sniffed. "It's safer than meeting him for real."

"Why?"

Simone's face turned crimson. How could she tell this grandmotherly woman that when she was with Nick, all she wanted was to make love to him? She evaded it by replying, "He . . . he'll hurt me again if I let him know how I feel."

"How can you be so certain? What has he done lately to make you believe that?"

Simone started to reply in indignation, but nothing came to mind that Nick had done lately to hurt her. Nothing! She sniffed again. "Well, he hasn't done anything, I suppose. But we haven't been together . . ." She felt the lie harden in her throat. "Yes, yes, we have been together," she confessed miserably. "He took me to dinner, and we danced, and then . . . I went to his place."

"You don't have to tell me all this," Esther said, relieving Simone's acute discomfort. "It doesn't matter. What matters is for you to sort out your feelings for him in the here and now, and not resort to using the perfume for escape, or for false answers. Look at what happened to John and Mary Rose."

"That's nonsense," Simone retorted. "I'm sorry, but I can't believe your story about them. There is bound to be some other explanation for their disappearances."

Esther stood up and went to the sideboard upon which rested Mary Rose's Book of Shadows. "I have seen a lot in my many years," she said, picking up the volume and opening it, looking for a specific page. "I am convinced that what happens in our lives is a direct result of what we intend and what we believe," she said. "Mary Rose tells us right in here what her intent was in creating the potion in the first place."

" 'I pray to obtain not only a sweet perfume oil, but a sublime one as well, which will allow us to transcend all that keeps us apart here on Earth.' "

"That's nothing more than a lover's wish," Simone replied, unconvinced.

"Mary Rose was no normal lover," Esther continued undaunted. "She had . . . certain powers."

Simone bit her lip to prevent a reply that Esther, the modern-day witch, might find insulting. Esther read on: " 'The very essence of my desire is that the union of his seeds and my soil will produce for us a "natural child," a potion that will have the power to unite us in love for all time.' ''

"What's a 'natural child'?'' Simone asked.

Esther laughed softly. "In our time, we'd call it a 'love child.' She meant a flower, born from the womb of the earth, the 'child' of their desire, that would bring them together. You see, what Mary Rose *intended* was a physical union with John, and I think she strongly *believed* that the *mahja* oil would bring this about, if not on earth, then perhaps in the land of dreams . . .''

"But that's impossible.''

Esther glanced at her slyly. "Is it?''

TWENTY-FOUR

~

The moon had reached its apex hours before and was sliding down the western sky toward morning. The motorway was nearly deserted as Nick raced back toward London. Beside him in the passenger seat was a ceramic crock, filled with the aromatic blossoms of the *mahja* that he had harvested in a frenzy from the five bushes in Mary Rose's garden. There was no way he could fail now. At last he had the genuine source of the perfume. But he must start the distillation process immediately, before the blossoms began to decay and lose their fragrant potency. He prayed he wasn't too late already.

Even though he'd covered the container with foil, their odor filled the small compartment of the car, making him lightheaded with an inexplicable sense of joy and well-being, a euphoria that was somehow connected to Simone. Her image kept creeping into his imagination, and with it, an awareness that regardless of what had passed between them, he was still in love with her. He wanted her, and oddly, inhaling the essence of the *mahja,* he illogically believed that they might possibly overcome their differences. If only she could forgive him. What could he do, what could he ever say to make her let go and forgive all that had happened in the past?

Just before dawn, he carried the crock and its precious contents into the lab at Bombay Fragrances and like a mad scientist began the process that would distill the essence from the trumpet-shaped blooms. He'd read in Mary Rose's diary that she'd used enfleurage to obtain the fragrant oil, but he didn't have time for that slow process.

Brenda found him still at it hours later when she came to work. She opened the door to the lab and smiled in surprise to find him there. Then she sniffed the air. "Ah, lovely! What is it? Our first perfume?"

Nick stood and stretched. "Could be," he replied, not allowing his hope to override his caution. After all, he'd come close before, in his efforts to synthesize the perfume. "Get me a cup of coffee, would you please?"

At last, droplets of a rich, brandy-colored oil began to rise to the surface of the container in which the product of the distillation was collected. Nick's heart hammered as he watched, mesmerized, as his future appeared before his very eyes. He had the perfume oil!

The droplets joined one another, forming larger drops that floated on the water base. He doubted if this limited batch of flowers would produce much of the *mahja*'s essential oil, unless the blooms were high in oil content. He'd had time to collect only those blossoms that had fully opened, not enough to fill the equipment to even one-third its capacity. The bushes were loaded with buds, however, and Nick planned to return to the garden tonight, with help, to collect a greater quantity.

When he felt the time was right, he drew off a few milliliters of the oil and placed it in a curved glass dish where it glowed golden warm in the morning sun.

It looked the same as Mary Rose's oil.

Nick placed two droplets onto a *mouillette,* and with a flourish, brought the slender white blotter to his nose. He smiled.

It smelled the same.

He waited, expecting the sensual arousal brought on when he inhaled of the ancient perfume. At the moment, he continued to experience that inexplicable glow of happiness, that feeling of well-being that had accompanied him on the trip back from Brierley. But Nick felt not a hint of sexual stimulation. He inhaled of the essence again.

Again nothing. Not even the slightest tingle of arousal, only a pleasant, light-headed euphoria.

Euphoria. Not a bad feature for a perfume.

Sexual arousal. An even better one.

But it wasn't here.

Exhausted and disappointed, Nick gathered the precious few drops of oil into a vial and tucked it into his pocket. There was one more experiment he must make before calling it a failure. "I'll check in later," he told Brenda. "Don't forward my calls. I'm going home to try to get some sleep."

At home, he showered and slipped into a pair of clean shorts, his mind all the while on the small red trumpets that dangled in orderly rows from each limb of the bushes in the garden behind the cottage. They *must* be the same flowers Mary Rose had used. He was certain they were identical in size and shape to the pressed flower that remained safely tucked away in his bank vault. Why hadn't they produced the same effect?

Nick's chemical analysis had shown Mary Rose's substance was not a blend but a single essential oil, just as he'd distilled in his lab. Somehow, it must be slightly different in its molecular structure. He would check on that later.

In the meantime he lay down on his bed and closed his eyes. Although he was exhausted to the bone, it wasn't sleep he sought. It was dreams. Would this essence take him into the dreams? To Simone?

With her senses as replete with the scent of the *mahja* as they'd ever been, Simone fully expected that she would enter the indigo mist of her dreams as soon as she fell into bed. Although she respected Esther's beliefs that using the perfume to meet Nick in dreams could be dangerous, in her heart, she felt it was the only way she could ever transcend the sea of mutual mistakes that continued to separate them. And even though she'd been unable to meet Nick in her most recent dreams, she thought perhaps, with the fragrance of the fresh *mahja* blooms in her soul, she could summon her dream lover once again.

But Simone slept soundly, her slumber uninterrupted by dreams of any sort, and she awoke just after dawn, feeling empty and depressed. The tears of the night before, shed as she unburdened her heart to Esther, threatened to resurface, and she tossed on the bed, hugging her pillow tightly.

What good is it, she thought bitterly, to have a prestigious job, to create perfumes that would make her father proud when her father would never know about them? What value was there in a life driven only by a desire for revenge? Even more depressing, what good was a life in which she could never be with the man she loved, not in reality, and now it seemed, not even in her dreams?

Her mood when she dressed and went down into the garden was as forlorn as the steely gray skies overhead. Perhaps it would rain today. The land wanted the relief of rain. It had been the hottest, driest summer on record. Simone wanted some relief as well from the parched feeling of loneliness that had settled somewhere around her heart.

By daylight, the *mahja* plants were nothing spectacular, rather weedy-looking bushes, except for the symmetry of the row of buds along some of the stems that tonight would open into their signature trumpet shape. Other than in photos, she'd never seen either a datura or a brugmansia, and she wasn't sure just how much this plant resembled its supposed cousins. Of course, if these innocuous-looking little flowers were hallucinogenic in nature, no one should ever use them to create a perfume for distribution to the mass market. She probably shouldn't even use the stuff to make Shahmir's concoction, but she'd already decided she would. She doubted if the tall Indian man would turn her in to the authorities, and she suspected that it was the hallucinogenic effects that he was after. She would make his perfume, but she'd return the formula to him and tell him not to come back for more.

After checking each bush in turn, Simone was certain that they would not bloom again until dark. There was time for her to complete an errand she needed to do in London and return to help Esther repeat the *enfleurage* process they'd started last night. Allowing the scent to be absorbed by the fat was only the first part of the process. To finish it, she needed ethyl alcohol, a commodity not readily available since it was the same ingestible alcohol found in liquor and therefore a controlled substance.

But Simone knew where there was plenty of it, for her needs at least. The perfumery at the House of Rutledge. She was nervous about going back there. She hoped she wouldn't run into Dupuis. Irregardless, she would take the opportunity to collect her personal belongings and turn in a letter of res- ignation. Later, if she had time, she'd take a specimen of the *mahja* plant to Dr. Wheatley and have him determine once and for all whether or not the essence of the *mahja* was dan- gerous. She clipped the end off one stem and returned to the house to tell Esther her plans.

"Aren't you afraid of your boss?" she asked.

"Ex-boss," Simone corrected her. "And I'm not afraid, although I'd just as soon avoid him. I don't want to give him the chance to try to manipulate me into doing what he wants."

"Which is . . . ?"

Simone shrugged. No use lying to Esther. "When Dupuis first got a whiff of Mary Rose's perfume, then started using it himself, he . . . well, sort of became obsessed with my de- veloping it into a fine perfume for the House of Rutledge."

Esther blanched. "But you see what it did to him!" she fussed, wringing her hands. "Surely now you can understand the danger. Simone, you must not make that perfume."

"I'm not going to. I told you, I'm resigning from the job. I have to go back to the lab, though. I have my personal belongings to collect, and I'm going to give myself a little bonus," she added with a wink. "I'll get the solvent we need for our project here."

Later that morning, Simone entered the corporate flat in London, fully expecting the rest of her belongings to have been removed, evicting her from the place. But everything was just as she'd left it. She let out a sigh of relief and called Sarah Addington at the House of Rutledge to tell her she wouldn't be in today and see which way the wind was blowing with Dupuis.

254 Jill Jones

"Mr. Dupuis has taken the day off," the woman told her. "He said he wasn't feeling well."

Simone grinned as she rang off. She'd *bet* he wasn't feeling well, especially in a certain place in the groin. Perfect. She could get in and out of the perfume lab quickly, and leave her note of resignation under the door to his office. She shuffled through her desk drawer and came up with a relatively presentable piece of white paper, dug in her purse for a pen, and composed a short, polite note to Mr. Antoine Dupuis.

"I herewith proffer my resignation as master perfumer at the House of Rutledge, effective immediately."

Nick awoke before noon, groggy from the heavy but dream-free sleep. He splashed cold water on his face and went downstairs for something to eat. There on the counter, where it had remained after he'd retrieved it from his front drive, was Simone's red slipper. The sight of it drew a ragged breath from him.

He picked it up and dangled it from his finger. So fashionable. So sexy. So Simone. Suddenly, his hunger for food vanished, replaced by a deeper hunger—for the woman he loved and had betrayed. He didn't care that she'd fallen under the influence of Antoine Dupuis. He'd done so himself. Nor did he blame her for having returned his betrayal in kind. And he did not for one moment believe that Simone had become the Frenchman's lover. She had too much class for that.

Nick's body felt the fire of arousal as if he'd succeeded with the perfume. But it had been hours since he'd inhaled it. No, this was not an illusory arousal. It was real, visceral, and raw. He wanted Simone, more than anything. Success. Honor. Even his Rutledge name.

Because, without her, all the rest had no meaning.

He must find a way . . .

Placing the shoe on the top of his desk in the study, he could think of only one thing. He picked up pen and paper. *My dearest Simone . . .*

A short time later, he folded the paper, inserted it in an envelope, and considered what to do next. It was midday. She would be at work. He decided to take it to the flat and leave it at her door. He'd rather not be present when she read his words anyway. What if the letter didn't work?

Nick dressed hastily, shoved the red shoe into his coat pocket, and drove swiftly to the lab at Bombay Fragrances. Leaving the car's motor running, he dashed in, found the specimen he sought, and left again, aware that Brenda was watching him in bemusement. He didn't care what Brenda thought of his madness. This might, just might, convince Simone of his sincerity.

He wove through the noonday traffic until he made his way to the high-rise tower in which the House of Rutledge had purchased a flat. Ostensibly, it had been meant for use as a hospitality suite when the company executives entertained business associates, but Nick knew that Dupuis had also used it to entertain the bevy of models from which he was able to purchase favors from time to time. The man was disgusting. He hoped he hadn't made any passes at Simone.

He greeted the doorman, who recognized him and didn't question his presence there. Nick took the elevator to the fourth floor, and only as he approached the door to the flat did he question what he was about to do. He could still change his mind. But he shook himself resolutely. Whatever the outcome, he must give it a try.

He knelt and took the red shoe from his pocket and placed it on the carpet in front of the door. He slipped the note beneath it, and then, as if adding an exotic decoration, he laid the single trumpet-shaped flower he'd picked up at the lab on the wide satin strap of the shoe.

Then he turned away and left the building quickly. It had to work. It just had to.

Antoine Dupuis lay in bed until noon, nursing his black and blue private parts and his equally injured vanity. But what had happened had been his own fault, he reminded himself. He'd lost control. In fact, he was appalled at what he'd done to Simone, and knew he must act quickly to make amends, or he would lose her.

Even though she had not yet produced anything dramatic in the way of a fine fragrance for the House of Rutledge, he knew she had the talent they needed. Her lack of productivity was also partly his fault, for he'd insisted she work exclusively on the perfume that had become his obsession. He'd never thought it would be so difficult to re-create the potion.

He glanced at the small bottle of the essence that beckoned to him from his nightstand. His nightly use of it had dwindled his supply to a dangerously low level. He could, of course, live without it. But he didn't want to. The magic of the perfume took him in his dreams to pinnacles of pleasure he could never know in his waking hours. There, he became a king, or rather a sultan, with a harem of beautiful women to attend his every want and need. There, he had a full head of hair and always a virile erection.

Maybe if he gave Simone a break, took her off the project for a while and let her work in another direction, as she'd asked, she would soon be willing to return to her search for its magic.

Only one thing bothered him about that. Simone knew about the "special effects" of this perfume. Even though he trusted her, Dupuis would not rest easy until the House of Rutledge had a protected formula for it. He knew the fragrance held more for him than sensual dreams. It held wealth. Once developed and properly marketed, it would change the way the world looked at fragrance. He did not want, accidentally or on purpose, for it to fall into the wrong hands.

Dupuis frowned. Simone wouldn't do anything like that, would she? Even though it was taking her an inordinately long time to come up with the formula, he didn't think she was holding back on him or would sell it behind his back to another bidder. Still . . .

He decided to keep an even closer eye on her. But first he had to get back into her good graces. He'd have to find a way to apologize for his animalistic behavior. *Mon Dieu!* Had he gone completely crazy?

After making a checklist of things he thought might resolve the untenable situation, he looked up the number of his favorite florist in his appointment book and ordered two dozen long-stemmed red roses. "No, don't deliver them. I'll pick them up later this afternoon. I want to hand-carry them to the young lady."

Flowers. Check.

Next he made a call to a friend who was a fine jeweler. "A tennis bracelet? Yes, that should do the trick," he decided, but winced at the price his friend quoted to him over the phone. "Don't you have one with some smaller diamonds?"

Jewelry. Check.

A third call secured him the best table in one of London's most expensive restaurants for dinner at eight.

An elegant evening on the town. Check.

Then he called his secretary, who informed him that Simone had not shown up for work yet. "She has been under tremendous strain," Dupuis told her. "I suggested she take the day off." He hung up, a crooked smile crossing his lips. He knew how his secretary's mind worked, and that she likely suspected that since both he and Simone had taken a day off, that they were spending it together. He liked the idea.

But it troubled him that she hadn't come in to work, even if it didn't surprise him. Had he frightened her so badly that she'd run, and he'd never see her again? His fingers picked up the phone again and dialed the number of the corporate flat. After ten rings, he hung up. Where could she be?

TWENTY-FIVE

꙳

Dupuis showered and dressed in a light summer suit with a natty pin-striped shirt and blue tie. He wore Italian loafers rather than the dressier shoes of an important executive. He was, after all, on his day off. He stopped in at the jeweler's and decided the bracelet was just the thing, despite the cost. Then he drove to the florist. The roses were *magnifique,* he assured the henna-haired woman who had arranged them. Indeed, they were splendid.

Dupuis looked at his watch. It was only two-thirty. Too early to begin the evening he had planned with Simone, a rendezvous that had become enticingly romantic as he fantasized over every minute of it. Or was it too early? Maybe he should call on her first, surprise her with the roses. Get on his knees and beg her to forgive him. Who knows? Perhaps she'd invite him in ...

The doorman at the tower greeted Antoine Dupuis with a formal nod. "Good afternoon, monsieur."

"Good afternoon, Alfred." He handed the man the keys to the Mercedes that was parked squarely in the middle of the only access to the parking garage. "Take care of the car, will you?" His request was accompanied by a ten-pound note.

"Certainly, sir."

The doorman went to park the car, and Dupuis headed for the elevator, the vase of roses sloshing onto the carpeted hallway. He reached the door to the flat and noticed something on the floor. It looked to be a lady's slipper.

A slipper. On top of a note of some kind.

Without knocking on the door, Dupuis knelt and set the vase to one side of the doorsill. He picked up the shoe, sending a red flower unnoticed from the shoe to the floor, where its color and shape blended with the floral decorations on the carpet. Deciding it would be a pleasure to place it on her foot later, he stuffed the shoe into his pocket. Then, with no compunction whatsoever about reading someone else's correspondence, he opened the envelope, and as he read its contents, his blood pressure skyrocketed:

My dearest Simone,

Since the night I held you in my arms once again, I have been unable to think of anything else. I have loved you from the moment I laid eyes upon you those many years ago, and I love you still, with all my heart and soul.

I have found it nearly impossible at times to live with myself for what I did to you then. I have no excuse for my actions, other than I was young, foolish, and desperate enough to listen to the counsel of the wrong party. I blame no one but myself for the entire incident. I knew in my heart it was wrong, but I was in too deeply—at least so I thought at the time—not to carry through on the plot.

Grief has turned my heart to stone ever since. Not a day has passed that I haven't thought of you and wished to God I could somehow return to that time and change what happened. But of course that can never be. I can only hope that somehow, someway, you can find it in your heart to forgive me.

I do not know how, if ever, I can make up for what I did, but I offer you this gift as a symbol of the love I still carry for you in every cell of my being. It is the flower of a plant that I have found growing near the mandala garden behind the cottage. You said you wished to create les grands parfums, *and I believe you have been seeking this elusive beauty the same as I. It will, I am certain, provide you with an ingredient that can be found in no other perfume, a scent that could almost be called magical. These flowers are growing in profusion in Mary Rose's garden and are ready for harvest immediately. Take them, they are yours.*

Godspeed in your endeavors, although I wish you were creating this divine fragrance for your own company rather than for a man for whom I can have no respect. The House of Rutledge, however, will provide all that you need to launch your premier fragrance, and I am gratified that even though I am no longer associated with the firm, my family name can in some way be of benefit to you.

With all my love,
Nick

"That bitch!" Dupuis snarled, wadding the note viciously and stuffing it into the other pocket. Even though that fool Rutledge had given over the ingredient that had apparently been missing in Simone's perfume, he couldn't stand it that they had obviously been intimate. She would answer for this. They both would! He pounded on the door. "Open this door, you conniving little whore!" There was no sound on the other side. Realizing he'd forgotten the key to the flat, Dupuis kicked over the vase in a rage, sending a dark stain of water across the deep red carpet.

He slammed his palms against the door until they hurt, but either she was not at home or not receiving visitors. Obviously, Nick had left his pathetic little love offering without having seen her either. What were they up to? When had they been together? The thought of Nick and Simone together, as lovers, almost drove him insane. But then, it had been he who suggested that she seduce Nick and find out what he knew about the perfume.

He just found it difficult to imagine that she'd actually done it.

But obviously she had gone to Nick, and who had seduced whom was immaterial. The plan had backfired on him. Nick wanted her back. Which proved Dupuis's suspicion that Nick had fallen in love with her in the past and that she'd obviously fallen for him. Would she fall for him again? Dupuis hoped she was smarter than that. But love did funny things to people. Made them do stupid things. Like give away formulas to important, expensive fine fragrances.

Had Simone given Nick her research? Had they together come up with the real thing, while she'd lied straight-faced to him, denying any progress on the perfume?

"I'll kill them both . . ."

He picked up the dripping vase and all its nodding red blossoms and strode back down the hall to the elevator.

Simone's last visit to the House of Rutledge was carried off without a hitch. She entered through the back door, using her key, unobserved by the receptionist. The door to Dupuis's office was closed. She hurried up the back stairway and with unruffled aplomb, pulled off her miniheist in the perfume lab. She not only helped herself to enough ethyl alcohol to achieve her ends in Esther's kitchen, she also pilfered the ingredients she needed to make Shahmir's perfume. She only wished she knew where Dupuis kept the bottle of Mary Rose's perfume so she could reclaim her property.

Consider us even, she thought, slipping her letter of resignation under Dupuis's door, deciding not to charge the old lecher for the ruined blouse after all.

Kew Gardens was her next stop. When she showed him the specimen she'd brought from Esther's garden, Dr. Thomas Wheatley confirmed her fears. "This plant shows every evidence of being as hallucinatory as its cousins," he told her. "I'll have to report its existence to the authorities, just as I would if it were marijuana. They'll want me to explain where I got this specimen."

Oh. Simone had never considered that might happen. She did not want to get the man in trouble, but neither did she relish the idea of the narc squad descending on poor Esther, tromping down her garden and ripping out the plants, maybe arresting the old woman in the process.

"Is that really necessary? I mean, I'm not using drugs or anything. And I can assure you that I will personally destroy them upon my return to where they are growing."

"Destroy them? But they are already so rare . . ."

"Maybe only in the West," she offered, recalling the swami-like appearance of the man who'd given her the seeds. "I . . . I think maybe the seeds from which those plants grew came from India or Nepal, one of those places. Maybe the species is not as near extinction as you might imagine." She flashed him her most alluring smile. "What if I promise to destroy all but one bush, which I'll send to you anonymously? That way, you can remain totally legal and still have the specimen to study. And I will protect from involvement the woman in whose garden these are growing but who knows nothing about the nature of the plant. Agreed?" She stuck out her hand as if he *had* agreed, and reflexively, he shook it.

"I . . . uh . . . well, it's highly irregular, you see, but, well . . . I suppose as long as there's no harm done."

"Very well, then," Simone said, and took her leave before he had time to change his mind. "Thank you."

She hurried to the underground station, now eager to get back to the flat and pack what was left of her things, and then . . .

And then what?

She stood on the platform, looking into the black tunnel where soon with a whoosh the train would emerge. Suddenly, her life seemed as black as that tunnel. Where was she going with it now?

To Esther's? Yes, for a few days. Then, feeling a dark depression wash over her, she supposed she'd just go on home.

The subway arrived and she stepped aboard, oblivious to the others around her, obsessed suddenly with the thought of home, and the notion depressed her even more. Where was home? New Orleans? She grimaced to consider returning there. *Come home to Provence,* she thought wistfully, recalling the travel poster. But her home was no longer there either.

Home. The last time she could remember feeling the comfort and security she associated with "home" was when she'd been in Nick's arms, in Nick's bed. With Nick a part of her. That was home—in truth, the only home she wanted.

But it was a home she could never have.

Unless . . .

A startling idea suddenly occurred to her, and by the time she reached her station, a plan began to form in her mind. She wasn't sure it would work, or that if she succeeded, she would find what she so desperately longed for. But given what she considered to be her limited options for "returning home," the plan beguiled her despite her reservations. As she hurried down the walk toward the ugly little flat, she put all else from her mind. It was, she decided firmly, at least worth a try.

Unlocking the front door, Simone noticed a dark spot on the hallway carpet and knelt to touch it. It was soaking wet. Rushing inside, she fully expected to find her pipes had burst. But all appeared to be in good order. No plumbing problems, no overflowed tub. She stepped outside her door again, thinking she must have imagined the puddle. But the carpet was thoroughly wet. Odd, she thought. But what did she care anyway? Where she was going, none of this would matter anymore.

If she could get there. And stay there.

Like a person preparing for an extended vacation, Simone bustled around the flat, collecting everything that belonged to her into her large suitcase. She stripped off her dress and packed it away, sweat and all. The only thing left was the bottle of perfume on the bedside table.

Then she took a refreshing shower, drank a glass of cool water, and walked naked into the bedroom. She turned back the bed, smoothed the sheets, and sat down. With reverence, she lifted the lid from the vial and inhaled a brief whiff. Instantly, she felt the familiar warmth of sexual arousal begin to suffuse her body, and she smiled.

Esther, a bona fide witch, had told her that what happened

in a person's life was a direct result of what that person *in-tends* and *believes*. Well, Simone intended to go home, to the only place where she believed she had a chance of being with Nick again—if he would only return to her there, in the per-fume-induced dreams.

Simone inhaled deeply of the essence. She opened her palm and let the fragrant liquid flow into her hand, where she used it like a massage oil, rubbing it into her breasts, her belly, along her upper thighs, down her arms, over her face, through her hair. She lay back on the bed, her sensitive nose nearly overcome with the scent.

"It is the essence of my desire," she whispered drowsily into the afternoon heat, imitating the quaint phrase that Mary Rose had used, "that this perfume take me forever into the realm of my dreams and reunite me there with my beloved Nick for all time."

If it had worked for John and Mary Rose, she thought as consciousness faded, perhaps it could work for her . . .

Nick heard a commotion, but before he could reach the out-side office, Antoine Dupuis burst into the laboratory, his face nearly purple from fury. "Where is she?" he bellowed. "Where is that bitch?"

Adrenaline surged through Nick. Simone must have done something royally wrong to piss him off this bad. He bit the inside of his cheeks to keep from smiling. "Exactly which bitch were you looking for, Dupuis?"

"Don't get smart with me, you insipid has-been aristocrat. I know you and the French slut have been shacking up to-gether, so don't try to play innocent with me. Where is she?"

"The 'French slut' told me she does not want to see you again, Dupuis," he said, making it up just to watch the man's reactions. To his surprise, he saw Dupuis's face grow pale, and a guilty look shifted into his eyes. What was going on here? Nick was seized suddenly with cold apprehension. Why would he come here, screaming like a madman, looking for his own master perfumer? "Why would she say something like that?" he pressed, all of his senses alert.

"Tell her she's fired," the Frenchman growled, evading the question. "And tell her if that perfume shows up with your label on it, I'll . . . I'll kill both of you."

He was gone before Nick could stop him. Nick stood in the door, scratching his head, wondering what the intrusion had been all about. Clearly, he and Simone had had some kind of blowup, something to do with a perfume.

His stomach knotted. Could it be *the* perfume Dupuis was referring to? Mary Rose's magical, sensual aphrodisiac? He'd bet his life on it. And he'd bet Dupuis knew all about its sexual magic. Why else would he behave so irrationally?

Nick surmised that Dupuis thought Simone had discovered the formula, and that she'd betrayed him and brought it to Bombay Fragrances. But surely Dupuis would know better than that. Simone must have told him how she hated Nicholas Rutledge. He could envision the little slimebag's face, all benevolent and understanding when she'd told him how Nick had so brutally betrayed her. He could hear him attesting to his own innocence, and offering his sympathy.

It made him want to throw up.

The whole thing made him very uneasy. Why had Dupuis blanched so suddenly when Nick intimated that Simone did not wish to see him? Had he done something to her? Hurt her?

Oh, my God.

He went into his office and grabbed his car keys. He had not thought Simone was at home earlier, so he hadn't even knocked. Had she been hiding behind that door after all, nursing bruises, terrified that Dupuis would come after her again? His imagination was running wild, he knew, but he had to go there. He had to know that she was safe.

Nick parked illegally, half the Triumph overhanging the curb. The doorman yelled at him to move it, but Nick didn't hear him. He ran up the four flights of stairs instead of using the elevator, and he was breathless by the time he got to her door.

"Simone!" He pounded on the door with his fists, then tried the lock, which held firm. "Simone!"

Down the hallway, the elevator doors whished open, and an icy-calm Antoine Dupuis stepped out. "I knew you two were in it together," he said, reaching into both pockets, coming up with a key out of one and a snub-nosed pistol from the other. "I forgot this earlier," he said, waving the key, "but it does save wear and tear on the hands."

"You have no reason to threaten me with a gun, Dupuis," Nick growled. "I'm not *in* anything with Simone."

"Oh, no?" The Frenchman scowled at him and brought another item out of his pocket, a paper wadded into a ball. "Sounds to me from this pathetic schoolboy's note that you are *in* love with her."

Nick started to lunge at him, wanting to choke the life out of him on the spot. Where had he come by that note? Had Simone given it to him, to taunt him somehow, or prove that she had access to the *mahja* flowers now? Or had he taken it from her? But he stopped when Dupuis raised the gun and pointed it into Nick's face.

"I wouldn't," the shorter man warned. Then he leered at Nick. "Shall we see if the bitch in question is in residence?"

Dupuis returned the balled-up note to his pocket and eased the key into the lock. The door opened, and Nick grimaced to think that this sleaze bag could have walked in on her any time he pleased. He bit off his reply and preceded Dupuis into the apartment.

It appeared to be vacant. The sofa and tabletops and chairs were empty of any sign that the place was occupied. The kitchen was clean, the countertops empty. In the fridge, there was only a half-empty carton of orange juice and a few cookies in a crumpled-up bag.

"Guess our bird has flown," Dupuis said, his tone sounding not altogether disappointed. Maybe he hadn't relished killing her after all.

Nick sniffed the air and followed a faint scent to the back of the flat, where its intensity increased until it became cloying. Dupuis smelled it too, and followed Nick down the short hall. "What has she done with that perfume?" he ranted.

Turning the corner, Nick feared the worst, that he would

come upon her dead in bed, murdered or by her own hand.

But the bed was empty. The room was empty. He felt the sheets. They were still warm. "Simone? Are you here?" he called, then went to check the bathroom. But she was not there either. Her suitcase stood on a nearby chair, and when Nick checked, he found it packed, as if she were ready to leave.

"She's probably gone out," Dupuis grumbled, losing some of his earlier rage. He pulled off the top sheet and held it to his nose. "My God, that stuff makes me horny."

Nick watched Dupuis lose concentration, visibly mellowing into a sexual fantasy right before his eyes, and in a flash, he kicked the gun from his hand and wrestled him to the floor.

"Get off me, you English bastard," Dupuis yelled.

But Nick's reply was a knee in his back. "What did you do to her, Dupuis?" he demanded, pulling the man's short arms sharply behind him. Dupuis screamed in pain.

"Let me go!"

"What did you do?" Another jerk, another exclamation of pain.

"Nothing. She brought it all on, the whoring bitch. Twitching that tight little ass right in front of me, knowing all the while what that perfume does to a man."

Nick couldn't bear it. With one chop remembered from a long-ago martial arts class, he cold-cocked Dupuis, whose body went limp beneath him.

Shaking, Nick eased himself up. He picked up the gun and stuck it in his own belt, then reached into one of Dupuis's pockets and came up with Simone's red shoe. From the other pocket he took the note.

"You sorry son of a bitch," he snarled, unrolling the paper, recognizing his very private note.

Nick placed the red shoe on the suitcase and picked up the phone and dialed the number of the detectives who had been assigned to investigate his two burglaries. "This is Nicholas Rutledge," he said. "Remember me? I've caught our thief. But I think now he should be charged also with attempted murder."

Nick hung up the phone, his stomach wrenching. Where

was Simone? She may have just gone out, as Dupuis said, to get some last-minute thing for her travels. In which case, they were going to look very foolish to the police who should arrive at any moment.

Then Nick's eye caught a glimpse of something under the bed, and he knelt to pick it up.

It was the amber vial that had held the perfume she'd stolen from him.

Empty.

TWENTY-SIX

꒰

Nick hastily jammed the perfume bottle into his pocket. He doubted the police would consider it a murder weapon, but Nick found it not impossible that it might be responsible for Simone's disappearance.

He heard the police at the door and left Dupuis long enough to let them in. Nick explained as best he could what had happened, about Dupuis barging into the offices of Bombay Fragrances, Ltd., threatening to kill both Nick and Simone. He told them about coming here to make sure Simone was safe and being attacked again by Dupuis, this time with a gun. By the time he was finished, he knew it would take the Frenchman some fast talking to get the charges of assault and battery, maybe even attempted murder, dropped.

"But where's the girl?" the officer wanted to know, sniffing the air. Nick saw the policeman shoot a sly look at his partner and hid his own grin, knowing the man was probably feeling some of the "effects" of the perfume. The uniformed man opened the suitcase. On top of the rest of her things lay her slender handbag, the contents of which he dumped onto the bed. Among them were her passport, money, a Louisiana driver's license, cosmetics, and a scribbled-upon scrap of paper. It was obvious to everyone that Simone Lefèvre had not just run out to the store for some last-minute things.

Nick's already overwrought nerves stretched until they hummed in his ears. "I don't know where she is."

The officer gave him an appraising look. "You have my card, Rutledge. If she doesn't show up in twenty-four hours, we'll need to talk to you."

"If she doesn't show up in twenty-four hours, I'll be on your doorstep demanding you do something to find her," Nick replied, glowering at the detective. "In the meantime, I'll search for her myself."

When the policemen turned their backs to rouse and hand-cuff Dupuis, Nick replaced the items into Simone's small handbag and slipped it into the inside pocket of his coat. She should know better than to leave her purse in the apartment where it could be stolen by an intruder. He gave a short, ironic laugh. An intruder like himself? But he took it only to keep it safe for her until her return.

On his way out of the building, Nick handed the doorman a large tip for not having had the Triumph towed away. Then he settled behind the wheel, trying to decide what to do next. *Had* Simone just gone out for a few moments? Would she be back momentarily? He drove around the block several times until a parking space on the street became available and he slid into it. He needed to think, but he could think and keep an eye on the building at the same time, just in case she returned home.

But Nick knew intuitively that Simone wasn't coming home. At least not back to that flat. He didn't know what Dupuis had done to her, but it must have been a terrible threat for her to have left without her suitcase and handbag. Either that, or . . . he took the perfume bottle from his pocket. He remembered Mary Rose's claims, in both her letters and the diary, that she believed this potion had the power to transport a person physically into the dreamworld. Had she been right? Was that what had happened when John Rutledge and Mary Rose Hatcher had disappeared on the same night from their homes half a world apart, their bodies never to be found? Could any perfume have such power?

Nick knew that was ridiculous. Yet, in his own dreams, he himself had been transported into another realm that was so intensely physically real, he was tempted to believe now that t was possible. Had Simone overused the perfume and been physically transported into that alternate reality? Was she here at the moment?

Rubbish! Nick did not believe in that sort of hocus-pocus.

But then, he recalled the voice from his dreams, warning him against using the perfume to supplant reality.

"There is grave danger of becoming lost here."

That voice. It had said something about a doorway, and becoming imprisoned, and . . .

"Your lady love visits her dreams too often as well."

Lady love. John Rutledge's favorite term for Mary Rose. Nick closed his eyes and fought his overwhelming desire to laugh at the ridiculous direction his thoughts were taking— that the voice was that of his ancestor, John Rutledge, and that like John and Mary Rose, Simone had experimented with the perfume too often and become imprisoned in her dreams.

Nick knew his fear for Simone's safety was eroding his reason. There was a logical explanation for all this, and likely it had to do with the hallucinogenic properties of the *mahja*. Nick made a note to take a specimen to Dr. Wheatley at his earliest opportunity. Perhaps Simone had overused the perfume and was experiencing some kind of hallucination that had made her leave the flat and wander off somewhere.

That thought gave Nick no comfort whatsoever. What to do? What to do? He drummed his fingers on the steering wheel. If she had wandered, where would she go? He took out her purse and went through her personal items again. There, on the slip of paper, was written, "Esther Brown," followed by a telephone number with the same prefix as Brier-ey Hall. Nick thought a minute. Simone had told him she'd gone to an inn in Redford when she left the cottage. Had it belonged to this Esther Brown? Redford. It was a long way for an hallucinating woman to travel, but it was the only place he knew to look.

He dialed Brenda on the cell phone and told her he was going to be away for a while on an emergency. Thank God the woman could hold down any fort, any time, on any given notice. "If by chance a woman named Simone Lefèvre should call, find out where she is, get her number, and call me right away.''

Then he dialed the number written on the scrap of paper. He let it ring more than a dozen times before disconnecting the call. Damn. With a last glance in the direction of the high rise building, he made up his mind. He would go to Redford. Surely this Esther Brown would return home soon. Maybe with Simone.

These trips between London and Redford were becoming habitual, Nick thought as he turned into the traffic. He might as well move to Brierley Hall and commute. He kept trying the phone number from the cell phone, finally reaching Esther Brown just as he approached the Redford exit from the motorway. At first Mrs. Brown was reluctant to tell him anything other than that she'd had a recent guest by the name of Simone Lefèvre, but when he identified himself, she seemed to ease up a bit.

''What do y' want of her?''

There was much Nick wanted of Simone, including her love and forgiveness, but at the moment, only one thing mattered. ''I want to know she is safe.''

''What's happened to her?'' Esther's voice prickled with alarm.

''I don't know. I hope nothing. But she's missing from her flat in London. She hasn't shown up for work, and . . . well, there are some, uh, unusual circumstances surrounding her disappearance.''

''Oh, dear,'' the woman said. ''I warned her, but she wouldn't listen.''

The hair at the back of Nick's neck stood on end. What did the woman mean? ''May I come to see you?'' he asked. ''I think we need to talk about this in person.''

Five minutes later, he was on Esther's porch, and she opened the door before he could ring the bell. He could tell by the look of sick anxiety on her face that she cared very, very much for Simone.

Over the ceremony of tea, a ritual that served to anchor an otherwise insane and impossible conversation in reality, Nick listened to Esther's story about her "craft ancestor," and of the old woman's firm belief that misuse of the perfume oil had cost Mary Rose and John their lives. "I . . . I think it's likely that our lovely Simone might have done the same."

"But why?" Nick was in agony, not because he believed the woman, but because he felt so helpless.

"Because she loves you," Esther said, leaning toward him, peering at him intently. "And because she believed that the only way she could be together with you was in dreams."

Nick stared at her, stunned. "She . . . loves me?" he managed at last. "She told you that?" Surely it was he who was hallucinating now.

"She told me everything," Esther said, patting his hand, grandmother style. "She wants to be with you, but she is afraid of getting hurt all over again."

Nick's heart lurched. "She has every right to feel that way," he admitted, "but I swear I would never hurt her like that again. I know it sounds . . . insufficient, but I never meant to hurt her in the first place. I made a bloody awful mistake." He looked up into the old woman's eyes. "What can I do to make her believe that?"

"First, you have to find her."

"I don't know where to look."

"You'll find her in the dreamworld."

Nick blinked. Batty. Esther Brown had to be nuts. But not wanting to offend her and wishing her solution made sense, he replied, "I have no way of entering that dreamworld now." He produced the perfume bottle from his pocket. "She used all the perfume."

Esther frowned and rocked back and forth for a long moment, as if considering something. "Wait here," she said at last. "It will take me a little while. Pour yourself some more tea." With that, she shuffled off in the direction of the kitchen.

Nick stared out into the garden while he waited. The beauty of the lush foliage and flowers belied the feeling of dread that gnawed at him. Why was he here, wasting valuable time on some old woman's ridiculous notion when he should be . . . ?

But he didn't know where he should be. There was no other

place he knew to look. Why not in the dreamworld?

His eyes focused suddenly on a nearby bush that looked familiar. Its gangly stems rustled in the early-evening breeze, and upon them, lined in a symmetric row, were reddish buds just ready to burst into bloom. My God, the old gal's got the *mahja* plant, right here in her garden, he realized, incredulous. That's where Simone must have learned about the perfume. From Esther Brown.

Long minutes later, Esther reappeared through the doorway, carrying a small jar with her. "I gave Simone all the potion that had been handed down to me, hoping she could make more, so I don't have any to give you. But I think maybe this might suffice."

She handed Nick the jar, which appeared to be full of chopped red cabbage or radishes.

"What's this?"

"Open the lid and smell it," she said, watching closely.

Nick did as she bade him and instantly recognized the scent of the perfume. He also felt the familiar tingle of sexual arousal spread through his body, the effect he'd tried to duplicate and failed. "Where did you get this?"

"Th' flowers are out there in the garden," she replied openly. "I just chopped some of them up to release the fragrance."

Just chopped them up. And they instantly gave forth the sensual effect he had been struggling for weeks to chemically re-create. Nick shook his head. No way. She'd added something else to the mix as well. The elusive "magic" ingredient that gave the potion its power?

But he didn't pursue it at the moment because the effect was strong and had him under its spell. "What should I do?"

"Take it home to Brierley Hall with you and use it . . . now, tonight, to find Simone."

The country house was closed and dark. Nick was glad he hadn't phoned the housekeeper ahead. What he was about to do defied all logic and reason, and he wasn't anxious to have any witness to his madness.

Hurrying up the wide old staircase, he made his way quickly along the portrait-lined gallery to the bedroom at the back. The room had slept his ancestors for over two centuries, and now he claimed it as his own, along with the recently elongated Rutledge family bed, although both room and bed were seldom used. When he died, there would be no heir to this place, and he wondered briefly who would next inhabit this rambling old estate. Who would want it?

He stood in the doorway, feeling his heart battering against his rib cage, his breath washing heavily through his lungs. His nerves were taut, his libido on fire, not only from his recent whiff of the essence of the crushed *mahja* blossoms, but also in anticipation of what might soon take place.

Drawing the heavy curtains fully over the window to seal out the remaining daylight, Nick wondered if he had any hope of success. Was Simone trapped in the dreamland? Was she truly in danger? For these and a hundred other questions, he had no answer. The only thing he knew was, he had to try.

For Simone had told Esther she loved him, and for her love, he would go anywhere, do anything.

He placed the jar of mashed flower blossoms on the nightstand and sat down heavily on the edge of the bed. Simone loved him. Did he dare believe the old woman?

Nick tugged the tie away from his neck. He unbuttoned his shirt, remembering the deliciously passionate undressing Simone had given him the night she'd followed him home. He closed his eyes and groaned aloud. *Did* Simone love him? He prayed Esther was telling him the truth, for Simone was the only thing in the world that mattered to him anymore.

Simone.

He *must* find her.

Nick reached for the mysterious, powerful *mahja* blossoms and opened the lid to the squat jar. Would the essence of these few coarsely ground blossoms be strong enough to take him into the dreamworld? If he went there, would he find her? Would she want him to find her?

He closed his mind to further doubt and took a giant leap of faith.

Inhaling deeply, he called forth an image of Simone in his mind. He saw her, naked in the golden sun, lounging beside the triple pools that trickled pleasantly from one to the next, down the terraces of the white marble temple. He felt her desire for him, her anguish over their separation. He heard her silent plea for him to come to her.

His heart filled with such love and longing he feared it might break, and he knew he must embark upon this journey without delay. It was his only hope.

Already in a near-trance, Nick managed to remove the rest of his clothing and pull down the bedcovers. Slipping between the cool, crisp linen sheets, he lay back against the pillows and brought the jar of flower petals to his nose. He breathed in their scent again and again, until he felt himself drifting toward the edge of consciousness. The essence of the *mahja* oil fueled his already passionate desire for Simone as he entered the dreamworld, and he vowed he would not return until and unless he reclaimed the woman whose love he had once so foolishly thrown away.

He must not, would not, lose her again . . .

Nick surrendered his consciousness and dropped into the subtle, shifting haze of the dreamworld. But instead of arriving among the familiar swirling indigo mists, he was instead enveloped by a heavy, hushed silence, a thickness in the atmosphere he hadn't experienced before. He hesitated, listening for a whisper, a sound that would let him know his beloved was nearby. But the only sound he heard was that of his furiously palpitating heart, echoing noisily in his ears.

"Come to me!" He summoned her with all his will, but no ethereal beauty heeded his call, and he sensed he was alone in this suddenly disquieting wilderness.

His eyes strained to see through the vapors, hoping to catch a glimpse of the graceful figure of the lover of his dreams. But he perceived only the changing shades of light and darkness that wove around him as the familiar colors of twilight commingled with brighter auroras he had not encountered before.

"Simone!" he called out again, panic rising in his breast. *"Where are you? Will you come to me?"*

The eerie whistle of a cosmic wind replied in a lonely, melancholy wail. Was he too late? Had she disappeared forever into the ether?

Nick closed his eyes and dropped his head back, struggling against the scream of despair that threatened to break from his throat. No! It must not be! He would not let it be!

Behind his closed eyes, he saw the image of Simone he'd brought to his mind before dropping off to sleep, and with it came the realization that she was not here, not in this dreamworld, because she was in that other higher realm, that holy, sacred space into which they had traveled together the night she had come to him.

The white temple.

He must go there, but he was unsure how he could reach that higher plane. Before, it had been the perfume that took them there. But now, he had nothing other than the love in his heart and his desperate desire that she be his always.

"I pray to all the powers in the Universe, help me!" he cried into the void of the encroaching gloom. *"Help me find her! Help me!"* At the same time, he summoned every ounce of the power of his own will to take him to the woman he knew he would love beyond eternity.

Suddenly, he was thrust abruptly and violently into a maelstrom as the muted, brooding mists swirled into a storm of vibrant colors—electric-blue, gold, violet, ruby, indigo, white, and the edge of midnight. He felt himself being swept into the vortex of an unnamable oblivion, and as if he were caught in a sandstorm on the desert, or in a blizzard in the Arctic, he was blinded by the totality of his surroundings. He was hurled through time and space, the continuum of infinity, with only one thought in his mind, only one name on his lips.

Simone.

He held the image of her face in his mind and called out to her with all the love in his heart. *"Simone!"*

As suddenly as the storm came upon him, it was over, and as the mists parted, he found himself on cool stone steps. He *was at the foot of the white marble temple. Above him, brilliant stars bejeweled the midnight sky. Below him a lush jungle forest glimmered in tropical splendor, and he knew therein lay a mystical glade he'd once visited.*

He at last sensed her presence, and his heart rejoiced. Simone! *He called out to her in the unspoken communication of the dreamworld. From far above, he felt the pull of a faint response, and he began to climb the tower of steps that suddenly appeared, chiseled from the crystal mountainside. When at last he reached the top he saw her, just as she was in his mental image, resting on the bench, waiting for him. Her lips curved upward in a dazzling smile when she saw him, and she stretched out her arms, inviting him to come to her.*

"At last, you've come," she murmured.

Nick ran to her, overcome with emotion. He drew her into his arms and kissed her. The feel of her body next to his reassured him that she had come to no harm. "Oh, Simone, my love, my love." He whispered his relief, kissing the words into her scent-sweetened hair. "I would have died if anything had happened to you."

She raised her gaze to his and touched his cheek. "There is no need to worry now," she said, returning his kisses tenderly. "Here we are safe and protected from all that has kept us apart."

Nick nodded, tempted by her soft assurance to follow her lead. "Nothing will ever keep us apart again," he told her.

"Make love to me, Nick."

She wanted no fantasy pleasuring as she drew him down against her on the cloud-soft bench. His every sense seemed filled to overflowing as he moved to honor her desire, and his own. He felt the heat of the sun's golden-white light penetrating his skin, warming them and releasing the lovely and familiar scent of flowers into the atmosphere. He tasted the hunger in her kisses for the love they had denied each other for so long, and as he entered her, he heard a light and lilting exclamation escape her lips, as if she were rejoicing in their oneness.

That oneness spiraled them higher and higher as they si-

lently but surely pledged their troth, in body, mind, and spirit, before all the powers of the Universe. They were truly one, here, in this divine and holy temple, and Nick no longer cared if they returned to—

"Return. You must return." *A voice echoed like thunder in his ears, and Nick sat up abruptly.*

"What is wrong, my darling?" *Simone frowned, the first unhappy expression he'd seen on her face in this place. He knew the voice, and he knew it spoke the truth, but the pain it brought him was indescribable.*

"We cannot remain here," *he told her, stroking his hands alongside her cheeks.* "We must return to . . . our world."

"We can only remain here," *she returned, a troubled look in her eyes,* "if we wish to be together. There is no other world for us."

"Together, we can make a world of our own, my love," *he whispered urgently.* "We can, if we wish it."

"No. I will not go back. I do not wish ever to go back . . . there." *She laid her hands on his arms and her cheek against his chest.* "Do not make me, Nick. It is not a good world."

Nick heard the fear and despair in her voice, and he regretted that the voice had broken the joy of their reunion. But he also knew the wisdom behind the voice. He understood suddenly and clearly that to remain in this place was to lose their humanity . . . forever. It was not the nature of their being, and they would become lost souls.

"There is grave danger of becoming lost here."

Nick didn't know whether he'd spoken them, or if the words had come from outside himself. But he believed them. "We must go, Simone," *he told her as firmly as his now-tormented heart would allow. For even as he knew they must return to their own world, he also realized that in so doing, they faced the risk of losing the oneness once again. He encircled her wrists and brought her fingertips to his lips.* "We must return to our own reality. We can make it work."

But she shook her head. "If we go back, there is no hope for us," *she whispered, her eyes searching his with a quiet desperation.* "Don't you remember? In that world, deceit and* *hatred and mistrust have built a wall between us too vast to conquer."*

"We can tear down that wall, Simone," he implored. "I love you, and I know you love me as well. We are pledged to each other through eternity."

"Yes, but there, that love is darkened by earthly events. Nicholas, don't you see? Here, there is no yesterday, no tomorrow. Only us, and now. This moment." Tears glistened in her dark eyes.

"Can you forgive, Simone? Can you forgive those earthly events? I have loved you, always. God curse the day I ever brought you sorrow. I have lived in torment since then, wanting you, knowing I could never have you again, knowing that you hated me. Can you forgive me, Simone?"

"I want to forgive you, Nick," she murmured, "but I am afraid. How can I ever trust you again?"

Nick gently placed his lips on hers, willing her to understand the love that overflowed his heart. "I would give up my life to regain your love and trust," he swore, holding her head between his hands. "But you must find it in your heart to forgive me. If you can do that, we will easily find our place together, on earth, in our own realm. Come home with me, Simone. Please. Give us another chance."

He searched her eyes, his own pleading with her. At last, her lips edged upward into a tremulous smile and she nodded, ever so slightly. "Yes, Nick. I want that too. Take me home."

TWENTY-SEVEN

Simone opened her eyes and lay very still, trying to decide where she was. She could vaguely see the shape of a large room, heavily draped from ceiling to floor along two walls. She was in a bed, a very large bed, and next to her was the man in her dreams. Then it all came back in a rush.

"Nick?" she whispered, terrified, realizing that she had left the safety and protection of the wondrous dreamworld. She reached for his hand.

"Yes, love." Nick put his arm around her and drew her against the warmth of his body. "Are you all right?"

As full consciousness returned, Simone's head felt light, and she was not sure that she was all right. There was so much to grasp, such overwhelming impossibilities to consider. "Hold me," she said in a small voice.

He tightened his embrace and kissed her forehead. "Don't be afraid."

But Simone shivered. She *was* afraid. "Where are we?"

"At home. In Brierley Hall."

Simone closed her eyes. Brierley Hall! How had she ended up at Brierley Hall? Or back in this world for that matter?

From her memory, she summoned the available fragments of her most recent dreamtime, struggling to comprehend how she got here. Nick had been in the dream. No, Nick had *come* there, and she had the distinct impression it was to find her. Then she recalled him telling her that he would give up his life to regain her love and trust. Yes, she was certain of it. He'd talked about forgiveness, begged her to forgive him. Her pulse quickened as the recall grew stronger. He had said those things, but had he meant them? Or was that memory just a trick of her imagination in its hungry desire for it to be so?

She lay very still, feeling his heartbeat next to hers, and thought about forgiveness.

Forgiveness meant giving up her anger. Her mistrust. All those thoughts of revenge that had been her constant companions for so long. Forgiveness meant opening herself to him fully, in every way. Becoming vulnerable to him again.

Forgiveness was fraught with danger.

She bit her lip. Could she do it? Could she really and sincerely forgive him from the depths of her heart? For if she did, and Nick betrayed her again, she would not survive.

But had he not come for her, sought her out and implored her to return to this world with him? There must have been a reason for him to want her back. She was certain it was not an adventure that had been undertaken lightly. He'd told her he loved her, that he believed if she would forgive him, together they could create their own paradise here on earth, where they belonged. Did she share that belief?

Simone drew in a deep breath. She remembered that she'd asked him to take her home. Before, she hadn't known where home was. Now, she knew. Home was here, with Nick. If she wanted that home, on every level of her being, then she must forgive him, make her peace with him once and for all.

"Nick?" she murmured again.

"I'm here, love."

Simone smiled at that. Yes, he was here. With her. For her. "Is it true? Can we really be together in this world?"

"According to Esther we can, if we have the intent and the belief."

Simone jerked her head to look into his face to see if he was making fun of her. But his expression was dead serious. "When did Esther tell you that?"

Nick smiled, and the look of love and tenderness on his face melted away Simone's momentary doubts. "I don't know. Yesterday. The day before. Last night. Depends on what time it is, what day. It doesn't matter. All that matters is that Esther gave me what I needed to come into the dream-world to find you.''

"Which was . . . ?''

Nick loosened his embrace only long enough to reach for a small, flat jar that rested on the nightstand. "These,'' he said, handing it to her. "And the courage to suspend my dis-belief and follow my heart to you.''

Simone held the jar in front of her face. It appeared to contain something that looked like pieces of old shoestrings. Shreds of something brown and wilted. "What on earth is in here?''

"Chopped flowers. *Mahja* blossoms.''

Mahja blossoms. Simone was astounded. "But the perfume oil is not yet ready,'' she blurted out, then stopped short, realizing she'd just revealed their secret to Nick. But then, if Esther had given these blooms to him, she must have told him about the plants and their efforts at enfleurage. Besides, Nick, she hoped, was no longer the enemy. That concept would take some getting used to.

"Apparently it does not necessarily have to be an oil for the fragrance to . . . uh . . . have its magical effects,'' Nick said, taking the jar from her and returning it to the table. Then he encircled her with his arms again, and she nestled into the warmth and security he offered her.

"Do you believe that's what it is, Nick? Magic?''

She felt him take a deep breath. "I don't know what I believe anymore, except that something magical must have happened for you to be lying here in my arms.''

Simone's heart leapt. "Nick?'' She said his name again, liking the feel of it on her lips.

"I'm here,'' he told her again.

"Forever?''

Nick rolled her onto her back and leaned on one elbow, looking down into her face. "Forever. I meant everything I said to you in the dreamworld. I love you. I always have. And I've lived in torment since I betrayed you in Grasse.'' He moved his face closer to hers. "I beg your forgiveness, Simone. I can't go on without it, or you." She saw the earnest urgency in his eyes and felt the openness of his heart. She reached up and touched the rough stubble on his chin, thinking she must still be in the dreamworld. God, how she had longed to hear those words. And believe them.

"If we want to make our own dreams come true, we must both let that past go now," she whispered. "I'm ready if you are."

He closed his eyes, his expression revealing an intense sense of relief. "Thank God," he uttered, lowering his lips to hers. "I promise you, Simone, I'll do anything in my power to make all of your dreams come true."

"Anything?" Simone smiled lazily and moved sensually in his arms, filled with a delicious anticipation. "Then prove to me that it wasn't the perfume after all that made those dreams so special."

Nick wasted no time in granting her wish. She felt his strength surge as he bent to his task, making magic wherever he touched her. His caresses were both tender and virile, and he played her body with the practiced touch of the lover in her dreams, bringing her to new exquisite heights. But this lover was real, and he indeed proved to her that they needed no perfume to feel the magic of the love that flowed between them.

Much later, Simone peeked from behind the door of the bedroom's adjoining bath where she had just enjoyed a long and luxurious shower. The heavy drapes that had earlier kept out the light of morning had now been moved aside slightly, and a slant of sunshine highlighted an old Oriental rug on the floor. The bed, though rumpled, was now empty. "Nick?"

But the room was empty as well. Simone frowned. What was she going to do now? She was stark naked and had nothing to wear. Where were her clothes? Her mouth suddenly went dry. She remembered packing her suitcase in the flat in London, before she'd entered the dreamworld. But she'd

come back from that dreamworld with Nick to Brierley Hall!
Was her suitcase still in London?

Wrapping her body in a large towel, she crept back into
the bedroom, her mind racing at the inference that the perfume
actually had the power to transport a human body through
space. But her logical mind fought the idea that she had dematerialized into the dream, then come back here physically
with Nick.

It simply could not be. Nick must have come upon her
asleep in her room in the London flat and brought her here.
It followed that her suitcase was nearby.

The whole business threatened to give her a headache.
Surely there must be a reasonable explanation for everything,
something more substantial than "magic." Simone sank into
a nearby chair and tugged at the edge of the towel that barely
covered her thighs. Despite their earlier intimacy and the fact
that she'd allowed herself at last to forgive and trust Nick, it
made her distinctly uncomfortable to find herself so weirdly
transported to a strange house, into a strange bedroom, a
man's bedroom at that, with no clothing available to her. The
whole episode had a certain dreamlike quality to it.

Determined to find her suitcase, she stood up again and was
almost to the door when she spied the jar of crushed flowers
on Nick's bedside table. She returned and picked it up, twisting the lid and lifting the container to her nose. The scent of
the *mahja* renewed her doubt and underscored her questions,
but it did not, she noticed, exert any "magical" effect over
her. She felt no sexual stimulation whatsoever. Why did the
essence work at some times and not at others?

Simone shook her head, more perplexed than ever, wondering if she would ever understand what had happened to
her.

She heard a door slam somewhere in the house, then the
sound of footsteps hurrying up the stairs. A polite knock
sounded on the door before Nick poked his head inside.

"Simone?" He called out her name breathlessly. A distinct
look of relief washed over him when he saw her, then he
flashed her a sexy grin that sent her heart rate soaring again.

"Oui, Monsieur Rutledge," she said, tucking the towel around her and using a playfully formal greeting to hide the sudden rush of shyness she felt.

Nick entered with two paper bags and several boxes. "I thought you might need these," he said, placing the boxes at the foot of the bed and removing the lids. "I didn't have much time, and there's not much in the way of fashion available in Redford anyway, but this should at least cover the subject."

He took out a simple red knit sundress, with spagetti straps and a bias skirt that on Simone would reach to her calves.

Clothes. So her suitcase wasn't in the house after all. "My favorite color." Simone smiled, fingering the texture of the towel nervously and wondering exactly where her belongings were. "It was thoughtful of you, Nick. Thanks."

The other box held something wrapped in tissue, and he handed it to her, an abashed look on his face. "I . . . I had to have the saleswoman pick these out for you. I don't know much about ladies' lingerie."

Simone cocked a curious eyebrow at him and took the box. Between the sheets of white tissue lay a pair of red silk bikini panties. In spite of all her uncertainties at the moment, she had to laugh. "Are you sure you bought these for me?" she asked, teasing him by holding them over the appropriate place against her scantily clad body.

"Well . . ." Nick grinned again and left the implication hanging. "I thought about buying a matching bra, but . . ."

She gave him a suggestive look. "I'm glad you didn't. I despise the things."

"They can be kind of sexy sometimes," he said solemnly, taking a step in her direction, all trace of embarrassment gone now from his expression. "Intriguing to remove, as well."

Simone's mouth watered at the thought of Nick removing any piece of clothing from her. Was he going to help her out of the towel? But instead he handed her the third box. In it were a pair of red strappy sandals.

Forgetting the questions that had so disturbed her only moments before, Simone wanted only one thing. Nick. Everything he'd given her screamed of the sexuality they enjoyed between them, and his suggestive comments tantalized her and whetted her desire once again. "You did pretty well for an old bachelor man," she said with a devilish smile, beckoning him with one slender finger. "You deserve a reward." Slowly, she raised her arms, letting the towel slide to the floor.

Nick followed her down onto the bed, where together they discovered new delights and rekindled the intimacy both hungered for. When they finally came up for air, Simone looked into Nick's face and felt as if she would explode with happiness.

"I am still in the dream," she murmured. "This can't be happening for real."

Nick cradled her in his arm, and she rested her head against his bare chest. "But it *is* happening. The voice was right. We *can* be together in our own reality."

Her hand froze where it had been making playful circles in the hair of his chest. "Voice?"

Cooking was basically foreign to Nick, but after he left Simone to dress, he went downstairs into the large, old-fashioned kitchen and, finding the microwave, warmed the now stone-cold coffee he'd brought from the village. Simone joined him moments later, glowing and fresh from their lovemaking, and stunning in the red dress.

He couldn't help himself. He had to take her in his arms and kiss her soundly to prove to himself she was real. "You're gorgeous," he told her, and she warmed him with her smile.

"You too," she teased, then eased out of his embrace. "But if we want to sort through things, we'll have to keep some space between us." She winked. "For a little while, anyway." She accepted a mug of coffee and a cold pastry and sat down at the wooden trestle table. "Now, about that voice . . ."

Nick took the chair opposite. He liked the way she joked with him, but he knew she was right. They had some serious ground to cover. Sitting at the rustic kitchen table in broad daylight, he found it difficult to talk rationally about disembodied voices speaking in a dream, but he knew that voice had been as real as the wood on the tabletop.

"After that night, when we . . . when you . . . came to my house, and then left without saying goodbye, my life fell apart," he said, admitting it to himself for the first time even as he shared it with Simone. "I started using the perfume, every night, trying to meet you in the dreamworld."

He heard her sharp intake of breath. "*Mais non!* I, too, went there, searching for you. But you never came." The last held an accusatory note.

"It was the voice that restrained me. Believe me, I wanted to be with you, and the dreamworld seemed the only place. But the strangest thing happened." He told her about hearing the man's voice warning of the grave danger of going too often into the dreamworld. "He told me that a doorway would eventually close, and I would be unable to return to the real world. I understood another message, although I'm not sure I *heard* it, that those who get trapped in that dreamworld lose their humanity, become lost souls . . ." His voice faded, and he wondered if Simone thought him daft. But her next question proved otherwise.

"Whose voice do you think it was?"

Nick leaned back in his chair and rubbed his forehead and his suddenly tired eyes. Then he told her his family's legend about John Rutledge, and about finding that ancestor's diary, letters, and the perfume in the old trunk. "In those diary entries, John Rutledge often referred to Mary Rose as his 'lady love.' " He took a deep breath. "When I started going into the dreams looking for you, I believe it was he who warned me, for he also told me that my own 'lady love,' meaning you, went there too often as well."

Simone set her coffee mug down with a thump. "You believe that John and Mary Rose are still alive and living in the dreamworld?"

He shrugged. "Sort of. I think our own experiences have proven that . . . the physical body can and does at times enter into another plane. Their bodies were never found. And from the information I read in his diary and her letters, I know it was their intention to run away together into the dreams, never to return.''

He saw Simone shiver and reached across the table and laid his hand upon hers. ''I know it's lunacy, but it's the only explanation I have to offer you.''

''I was hoping you had come to the flat and carried me unconscious back here to Brierley,'' she said softly. ''It would be a lot easier to accept than thinking I was physically transported here through the dreams.''

A protracted silence fell between them. Then Simone spoke again. ''Esther thinks that John and Mary Rose overused the perfume, and that it killed them and dematerialized their bodies,'' she said. ''I'd rather believe they were still together in the dreamworld.''

Nick let out a heavy sigh. ''Yes,'' he agreed, ''I would rather believe that too. But that brings us to the perfume.''

''It's dangerous, Nick,'' Simone said abruptly. ''At first I didn't believe Esther's warnings, but now I know better. Dupuis—''

''What about Dupuis? What happened between you and him? He came barging into my lab like a madman, threatening to kill us both.''

''He has tried the perfume, Nick. He's used it, and now he's obsessed with having it.''

Nick's stomach balled into a hard knot. Of course, he'd suspected Simone was working on the substance at the House of Rutledge, but he hadn't considered how Dupuis would react to it. But then, considering its effects, what man wouldn't become obsessed with having it? That idea aroused an earlier and terrible suspicion. ''He didn't . . . uh . . . come on to you, did he?''

Simone frowned, then related the whole sordid incident to him, and when she finished, Nick felt as if he could kill Antoine Dupuis with his bare hands. ''If I'd known what he did to you, I swear I would have used his own gun to blow him apart.''

Simone touched his arm. ''I'm glad you didn't. You would

have ended up in jail, and I would have been stuck forever in the dreamworld, waiting for you.''

Nick stared at her, distinctly glad he hadn't murdered Dupuis, no matter how he hated him. For it could have happened just as she said.

Coming to his senses, he told Simone about the Frenchman's arrest. ''Dupuis is likely the one in jail, although with his connections, he's probably managed to free himself on bond.'' Then another thought occurred to him, and he scowled. ''Do you think there is any chance he might be able to re-create the perfume?''

Simone shook her head. ''As I'm sure you know from our mutual acquaintance at the Botanical Society, the flower Mary Rose used to make her perfume is extinct. At least it was thought to be so, until I was given those seeds.''

What seeds? What was she talking about? Nick made a mental note to question her about them, but didn't interrupt what she was saying.

''I doubt if Dupuis could ever come up with the flowers, and I had no success trying to synthesize the perfume oil,'' she continued.

''So you had no better luck than I.'' Nick smiled ruefully. ''I've never been so frustrated with a perfume in my life. In fact, even once I had the actual blossoms to work with, I still was unable to distill a fragrance that had the, shall we say, the 'powers,' of Mary Rose's perfume.''

Simone looked up at him sharply. ''Blossoms? Where did you get *mahja* blossoms?''

''Come. I have something to show you.''

TWENTY-EIGHT

❧

The afternoon sun was warm on her face as Nick led her across the meadow. The lush yet serene surroundings and her own deep sense of joy filled Simone with the sense that they were still in some kind of magical world, where time did not exist and the past had dissolved into a vague darkness that need not be entered again. Except this world appeared to be the real thing. The sky was pale blue, the meadow English-summer green. There was not a wisp of indigo mist in sight, and the only pleasure palace around was the dilapidated but lovely old manor house, Brierley Hall.

And moments ago, Nick had asked her to become the lady of that manor. Lady Rutledge. Madame Rutledge. Mrs. Nicholas Rutledge. Any way she said it, she found it incredible that it would soon be her name. Her oldest and most impossible dream was at last to come true!

They trod down the path through the woods until at last they reached the garden behind the cottage. Nick opened the gate, which gave a rusty squeak under his touch. "Remind me to replace that," he remarked.

"No, don't replace it," Simone answered, touching the sun-warmed iron bars and almost feeling the vibrations of the woman who once lived in this place. "It belongs here. Likely Mary Rose went through this very gate to enter her garden every day."

"Romantic."

She tossed him a light laugh. "Yes, very. Now what mysterious thing have we come here to see?"

He led her across the enclosed garden to where five shrubby bushes grew along the opposite wall, and Simone's eyes nearly popped from her head. *"Mon Dieu!"* she exclaimed, touching the ripening buds on one stalk. "The *mahja*! Were they here all along?"

Nick plucked a bud and held it to his nose, then tucked the unopened blossom behind Simone's ear. "I guess they've been here ever since Mary Rose planted them." He told her about the entry in John Rutledge's diary that revealed where he'd obtained the original seeds. "And you read in Mary Rose's own diary what she did with them."

"Book of Shadows."

"What?"

Simone laughed at Nick's perplexed expression. "That's what a witch calls her record of charms and spells. A Book of Shadows."

"Oh." He laughed uncertainly. "Esther told you that, I suppose? Is she a witch?"

"Most definitely."

"I saw these flowers in her garden as well. Did you first learn about the perfume from her?"

Simone shook her head. It was her turn to fill him in on the incredible chain of events that had brought her to England, and ultimately, into his life once again. She told him about discovering the perfume in the crystal antique vial, about tracing the shipment to its source, and about coming to the cottage to see if she could find out more about it. "So, I must confess, my rental of the cottage was not quite coincidental," she said with a lift of her brow. "But I did not know it belonged to you."

Nick laughed. "I'm becoming a believer in the notion that there are no coincidences. But tell me, where did Esther get the *mahja* bushes?"

After telling him that her hostess had given her a sample of the same perfume, claiming it had been made by her "craft ancestor" and hoping Simone could make more of it for her "medicinal" purposes, Simone shared with him the strange story of Shahmir and the seven seeds. "Those are new plants in Esther's garden. We only put the seeds in the ground a few weeks ago."

They began to stroll around the circular bed in the center of the garden. Nick took her hand.

"Well, where do we go from here? We have the plants. We have the expertise. We have the equipment. Shall we continue to try to replicate old Mary Rose's potion?"

"Nick, you know that Dr. Wheatley believes the *mahja* is a hallucinogenic plant. A cousin to the datura. We can't make a perfume that could be harmful."

"Nobody has proven it harmful yet."

"Think of how it affected Antoine Dupuis," she argued. "What if we were successful in reproducing what Mary Rose created and it affected everyone like that? The world would be overrun with horny old men."

Nick laughed and led her to the bench, where they sat basking in the warm sunlight. "You're right. *That* could be dangerous. But, as I said, I've never been so frustrated with a perfume in my life. Even when I distilled the essence directly from the fresh flowers, it still didn't work like . . . Mary Rose's."

He leaned back against the wall and drew her securely into his arms, then exhaled heavily, as if in resignation. "I guess we'll never know what her secret was, but because of the potential danger inherent in using the *mahja*, I suppose you're right. We ought to give up on it. But I've been thinking. You've told me you wish to create fine perfumes in the tradition of your father. Since you no longer have the facilities of the House of Rutledge at your disposal, it occurred to me you will need another perfumery."

Simone looked up at him, perplexed. What was he getting at? He kissed her, and she felt him press something cold and metallic into her palm. She looked down and saw it was a key. "What is this?"

"It isn't much, but if you'll have it, Bombay Fragrances is yours."

Simone straightened in his arms. "What? You must be out of your mind. I know what it has cost you—"

He cut off her protests with another kiss. "I am only a nose, with perhaps a nose for business as well. You are an artist. Let me help you. I know the people you will need to create the bottles, the packaging. I know how to organize the promotion. It's what I did for Dupuis. Let me do it for you."

She once would have been suspicious that he was just trying to use her talents as a perfumer for his own gain, as he had her father's. But the remarkable events of the past few days had taken away any such notion. Now, she saw his offer for what it was . . . he was ready to give up everything, just as he'd said, for her love and forgiveness. Tears welled in her eyes.

"What makes you think I want to remain in the perfume business? Maybe I would simply like to retire and become a country witch, like Esther."

"If that is what you'd rather," Nick replied, nuzzling her ear, "then become a witch. Brierley Hall may not be the grandest estate, but I've been thinking lately that I'd like to move to the country anyway. I'm rather worn out with the whole fragrance business myself. I'll find some other way to support us . . ."

"Who said I couldn't be a witch *and* a perfumer?" Simone teased, wondering what it took to become a witch. But she knew that was not her calling. "Why couldn't we move the perfumery from London and set it up in Mary Rose's house?" The thought appealed to her for many reasons. "I don't want to stay in the city. The air is so foul. Here, it would be . . . a little like in Grasse."

She could see that her enthusiasm had spilled over into Nick, and he beamed at her. "Do you mean it? You'd move to the country?"

"I love the country. I guess I'm just a peasant at heart, although I'm about to marry an aristocrat." She smiled at him wistfully. "I'm glad times have changed since the days of poor John and Mary Rose."

* * *

Later, Simone telephoned her friend Esther to let her know she was alive and well and living firmly on Planet Earth. "Thanks for encouraging Nick to . . . come for me," she said in a low voice, as if someone might overhear what could seem to be a rather mad conversation. "We're to be married soon, and we are going to move here, to Brierley Hall."

She could tell that the old "white witch" was thrilled at the news, and wondered if she'd cast any sort of charm or spell to bind the two dream lovers together. She didn't dare ask.

"What about 'our' perfume? Will you be able to finish it for me?" Esther wanted to know.

"You won't need me for much. When the enfleurage is completed, I'll come over and use the ethyl alcohol to extract the pure absolute, the perfume oil. But . . ." She hesitated, not wanting to disappoint her friend. "I have to warn you, I can't guarantee it will have the same . . . effect . . . as Mary Rose's." She told Esther about the *mahja* bushes growing in the cottage garden and how Nick had distilled the essential oil only to find that although it smelled sweet, it had no special powers.

She expected Esther to express concern or disappointment and was surprised to hear instead a low laugh from the other end of the line. "Oh, I'm sure it will do, my dear. Now what about the other perfume? The one you promised to make for . . . what was his name?"

"Shahmir? Oh, I intend to make it too. Right away in fact. Nick has quite a few things to wrap up in London. He plans to put his town house on the market and get things organized to move the perfumery into the cottage. While he's busy with that, I'll use the present facilities to assemble the blend listed in the formula created by my father. Nick has said I can use the oil of the *mahja* he distilled, and I took the rest of what I needed when I went back to the House of Rutledge." She paused, then asked, "You don't believe it would be dangerous, do you?"

Esther did not answer right away, and when she did, her words were measured. "As you know, I believe the oil of the *mahja,* wrongly used, can be dangerous. But I suspect that Shahmir and his 'master' know the dangers and are willing to accept the consequences. I would advise you to fulfill your obligation to him, then return the formula and seven seeds if you can find them, and ask him not to bother you further.''

Simone liked having her own personal wise woman, if only to confirm the decision she'd already made. ''Good idea.''

A few hours later they entered the suburbs of London, and Nick made straightaway for the high-rise tower and the corporate flat. They pulled up in front, and Simone used her most charming smile to convince the doorman to let her into the flat. ''I went out of town for a few days, and I locked my key inside,'' she told him.

He escorted them up the elevator, and she snickered when she saw him keeping a suspicious eye on Nick. While she waited for him to unlock the door, she tapped her foot on the hallway carpet and felt a bump beneath the sole of the soft sandal. She looked down and saw what looked like a little red worm. She moved it with the toe of her shoe and realized instead that it was a wilted flower. A wilted *mahja* flower. She glanced around furtively, halfway expecting to see the tall figure of Shahmir materialize from the ether. Although curious about her discovery, she bent without remark and picked up the blossom, then followed the others into the flat.

''The place has been under guard since the, uh, trouble,'' said Alfred. ''Everything should be just as it was.''

Simone went swiftly into the bedroom. Everything was just as she'd left it, except that the red shoe she'd dropped making her escape from Nick's was on top of her suitcase. She slipped it inside the luggage without comment. ''I'm ready,'' she said to Nick. ''Let's get out of here.''

Outside, Simone heaved a sigh of relief. ''Thank God that is all behind me,'' she told Nick as he placed the suitcase in the back of the car. ''Thanks for returning my shoe, by the way.''

He kissed her and helped her into the small roadster. ''I hated to part with it.''

When he was in and settled, she showed him the wilted

mahja blossom. "I found this on the carpet in the hall."

"I put it on your shoe when I left it by the door."

Simone was puzzled. "A peace offering?"

Nick steered into the heavy traffic. "I wanted you to know then what I told you later in the dreamworld, that I would give up everything for you."

"And you had no way of knowing I already had *mahja* blooms to work with . . ." she thought out loud. "You were handing over the perfume, weren't you?"

Nick only nodded. They drove in silence, then Simone asked, "But why didn't I see the shoe when I came home?"

"Because Dupuis got there first. He found and took your shoe, and something else I'd left for you. I guess he didn't see the flower, or he would have taken that too."

"What something else?"

Nick took one hand off the steering wheel and reached into the pocket of his coat, the same one he'd been wearing the day he discovered Simone was missing. He handed her a ball of wadded paper.

Before she finished reading the note of apology Nick had written her, the words swam before her tear-filled eyes. If there had been any remaining doubt in her mind of Nick's intention toward her, it vanished into the blue. For here in her hands was proof that everything he'd told her, promised her in that other realm, he'd first tried to tell her here on earth.

The next morning, Nick laid the *Times* on the kitchen counter and poured himself a cup of coffee. Upstairs, he could hear the shower running, and he smiled and shook his head, still not believing that Simone was here, with him at last. It couldn't get any better than this.

But it did. He laid open the paper, and a headline jumped out at him: "Executive Missing. House of Rutledge CEO Charged with Battery, Suspected of Embezzlement."

Nick stared at the story, stunned. According to the article, Antoine Dupuis had not been seen since being released from jail on bond after an incident involving a suspected assault on an employee. In addition, several members of the firm's board of directors, who had been auditing its operations, were charging him with embezzling money from the company. Nick let out a low whistle, but he couldn't resist a grin. It looked as if Dupuis were about to get his after all.

When Simone joined him for coffee, he read the story aloud to her.

"Oh, Nick, I'm so sorry," she said softly, settling into a chair across from him. "Not for Dupuis, of course, but that your family name is being dragged through another puddle of mud."

Nick shook his head and grinned broadly across the table at her. "You don't understand. All that doesn't matter anymore. Everyone I care about knows it's not my family's business any longer. As you said, companies change hands all the time. But where do you suppose Dupuis has gone?"

"I'll give you one good guess," Simone said, shooting him a knowing look.

Nick stared at her. "You don't think . . . ?"

"I know he used the perfume. All the time. But he must have had enough left to cross into the dreamworld one final time, with the intention never to come back."

"The perfect escape," Nick murmured, astounded and somewhat disappointed that the Frenchman's destiny might not include a jail sentence after all. Then he remembered the other article he'd found, this one in the financial section, and he turned to the page. "Well, listen to what else is going on at Rutledge. 'House of Rutledge Slated for Public Offering.' "

The story responded to the Dupuis scandal, with one of the directors assuring investors that with Dupuis gone, things would be set straight within the company, and that the lucrative fragrance house would offer a prime investment potential on Fleet Street.

Nick laughed bitterly. "If my father could only see this. He was such a snob, he would never have dreamed of selling shares in a 'Rutledge' operation to commoners, even if it had given him the means to keep it afloat." He shook his head. "I wish I'd been smart enough to go public, instead of selling to Antoine Dupuis."

TWENTY-NINE

Simone completed Shahmir's perfume using the oil Nick had distilled from the *mahja* blossoms. She sniffed her final arrangement of scent, satisfied that it not only followed her father's formula, but also harmonized with the heretofore missing ingredient. It was an exquisite fragrance, a truly *grand parfum*, and although it had a certain euphoric effect, enough to bring on a smile, it did not seem to be aphrodisiac in nature.

Carefully, she packaged two small bottles of it, all that she had made. Now, how to get Mr. Shahmir to come for it?

It was Saturday, and she had the place to herself. *"Entendez, s'il vous plaît,"* she said aloud, grinning and holding up the bottles. "Your 'master's' perfume is ready for you, Mr. Shahmir, wherever you are. Please come for it soon so I can get on with my life."

Before leaving the lab, she looked around and was glad this was not to be the place where she would create her *grands parfums*. It was too stark, too sterile. Mary Rose's cottage would be perfect. Simone turned out the light and left, locking the door behind her.

She had Nick's Triumph and started to get into the left-hand seat before she remembered she was in a British vehicle. She didn't relish the drive home in traffic, even though it wasn't far.

Cautiously, she pulled out into the street and used the technique that had brought her safely to the perfumery: she spoke aloud to herself as if she were teaching a student driver. "Stay in the left lane, stay in the left lane." She glanced in the rearview mirror and noticed a black Mercedes behind her, following a little too closely. She tapped on her brakes, just enough to flash the taillights without slowing down, and the trick worked. The car backed off, but it stayed behind her, following every turn. Simone grew uneasy. It seemed as if she were being tailed.

That's ridiculous, she thought. Who would want to follow her? Could it possibly be Antoine Dupuis, not lost in the dreamworld after all and bent on some sort of sick revenge? Her alarm turned to terror when at last she reached Nick's driveway and the black car followed her onto the gravel and parked behind the Triumph.

Heart racing, she locked both doors and sat behind the wheel, ready to blow the horn to summon Nick if she had to. Then the door to the other car opened, and Simone's fear turned to an hysterical laugh. Stepping into the afternoon heat, dressed in full bejeweled regalia, Shahmir bowed low in her direction.

"Mon Dieu!" Simone murmured, swallowing her giggles at his affected attire. "He heard me."

She unlocked her door and got out of the car, then retrieved her tote bag containing the items she had ready to give him.

"My father's work is complete, Mr. Shahmir," she said, handing him the two bottles of perfume. "And along with these, I want to return to you the formula,"—she handed him the manila folder—"and seven newly picked seeds to replace those you gave me that produced the flower we needed to make this."

He accepted the items, especially the perfume, as if he were accepting the crown jewels. "My master will be eternally grateful," he said, nodding his enshrouded head solemnly.

"Eternally?" Simone replied lightly. "Isn't that a bit much for two bottles of perfume?"

His eyes twinkled. "I suspect you have learned something of the power of the *mahja,*" he said with the enigmatic smile to which she'd become accustomed. "It has enabled my master, and myself, to live longer than any others on earth."

"Who is your master, and how old is he?" Simone felt she'd earned some answers from this strange man.

"My master is a holy man who has lived for over two hundred years in a monastery at the foot of the Himalayas. He is also my uncle. Once the monks of his order raised a plant called the *mahja* and from it concocted a liniment which, rubbed into the skin, greatly extended life. But in the middle of the last century, some seeds were stolen, after which the bushes would no longer grow."

"I see," said Simone, although she did not believe a word he was saying. His storytelling, however, was as rich as his dress. The jewels on the red coat glittered when he moved.

He continued. "Several decades ago, the supply of liniment oil was so depleted that the monks began to add other oils to it to extend it, those in the formula I presented to your father. But even that was not sufficient, and at last, they sent me into the world to find more of it. That is when I came to your father. His reputation for knowing how to extract plant essences reached even into my far country."

"But he didn't have the *mahja* plant, so he couldn't make the perfume," Simone said, sorting out as much truth from the fiction as she could. "Where did you get the seeds you gave me?"

"Long ago, I was the servant of the one who stole the seeds from the monastery. He was a foreigner, who sought to use the *mahja* for his own gain. Alas, he misused it, not understanding its power, and he vanished from the earth. I was accused of murdering my employer, and I ran away to the protection of the monastery." He gave her a soft smile. "I owe my life, many, many years of it, to the monks. Their need for the oil is great, for without it they will die.

"After I once located you and heard that your father had failed to synthesize the essence, I returned to the city where my foreign master once lived, to the place where his house once stood. It has been torn down, and the area is now deserted, as water there has become scarce. However, upon walking the grounds, I came upon five bushes, growing in a row. My heart was overjoyed, for I believed them to be the *mahja* plant. The flowers had turned to seeds, and I harvested them all."

Simone wanted to call Nick to come and hear this tale, but she was afraid if she did, Shahmir would vanish without finishing his remarkable story. Instead, she questioned the tall man. "Why didn't you just take the seeds back to the monastery and plant them there and make the liniment as they used to?"

"I did plant some there, but still they would not grow. That's when I brought them to you. Time, for once, was of the essence for my master. Henceforth, I believe we can survive by harvesting the flowers of the plants that grow in the old place, but I needed these"—he held up the two bottles proudly, the crusader accomplishing his quest—"to sustain us until then. And now, I must go." He bowed until his turban disturbed in the pebbles in the drive. "My gratitude, Mademoiselle Lefèvre."

As Simone watched in amazement, Shahmir uncorked one of the bottles, inhaled deeply of the perfume, and was gone. Vanished, literally, into thin air.

The driver of the Mercedes jumped out of the car. "Damn that fellow," he screamed, running around the car, looking beneath it. "He's done it t' me again."

"What's wrong?" Simone asked calmly, as if it made all the sense in the world to have witnessed the vaporization of a human being.

"Th' bloke's hired my car twice now, and both times he's left me without paying th' fare." He opened the back door and searched the upholstery where Shahmir had sat. "That's what I thought," he said in disgust, holding up a green rhinestone. "That's what 'e left behind last time. Th' bugger's nuts if 'e thinks this is some kind of pay."

Simone watched in bemusement as the driver got back behind the wheel, mumbling curses beneath his breath. When the driveway was empty, Simone stared at the spot where

Shahmir had vanished. She wasn't surprised to see a red rhinestone shimmering there on the pebbles.

Nick thought he heard a commotion in the drive, but he was on the telephone with his estate agent so he didn't investigate. Several minutes passed, and he decided he'd been mistaken, until Simone came bursting into the house. "Get off the phone, *allons*! Quickly!" she said, her face flushed and her eyes bright.

Nick made an excuse to the agent and rang off. "What's the matter?" he asked, taking her by the shoulders, feeling her excitement beneath his fingertips. "Are you all right?"

Simone exploded with laughter. "Physically, I'm all right, but mentally, I think I'm going off my head, as you say here. You're not going to believe this." Breathless, she told him what had just taken place in his driveway—Shahmir's wild story about the monks and the liniment and the *mahja* bush and his "foreign master's" disappearance, and with each word, Nick's heart beat faster even as he felt the blood drain from his face.

Simone stopped at last and looked at him with concern. "What's wrong, Nick? I mean, other than that your fiancée has become a raving lunatic?"

Nick's knees were suddenly weak, and he needed to sit down. He took her hand and led her to the sofa in the front living room. "Simone," he said, trying to gather his wits, "we've been so busy getting to know one another again, I haven't had time to show you the items I found in that old trunk with the perfume."

"What does that have to do with Shahmir?"

Nick shook his head, feeling dazed. This whole episode with the perfume kept getting more and more curious. "Maybe nothing. Maybe everything. I can't explain. There's something I want you to read. I'm almost finished here. Get your things together. We're going to Brierley immediately."

Simone unfolded her hand and held it out in front of him. Upon her palm lay a large red jewel. "He's dropped another one."

Nick stared at it, glimmering even in the diffused light. He'd seen a lot of jewels in his lifetime adorning the rich and famous at galas and balls he'd attended as the son of Lord and Lady Rutledge, before the disaster with his father. This looked like a ruby. A very large ruby. "Who dropped it? What are you talking about?"

"Shahmir. It came from that Mardi Gras sort of coat he wears. It's a rhinestone, I imagine. He's left one behind every time he's, uh, dropped in on me. I have three of them." She laughed. "Guess he figures they're a tip."

"Let me see it." Nick took the oval-shaped stone and turned it over between his fingers. "This is no rhinestone, sweetheart," he told her, holding it up to the light. "Unless it's a very good fake, it's the biggest ruby I've ever seen."

A light misty rain began to fall before they arrived at Brierley Hall, bringing a welcome relief from the heat. Nick carried in their bags and asked Simone to wait for him in the drawing room. She shivered in the gloom of the rainy afternoon, wishing it wasn't summer so they could build a fire to cheer the somber old room. Instead, she turned on all the lights, but even that scarcely managed to dispel the shadows. Could she live in this place? Not without a lot of changes to brighten it up, she decided.

But, she thought, her spirits lifting, after learning of the incredible value of Shahmir's "gifts," she knew she would have the money to do whatever she wanted, both here in the manor house as well as at Mary Rose's cottage. Together, she and Nick would restore Brierley to its one-time splendor, and create a small but perfect perfumery.

After having had a taste of commercial perfuming, Simone realized why her father had never expanded his operation. He'd preferred to do it his way, and she would follow in his footsteps, creating exquisite all-natural, very expensive perfumes. Their very quality, Nick had told her, would create their own market.

Nick came into the room carrying a quaint, old-fashioned trunk which he placed on a table in the center of the room.

Simone went to it and watched as he opened it. Even after the eons, a faint hint of an aroma filtered past her sensitive nose, a scent that she recognized instantly. *"Le parfum,"* she uttered.

"From the source," Nick replied, reaching inside and bringing out the cameo necklace and fastening it around her neck. "I want you to have this," he said, explaining his theory that it contained the entwined locks of the star-crossed lovers. Then he handed her a faded red book. "And this will tell you their whole story. It's John Rutledge's diary. Get started on it while I make some tea. I think water boils in a microwave."

She laughed and fingered the cameo as she watched him leave the room, her heart full and open and joyous. How their lives had been transformed by the magical perfume!

Then, taking the diary to a settee beside the brightest lamp, she nestled against the faded brocade and began her work. The brittle pages crackled as she opened the book. "For the eyes only of John Hamilton Rutledge. Do not trespass."

"Are you sure we should go snooping into this?" she called after Nick.

"Too late. I've already been there. Read on."

Simone did so, eagerly. Here at last was a glimpse into the lives of those remarkable, mystical lovers. But from the first page, it was a sad story, filled with the passion and despair of a lover cruelly torn from his beloved and so desperate to be reunited with her that he would risk everything, even his very life. John Rutledge's words tugged at Simone's heartstrings until she thought she would cry.

She read several pages, then suddenly came across an astonishing entry:

> *My young assistant, an Indian native, is witness to my torment, and he has been urging me to visit his relative who lives in a monastery high up in the mountains. He tells me the monks there concoct some kind of potion, an oil made from the blossoms of a so-called*

magical plant, that massaged into my skin will take away my pain and relieve the loneliness.

Simone let the book fall into her lap as Shahmir's story exploded in her mind. Monastery. An accusation that he'd murdered the man he served. A magical oil. It all fell into place. Nick returned with the tea tray, and Simone jumped off the couch. "This is incredible, Nick! Do you think Shahmir was John Rutledge's servant?"

Nick raised his eyebrows and shrugged. "I'm beginning to believe anything's possible. Let me find another passage for you quickly," he said, setting the tray on a table and taking the book from her. He flipped through a few pages. "Read this."

Simone read aloud: " 'I have sown the seeds of the *mahja* plant outside the walls of the compound, in a row of five, as Mary Rose instructed. I cannot expect that they will grow, it is so confoundedly hot and dry in this place . . . '

"Shahmir told me he'd picked the seeds he gave me from five bushes that were growing in a row, where his 'foreign master' once lived. My God, Nick, this is too much. Nobody can live for a hundred and fifty years."

"John and Mary Rose believed they could live forever. Skip to the end," he said, turning to the last entry in the book. Simone's eyes watered and she sank back onto the seat as she read what the lovers, in their desperation, intended to do:

The perfume of the mahja *sent to me in the late summer by Mary Rose has indeed fulfilled the promise of the monks to alleviate our private suffering, as it has taken us in dreams into a world that knows no parting. In that place, there is no society to enforce its insipid rules against our marriage. There is no distance across land and sea dividing us. There is only us, and eternity. We have decided to enter that world, never to return to this one. It is a desperate experiment, but one to which we are both committed as our only hope of being physically reunited. Will it be possible to step over the*

*boundaries of our mortality and take with us our bodies
as well as our will? Only one in all of the history of
mankind has succeeded, and neither Mary Rose nor I
would dare compare ourselves to Jesus Christ. Yet from
repeated use of the perfume, we believe we have already
on many occasions succeeded. This time, we intend to
cross that boundary never to return to the mortal world
again. Mary Rose has written specific instructions. Tonight is the night—*

Simone closed the book gently and laid it on her lap, her
eyes shimmering with tears. "If I'd read this before I came
across the perfume, I would never have believed any of it.
But having been to that dreamworld myself, I believe that
John and Mary Rose were successful in their journey. I can
actually believe that Shahmir is a century and a half old.
And," she said, taking Nick's hand and drawing him onto the
settee beside her, "I *know* that the perfume has the power to
heal, just as Esther described it to me." She entwined her
small fingers into his larger ones and gazed up at him. "All
that anger, all that hurt and desire for revenge I held against
you all those years." She touched their two hands to the place
on her breast above where her heart beat steadily. "It's not
there anymore."

Nick drew her onto his lap and held her tightly as they
leaned back against the soft cushions. "I'm so grateful to have
you back in my life," he whispered. "I can't explain any of
what has taken place, but because it brought you to me, the
perfume has made me a whole man again."

They lay together in tender silence. "What makes it work,
Nick?" Simone asked at last. "Neither of us was able to re-
create Mary Rose's potion. Not fully. What was the magic of
her perfume?"

Nick kissed her forehead. "That, my darling, is a secret
likely no one will ever know."

Esther Brown hurriedly gathered up the items she needed for
the night's work. It was Lammas. The first harvest. The perfect night for working her spell.

Going to the drawer where she had secreted her craft ancestor's Book of Shadows, she took it out and turned to the page where Mary Rose had made certain notations. There was a short poem, a sketch of two corn-husk "poppet" dolls that she supposed represented the lovers John and Mary Rose, and some special instructions for casting the spell.

Tucking the book into her apron pocket, along with two dolls she had made from husks of corn according to Mary Rose's directions, the old witch drove the short distance to the cottage where Mary Rose Hatcher once lived. She parked on the lane so as not to arouse suspicion, then hurriedly made her way to the garden behind the house. She winced as the metal gate squeaked noisily when she entered.

She scanned the garden and immediately spied the *mahja* plants Simone had told her were here. Her excitement grew when she went to examine them and saw that although they were no longer in bloom, the branches were lined with the same small, black seeds as Simone and she had planted in her own garden. Esther grinned.

Simone had insisted that they uproot her *mahja* plants when they were finished blooming, because she'd promised somebody up in London she would destroy them. Apparently that person understood the potential danger in the essence of the *mahja*.

Still, Esther knew it was only dangerous if it fell into the wrong hands, and she was unhappy because her uprooted plants left her with no way to make more of the precious healing perfume. Her own plants had not had time to go to seed, but here before her lay the answer to her dilemma. She was glad she'd come tonight, for she knew Simone also planned to destroy these bushes soon.

She plucked seven seeds and hid them securely away in her purse. The world need never know what grew in a witch's garden. She would tell only her protégé to whom she would also teach the technique of enfleurage. This would insure that the *mahja* oil would be available for the right and correct use in healing.

That is, if she were successful in this night's affairs.

Esther had never seen this garden cleared of weeds and debris, and as the late-summer night began to fall around her, she studied the mandala she'd known was hidden beneath the web of vines and brambles. She walked the entire circumference, examined the shape of the wedges, then saw a bench nearby. Taking great care not to fall, she managed to climb onto the bench, which elevated her sufficiently for her to see the entire pattern of the garden.

Its design did not surprise her. Mary Rose had laid out this garden in the shape of a pentagram. The pie-shaped beds within the outer circle were the lines of the five-pointed star that was the symbol of the witch. Each of the points represented the four basic elements—Earth, Fire, Air, and Water. The fifth stood for Spirit. The center of the pentagram, where all of these things work in perfect balance, was where magic happened.

With sudden clarity, she knew what she must do.

Clambering down again from the bench, she went into the center of the circle, where an inner pentagon-shaped circle was formed by the white rocks. Just as she'd suspected. The rocks of this circle were charred. She took out the Book of Shadows and turned to the page she'd marked, where Mary Rose had written the charm that had cast the spell:

Fire high, flaming bright,
Remove the darkness of our plight,
Burn away the harsh divide
That keeps me from my true love's side.
Fire high, banish fear
And bring me close to him I hold dear.
Twice round two, and my work be done
As into the flame we melt into one.

Esther regarded the charred rocks.

Fire high, flaming bright . . .

She gathered a handful of nearby twigs and brambles and put them into the inner circle, stacking them ready to light.

Twice round two . . .

Two lovers? Two corn-husk dolls? *Twice round two . . .*
Two circles.

As the light of the rising moon lit the night sky, the glow
from Esther's fire illuminated the mandala garden. In a ritual
older than time, the crone performed an incantation, then followed the directions given in Mary Rose's charm. First she
walked the outer wheel, then crossed into the inner, circled it
and stopped directly before the pyre. Taking the two doll figures from her pocket, she anointed each with a drop of the
perfume oil, then cast them into the flames.

In a voice that cracked with age, Esther Brown began walking round the fire, chanting the words Mary Rose Hatcher had
written long ago. She repeated them over and over as she
gazed into the firelight's glow, watching mesmerized as the
dolls melted together, then burst into a last bright flame before
turning to ash.

Esther's work was done. She was confident the spell she'd
cast using Mary Rose's enchantment had now empowered the
newly extracted *mahja* oil to serve her purposes. She had an
abundant supply now to use in healing the emotional wounds
that prevented those who sought her help from knowing the
beauty and joy of the physical aspects of love.

As for its other, more dangerous side, the secret of the
perfume's magic would remain forever hidden safely in her
witch's heart.